THE LUCID NYMPH

RICHELLE P GIST

Printed in the United States of America

Hardcover ISBN: 979-8-987670-0-6
Paperback ISBN: 979-8-987670-1-3
eBook ISBN: 979-8-987670-2-0

Canoe Tree
Press

4697 Main Street
Manchester Center, VT 05255
Canoe Tree Press is a division of DartFrog Books

ACKNOWLEDGMENTS

I did it. It's finally done, this book of mine. It's been over a decade, with endless editing, multiple structure changes, and too many re-writes to count. There have been tears of frustration, rejections from agents, and days when I thought I would never get here.

Through all the craziness, I have had support.

This book would not have structure, a fully formed plot, or the voice of Hazel if not for my writing coach, Janna. We spent many hours together in coffee shops, at my kitchen table and on FaceTime creating a world for Hazel to navigate in. It is with her I painstakingly learned how to write as both a thirteen-year-old and as an adult. We cringed at the awkward fashions from the eighties and seethed over the actions of Teddy. Without Janna, this book would be in shambles.

For Rowan, my lovely editor who dotted all the I's and crossed all the T's. Crossing back and forth between decades is difficult, especially when you stink at math and years and dates all get confused. She does not mess around, catching the teeniest, and the biggest mistakes overlooked by myself and many others. Thank you for polishing up the jumble of words I created and tying it up in a pretty bow.

To my writing partners and instructors whom I met in New York City at Gotham Writer's Workshops, specifically: Masha, Christine, and Fran. They've been instrumental in critiquing the hell out of this book.

For all my beta readers whom I've sent terrible first drafts. Reading five-hundred pages of chaos is not easy and I imagine there were glasses of wine involved. I appreciate all of you. I will need you again for the next book.

To Jenni, my writing friend whom I've never met! We started out online critiquing each other's work and that turned into a camaraderie that I never expected. I would never have had the courage to self-publish were it not for her. After years of rejection by agents, I turned to her for advice as she has self-published four books. She has guided me through the entire process—which can be daunting—and I am forever grateful to her. Hopefully someday we will meet in person.

For my life coach, Julie, whom I inadvertently converted into a line editor, thank you for helping me cut eighty pages out of an already hefty book. You really believed in me, always telling me my story needed to be out in the world. You loved Hazel as if she were your own daughter, and you've been a great cheerleader—and new editor!—to me.

To my supportive family who have patiently waited for this theoretical book I've talked about for years. Special thanks to my aunt Chris and my mother-in-law, Laura, for reading the manuscript (sometimes multiple times!) and editing my messy drafts.

And, of course, to my husband, Brian, who has been an endless support to all the craziness attached to this process. I have become a master of procrastination, and he's become quite good at pushing me through it. He has celebrated in my exciting moments and comforted me during the rejection and depression that goes along with this. His love and encouragement mean everything to me and I'm so lucky to have him.

And last, but not least, the cats in my life, past and present, who have curled up on my lap, stretched out beside me and gave me comfort through some tough times. Thank you to Harrison, Amira, Bjorn and Eleanor.

CONTENTS

1

SLITHER

ANN ARBOR, MICHIGAN 2005

I never knew Teddy in the winter. I only knew him in the blistering shadows of the summer sun, our bodies slick from sweat. Crunching through icy snow, I wondered what it would have been like, warm and cozy and curled up together beneath a blanket in our secret apartment. What it would have been like for Teddy to touch me as a woman, and not as the child I had been back then.

I had no idea if he lived here anymore. Whether he was married or had children, and I told myself not to care. I wasn't here for Teddy. I was here for Harper.

A blast of wind whipped up, and the muscles in my neck seized into an angry knot. It was a familiar and agonizing feeling that always came with brutal cold. I clenched my jaw and propelled myself forward, pulling my newsboy cap farther down over my ears.

I reached the intersection of the Diagonal Green, better known around the University of Michigan grounds as "the Diag," and stopped. The iconic crisscross of diagonal sidewalks, snuggled between pristinely cut grass, was the epicenter of campus. The university's most frequented libraries and halls surrounded the peripherals of the Diag. During warm weather months, the open space was flooded with students—studying, smoking, picnicking, lying on beach towels soaking up the sun, and even enjoying concerts in the evening.

A twinge of sadness pulled at me. I could have attended school here as my parents and sister did, experiencing growing pains the more traditional way. But my need for love and attention dominated the summer of 1986, and the idea of college had been a distant one.

What would my life have been had I never met Teddy? Maybe if I *had* known him in the winter—when the frigid air twists your breath into icicles, when your muscles ache from the sting of the cold and it hurts to laugh, and when your skin is so chapped and scaly that no one wishes to be touched—maybe then, none of it would have happened.

As I crept along the sidewalk, the lingering bite of juniper gripped my tongue, and my head was pulsing with the beginnings of a gin hangover. I had been tasked by my drunk and belligerent best friend Harper to go on a cigarette run as she sat alone back at the bar. Her marriage was a mess and the reason I had driven back home from Chicago—to help her untangle it. It was foolish, considering my past, to think I could help at all. My own marriage was riddled with secrets, but at least this time, it wasn't me feeling the brunt of poor choices.

I reached my destination and pushed through the door of the convenience store, fluorescent lights humming overhead.

"Smooth Operator" by Sade filtered softly through speakers in the ceiling. The place was empty except for a young cashier, his face pocked with acne. He was thumbing through a magazine when he acknowledged me with a nod.

I headed towards the refrigerators in the back. Once the hangovers kicked in, we were going to need some Gatorade. My legs wobbled as I passed bags of Doritos, beef jerky, and rows of candy. I was drunker than I thought. I spotted the bottles in a rainbow of colors and flavors, packed together on the shelves behind the glass doors. In the reflection, I caught a glimpse of my frosty crimson cheeks and equally red earlobes peeking out from under my hat. It was a typical heinously cold Michigan night, and I was grateful for my long down jacket.

Bells jangled from the front of the store. I yanked the refrigerator door open and grabbed two of the plastic bottles—Fruit Punch and Orange. The door closed with a smack, startling me, and the image of a man appeared behind me in the glass.

My recollection was slow, the resemblance of this phantom crawling through my memories. I gasped. The blood drained from my arms, and the bottles of Gatorade tumbled to the ground. I watched in slow motion as they rolled in opposite directions.

Teddy. He was older now, his dark hair peppered with gray, cut short and slicked back with gel. Deep lines creased the corners of his eyes. He had to be around forty years old. The last time I had seen him was back in 1990 when I was just seventeen years old. A flannel shirt hung from his lean frame under a fleece jacket. Black jeans hugged his legs, and on his feet were Timberland boots, crusted with snow.

I knew there was a possibility of running into him; Ann Arbor is a small college town. But my first night back? It seemed an impossible coincidence.

"Hazel," he whispered, and a smile spread across his face. The crooked smile that housed a thousand lies. Gooseflesh prickled my skin.

"Excuse me, Miss, I need to get in there. Do you mind?" A woman was suddenly beside me, pointing to the cooler doors.

"Oh! Yes, sorry!" I scooped up the bottles and spun on my heels to face him.

"What are you doing here?" I whispered.

"Shit, that's no way to greet me, is it?"

"Sorry," I shook my head and avoided his gaze. Greasy slices of pizza spun around lazily in their case at the front counter. "How's it going?"

"Great, thanks for asking," he laughed, his eyes narrowing as he moved in like a python, squeezing himself around me.

I stiffened at his touch, the heat of his fingers penetrating my jacket. Holding the Gatorade bottles tight to my chest, I tried to place space between us. The scent of a campfire on a cool night rose from his skin.

As I wriggled myself from him, he grinned at my unease.

"You look amazing, Hazel," he said, holding my gaze. "What are you doing here? I heard you moved to the big city."

He heard? From who?

"Thanks," I murmured, and glanced at the floor. "Big jackets are always a great statement piece."

"Well, I guess snow looks good on you. We never hung out in the winter, did we?"

"Nope, we didn't," I replied quickly. "What are *you* doing in Michigan? Don't you live in Indiana?"

He picked up a packet of Oreos and fiddled with it, turning it over and over.

"Yeah, well, I did. I came back a while ago. My job at the refinery sucked, and Indiana is fucking depressing. My folks are down in Florida, but I got my own place here a couple years ago."

This news was not surprising. The rich kid who had never lifted a finger in his life couldn't handle hard work.

"Oh, I see."

Asking him where he lived or where he worked or anything about his life was a bad idea. I needed to get back to Harper and away from him. A sharp pain darted from the back of my head and traveled up around my ears.

"Well, it was good to see you, I have to go now."

I began to move past him, but he grabbed my arm. His dark eyes locked on mine, and butterflies battered their wings against my stomach.

"Oh, come on. Come have a drink with me, just one. We can catch up. I'd love to know what you've been up to and what you're doing here now. I still think about you, you know."

He's trying to pull you back to that time; don't do it.

All signs pointed to me leaving. I should have walked out the door. But, the thirteen-year-old girl in me was reemerging, vulnerable and smitten.

"I can't. Harper is waiting for me over at Red Hawk."

"Harper! Aw, how's she doing? Is that why you're in town? She could join us! Come on, just one."

"I don't think so, Teddy, I really need to go. Good seeing you."

I set the bottles on the counter, and the cashier began ringing them up.

"Why don't I join you guys then? Come on. I haven't seen her in years."

You barely knew her.

My cell phone beeped from inside my bag. I handed a ten-dollar bill to the kid at the counter and dug my phone out. I flipped it open. It was a text from Harper:

Where R U? I met this really hot guy and he's going 2 give me a ride home. If U know what I mean :-). He's super nice, don't worry. He knows 1 of my friends from cheerleading from high school! Can U believe that? Anyway, thank U SOOOOO much for coming out with me tonight, but I'm going 2 get LAID!! Call me tomorrow!

Being as drunk as she was, it must have taken her a half hour to type all that out.

Teddy stood close to me, his breath tickling my neck. Images of his mouth kissing my neck, my stomach, and my tiny adolescent lips generated a shiver inside me, and I shook my head.

Fuck. Now what?

When it came to Teddy, I never made the right decisions. My whole life had been one big consequence of those bad choices.

"Everything okay?" Teddy asked. I snapped my phone shut and reached for my change. The cashier handed me the bag. His eyes ping-ponged between me and Teddy.

"Yep. It's fine, thanks. Oh, wait, shit, I'm sorry." I looked up at the cashier. "I need two packs of Marlboro Menthols too."

"Menthols? Wow, that's brutal, Hazel," said Teddy.

"They have a minty aftertaste." I smirked at him.

He laughed. I paid for the cigarettes and headed for the door. Teddy pushed it open for me, a burst of frigid air knocking me backwards into his chest. He grasped my hips and gently grounded me. Visions of his rough hands tugging and pulling at my pants spun around my head.

Twisting away from him, I slipped from his grip.

"So, did your plans just change?" he asked.

My car was at least ten blocks away. I was freezing, and my face felt coated in frost. Trying to focus, I shifted my weight back and forth in my boots. A police car and an ambulance came barreling our way, sirens screaming down State Street.

"Yeah, sort of. Harper decided to go get laid."

"Good for her," Teddy chuckled and zipped up his jacket. He nodded towards the emergency vehicles.

"That your ride comin'?"

"Ha-ha," I said, and rolled my eyes.

"Well, then, Harper's about to go get busy, and it's fucking cold out here. How about we go get that drink?"

2

INITIATE

ANN ARBOR, MICHIGAN 1986

T he first time I met Theodore Michael Spencer was a warm spring night in May. I was upstairs, propped on my elbows across my bed, scanning through the summer reading list assigned to us. Eighth grade was winding down, and I was anxious to start the task. Twisting my hair with a pencil eraser, I pondered the order to read them in. *The Lion, the Witch and the Wardrobe* or *The Road to Terabithia*?

"Secret Lovers" by Atlantic Starr played from my boom box, and I gazed up at my *Miami Vice* poster. Sonny Crockett and Rico Tubbs leaning against a convertible in white blazers and woven boat shoes made me smile. I couldn't wait for the next episode. Downstairs from our living room, I heard my sister, Isabel, shrieking with laughter. What was so hilarious on TV? It was too quiet to hear, and I couldn't make out what was on.

A strange boy's laughter trailed hers. I frowned and gnawed at my lower lip. Isabel was breaking two of my mother's major rules. First, we were allowed only two hours of television a day, which she had surpassed, and second, no boys were allowed inside without one of our parents home. The TV had been on since my parents left for dinner.

"Television and boys lead to recklessness and teenage pregnancy," Mom said.

I didn't care that Isabel was watching too much TV. It was better than her bossing me around. I was thirteen and practically a woman. She was eighteen, and our relationship had sadly changed. As kids, she enjoyed having a baby sister to carry around like a doll. Now she was just moody. The hormones, boys, and coping with my mother's erratic behavior had turned my sister sour. Spending time with me was as loathsome as doing the dishes.

The laughter from downstairs grew increasingly louder. I made another adjustment moving *To Kill a Mockingbird* to number three and *Anne of Green Gables* to number five. I put my pencil down and snuck from my room to the top of the stairs to listen.

What was going on down there?

From the television set, Tony Danza called out for Angela, and I could picture the *Who's the Boss?* star chasing after Judith Light in an apron and kitchen towel slung over his shoulder. Peering through the stairway spindles, I watched Isabel practicing her flirtatious act of laughing and squealing in a high-pitched tone while tossing her hair around.

I rolled my eyes.

Curled up on the couch, her legs under a blanket, her toes poking out, she wriggled them against the boy's leg. This was so gag worthy. My sister had her share of boyfriends but didn't usually invite them home as our mother would either show cool indifference to them or lash out at Isabel and embarrass her. The boy's voice was rumbly, unrecognizable. I silently begged the creaky stairs to stay quiet to get a closer look. Even sitting down, he appeared tall and lanky. Thick dark hair fell across his eyes. His skin was slightly bronzed, a complete contrast to Isabel's pale complexion. He held a can of beer. As he tilted his head back for a sip, he spotted me.

"Hey there!"

I gasped aloud. Isabel followed his gaze, scowled, and shook her head as I awkwardly descended, the stairs creaking with every movement.

"Are you spying on us, you weirdo?" Isabel demanded, attempting to hide her beer.

Nice try, sister! At my age, I knew what beer was. My confidence grew as I evaluated the situation. Entertaining a boy (or whatever you called toe-rubbing a stranger,) and drinking! And the lesser offense of the TV, yet another rule being broken. My head spun with an abundance of blackmailing possibilities.

Meanwhile, the boy playfully shoved Isabel.

"Aw, leave her alone. You weren't spying, were you? I'm sure you just wanted to see what was going on. Right?"

Isabel elbowed his ribs. "Like you would know! You have no idea how annoying she can be! She's sneaky and a tattletale." Her high-pitched flirting voice was now pelted with irritation.

"I am not!" I straightened up and tried to look mature in my Garfield the Cat T-shirt and stirrup pants, my after-school attire.

The boy stood up, tall, like I had imagined. Wow! He was not a boy, but a man. A very handsome man. He wore black jeans that clung to his long legs and a dark-gray T-shirt. Lean muscles rippled from beneath his shirt sleeves. He strode towards me and extended one hand. As he grinned, the right side of his mouth raised higher than the left, resulting in a crooked smile. He held his beer in the other hand, casually.

"Aw, don't listen to Isabel, she's just kidding around! My name is Teddy. You must be Hazel." All at once, I was shy. I hesitantly extended my hand, feeling woozy. His palm was so large it engulfed mine. My knees buckled, and I gripped the banister to steady myself.

"Yeah, I'm Hazel."

He held my hand for what felt like the entire Cheerios commercial faintly jingling behind us.

Isabel jumped up, snatched Teddy's beer, and placed it behind her back with hers. Her eyes narrowed, goading me to say something. I smirked back. *Just try me.*

She was wearing the soft-pink, off-the-shoulder angora sweater my mother bought her last Christmas and jeans with strategically placed rips in the knees. Her bangs were teased up high, stuck together with Aqua Net, and her tight, permed curls were pulled back with a matching pink scrunchie into a neat ponytail. She looked prettier than usual.

She must really have the hots for this guy.

"Go back upstairs, Hazel. We were . . . talking. Nobody invited you!" She walked towards the kitchen to hide the forbidden beer cans.

Teddy held my gaze, his eyes so brown they seemed black. I searched his face for answers. *Who was he? How old was he? Was he her boyfriend?* He was so cute. I could barely process thoughts. He made Ricky Schroder and Kirk Cameron look like troll dolls.

"Nah, why don't you join us, Hazel? We're having some very deep philosophical discussions about music videos."

His baritone voice resonated around the room and came to settle around me.

"Okay, sure, I guess so."

Isabel was going to freak. Whatever. It was not often (or ever) that a cute guy invited me to sit with him. I eased into the couch and Teddy plopped down next to me. Glancing nervously at the television, I twirled a strand of my dark straight hair and swallowed hard. Feeling his eyes on me, I stared at Tony Danza making wise cracks on TV.

Isabel appeared with a glass of chocolate milk and aggravation on her face. She set it down with an exaggerated thud, sloshing light-brown liquid on the glass coffee table. She ignored the mess and glared at me.

"Here is chocolate milk for upstairs. I know you still have shit to do for school, so why don't you go work on that?"

"I'm not a baby. I don't need milk," I said, defiantly. "And I'm done with my 'school shit' anyway."

Teddy sank back into the couch and slung an arm onto the back nearly touching my shoulder. Feeling the heat of his body tickled the hairs on my bare arm.

"See, she's all done," he said, flashing a sly smile. "No harm in her hanging out with us. And maybe I could get another beer, Izzy?"

Isabel pursed her lips—heavily coated in frosted-pink lip gloss—and placed her hands on her hips. I smirked at her as if she were merely a waitress. I had no homework and putting a reading list in order could wait. I had plenty of time to hang out with her and this hot guy next to me. Here I sat, all of thirteen years old, in a cartoon T-shirt, ruining her night. She stared at me like I was competition.

Wait, was I?

Isabel opened her mouth to speak, but Teddy interrupted.

"So, Hazel, what do you do for fun?"

My insides squirmed, baffled by his attention. I picked a piece of fuzz off the blanket and stared at my feet, bare and small. Everything about me was small next to him.

"Um . . . well . . ." I started, but Isabel, unable to control herself, blurted out, "What the fuck do you think she does for fun? She's thirteen! She reads and plays with dolls and shit."

"I do not play with dolls!" I lied. It wasn't a total lie; it *had* been a couple weeks since Barbie and Ken had hung out barbecuing in the Dreamhouse.

"Well . . ." I had to think. My mother forced me to take piano lessons that I hated—my piano teacher smelled like sunflower seeds and soap, and my fingers cramped. I had tried 4-H but discovered that horses scared me, milking cows was disgusting, and the trip to the countryside in Saline from Ann Arbor stressed my mother out. My idea of fun consisted of reading, listening to music, writing stories, hanging out with friends, and playing with my cat, Coconut—and yes, sometimes Barbies.

"I like to read and write a lot."

Isabel rolled her eyes and plunked herself down next to Teddy. She leaned back and flung her feet onto his lap, marking her territory. Teddy absently rubbed one of her feet but looked at me.

"That's cool. I like reading too. What are you reading now?"

I was currently finishing *Blubber* by Judy Blume, but I could not tell him that. The name alone was embarrassing. I tried to recall one of my mother's literary novels that lined her bookshelves upstairs and could not think of a single title. Before I could answer, he leaned over my sister and picked up a book from the coffee table: *Fear and Loathing in Las Vegas* by Hunter S. Thompson.

"This, Hazel, this here is a fucking phenomenal book. I *highly* suggest you read it."

Teddy and Isabel laughed hysterically. I was missing the joke. I glanced at her and then to him only to notice that both of their eyes were glazed red and shiny.

"But seriously, I'm talking about real fun. What do you do for real fun, Hazel?"

What did he mean, real fun? Did he mean drinking? Sex? Feeling flustered, I didn't know what to say, how to act. They were drinking and had inside jokes. I was the little sister, a trespasser in my own house, who didn't comprehend the question. I wasn't in on the joke —I *was* the joke.

"Like, what kind of fun?" I asked.

Why didn't I know the answer? Maybe I had it wrong, and he meant water skiing, or something. In answer, Teddy pulled a baggie of pot from his back pocket and threw it onto the coffee table. *Oh. That kind of fun.* I glanced at Isabel and raised my eyebrows at her. *Are you serious?* She narrowed her eyes and smirked, digging her toes into Teddy's thigh, creeping them towards his crotch.

My options were limited. If I stayed and tried the pot, I would pass the cool test with Teddy, but my sister was provoking me and surely consequences would follow. I had my own ammunition; I could tell on her if I had to, but she would make my life hell.

Teddy was pulling me with his eyes. If I stared too long, he could get me to do anything. He seemed genuine, but I knew from watching my sister and her friends how people acted when high; they could not be trusted. Isabel wanted me to look stupid. She wanted me to say no and run upstairs and leave them be. She was jealous because Teddy was talking to me and inviting *me* to be a part of their fun night.

I should have stayed upstairs. This decision was a thousand times tougher than picking out my next book. I could be petting Coconut and listening to music, oblivious to my sister breaking the rules and being thrust in the middle. They were waiting for my answer.

My heart raced, and I floundered in the couch cushions; they felt too soft, too constricting. I spotted a quarter and a button wedged between them. Teddy grinned my way and pulled out an aromatic chunk of pot.

"Oh, that. Um . . ." I sat upright and took a deep breath. "God, that stuff stinks!"

As he moved, I inhaled his musky scent of sweat, cigarettes, and beer.

I watched Teddy tear the pot apart. It stuck to his fingers as he separated tiny little branches and seeds from leaves that cascaded into a small pile. I had seen pot only once before at my friend Kathy's house. Her older sister and a friend were smoking it.

"Oh, you get used to the smell after a while. Besides, it's worth it," said Teddy, who was now pushing the pot into a pile.

Of course, it stinks, you baby, it's grass!" said Isabel.

She laughed loudly, flipping her hair. She was getting her confidence back, probably feeling foolish for being jealous of her little sister who said stupid things.

"Hey now! Don't call her a baby. You're not a baby, are you, Hazel?" Teddy cooed softly in my direction.

My stomach churned. Teddy was drawing me in, expecting me to join in. If I refused, they would laugh, go back to their fun and forget about me. I would disappear.

"She's thirteen years old, Teddy!" Isabel rolled her eyes. "She's totally still a kid! Right, Hazelnut? Listen, you can totally just go back upstairs and forget this whole thing happened. But tell Mom and Dad, and you're dead!"

I glared and crossed my arms.

"I'm not a kid!" I protested, but the truth was, I did feel more like a kid than ever.

"Girls, girls, girls. Let's not fight. Let's smoke up this joint. She's a beauty." Teddy rolled the joint between his fingers and gave it a long whiff, held it out to me, and smiled that crooked smile. "Would you like to try it, Miss Hazel? You can take the first hit. Buy the ticket, take the ride."

I had no idea what that meant, but I imagined my mom and dad coming home, smelling the foul smoke, and demanding answers from my sister. She would lie, so they would corner me. It was nearly impossible for me to lie. My father would use his charm and wit to persuade the truth out of me. My mother used different tactics, mostly chastising me until I folded. Disappointment might cross my father's face, while my mother would indulge in exasperated drama, her eyes to the heavens, asking no one in particular why her children were so deplorable. Privileges would be rescinded, tears would be shed, and Isabel would lash out at me. I would cry and tattle that it was Isabel's friend, and that he brought the pot, and round and round this would go until both Isabel and I hated each other.

"Um, I really appreciate the offer," I said with a polite tone my mother might use, "but, no thanks. I remembered I do need to work on some school stuff."

"You sure?" asked Teddy.

He brought the joint to his lips and pulled a Zippo from his pocket. A raised emblem of a Playboy Bunny covered the lighter and I thought I saw her smile at me.

"Um, yeah, thanks. It was nice meeting you." I glared at Isabel. "And besides, Mom and Dad will be home soon."

Before he could respond, I scrambled off the couch and bounded up the stairs, two at a time. Echoes of laughter chased my footsteps until I reached my room and shut the door. I looked around my room—books from my summer reading list sprawled across my bed, walls covered in childhood posters and dreams. My cat, Coconut, curled into a white ball of fluff on my pillow. Tears of frustration and confusion fell down my cheeks. I felt like an idiot and a baby. He would never invite me to hang out again. I blew it.

3

CRUSH

ANN ARBOR, MICHIGAN 1986

"Just *look* at these ravishing flowers! Oh, Teddy, my daughter is one lucky girl."

Spring was ripe with flowers. Teddy often came with bundles—gorgeous stargazer lilies and stunning birds-of-paradise—their stems intertwined. He frequently gifted them to my mother. She was thrilled in her usual dramatic way.

I would frown, and Isabel would beam proudly at me. She and Teddy were easily pulling the wool over my mother's eyes. Our mother was intrigued—a giddy college girl again, elated when he showed up. He was handsome, funny, and charming. His knowledge of literature impressed my mother, an English professor at University of Michigan. Despite his leather jacket and black T-shirt tough act, his shoes were polished, each hair was strategically placed, pulled back in a ponytail, a few stragglers in his eyes for sex appeal—and it worked.

Isabel told my parents she and Teddy met at a party. After talking, they discovered that his dad and our dad went to college together, which made him a shoo-in. Dad was thrilled, and soon the dads went out a few times a month to have beers and catch up. Dad would slap him on the back and say, "Good to see you, Teddy!"

He was too nice to be my sister's friend. He laughed when I told stupid jokes and complimented me, whether it was my hair, my newly expanded vocabulary, or even my clothing. He never treated me like a baby, the way Isabel did. But his darker side? That was what intrigued me. His eyes could hypnotize me into doing anything he asked of me.

Rob a bank? Sure!

Swim deep in the lake with no life jacket? Sure!

Sneak off with me into the woods and . . . sure!

I once asked him where he went to school, and he laughed with that crooked mouth. He said he graduated from the "fancy rich kid" school last spring. He was named after Teddy Roosevelt, his father's favorite president. He had one sister, Liza, named after his mother's favorite Broadway star, Liza Minnelli. His mother, Evette, had always been a stay-at-home socialite mom, and his father, Robert, like my dad was an urban developer, and according to Teddy, they were awful parents.

Teddy described the details of his life in an agitated way. When he spoke of family, his eyes clouded into smooth black circles. Like most thirteen-year-old girls, who liked boys their age, I should have been awkwardly passing notes to my latest crush and blushing when he read them. But the boys in my grade who ran around the playground punching each other and calling each other names seemed immature. None of them held secrets in their eyes.

The way Teddy stared at me with silent eyes when Isabel wasn't looking hinted that we shared some past, deep secret. He would touch my arm sometimes when he spoke to me, the heat running through me like little bolts of electricity, settling in my stomach and staying until he left. I was both scared and excited.

Often, he brought his guitar and effortlessly belted out classic rock songs, including Led Zeppelin. My favorite was "The Rain Song." He would close his eyes and lean down over the guitar and then roll his head back up and down when he really let go. He played with passion. My knowledge of passion had been limited to my mom's Cosmopolitan magazine, which referenced sex. I saw, though, that passion could also mean something else.

He and Isabel would get high and play records, and he would read poetry. I didn't know anything about poetry, except that Oscar Wilde was his favorite poet and "Her Voice" his favorite poem. I knew little about romance, but when his words flowed, I felt warm sensations prickling through my body. He would push stray strands of his long hair behind his ear and gaze up with sparkling dark eyes, transfixing our attention.

I paid closer attention to my appearance. I never knew when he was coming, but I prepared myself after school, curling my straight hair, applying double coats of Strawberry Lip Smackers, and ditching more childish clothes.

Sometimes, he slid next to me on the couch as I read an assigned summer book—close enough to feel his breath on my neck. His hands brushed mine when he grabbed my book to study the back. He would tease me if he thought it childish, and I would pretend to agree, rolling my eyes and bemoaning my fate. Anytime Isabel walked into the room, Teddy would straighten up and pull away.

"What is your problem?" She would come at me as soon as he'd leave. "You don't need help reading books! Are you asking him to explain words to you? He's my boyfriend, and he comes over for me. Why are you throwing yourself at him?"

"What? I'm minding my own business! He's the one who sits down next to me."

"Bullshit! You need to stop being so obvious with your little crush on him. It's ridiculous. He's an eighteen-year-old man for God's sake! He would never have any interest in you."

When I opened my mouth to protest, she waved her middle finger at me and left.

◦◦◦

Spring was winding down, signaling the end of eighth grade. The summer heat was rolling in and I felt restless.

Whenever her sister could take us, my best friend Harper and I would hit the mall. I bought clothes just like what my sister and her friends wore, and I cut the legs off my jeans into shorts that grazed my bottom butt cheeks. I started jogging. I decided to build muscle and not gain weight before high school, so I bought running shorts and tennis shoes and sports bras. After running, I liked how exhausted and exhilarated I felt. The sweat that made invisible tracks down my face and between my blossoming breasts felt sexy and powerful.

One night, I was finishing a run when my mother and Isabel stormed out of the house after a fight. Mom paused to mention she was going to dinner with a colleague, and she had no idea where Isabel huffed off to. A few minutes later, as I was gulping down water, there was a knock at the side door. I wiped the sweat from my face and opened it to a smiling Teddy. He was wearing a navy-blue oxford shirt with khaki-colored shorts and K-Swiss tennis shoes, his long hair pulled tight in a ponytail. Depending on who he needed to impress, he alternated between his leather-jacket-bad-boy look to the preppy, rich-kid outfits that he grew up in.

Despite my parents being charmed by Teddy, Isabel made sure our parents were gone before he came over. A few nights a week, my mom went out with friends or colleagues from the university, and my dad had weekly city development meetings at the steakhouse, after which he was often perfumed with whiskey. And, sometimes, he ate dinner with Teddy's father.

My parents trusted Isabel to care for me, including feeding me. When Teddy was there, she would make grilled burgers or macaroni and cheese. Or I made myself peanut butter and jelly. I felt old enough to take care of myself. Their drinking was the norm, mostly beer or liquor that, despite being underage, Teddy supplied.

After dinner and many drinks, they'd go outside to smoke cigarettes and pot, the scent wafting through my open windows. And then sex. They would go to Isabel's room and weren't subtle about it, forcing me to turn the TV up or escape to the garden. It lasted about twenty minutes. The sounds of sex were new to me, and I wasn't sure if he was hurting her or if she was enjoying it.

I kept distance from Teddy. I didn't want Isabel madder at me.

But any time I was downstairs, he would talk to me, asking a million questions:

How's school going?

Well, it's almost over, so I guess fine.

Right, right. How's your cat?

He's fine.

How's the reading going?

Okay, I guess.

Do you have a boyfriend?

Um, no.

Do you want to smoke pot with us?

No, thanks.

How could I avoid him now? His clean-shaven face soft and the color of tanned olives. Teddy's eyes roamed my body—my striped running shorts, a tank top covering my sports bra, and bare legs, shiny with beads of moisture. My hair was in a high ponytail, and undoubtedly, I wore the rosy-red face of exhaustion.

"Hi there," he said, his smile drawing up his cheekbones.

"Hi yourself," I managed.

I wiped my damp neck with a towel, lingering above my breasts. He didn't even try to hide that he was staring, and I smiled slyly.

"What are you doing here?" I said, heading into the kitchen.

"Your sister and I are going to the movies."

"Oh, really?" I picked up an orange and started peeling, picking the waxy rind with my fingernails. "I'm not sure that's happening."

"What do you mean?"

He stood close, pretending to have interest in a photo stuck under a refrigerator magnet, a snapshot of a younger me and Isabel at Disneyland. Even then, Isabel oozed attitude. Her arms were crossed and her face sour as we sandwiched a life-sized Donald Duck. I was wide-eyed and grinning. I popped a section of orange in my mouth and bit down. Sweet juice filled my mouth, and I shrugged.

"Well, she and my mom got into a fight, I guess, and they both took off. Mom has dinner plans, but I have no idea where your girlfriend went."

"Great," he sighed. "She didn't say where she was going?"

"Nope."

He tossed his keys on the counter.

"Mind if I stick around and wait? We definitely had plans."

"I guess."

I threw the orange rinds away and headed upstairs.

"I gotta shower, so, do what you do best and make yourself at home."

I smiled, and his eyes trailed me as I glided upstairs.

I turned on the shower, undressed, and examined my face in the mirror while the water heated. Isabel and I looked similar in the way sisters do of course, but she was what my mother called, classically beautiful. She had a perfectly symmetrical face with high cheek bones and large expressive eyes and full lips. She was confident and alluring—cool as a cucumber. My dimpled face was rounder with a little pug nose. I loved my dimples, but now I questioned if they were babyish. My lips were thin, and I prayed to the beauty gods for them to plump up. My eyes were my best feature, dark green in the center with a light ring of blue around the iris. My sister had them too, but I thought mine sparkled more.

I ran regularly, but the fleshy body glaring back was not yet muscular. Thankfully, my breasts were sprouting into the size of plums.

My shower was hot and long. I drifted in between daydreams, imagining what it would be like to have Teddy for a boyfriend. I wondered what sex was like and if my sister gave him blow jobs. None of my friends had yet and I was petrified at even seeing a penis. I wrapped a towel around myself and tip-toed over to the staircase banister to see Teddy sitting with a glass of ice tea in hand. The wood squeaked, and his eyes shot up to see me spying at him with dripping hair and just a towel on.

His eyes softened and his lips curled into a smile.

"Yeah, I'm still here," he said, sipping tea, while watching me over the glass.

"Oh, yeah, I was just checking if Isabel made it back."

"Nope, no sign of her yet. Come down and keep me company?"

"Um, sure. After I get dressed. Back in a few."

I skittered across the floor, stepping back over my wet footsteps and into my room. I leaned against my closed door, my heartbeat smacking against the folds of the towel. I hurriedly stepped into underwear and jeans and scrambled into a tattered old Pink Floyd T-shirt that belonged to Isabel. I combed through my wet hair and slicked on some lip gloss.

Get to him before she gets home.

"Feel better?" he asked as I walked towards the kitchen.

"Yep!" I said, as I opened the fridge for the ice tea. I poured a glass and went to the living room. I sat in a chair in the corner.

He set his glass down and placed his elbows on his knees and folded his hands beneath his chin.

"So, Hazel, tell me about your day."

The pale-pink light of dusk streamed through a window and cast a radiant glow across his face. I swiped condensation on my glass with my thumb and stared into the floating ice cubes.

"Um, my day was fine, thanks."

Is this what he asked Isabel every day?

"Just fine? That's not an answer. What did you actually *do*? I'm interested to know."

"Okay, well, I went to school and took some tests and came home and did some homework and then went for a run."

This is boring. This can't be what boyfriends and girlfriends really talk about.

"I see," he sat back again and licked his bottom lip. "Well, did you learn anything new?"

"Not really. It's the end of the year. You know, time to show what we learned by taking tests. You remember tests, don't you?"

He chuckled and took another sip.

"I do. But all that shit they teach in school is garbage. You'll never use it again. What you need is real world experience. Information to get you through life."

What was he talking about?

I looked at the clock on the dining room wall.

Seven thirty.

Where was Isabel?

"What do you mean?"

"You know, traveling around the world, reading books, watching documentaries, maybe even trying pot sometimes. It expands your mind, Hazel. Makes you think, gives you perspective."

Here we go again with the pot.

"I see. So, what books should I read? Because my summer reading list is already long. I'm not sure I can fit in your worldly knowledge."

I smiled and poked at an ice cube.

"Well, you should start with *The Catcher in the Rye*, I think. It covers complex issues like innocence, identity, connecting with people. It's a subjective point of view from the main character, Holden Caulfield."

"It's on my list already," I said, smirking. "Guess my teacher wants me to be worldly too."

He laughed.

"Fair enough. When you read it, I can help you decipher it."

I rolled my eyes. *Did he think I couldn't understand books?*

"Okay, sure, I'll let you know if I need help."

"Well, Hazel, I'm here to help, when you need it."

Suddenly, the back door opened and Isabel blew in like a windstorm. She was carrying a bag of groceries, chips peeking out the top, and her friend Abbey came in behind her carrying a six-pack of beer.

"Sorry!" she said spotting Teddy. "My mom was being a bitch, and I thought we could skip the movie and hang out. And Abbey had some beer and a bag and I . . ."

She stopped short when she saw me in the living room.

"What are you doing? Is she bugging you?" She looked from me to him.

"No, no, of course not. We're just talking about school stuff," He smiled and got up to kiss Isabel. I watched their lips connect, in slow motion.

"Hey, Hazel," said Abbey, setting the beer down and plopping into a chair. She had long black hair, tightly wound from a recent

perm and smoked Parliaments, which showcased her round, full lips
—the kind I wanted. Acne sprouted around her hairline and chin.

"Hey," I said back and ignored Isabel.

Teddy grabbed a beer and nodded at Abbey. She flashed a smile
as her cheeks turned the color of Pink Lady apples. She, too, was
enamored with Teddy.

Who wouldn't be?

"Teddy, *what* are you wearing?" Isabel screeched from the dining
room.

"We were supposed to go to the movies, remember? I dressed up
for you. You don't like it?"

They laughed, and bottle tops twisting open was my cue to go
upstairs. The party was beginning. I brushed past them and took my
empty glass to the kitchen.

"Where did you get the beer?" Teddy asked Abbey.

"Our garage. It's my dad's. But the 'rents are in Paris for a week,
so it's mine now," she said, and they all laughed again.

"Why the fuck are we here, then? You have that awesome pool
and game room. If we're not going to the movies, we should split.
Izzy, your parents *are* coming home at some point. Hers are not."

"Yeah, good point. Gonna grab some clothes. No need to come
home tonight?"

"Definitely not," said Teddy with a mischievous laugh.

"Oh, gross, you guys! You can sleep in the guest house. I don't
want to hear you banging all night!" Abbey griped.

More laughter.

"Ha-ha. Okay, be right back!" said Isabel, and she scrambled up
the stairs.

Teddy appeared in the kitchen.

"There you are."

"Oh, yeah, hi."

"Sorry to desert you, but we're going to Abbey's house. No
parents and all."

"Yep, I get it. Have fun," I said, attempting to push past him.

He grabbed my arm lightly and peered into my eyes.

"Hey, don't forget. *The Catcher in the Rye.* And watch a

documentary, *The Killing of America*. A little depressing; it's about the downfall of the United States, and there's some good interviews with some convicted killers. It's awesome."

"Um, okay? The book, sure, if I have to. That movie sounds horrible."

He laughed, let go of my arm, then winked.

"Yeah, but we'll have something to talk about other than school, right?"

His fingers left warm imprints, and I felt a tingling sensation between my legs.

4

NYMPH

ANN ARBOR, MICHIGAN 1985

A n early sun sliced through thick layers of leaves from the black oak tree next to my bedroom window, casting fragmented shadows across the walls. I was stretched out in bed, and Coconut purred loudly as I pet him with sleepy hands. The notes of Charles Mingus floated up the stairs, tiptoed beneath my door, and brought with them the bitter fragrance of coffee. The cat rolled over and showed me his belly. I smiled and gave it a soft squeeze.

"Okay, okay, I get it. You need a lot of petting."

I heard a tap on my door, then a creak as it opened. It was my father, smiling, holding two mugs. I grinned as he walked over and sank onto the edge of my bed, leaned over, and kissed my forehead. His scent of fruity shampoo and spicy aftershave lingered.

"Good morning, pumpkin. Sleep well?" I rubbed my eyes and nodded.

He set the mugs on my nightstand, mine filled with a combination of hot chocolate and a little coffee—toffee colored with cream swirls.

"Get dressed and come downstairs? I have a surprise."

"Okay." I said, pulling back the covers.

I took a sip of my coffee concoction, the sugary liquid coating my tongue. He tousled my tangled brown hair and left me to get dressed. I yawned and pulled on jeans and a sweatshirt.

On my way out, I peeked into my sister's room. She lay sleeping, covers rumpled and the shades drawn. Across the hallway, my parents' door was cracked open, and I could see the outline of my mother sleeping, one leg outside the sheets, dangling towards the floor. An empty wine glass sat on the nightstand, and she was snoring. I clicked the door shut. As I headed downstairs, the music got louder, and the aroma of coffee, stronger. My father was at the kitchen table, browsing the newspaper, reading glasses perched on the end of his nose.

"Coffee good?"

I nodded.

At age twelve, I was allowed a coffee and hot chocolate combination on the weekends. Same for Isabel, but now that Isabel was seventeen, she drank black coffee. Our parents didn't see any harm in a little caffeine in the mornings to jumpstart our brains.

He folded the paper, stretched his arms up and out, and let out a loud yawn and got up. He opened the backyard screen door, and we stepped out into a mellow morning sun.

"Okay, Hazelnut. It's a beautiful morning, and we've got things to do and things to see."

The lush backyard greenery had sealed the deal for my parents when they bought our house. Beautiful flowers—black-eyed Susans, swamp milkweed, and cattails circled our small pond, rich with water lilies. The landscape was a perfect backdrop for attracting diverse wildlife and insects. Ducks quacked cheerfully, and bushy-tailed squirrels chased each other up and down the American beech trees that separated our property from the neighbors. Trembling Aspen trees with beautiful bright-yellow leaves and smooth gray bark outlined the pond and attracted white-tail deer. My father told me they liked to eat the bark, which sounded chewy and awful.

The sights and sounds and smells of our own cloistered paradise brought a welcome reprieve from the family chaos. And this morning, to have my father all to myself was even more special. A remarkable man. He was good to us girls and always comforted my mother, even when she lay in bed for days, lamenting about her failed writing career. Her *novel*. The "unfinished manuscript," the bane of my mother's all-inclusive world.

On good days, the pages of her novel were spread on the bed and her emerald eyes glistened wild with creative passion. My dad brought her coffee and croissants from Zingerman's bakery in the morning and wine and cheese in the afternoon. She was, after all, an artiste; this was her process. Pajama clad, her long red hair spilling over her shoulders, and a pen in her hand writing feverishly. "Oh, Richard, listen! This is good. This is so good! Girls, I'm telling you, this chapter is brilliant!" she would say, beaming, as Isabel and I stood waiting and wishing she would instead take us to the park. We had no idea what a novel was or what hers was about, nor did we care.

On bad days, there would be her favorite wine—Bordeaux, she called it—on the nightstand, and my mother would be splayed out on the floor, arms and legs star-fished, her eyes traveling across the ceiling. Her skin ashen in gray tones, her russet hair stabbed with bobby pins in a messy up do, and mascara staining her cheekbones as she sobbed for inspiration.

The absence or existence of words could cause my mother to either crumble to pieces or to laugh and smile and make promises of ice cream or new dresses. It was confusing to manage my emotions back then. Was this normal? We looked to our dad for guidance and normalcy. He assured us that she was fine, that creative people were—unpredictable.

"Let's go to the bench," my father said. "Best seats around this place!"

The Thinking Bench. My mother's flea market find. It was nineteenth century and cast iron. Its curly-pawed feet were engraved with birds along the length of the arms and curved upwards into a floral carved back. Beautiful. To get it home, my parents had to enlist the neighbors and their truck. When they lowered it to the ground, it seemed to sigh as it sunk into the soft dirt, as if it needed us as much as we needed it.

We sat on the steely surface, warmed from the early morning sun. My dad sipped his coffee and squinted toward the water, his eyes searching.

"Keep your eyes peeled to the reeds." He lifted his chin to the right side of the pond. Our hummingbird feeders were active with the nimble little birds buzzing around. Their wings beat in rapid succession as they flew in and out of the sugary basin.

"The hummingbirds?" I asked.

He shook his head.

"No, just keep watching, you'll see."

I waited. I took another sip, the light buzz of caffeine peeling my eyes open. As far as I was concerned, nothing could happen, and I would be happy. My mother and Isabel were missing out, snoozing away.

Suddenly, hundreds of tiny helicopters rose from the surface of the water, and I leaned forward, in awe. Dragonflies. Blue and green wings sparkled and whirred in the rich glow of the morning sun, and their shadows bounced and reflected over the pond. Spinning forward and backward, air dancing. In and out, weaving between the grassy reeds, nose-diving only to hover inches atop the water, as if dipping their toes, and then rocketing back towards the sky, seducing one another with a circular airborne waltz. As if my mother's shiny jewelry was being cast into the air and sprinkled down, glittering and twinkling. They flew in pairs, playfully teasing each other in this sacred, secret tango. I caught my father watching me, grinning.

"Aren't they amazing?"

"So cool! How come I've never seen them before?"

He crossed his legs and reclined. "Well, we probably weren't out here when they were becoming adults."

"What do you mean?"

"Well, the dragonfly has a life cycle, like everything. When their eggs hatch, a baby begins its life as a 'nymph.' They resemble little aliens, with no wings, and they have this little crusty hump on their backs."

"Ew!" I scrunched my nose, and he laughed.

"I know, sounds kind of gross, huh? Well, they are smart little guys. Ducks, frogs, and fish, and even other nymphs try to eat them, and how they protect themselves is by pretending to be dead or swimming away fast. And if a predator happens to catch them, the nymphs will shed their limbs right off! They grow back during molting. You remember molting, like what snakes do? Shed their skin? But these guys lose their legs. Isn't that cool?"

"And pretty gross, Dad!" I said, making another face. "I wouldn't want my legs to fall off."

He laughed, "I wouldn't want your legs to fall off either! Dragonflies are ruthless about feeding. They devour mosquitoes, which is good for us, but also butterflies and moths, and I saw in *National Geographic* that they can even take down tadpoles! Those tiny little nymphs can scoop up moving fish! It's very impressive. And, they have two sets of wings—very delicate wings, and as adults, they fly up to thirty-six miles per hour!"

My dad, the walking encyclopedia. He loved facts about anything. Sometimes, it was weird stuff. We once sat through dinner listening to him explain how elevators worked. His enthusiasm was contagious even if the topic choice was odd. By the end of the meal, we were all astounded to learn that no matter how many times you pushed the button, it did not make the elevator come any faster. There is only one switch to signal it to go, yet people always frantically jam the buttons as if willing the doors to open faster.

"How long do dragonflies live?" I asked.

That's the sad part. Typically, two months."

"Two months? Really? That's so unfair."

"It's a shame," he said, shaking his head.

"The babies don't get to know their parents either?"

He chuckled.

"Nope! They leave that little crusty clump of themselves on the plant it crawls on. That clump stays for a while. The little nymph may be leaving home, but part of them will remain. Like you girls. When you get older and head to college, I bet you will leave something gross behind too, maybe a crusty old tube of toothpaste!"

"Ew!" I giggled. "Isabel probably will! Not me! I always put the cap back on!"

He smiled and squeezed my knee. "Of course, you do. But someday you will shed your own skin, leave home, and go into the world. You'll have to make good decisions and decide what's safe and what's not. All kinds of ducks and frogs and fish will try to eat you up, and you must learn to bite back. Lose a limb or two to protect yourself."

"Okay, Dad, I'll be careful," I said, imagining running away with my legs falling off, one by one.

I linked our hands and swung my legs. I didn't want to leave home. We sat in silence while the dragonflies rose up and skimmed delicately in search of their next meal.

～

My mother remained upstairs for the morning. Around eleven o'clock, my dad delivered fresh squeezed orange juice, an almond croissant, two pats of butter, and the newspaper to her. After lunch, I sat on the divan out back watching the clouds open their pillowy arms and build stories on top of each other. First, an alligator chasing a horse and a long sharp sword piercing a cactus. As soon as the characters materialized, the wind blew them apart, and new ones took shape.

A clatter came from the kitchen. I recognized the sound of Isabel moving dishes around. She would pile them in neat stacks to look less chaotic and promise to get to them later. After a few minutes, the screen door creaked open and slammed shut, and there she stood, barefoot, wearing a faded red T-shirt and flannel pajama bottoms. Her matted brown hair hung limp past her shoulders, and yesterday's mascara smudged black racoon rings under her eyes.

"There you are." Her voice was gravelly, like after a night of smoking cigarettes and drinking. "Clean your cat's gross litter box. It smells disgusting. It actually woke me up. Why can't he shit outside seeing that he is out here half the time?

"Gee, I don't know. Would you dig a hole if you had a toilet inside? He is the *family's* cat. We all are supposed to help do chores! Dad said—"

"—Yeah, I know what Dad said. But he's more your cat than anybody else's. He's always by you—like right now."

Coconut had come from the woods and wove in and out of my legs.

"Maybe he doesn't like you very much."

Isabel rolled her eyes. "Whatever. Dogs are better anyway. Just clean it up while I do the stupid dishes."

She scowled at Coconut and let the door slam shut. This was my sister lately—an angry tornado, hurling insults and complaints, then gone in a gust. Did she hate me these days? What had I done that was so awful? Or was it that my mom and sister were continually battling, and the war trickled down to me?

Late afternoon, my mother appeared. She was freshly showered, her face shining in a cinematic glow—fully made up with her signature red lipstick and her hair wrapped in a tight French twist. Equal parts intoxicating and nauseating, the aroma of Christian Dior Poison elbowed its way into the room before and after her. She wore white capri pants, and a soft, fuzzy cashmere sweater. She was barefoot, her toes sparkling with cherry-red polish. My mother was beautiful. She flowed into a room effortlessly—like a wave of hot lava. Her insecurities were masked with convincing charm, and to know her and love her was to play along and grant her your full attention. *Today* was a good day. She padded across the kitchen floor on her delicate feet and poked her head around my father's shoulder as he stirred a large pot of Bolognese sauce.

Sunday night family dinners were my dad's idea, and he spent hours preparing for it. On Italian night, he began with the lengthy process of making homemade pasta. A moat of flour and salt surrounded several eggs, and as he slowly whisked them, he would gradually pull in flour from the bottom and sides until soft dough formed. His fancy machine with rollers and blades would cut long stretches of dough into noodle-length sheets. He then dried them on the rungs of my mother's accordion-clothes drying rack, the backs of kitchen chairs, and even coat hangers he hung from cabinet doors. It was as if dozens of Hawaiian straw hula skirts shimmied around the room.

Luciano Pavarotti's rendition of "Largo al Factotum" boomed from the speakers—the infamous Bugs Bunny sketch was one of Isabel and my favorites. We had long ago incorporated the song into these dinners. While the noodles dried, and the sauce simmered, my dad would take turns waltzing with us, singing with Pavarotti at the top of his lungs. He sipped Chianti and filled two wine glasses with sparkling water and lemons for us. Isabel and I felt sophisticated with our "wine" and opera and fancy spaghetti. Holding up our glasses, we made silly toasts and said silly things like, "I would like to thank the Academy" and "I couldn't have done it without my agent."

Lately, my mother had been missing from these ceremonial Sunday nights, but now, here she was, smoldering and seductive, drawing us in. As she bent forward to taste the sauce with a wooden spoon, my sister and I nervously glanced at each other.

"Oh, Richard! That is simply divine! You really do make the best Bolognese! I just can't get enough basil. Can you girls ever really get enough basil?" she exclaimed, glancing back at us. "You are so lucky, you two. Your father spoils you two every Sunday! So spoiled my girls are!"

My sister raised her eyebrows and shrugged. I stared at the lemon slice in my fizzy water, the bubbles climbing the sides of the glass. My father shot me a look, imploring patience.

"Yep, we are!" I replied.

My mother looked at me, her brow furrowed.

"Hazel, you know I don't like it when you say 'Yep.' The answer to yes is always yes. Anyway," she shooed an invisible fly from her ear and turned to my father, "I'm so sorry, Richard. This looks divine. But I must run to work. I forgot some papers yesterday that I left on my desk . . . I'm always in a rush . . . and well, you know I can't eat this anyway. I'm doing that grapefruit and cabbage soup diet . . . I know, I know, they're two different diets, but I'm combining them for maximum results."

She plucked a piece of romaine lettuce covered in Caesar dressing from the salad bowl and sniffed it. Without tasting it, she dropped it back into the bowl. "Sometimes, I swear, I wish I had a big old tapeworm inside me . . . no, no . . . I would never do that . . . But did you know that the tapeworm actually attaches to your stomach and eats your food for you? Imagine! It's like your own internal garbage disposal! I know, I know, disgusting! But to not have to think about what you're eating . . . the damn thing does it for you!"

My father tried to speak, but she was in her own world, oblivious to our presence.

"Anyway, finals are soon, and I have to make sure I'm prepared! I still have last week's papers to grade—Richard, this counter has a sticky spot on it over here." My father glanced at the spot, but she continued, "I suppose you'll get this later when you clean up. You know how I can be when the tiniest things drive me insane!"

I held my breath, waiting for my father to say something, anything. But he didn't, and his shoulders fell as he attended to his sauce. I looked again to Isabel, but she was flipping through the latest issue of *Time* magazine, pretending to be interested in the cover story of Bill Gates, "Computer Software: The Magic Inside the Machine."

"Joanne, you said—"

"—Yes, I know, Richard, you are not happy, but I promise, I won't be long and you lucky three will have a marvelous dinner and won't even notice I'm gone!"

Her voice drifted off as her eyes darted around the room. She took a large gulp of my father's wine and waltzed over to the back door where she cleared her throat and pulled her keys from her purse.

"Like I said, darling. I won't be long. Enjoy your dinner. Girls, I'll be back in time to tuck you in, I promise."

5

VACILLATE

ANN ARBOR, MICHIGAN 1985

"Girls! It's time to go! Are you ready?" my mother called up the stairs.

"Almost!" I yelled, as I stuffed clothes into my backpack.

"Yep!" my sister hollered.

We were heading out to a "girls" weekend to visit my mom's college friend, Mavis Flowers, referred to by my father as my mom's weird hippie friend. Our destination was north of the Sleeping Bear Dunes in a tiny town named Leelanau. This place was the stuff of legends amongst my classmates. Many of them spent summer vacations there trudging up the thick sand to the pinnacle of vast formations, and then like miniature barrels, they tucked and rolled down the giant hills, their mouths and hair and clothes covered with gritty granules of sand. For me, I was excited for the gift shop at the base of the dunes, replete with old-fashioned candy sticks flavored like root beer, butterscotch, and cinnamon, and jewelry carved out of Petoskey stones and miniature Michigan-shaped key chains.

I dragged my backpack off my bed, gave Coconut a rub under his chin, and headed downstairs to say good-bye to my dad, who I desperately wished was going with us.

"I guess we're leaving, and it's not going to be the same without you!" I whined.

"Hazel, your mom is a lot of fun. Do you think I'd have married a boring girl? Now go get your sister and get moving!"

"Fine," I grumbled.

Downstairs, my mother and Isabel were packing the car, a striped brown and beige Ford station wagon. Our cooler was filled with sandwiches, chips, and cans of Vernors Ginger Ale and Faygo Rock & Rye. Two bottles of wine were nestled in ice.

"There you are!" exclaimed my mother, who was dressed in hippie attire and a bandanna tied around her hair. Sweat beaded her smiling face. The humidity was a soggy blanket draped around us.

"Sorry," I said, "I was saying bye to Dad. Need any help?"

"Nah. There's not much to bring and it's almost all packed." She snapped the lid on the cooler and motioned to my sister, who was standing behind me.

"C'mon Isabel! We can lift this up together."

Isabel rolled her eyes and sighed.

"It's not that heavy, Mom. But, sure, no problem. I don't mind working for free as a child laborer." She dragged her feet towards the car, and the two of them hoisted it inside.

"Enough with the attitude," my mother said, narrowing her eyes at her. "Let's hit the road."

Soon, Isabel snuggled into the back seat corner as far from me as possible. Once her Walkman was on and headphones in, she stared out the window. I sat behind Mom and could see her eyes in the rearview mirror. The little lines around them creased and puckered when she smiled. The pointy end of her bandanna jutted out and brushed the head rest when she moved. She sang softly to James Taylor.

"Are you excited, Hazel?" she asked, straining her neck to see me.

"Yes," I said.

My mother looked at Isabel, who was faking sleep. My mom pursed her lips and shook her head.

The drive was uneventful. Big, full trees along the expressway passed in a blur as my mom chatted with me about my piano lessons (which I hated), the trip we planned into the city to go to the Detroit Institute of Arts again, dinner at Lelli's—and how she needed to weed the garden. She kept one hand on the wheel and waved the other one around in excited gestures. It was surprising to me how easy it was to talk to her sometimes and how happy it seemed to make her. Eventually, Isabel's fake sleep slipped into the real thing, her head smooshed up against the door, one earphone off. I watched her, wondering about her dreams as her face gave away nothing, and wished she would wake up a nicer person.

∼

A beat-up wooden fence with chipped white paint bordered the two-track dirt driveway. Thousands of wildflowers and weeds climbed from the ground on either side of us as the car crawled towards Mavis's house. Halfway up, a gutted and rusted-out VW Bug sat on some tall grass. I was astonished to see it had gained a second life as a chicken coop with wire fencing and hens scratching around piles of hay.

I spied the house, splashed in a kaleidoscope of colors that resembled a tie-dyed T-shirt. Isabel removed her other headphone and pressed her face to the window.

"What is this crazy place?" she asked.

My mother laughed, eyes sparkling in the mirror, and her face glowed with anticipation.

"This, this is my beautiful, amazing friend Mavis's house," she said. "She's a wild one! You girls will love her!"

Isabel frowned, "I don't know, Mom, this place is nuts!"

"Listen. Mavis is a bit of an . . . eccentric." She turned to face us after she parked. "She's unique and different and so much fun! She moved up here after her divorce to reclaim herself."

"If you say so," Isabel muttered.

As I opened my door, two chickens came running over to the car, like dogs. They circled and pecked near my sandaled feet, making cute clucking noises. Wooden wind chimes swayed on the porch, emitting a hollow and melodic jangling that echoed in the air. The front screen door creaked open, and a tiny woman with long braids on each side of her head came sprinting down the stairs.

"JoJo! You're here!"

She embraced my mother as if she might break her. The woman was barefoot, wearing a long paisley-print dress, blue and green crystals dangling around her neck, and large turquoise and silver rings on each finger. My mother placed her hands on Mavis's shoulders and smiled warmly.

"You look beautiful! Refreshed. Happy!" My mother twirled Mavis around like a man fast dancing with his lady.

Isabel raised her eyebrows at me, and I shrugged. Our mother never acted like this, not even with our dad. And, *JoJo?*

"Mavis, these are my little darlings!" She motioned us to come closer. "This one here is Isabel," she put an arm around my sister, "my oldest, and seventeen for God's sakes, if you can believe I'm that old! She's growing up so fast. And this one," her other arm looped around me, "is Hazel, my little girl, twelve years old, who I am desperately hoping will stay my baby!"

I knew Isabel was cringing inside, but she stretched a phony smile across her face and nodded her head at Mavis.

"Hello," she said.

"Hi," I waved.

Mavis grinned at us with sparkling blue eyes and sun-burnished skin.

"Oh, Joanne, your girls are lovely! Just lovely! And, girls, mind the chickens, they like to peck toes!"

Tiny mounds of chicken poop were scattered all around. Looking at Mavis's bare feet, I imagined how filthy the bottoms must be.

"Come on, let's get your things and get inside." She slung an arm around my mother's shoulder and led her to the back of the car. "I made some ice tea and brownies. We have so much to catch up on, JoJo!"

Isabel twirled her finger by her head and mouthed, "cuckoo!"

We followed Mavis and my mom up the stairs to a porch with a wooden swing and potted plants in various stages of health. Oddly-shaped rocks and broken pottery leaned against the house while neglected tubes of oil paints and used brushes filled a bucket. A sign above the door read, "Hippies welcome." Inside, a large chocolate-colored dog unfolded his legs and sauntered over to us, limping. It pushed its nose into my hand.

"That's Earth Gypsy," said Mavis, "but call her Gypsy. She's a sleepy old gal. I rescued her a while back. No one wants to tend to older dogs. She's a sweet girl."

Scratching the dog's head, I looked around. In a continuation from the porch, plants littered every surface. Hanging-spider and creeping-ivy in macrame holders dropped from the ceiling, tiny cacti and herb pots filled with basil and cilantro perched on the kitchen windowsill, and a giant palm flopped over the floor in a corner.

Incense burned on the lip of an ashtray on the stove top, filling the room with a pungent aroma, while stringy ropes of smoke flowed upward. A curtain of wooden beads guided us into the living room. Fastened to the walls were tie-dyed sheets covered in spray-painted peace signs. A poster of a bare-chested man with high cheekbones, long curly hair, and a strand of oblong beads around his neck stared at me with eyes dark as mud. My mother said his name was Jim Morrison. I felt swallowed up by his gaze and had to look away.

Weird thick purple carpet tickled my exposed toes. It could easily swallow up dropped items. Bye, bye Barbie shoes! Big fluffy cushions in purples and blues were strewn around the room while oversized pillows piled on top of them in a rainbow of oranges and reds. There were small low tables covered with candles and more incense. This room, heavy with competing aromas and clashing colors, made me feel like I was swimming underwater in saltwater taffy with candied fish.

"Okay, take your pick, girls," said Mavis, nodding towards the piles of stuffed cushions. Apparently, this was her couch. "Your mom is going to sleep with me in my room, and you young ladies will be out here. It's super comfy!" She turned to my mother and smiled, "It will be just like college! Up all night giggling and stuff. Only this time we aren't going to try to save the world. We see how that turned out."

"Alright, alright," my mother chuckled. "No politics tonight, please. This is going to be a fun weekend with just us girls!"

"Where do you want to sleep?" I asked my sister.

She looked around and shrugged her shoulders.

"I guess I'll take the purple one."

~

That night, Mavis prepared a vegetarian dinner—bean salad, basmati rice, roasted vegetables, pumpkin soup, and brownies with ice cream for dessert. We ate outside on a picnic table she set up with dozens of flickering candles and Ball jars filled with wildflowers. On the left side of the yard, a sizable patch of garden grew cucumbers, spinach, tomatoes, radishes, butter lettuce, and pumpkins. The Moody Blues sang to us from the house through open windows, and Mavis and my mother chatted on endlessly about their gardens.

Where Mavis's yard stopped, thick woods began. Between the two was a fire pit with mismatched benches circling it. She said we could have a bonfire and s'mores after dinner.

"No way! S'mores?" I exclaimed.

"Yes! Of course! It's not often that I have kids around here, so I wanted you girls to enjoy yourselves," Mavis said with a big smile. Her skin was bronzed from the sun, and freckles dotted her cheeks and nose.

"Well, that's very nice of you, Mavis, isn't it, girls?" my mother asked, putting her arm around me and squeezing. She and Mavis were sipping wine, my mother on her second glass, her eyes wide with energy and edging into the familiar slippery gray globes.

"Yes, thank you!" I said.

"Yes, thanks," Isabel said, pushing her food around her plate.

My mother gave us a satisfied look, turned back to Mavis, and began lamenting about President Reagan and something called Sandinista.

Isabel hunched down to whisper across the table to me.

"Wanna go into the woods later?"

My eyebrows shot up.

"Later? When?"

"After dark, I guess. Or right after we have our s'mores. This food is making me want to ralph," she said lifting her chin towards the dense forest. "I want to get away and hide."

"Hide? From who?"

"From that wastoid," she hissed, narrowing her eyes at our mother, who was tossing back the last large gulp.

"Geez, Isabel! Don't call her that!" I whispered back.

"I hope you have more wine!" my mother shrieked. "I only brought one more bottle!" The bandanna from her head was gone and her fiery auburn hair spilled over her shoulders. I noticed she had put on her signature red lipstick.

"Don't worry, JoJo. I've got plenty. I know how you like your wine," Mavis said, grinning and trotted inside to get another bottle.

"Seriously?" Isabel pursed her lips and crossed her arms. "It's just the woods. Take a chill pill, and don't be such a chicken. There are already a bunch of those gross things running and clucking around here!"

The third bottle was popped open, and Isabel and I roasted marshmallows on flames as Mavis flitted around her yard plucking wildflowers and ivy that crept up the house. She produced ribbon as if from thin air and wove the flowers and vines into crowns meant for our heads. For a moment, I felt like a fairy princess. Isabel was too cool to be a princess, and, under her breath, told me that only a dork would wear one as she discarded hers. Ignoring her, I kept mine proudly perched on my head as I tackled my second s'more smiling as rivers of the sugary treat trickled down my hand.

When the fire died down, my mother and Mavis carried in the dishes and told us not to stray far. Isabel took that as our cue to head to the woods. Wispy clouds dotted the sky, and the sun descended in the West. The heat hadn't broken yet and mosquitoes began to feast on our arms and legs.

"Come on, slowpoke!" Isabel called to me as I stopped to examine a rock that was shaped like a heart. I picked it up and put it in my pocket.

"It's getting dark, I just think—"

"That's what you get for thinking, lame-o!" Isabel hollered as she kicked at the leaves and stones on the ground.

I put my hands on my hips, trying to appear intimidating.

"Why do you have to be so mean all the time? Stop calling me names!"

"Or what? You going to tell Mom? Because she is sure as shit not going to care right now. She's too busy in there with her girlfriend getting drunk again—"

"—What do you mean? She cares!"

"Oh, Hazel. You have no idea."

"Idea about what?"

Mosquitoes buzzed around my ear, cutting through the otherwise noiseless air around us. Isabel paused, and stared at the ground. I waited; anticipation caught in my throat.

"Her drinking. She drinks way too much. She's embarrassing. She's mean. Then, she forgets the whole ordeal the next day and acts normal. Our mom's a drunk, Hazel."

She said these words as if they were truth. So matter of fact. *Drunk.* The word was sour in my ears. I didn't want to believe it. A girl at school had a dad everyone called a real drunk. A day-drinking, fighting, getting kicked out of bars type. My mother was not like him.

"No, she's not!" I argued, picking at sticky strips of tree bark.

"Think about it. She sleeps in the afternoons. You hear how she slurs her words, right? Remember when she almost fell down the stairs that one time, but Dad grabbed her arm and saved her? It's serious, Hazel."

Like tiny thorns, her words stung, like I was somehow responsible for my mom's behavior. My instinct was to protect her.

A glass of wine in my mother's hand was like a cup of coffee in my father's. Normal.

"But she doesn't go to bars all day or anything," I whispered and stared at my damp and smudged fingertips.

Isabel smacked a mosquito buzzing around her ear. "You don't have to hang out in bars to be an alcoholic. You're too young to understand all this shit, but just know, it's not going to get any better. I am sick of how she acts. She's mean one day, and now, she's being all fake at her crazy friend's house, all lovey-dovey and so proud of us. She can't be trusted."

Can't be trusted.

"Don't say that! She's not being fake! She was really happy the whole drive here. You were sleeping, so you wouldn't know. We talked and talked, and she—"

"—I'm sure she was!" Isabel exclaimed. "Because it's all about her. This is her weekend, no matter what she tells you. That we're here to see the dunes because you want to go? No, this is her getting to see her friend, and drink, and we're just along for the ride. To make her look like a good mother."

"Stop it, Isabel! I don't wanna hear anymore!"

Tears stung my eyes. Why was she ruining everything? She was completely wrong.

"Listen, Hazel," she leaned against a tree. "I just want you to be prepared. You're still young. Mom can be great sometimes, but she is selfish. She loves us; she does. But she loves herself more. I'm not trying to be mean, just honest. No one was there to warn me, but I'm here to warn you. You're my little sister, and a total pain in the ass," she chuckled, "but I want you to know why she acts like this."

A sharp pinch nipped my ankle. I bent down to swat at a feeding mosquito. Blood smeared and blended with tree sap.

"We better get back," was all I managed.

Isabel grabbed my arm.

"I'm sorry, Hazel. I really am just trying to protect you."

I twisted away from her and peered into those green eyes that mirrored mine.

"I think we should go back now. It's getting late."

Isabel put her hands on her hips. "Look, Hazel, don't say anything to Mom about what I said. Okay?"

"Fine!" I sprinted toward the dim light coming from the house. I wanted to hug my mom. I needed her to be okay. She must be worried. I passed the smoldering fire, the open box of graham crackers next to it, and blinked through tears as the blur of wildflowers caught my watery eyes. On the picnic table, wax from the flickering candles had melted into blobby volcanoes.

Gypsy joined me as I headed in. I glanced behind and saw Isabel swinging a long stick, slicing through the air at nothing.

The door groaned, and I crept through the kitchen gingerly. A foul stench struck me, a road-killed skunk. I peeked through the beads. There, amidst the living room clutter, were my mother and Mavis, dancing. Giggling and twirling each other around, both off-balance and tripping over themselves. I held my breath. Abba's "Dancing Queen" swallowed up my ears as they sang along.

Mom's face was rose-colored as she tossed her head back and scrunched up her hair, her lipstick merely a stain now. She swayed her hips in seductive circles, her hands resting on Mavis's shoulders their eyes locked in a rhythmic stare. Mavis's lips were tangled in my mother's hair, and she was saying something that I could not catch. My feet stuck in invisible glue, panic rising up into my throat, as I heard the back door slam. I whipped around to see Isabel, fanning the air.

"What the hell is going on in here? They're smoking pot? Of course they are!"

The music whooshed to a murmur, and my mother came crashing into the kitchen.

"Girls! Where have you been? Come dance with us!"

Her eyes were globes of glass, and she wobbled towards a countertop, attempting to steady herself. My twelve-year-old brain snapped a mental photograph of this scene. My mother was messy drunk and high and dancing and almost kissing her friend, who was a woman. I couldn't process any of it.

"Upsy-daisy!" Mavis said to my mom, laughing. "We might have indulged a bit much tonight, girls! Sorry about that! I'll get her to bed."

"I'm fine! I'm fine!" my mother slurred and slapped her friend's hands away from her. "Where have you two been? In the woods? It's so dark in there, and—"

"—You are unbelievable, Joanne!" Isabel spewed, calling Mom by her name. "Can't you go one day without drinking? And now you're getting high too? While your kids are here? What the fuck is the matter with you?"

I clamped my hands over my ears. Her voice was shrill and angry, and xylophones vibrated in the background as Abba continued the happy chorus of melodies. My mother squinted and tried to focus on my sister. She smoothed her hair and licked her lips.

"Oh, yeah, yeah, we had wine and smoked dope. So what? I bet you do it all the time. I've got your number, Isabel. Don't act so innocent, and, by the way, you are not allowed to yell at me or call me by my name. You better just watch your tone and show respect!"

Inches away from each other, Isabel jabbed her index finger into my mother's shoulder.

"Respect *you*? What a joke!"

Before my mother could respond, Isabel spun around and headed towards the back door. My mother looked stunned; her eyes blinked rapidly as Mavis rubbed her shoulders.

"You get back here! You can't speak to me that way! I am your mother!"

Isabel put one hand on the screen door and exhaled a long breath of air. Turning away from the three of us, she said, "Unfortunately, I can't do *shit* about that!" and shoved the door, crashing it on its hinges.

～

T he next morning, my mother emerged from Mavis's room in an orange blossom kimono, her hair in wild tangles. Yawning, she passed through the living room, stepping over us in our velvety beds and glided into the kitchen.

"Rise and shine, girls!"

She began opening cabinets in search of coffee. Mavis materialized next in a thin tank top with no bra, showcasing her upturned nipples beneath, and lacy shorts that barely covered her butt. Her graying hair hung in long spiral curls down her back.

"Well, good morning, young ladies! I hope you slept well! Were you comfy?"

"Yes, it was good, thanks," I said.

Isabel just nodded and closed her eyes. She flung an arm over her face and let out a long sigh. We had already been awake for an hour, arguing in whispers about what our mother would say and do in the light of day.

"Great," Mavis said, ignoring my sister's dramatics. "I'll make us some breakfast in a bit. You kids drink coffee?

"Yes," Isabel moaned.

"Yes, please."

Isabel rolled over and faced me with a smirk on her face.

"I told you," she boasted. "They're both going to pretend nothing happened last night. They were drunk and high, and this is mom's M.O. anyway."

"What's M.O?" I whispered.

"Modus operandi. How she operates. Acts like an asshole and then never apologizes. You should be used to it."

The bitter scent that perfumed mornings at home wafted into the room. The machine gurgled and sputtered and then became still. An unintelligible conversation was happening between my mom and Mavis.

"Girls! Coffee's ready!" Mavis called to us.

"Come on," Isabel threw the afghan aside. "If we're going to play pretend all day, I'm going to need some fucking caffeine."

~

We sat outside, drinking our coffee and eating toast with soft-boiled eggs fresh from the chicken coop while Mom and Mavis chatted about astronomy and rare butterflies that inhabited their gardens. Our mother flashed smiles at Mavis in between giddy laughter and repeatedly combed her fingers through her hair. Isabel and I ate in silence, dipping our bread into the gelatinous and weirdly bright-yellow yolks of our eggs. Her irritation was palpable. From the corner of my eye, I saw her stabbing at her egg with her toast, both barely eaten. Mom didn't notice I was drinking coffee, to which I had added gobs of rich cream and two heaping teaspoons of sugar to cover up what I suspected was nasty. It bothered me that she didn't even notice my blatant defiance.

Neither Mavis nor my mother noticed our lack of conversation, and as they finished their breakfast, our dishes were abruptly taken inside. They were now discussing ceramics and folk dancing. Before we left, Mavis pulled my sister and I in for an awkward embrace. She planted wet kisses on our cheeks as we said good-bye to her and her strange little home. She gushed about what well-mannered guests we had been, and we were welcome back anytime. A pair of moccasins were gifted to Isabel and me, and we both muttered thank-yous and small smiles. My sister and I exchanged glances, knowing we would never wear them. I watched the chickens pecking, pooping, squawking, and strutting back and forth from their VW Bug home to our feet. Mavis and my mother embraced far too long. Isabel and I rolled our eyes at each other in disgust.

~

In the car my mother cranked her music—Crosby, Stills & Nash crooning about "Judy Blue Eyes" and Jimi Hendrix wailing to an "American Woman" to stay away from him. My mom's single braid, Mavis's handiwork, swung around as she belted out the lyrics. We sped towards the Sleeping Bear Dunes under a brilliant indigo sky. Little smudges of mascara streaked from the corners of her eyes. I wanted to be angry at her. She spent the evening rehashing the good times with her dear college friend, ignoring us, doing as she pleased. Just as Isabel had pointed out, she did not take responsibility for the harm she caused.

Rolling into the parking lot of the Sleeping Bear Dunes, my mother squeezed my leg, and I shook off thoughts of the night before. Her eyes glistened. In front of us, decades of cultivated and abundant sand appeared relaxed as it posed in a series of pyramids surrounded by Lake Michigan. I thought I knew what to expect, but the sheer size of it all amazed me. I was a tiny person peering up at years of nature churning pieces of glass into sand.

Isabel, for all her resentment and sourness, was also in awe. Her expectations had been low, and I could see from her wide-eyed expression that she was impressed. She slid off her headphones and got out of the station wagon and stood next to me with a goofy grin on her face.

"Here we are, girls! Isn't this gorgeous?"

Before we could answer, she dragged her purse from the car, slammed the door and immediately lit a cigarette. As she exhaled a plume of smoke, she smiled and nodded towards the mass of sand before us.

"Come on, run up that hill, we can go to the gift shop after. Run up there and roll down! Isn't that what the kids do here? You girls go on, I'll be here waiting. Have fun and don't get hurt please."

She had settled in at a picnic table and sipped on a can of Faygo from our cooler with a book.

"You're not coming?" I asked.

"No, honey, you know how I feel about getting dirty. I'll be here reading all about the wonderful lakes around here."

I frowned and turned to see Isabel trudging up four-hundred and fifty feet of thick sand. Everywhere, children scrambled up effortlessly, some with their parents right behind them, laughing. One small boy had plopped down halfway up and was crying. His mother wrapped an arm around him and was doing her best to prop him back up again. I turned around and peered down to where our mother sat, smoking. The book was closed, and a man was at the opposite end of the table, smiling and flailing his arms around as he spoke to her. She was laughing and crossing and uncrossing her legs. Isabel followed my gaze and grabbed my arm.

"Come on, we're halfway up. Don't worry about her."

I sighed and faced the mountain of sand again and pushed forward.

"Why won't she just come up with us? Why is she like this?" I asked, gasping for air.

"Who knows?" she huffed. "I read . . . in one of Mom's self-help books that your parents affect everything you do . . . and basically . . . whatever happened to her with Grandma and Grandpa probably fucked her up."

"Really?" I gasped for more oxygen. "She never lets us see Grandma. What do you think they did?"

"No idea," she shrugged again, and stood still a moment. "After her dad died, I guess she just decided not to talk to Grandma anymore. Don't dare ask her either, she'll bite your fucking head off."

We were panting as we reached the summit and plunked down into the scorching, hot sand with sweat dripping down our foreheads. The dunes were bustling. Families were spread out, climbing up, rolling down, tucked like barrels in dust clouds, or at the bottom, enjoying picnic lunches near our mother, who continued to talk to some strange man.

"Sometimes I just wish things were different with her." I scooped up handfuls of sand and let it flow through my fingers; it was hot, and the minuscule grains were crunchy.

"Me too, Hazelnut."

Our view spanned for miles and miles of the expansive Lake Michigan. I felt a sadness seeing the Manitou Islands popping up out of the water, remembering where the dunes got their name. According to the legend, an enormous forest fire on the western shore of Lake Michigan drove a mother bear and her two cubs into the lake for shelter, determined to reach the opposite shore. After many miles of swimming, the two cubs lagged behind. When the mother bear reached the shore, she waited on the top of a high bluff. The exhausted cubs drowned in the lake, but the mother bear stayed and waited in hopes that her cubs would finally appear. Impressed by the mother bear's determination and faith, the Great Spirit created two islands (North and South Manitou Islands) to commemorate the cubs, and the winds buried the sleeping bear under the sand dunes, where she waits to this day.

Isabel hooked her arm around me and put her head on my shoulder. I leaned into her, and we watched tiny sailboats bob back and forth between the waves.

6

RUIN

ANN ARBOR, MICHIGAN 1986

One night, while my dad was at a developer meeting, and my mom at work grading papers, I was alone at home, lying on the couch with Coconut, reading *The Catcher in the Rye*. Isabel was at her catering job.

The knock at the side kitchen door startled me. The book slipped from my hands onto Coconut, who, now also startled, jumped down. Before I could get up, Teddy came through the door, his leather jacket pelted with water and his hair slick from the raging June thunderstorm. He smiled when he saw me and kicked off his boots.

"Teddy! God, you scared the shit out of me! I guess you don't wait to be let in after you knock, huh?"

"But I'm like family, Hazel! I practically live here."

"Yeah, right," I said. If Mom and Dad knew how much he was here, they would be boarding the windows up.

His clothes were sopping wet and forming a puddle beneath him. I quickly headed towards the bathroom.

"Let me get some towels, you're making a mess!"

"Thanks! I'm soaked! It's nuts outside."

In the bathroom, I looked at my reflection. My long brown hair was in a ponytail and my bangs pushed back by a plastic headband. A sudden heat flushed my face—I was home alone, and Isabel hadn't mentioned he was coming over.

What was he doing here?

I grabbed towels and as I turned the corner, suddenly, a flash of skin appeared—Teddy, with his shirt off. He was glistening, and I immediately saw every chiseled and woven muscle in his chest and stomach stretched across his lean bones. The heat from my face flowed to the rest of my body. I looked away and thrust the towels towards him.

"What's wrong, Hazel?" he chuckled. "Never seen a half-naked man before?"

I was speechless. Even if I could speak, what would I say? I longed to be flirty and sexy but was caught off guard and melted into the insecurities of a little girl. With great strain, I pretended it didn't bother me, went back to the couch, and resumed reading.

"Isabel's not here," I said. From the corner of my eye, I watched him toweling off his chest and arms.

"Oh, she isn't? Huh. Where is she?"

"Working. Not sure when she'll be back."

"Huh. I didn't know she was working tonight," he said, "I thought we had plans."

"I guess you didn't."

"Yeah, no cars in the driveway. I guess Mom and Dad aren't home either?" His voice was softer now with the sudden realization that they could come home and catch him standing in our dining room shirtless.

"Um, no. Mom's at work, and Dad's at a meeting. I guess Isabel forgot to call you." I tried not to smirk, but I felt victorious.

"Guess so," he chuckled, and the way his eyebrows knitted together, I could see his irritation. "She's doing that a lot lately."

He squeezed water from his long hair into the towel and shook his head like a dog.

"Man, it's coming down out there! And the wind is crazy! Can I throw my stuff in your dryer? I'm freezing."

I stared at the pages of my book while pondering. If I let him stay, and either my parents or Isabel came home, I would be in deep trouble even though it wasn't my fault he just showed up. But if I told Teddy to leave . . . I would seem childish, afraid to be alone with him. I didn't want to disappoint him, and I wanted him to like me.

"Okay, sure," I said, and grabbed the soggy black T-shirt he was holding, brushing his slick wet arm as I passed him towards the laundry room.

"But you can't stay long," I called out, "since I'm alone. They would be super pissed! You know, Mom's rules and all."

He laughed from the other room.

"Yeah, okay, Hazel. We always stick to the rules!"

What a dumb thing to say. He was here all the time without permission.

I threw his shirt in the dryer, turned it on, and leaned against it, stalling for time.

"Hey, whatcha doing in there?" he called out.

"Oh! Nothing, I'll be right there." I took a deep breath and headed back.

He was sitting on the couch, in just his jeans, holding my book. He smiled when he saw me.

"So, Hazel, I see you finally took my advice!"

"And I told you, it's on my summer reading list, so I had to read it anyway."

"Ahh, but you have a whole list of other books, and you chose this one to read now. Why is that?"

The corners of his lips danced into a wicked smile, and I couldn't help but laugh.

"It's a short read. The others are much longer. I like to do easy things first, then move on to the more challenging things."

"Is that so?" he grinned, and put the book down. "What else have you been up to lately?"

"Just reading and running and hanging with friends. You know, just stuff."

The movement of his muscles distracted me, and I had a strange urge to reach out and touch him.

"Listen, I need to grab something upstairs. I'll be back soon," I said, feeling myself blush.

"Something I said?"

"Nope!" I called, as I dashed up the steps.

I raced up to my bedroom and shut the door behind me. My head was spinning. What should I do? I wasn't doing anything wrong, really. He came to our house uninvited. And what did it matter? I was a kid, and he had no interest in me. Or did he? I had no time to answer my own questions, before he knocked on my door.

"You okay in there?"

"Yes, I'm fine. I was just looking for something," I lied.

The doorknob turned, and before I could stop him, Teddy was in my bedroom. He was so hot. His hair had dried in thick chunks, and the strands where the sun had streaked it blonde were tucked behind his ears. His dark eyes searched my face, and a sense of alarm came over me.

This was so wrong. He was here in my room—my girly pink room with posters of celebrities and bands and frilly white curtains. He took one long stride and lifted my chin up to meet his eyes, his long limbs twice the size of my body. He was a giant, and I was a tiny pebble in a sea of adolescent fantasies.

"Did you find what you were looking for? Because I'm right here and happy to help."

Before I could think, my face was cupped in his hands. My world shrunk as his eyes bore into me, and I searched for cues in them. He turned his head sideways and gently pressed his lips against mine. They were soft like silk, but much bigger than mine so it felt like he was kissing my entire chin, too. I had no idea how to kiss back, so I let my jaw go limp as the rest of my body stiffened, and blood rushed to parts of me never activated before. Goosebumps flooded my dangling arms, and I was not sure where to put them.

What is happening? Is he really kissing me?

He pulled away and stroked the side of my face and smiled.

"You okay? Did you like that?"

My freshly kissed thirteen-year-old mouth had no words, so I simply nodded. I was paralyzed with fear, not of him, but of what I was supposed to do next.

Do I kiss him back now? Hug him?

"Good, me too. Want to try it again?"

I nodded and closed my eyes. This time he held the back of my head in his hands and pulled me close, his tongue prying my lips open. It felt huge in my tiny mouth, gliding over my teeth and pulsing down my throat. I felt like I might throw up, so I pushed him away, coughing.

"Sorry. I was getting carried away," he chuckled. "You're just so . . . beautiful, I can't control myself."

He took my hand and placed it on the crotch of his jeans. "See?"

A stiff bulge protruded from it, and for some reason I thought of his lighter with the Playboy Bunny on it that he always carried. I quickly released my hand. I felt dizzy. Did he just call me *beautiful*?

"It's okay, Hazel." He laughed again. "You can touch it, it won't bite, I promise. And it feels good. Go ahead, try again."

My head was spinning. He was looking at me, waiting. All the things that I had read about sex jumbled in my mind. I wasn't prepared. I both wanted to please him and run and hide. Rain battered the window, and the long branches of the tree beside the house whistled in the sharp winds. Was losing my virginity just a hurdle I had to get over? Would it be painful and bloody? After the first time it supposedly got better. But, with Teddy? He was a grown man and my sister's boyfriend! This wasn't how it should happen. Was it?

All in one movement, he gently pushed me back onto my bed, pinned my shoulders down, and straddled his legs around my body. He hovered above me and his hair fell forward and brushed my forehead. The irises of his eyes were black now, shining with anticipation, the way a dog waits for the signal to chase a ball. I squirmed from side to side, but he was holding me tight.

"Hey, hey . . . don't be afraid," Teddy whispered. "I won't hurt you. I would never hurt you, Hazel. It's going to be special. I want to be your first. I am your first, right? I'll go slow, I promise. We have a connection, the two of us . . . you know that, right?"

I felt myself panicking. How did this unravel so quickly? I thought we were just kissing. Of course, he knew I was a virgin. All the times I acted like a child and then my sister telling him I still played with dolls . . . Oh God, and Isabel! She would kill me if she saw this. And, connection? We certainly had something between us, I could not deny that. But, I never, ever suspected it was *this*.

"You can feel it too, Hazel. I know it. I can't ever stop looking at you . . . I want to be inside of you . . ."

I wanted him to leave. None of this felt right. The butterflies I usually felt in my stomach when I saw Teddy were different now; they were replaced with knots twisting and pulling. I wanted my dad to come home and rescue me.

"Teddy . . . I . . . I don't think I want to do this," I stammered. "And what about Isabel?"

He paused and sank back on his legs, pinning mine in the process.

"Don't worry about her," he said. "We're pretty much broken up. She doesn't really care about me. You see how she treats me. Not like you, you always talk to me, and we have fun together, right?"

He was still sitting back, still holding me down.

"It's okay, Hazel. Once you feel my skin on yours and me moving inside you, you're going to love it. We'll be bonded by this experience forever. And then, maybe, we will start to love each other. I'll go slow, you just need to relax."

Love each other? He was going to love *me?* And my body—he wanted to see it and touch my skin? I barely even looked at my body; it was too embarrassing. I was just starting to get boobs and would need a real bra soon. I still had the training bra my mother bought me last year, and it was ugly. Thankfully, today, I had a sports bra on.

"But, Teddy—"

His lips and tongue were all over my neck and face, and he gripped my tank top with one of his hands and was propelling it over my chest. I started to protest, but he put a hand over my mouth.

"Shh, it's okay, I promise. I want your beautiful body and you want mine—I know it. Please relax and let me show you how much you mean to me . . . you can trust me."

I swallowed hard and nodded my head. Tears stung my eyes, but he kept going. *Just get through it. You won't be a virgin anymore*, I thought as he panted like a wild animal and rubbed himself on me.

He lifted my bra up and started licking my nipples. I was numb. I knew I was supposed to like it, but I felt nothing. He shifted his weight and released my hands and hastily shoved a hand down my shorts. They were elastic, so it was easy. He pulled my panties over to the side and started probing between my legs. I held my breath and closed my eyes tight as his eager fingers jammed inside me. He thrust a finger deep inside me; my bellybutton felt the jab. I cried out in pain and surprise.

"Shh, shh, it's okay. I'm sorry, it might hurt some. But it will get better, I promise. It's like breaking in a new pair of shoes."

What? Was he serious?

I tried to sit up to stop him, but he crushed down on me again and began unbuttoning his jeans. His hands were quick; they made me think of the garter snake in our science class slithering around in its glass cage. Once he had wrangled his pants down around his ankles, he was right back at me, this time jamming his tongue back into my mouth. I could barely catch my breath. I opened my eyes halfway and saw that he was wearing red boxers with white polka dots. I thought of the Minnie Mouse costume I wore for Halloween years ago. I would have laughed if I wasn't so scared, so embarrassed. His legs were giant tree trunks next to mine, the size of a fawn's and just as shaky.

His underwear was down past his knees, and I caught a quick glance of his penis—the first real one I had ever seen. It was big and tangled in a cluster of hair and shot straight out from his body like a drill that was ready to punch through a wall. Or me! He reached between *his* legs now, and, suddenly, I felt this foreign object rubbing against my legs and stomach. It felt both soft and hard at the same time. He moved in circles, gyrating his hips—so diligent in this mission that he forgot me. I wasn't there; I was watching this scene as if it were on television, happening to someone else.

His breathing became more and more labored, and the muscles in his arms twitched as he held himself up and grabbed his penis, ready to pry me open with it. He poked at my vagina, so I opened my legs a little to help.

"That's my girl." He looked up and smiled at me. "It will hurt less if you just relax."

I gulped and nodded. I needed it to be over soon. He said we might learn to love each other. I wanted him to love me. So, I closed my eyes. A sharp pain stabbed my insides, and I shrieked.

"Shh, it's okay." He put his hand over my mouth again. "It might hurt a little when it first goes in, but you'll get used to it, I promise. And then you'll like it."

I grasped the flesh of his arms and bit my bottom lip hard. He looked into my eyes. He smiled, but it was distant, like he was looking through me. The hair falling in his eyes was sticky with sweat. I clutched a handful of my bedspread that lay under us while Teddy continued pushing farther into me, chafing me, shredding me apart. I opened my eyes, wet with tears now, and stared at the ceiling, at the spidery cracks that grew from the flaking paint in the corners, reminding me of a croissant, the kind Dad sometimes bought from Zingerman's bakery on Sundays.

I smelled his fruity shampoo when his hair spilled over my face. His skin was glossed with sweat and Polo cologne. He had three moles on his right shoulder. The veins in his neck were blue and bulged out as he strained and pushed. I bit my lip harder, exhausted. My guts felt pulverized. Then he stopped. I looked up to see his mouth open into a contorted shape, his eyes rolled back, and he let out a long groan. He shook a little before his body went limp, a dead weight on top of me. His heart thumped and thumped against my chest, and I could feel his penis twitching inside me.

"Um, you're really heavy." I gasped for breath and pushed at the mass of man covering me. "I can't breathe."

"Oh, sorry!" he rolled off me and onto his back. "You okay?"

Teddy was sprawled out, panting. His legs were too long for my bed, and his feet dangled off the edge.

"Yeah, sure."

I pulled my bra and shirt back down. Teddy propped himself up on his elbow and smiled. He ran a finger down the side of my face and wiped a tear from my cheek.

"I'm sorry. The first time isn't ever great, especially for girls. I'm sorry if I hurt you. It gets better the more we practice."

He winked at me.

Practice? I couldn't imagine doing this again. When he slipped his penis out of me and dragged it across my legs, it was limp and had shrunk to half its size, the color of an eggplant with a large bulging vein. It was so ugly, I recoiled.

"Yeah, that hurt a lot," I said searching for my underwear.

I felt sore and tired, and when I sat up, a gush of something oozed out of me and onto my bedspread.

"Shit! Gross!"

A thick puddle of goo swirled together, the color of cream and roses, soaking into my bedspread. I crawled backwards, afraid it might attach to me.

"Relax," he reached across me and pulled tissues from the box on my nightstand. "You were a virgin. You know the saying, break the cherry? That's the red, and that white stuff is what happens when you feel good. You'll get to liking it."

"I know what it is, Teddy," I said, annoyed. I wasn't that naive.

I was dirty and wanted to shower to wash him off me, and out of me.

"It won't hurt as bad next time, and there won't be blood."

What did he mean, next time? I was both thrilled and petrified. What about Isabel? Or my mother finding this giant red spot on my bedspread? I could tell her I got my period, but then she would make a big deal about it. I sat stunned as the mixture seeped into the fabric of my bedspread. There were smears of the mess on the insides of my legs. He sloppily wiped his penis down with the tissue and began to rub at the spot on the bed with it.

"No! Don't do that!" I said.

I knew that you never rubbed at a stain. The blood would settle in deeper and would set.

"What? I'm trying to help. We can throw this in the wash before anybody gets home."

Before anybody gets home.

"Shit."

I scrambled to put my shorts back on, my hands shaking. Teddy shrugged and dressed.

His skin was still damp, and he struggled to pull up his pants. I ripped the bedspread off the bed and bunched it into a ball.

"I'll take care of it. You need to go before anybody comes home!"

As he gathered himself back together, he delivered more promises—about how the next time would be better, how he'd find a way for us to meet, how it was our secret.

"See you soon, babe."

He pecked my cheek before leaving, and I watched through the window as he slipped into his bright-orange IROC-Z and lit a cigarette with his Playboy lighter. I heard him adjust the radio as he drove away. He blew smoke from the window and never looked back. What just happened? The stickiness between my legs and shorts stuck to me. My lower belly throbbed. The thought of the blood made me dizzy. I considered crying, but there was no time. I ran back upstairs, tore the bedding from my mattress, and then rushed down to the laundry room. I stuffed my shorts in with the bedding and poured an excessive amount of detergent on the pile. The dryer was still open, so Teddy must have grabbed his shirt on the way out. I slammed it shut.

As I came into the kitchen, I saw a pair of headlights in the window. The interior light of the parked car illuminated Isabel's head as she rooted around the back seat.

"What is she doing home already?" I said, realizing she couldn't catch me standing around half naked.

I hurried upstairs and into the shower, hearing the side door bang as I scoured with soap under scalding hot water.

"Hey, Hazel? Is that you?"

Isabel slapped her palms against the bathroom door.

"Yeah, it's me."

"You left the back door unlocked! You can't do that when you're home alone, remember?"

Except, I hadn't been alone.

"Oh, did I? I went running and must've left it open. Sorry!"

"Oh . . . okay. And what's in the washer? It's too big and throwing the machine off balance and making crazy noises."

Think, think.

"Um, I spilled ice tea all over my bedspread." She was quiet for a moment, and I held my breath. "I didn't want Mom to find out. Besides, it needed to be washed."

"Okay, just go fix it when you're done because it's all fucked up right now."

"I will! Why are you home so early?"

"My manager is an idiot and overstaffed us for this party. I'm fucking tired. Gonna go hang in my room. Don't forget about the washing machine!"

"I won't."

Cramps pinched my guts. Blinking back tears, I touched the rawness between my legs. I needed to wash away the evidence of what happened. I felt so dirty.

7

SPOIL

ANN ARBOR, MICHIGAN 1985

"Happy birthday, Hazel!" my best friend Harper squealed. I cringed at her high-pitched phone greeting and laughed. "Thanks!"

"Are you super excited about your party?"

"Yeah, when are you coming?"

"Noon," she said, chewing loudly—probably potato chips, her favorite snack—"that's when your mom said. Want me to come earlier?"

"Definitely. Like at least twenty minutes. My mom is driving me crazy!"

"Already? Parental units are a pain. Okey-dokey, I'll have my dad drop me off early. Did you read the books?"

In preparation for the day and my impending womanhood, I consumed any information available. In the den, my mother had a section of books that Isabel called, "feminist shit." I paged through *Our Bodies, Ourselves,* and I squirmed as I learned how my uterus would shed its lining. I discovered words like empowered and informed and unite peppered throughout. How did bleeding in my underwear equate to empowerment? It seemed more embarrassing than anything else. When I told Harper about it, she insisted that I go to the library and check out, *Are you there God? It's me, Margaret,* which I read from beginning to end on a rainy Saturday, only to realize how behind I was. I was going to need a "real" bra soon — although my small boobs were barely visible—probably a diary, and a few things to help me with my first period. I thought I might need extra underwear in case severe "shedding" occurred, and I swiped an entire box of Isabel's Stayfree maxi pads and stowed them in my room. I had no idea the amount needed. My mother's heating pad, a bottle of aspirin, and Pamprin were handy for cramps and headaches.

My mother clattered around the kitchen. The early morning air wafted mixed scents of homegrown fresh herbs and sweet fragrant chocolate. She was making my favorite, German chocolate cake. I went downstairs and was shocked by the barrage of party hats, bags of balloons, noisemakers, confetti, streamers, and board games. The couch was pushed against a wall so that the card tables, covered in birthday tablecloths of the Peanuts characters, would fit.

I stormed into the kitchen where my aproned mother sang to Carole King on the radio and pulled vegetarian lasagna out of the fridge. She wore a floral dress and leather sandals and loosely braided hair. Gold earrings dangled from her ears, and large rings covered her fingers. "Mom, what is all that stuff? Don't you think I'm too old for this babyish stuff? I'm not into Snoopy anymore! Besides, that was Isabel's favorite."

My mother smiled and pulled me close. A scented blend of garlic, vanilla, and basil clung to her. She stroked my hair and kissed my head.

"Happy birthday! Thirteen today! You are growing so fast!"

I rolled my eyes.

"Mom, stop. Please don't act this embarrassing around my friends."

She shooed me away and opened the oven to check the cake. Two pans of chocolate batter had baked, all toasty brown, and the sweet heat wave brought comfort.

"Nonsense. I plan to make your day perfect. Now, I don't know what your friends like, but you've always loved balloons and games. Why should this year be any different?"

"Because I'm thirteen today, Mom!"

"Do you want regular chocolate frosting or the German? I bought both having no time to make it from scratch."

She hummed with Carole as she began removing refrigerated items: a chickpea salad, a tomato and basil pasta dish, and a vegan shepherd's pie. She peeled back the plastic wrap and began to stir them up and arrange them, ignoring me.

"We're not wearing those dumb hats!" I huffed. "We're not babies! Where's Dad?"

"You are always going to be my little Hazelnut!" I cringed when she used the nickname my dad gave me—it wasn't hers to use. "He ran out for helium for the balloons. I don't have time to blow them up, and your father would probably pass out trying."

She was all smiles and rapidly moving about in the kitchen. It was hard to be mad at my mother when she felt purposeful, needed, and appreciated.

"Oh, okay. Did . . . you know. . . make any dishes with meat? Elizabeth is the only vegetarian."

Her jaw tightened over by the sink. She washed her hands deliberately, rings clinking. I knew what this was. My mother was on yet another diet, and my birthday coincided with vegetarian week. My body tensed and I waited. She took a deep breath and relaxed her shoulders. With a loud sigh, she faced me.

"No, Hazel, I didn't. I've been shopping and cooking for two days to make this a perfect party. I didn't consider each of your *nine* friends' appetites for fattening living creatures. Everything I made is delicious, and well, it's one meal for one day in their lives. I'm sure they will survive."

She forced a tight smile and turned back to the sink, scouring it in aggressive messy strokes. I swallowed hard and ventured closer. I had to save this now or my birthday could be ruined.

"I'm sorry, Mom. Everything looks great, and I really appreciate what you've done. You're right, they will be fine."

As I hugged her from behind, she softened and turned and

peered at me. Her face was blotchy, and her green eyes were building the gray hue that signaled darkness would follow. Her fingers clenched the sponge, and soap trickled down her hands.

"Okay, honey, go shower and get ready. When your father gets back, you can help him with the decorations."

My entire uterus could start shedding soon and my mother was on the verge a meltdown. I checked my underwear three times, and after my shower, I had decided to put a maxi pad on just in case. It was awkward and crinkly and felt all wadded up. What was taking so long?

I heard the familiar pop of a cork and the glugging sound of wine being poured into a glass, then my dad said something indistinguishable to Mom.

~

The doorbell chimed.

"I'll get it!" my mother announced as she whisked by, stacks of bracelets on her wrists jangling.

"Happy birthday, Hazel!" Harper squealed, and ran past my mother carrying a present with a big red bow tucked under one arm. Harper had wild tight spirals of curly hair that bounced when she spoke and giant shimmering blue eyes that revealed every emotion.

"Thanks!" I hugged her.

"Does thirteen feel different?" she asked as we walked towards the kitchen.

"So far, no. Not a thing. And . . ." I motioned to the folding tables with Charlie Brown tablecloths, "I'm being treated like a little kid."

"Yeah, what's up with that?" she laughed.

"Don't ask me. My mom thinks I'm still into that crap, but she has no idea what I am into."

"Tell me about it," Harper said, whispering. "My parents think I'm still into Snoopy too!"

We rolled our eyes in unison. Isabel, who had slept in most of the morning, was arranging the punch bowl and cups on the dining room table.

Soon, my girlfriends were gathered, and the energy became light and airy and giggly. They admired the sweater my dad got me and chased Coconut around. A *Teen Beat* magazine circulated, and we chatted about the cutest boys in class and how dreamy John Stamos and Matt Dillon were. They even tolerated the silly hats and blew the noisemakers my mother insisted on buying.

"Shh."

Harper motioned for everyone to form a circle on the living room floor.

"Okay, so, did it happen yet?" she whispered.

I glanced around, all eyes on me, my face felt hot.

"No, but I've been checking all morning. I have pads in the bathroom and I'm wearing one right now. I am ready."

My friends all giggled, putting hands over their mouths to stifle the noise.

"Well," Elizabeth said, "I have mine, and it is life changing." She propped up, imposing her womanly body on us. Her breasts were larger than the rest of ours, and we all moved closer to soak up her knowledge.

"Evvvvverything changes!"

Elizabeth was dramatic.

"Like what?"

"Well, you just feel . . . different. Like a woman, with real emotions. Boys start to notice you, and well, you get cramps, which are horrible, but mostly, it's no big deal!"

I already had plenty of emotions, including unwanted ones. I had a loose cannon mother and a sister who mostly ignored me, and I had no idea how to handle any of it.

Angela piped up. "I heard that if you stand in your bathtub when you think it's coming, it will come faster."

By the looks on my friends' faces, this was news to all of us. I wished I could ask Isabel. She would probably say it was nonsense.

"Really?" I said. "Where did you hear that?"

Angela twirled a piece of her shiny-brown hair.

"Well . . . um, my big sister. I haven't gotten mine yet, and she said she was in the shower when she got hers. She said she could feel it coming . . . so she went in there, and she got her period."

We searched each other's faces, confused, but Angela's sister was a very popular senior, so it must be true.

"Hazel! Girls!" my mother called from behind the kitchen door. "Time to eat!"

"Okay, Mom!" I yelled. "We'll be right there!"

Looking at my friends, I broke into a mischievous smile.

"After we eat, I should go stand in the bathtub and see if it works!"

Laughter erupted, heads nodded in agreement, and we headed towards the kitchen. My dad and sister were setting out plates and silverware.

"Happy birthday, squirt," Isabel said, with a hug. "Welcome to the teenage years. Now you're old enough to know everything."

She was wearing a turtleneck, and I saw a faint purple bruise peeking out. Dark eyeliner from the night before still clung to her skin.

"Okay, girls, there's plenty of food here, help yourself, please."

My mother appeared frazzled, wiping her hands on her apron.

"What is this stuff?" my friend Sarah asked, looking at the chickpea salad.

A rush of heat came to my face.

Kimberly stared at the shepherd's pie. "Yeah, and what's this?"

"Um . . . it's all vegetarian . . . my mom is eating that way lately . . . it's all really good I promise." Why couldn't my mother serve normal party food? It wasn't fair to drag me into her stupid diets, especially today. The girls looked at each other and then back at the meatless dishes.

Suddenly my mother was back, red wine in hand. Irritation thinned her smile.

She leaned against the counter, sipped her wine, and clearly having overheard us said, "Ladies, I know this is not your normal diet but take comfort that this food never breathed or had a face. And, most importantly, it's healthy and low in calories."

My jaw dropped. My friends looked down at their plates and silently waited for my response. My stomach seized into a tight ball.

"Mom! Stop it!"

My mother just laughed and waved her hand around in the air.

"I'm sorry . . . I thought you girls might find that funny. Wrong audience, obviously. Please, just try it, it's all very delicious. I promise you won't die from any of it."

I began to speak, but my dad, thankfully, grabbed her wrist, causing the wine to slosh. A couple of crimson drops plopped on the floor.

"Come on, Joanne, let's let the girls make their own decisions and go sit in the garden."

My mother scoffed and tossed back the remaining wine then slammed her glass down. Was she drunk already? On my birthday, and in front of my friends? Isabel had been right. My dad gave us an apologetic look, one all too familiar, and shook his head. He guided my mother away. Tears stung my eyes.

My friends all stared at me, paper plates in their hands. Harper put hers down and faced us.

"Hey, this all looks great, you guys. It's Hazel's birthday. We should all try it. I'll take pasta with no face!"

The cluster of girls laughed nervously but began to eat and proclaimed everything was delicious, and no one mentioned the awkward exchange. My emotions swirled. I felt nauseous, angry, confused, and relieved, simultaneously.

Angela whispered to no one in particular, "Hey, maybe Hazel should try the bathtub thing now!"

"Yes, let's go!" I said.

I corralled everyone quickly to the downstairs bathroom. I stepped into the tub and pulled the shower curtain across.

"Do I take my pants off? Like, do I need to have my underwear on? Are you sure about this?"

The girls giggled loudly.

"My sister was in the shower when it happened," said Angela, "so maybe turn the water on? It might make it happen faster, you know?"

I turned on the faucet. The water was cold on my toes. Seething inside, I knew once I became a woman with a period, I would tell my mom exactly what I thought of her and her antics. If I was a woman, I would get a loving boyfriend who would escape with me. If I was a woman, no one could boss me around anymore. I slid my jeans down to my ankles and peeked in my underwear. The maxi pad had shifted and was still clean, bloodless.

"What's happening? Anything?" Harper asked through the curtain.

"No. Should I *take* a shower? You guys can wait in the other room. Otherwise, it's weird."

Like this situation could get any weirder. Me, standing in the bathtub, with my new sweater on, minus pants.

"What on earth are you girls doing?" My mother's voice sliced through our laughter. "Why are you all in the bathroom? Where is Hazel?"

My heart thumped loudly as her footsteps grew closer. I bent down to pull up my jeans, but it was too late. She whipped the curtain aside, shocked and repulsed.

"What in the hell are you doing, Hazel?"

All my friends were either looking at each other or at their feet. Slowly, those in the hallway slinked back to the living room.

"Joanne?" My dad's voice. "Joanne? What's going on?"

I tugged my pants back up before he got there. Sweat trickled down my neck. My mother stepped back from the shower, as if to put me on display.

"Well, your daughter is half naked in here with her friends. I have no idea why. Is this some weird game you are all playing? Because this is not normal. And I won't allow it in my house."

Her eyes were wild and glossy, and the smell of stale wine hit my face with her every breath.

"What were you thinking, Hazel?" She wagged a finger in my face. "This is perverted and unacceptable!"

I had never seen her so angry. She turned to address my friends.

"Girls, get your things. Your parents will be coming soon."

She had ruined my birthday. I hadn't even blown out candles on my cake yet. There had been no singing in my honor. She had lived up to my biggest worries. I was angry too.

"Hazel, what is going on?" It was my dad now. "Why are you in the bathtub? What are—"

"—Richard! I'll handle this."

My mother slammed the door in his face, trapping us in the bathroom.

"You have some explaining to do, young lady!" she growled, hands on her hips.

"Just leave me alone! You ruined my party! You made stupid food, you got drunk, and then totally embarrassed me! I hate you!"

"Hazel!"

Smack.

I gasped. I slowly brought my hand up to my cheek, my flesh hot from the imprint of her hand, stinging.

"I . . ." tears blocked my words.

My mother stared at her hand as if it was foreign and looked at me. Smudges of mascara clung beneath her left eye, and her lipstick had bled out of its previously perfect pout.

"Oh my God, I'm so sorry, Hazel! I didn't mean to . . . do that . . . I . . . I . . ."

She reached out with the same assaulting hand, now shaking, but the door flew open. My father rushed to my side.

"What the hell just happened in here? Hazel? Why is your face all red? Why are you crying?" He glanced at my mother, staring at her hand. "Joanne. Joanne! What did you do?"

My mother stood silently as her tears flowed, and she kept shaking her head.

"I . . . I don't know . . . She just . . . oh, Hazel, . . . please forgive me!"

I put my arms around my father and cried into his shoulder.

I will never forgive you.

8

CORRUPT

ANN ARBOR, MICHIGAN 1986

E veryone said your first time should be with someone you love. I didn't have Teddy's phone number. I knew he lived in Barton Hills, but no idea where. He was my sister's boyfriend. I was a kid, and he, a full-grown man. But I was special. I had to be—he had sought me out.

I waited, but Teddy did not stop by, and Isabel didn't care. She worked late, slept late, and partied with Abbey.

"I don't get why you stay with that loser."

I overheard her talking with Isabel one night while washing dishes after dinner.

"No idea. He acts like a dick, comes crawling back, apologizing and shit. He had flowers delivered to the restaurant yesterday. That shit might make my mom wet herself but I see through that crap."

"Yet, you still haven't told him to fuck off."

"I know. He's hot and good in bed. Until I find someone better, I will deal with him."

They laughed.

"He still lives at home, Abs! He's eighteen, for fuck's sake! He called me at work like five times the other day. My boss was getting so pissed."

Maybe they will break up, I thought as I tiptoed from the kitchen and went up to my room.

The next morning, I saw my mother in the frame of the back door, smoking a cigarette, with a patterned silk scarf around her neck. She was off to a conference for English professors at Notre Dame, which she pronounced Noh-TRA-Dahhhm, as if she were French. She tapped her foot impatiently, as if my father was her chauffeur, as he loaded her suitcase into the station wagon. I was excited to have my dad to myself.

I made sloppy joes that night—my specialty—and my dad and I put Kraft Singles on them, which Isabel said was disgusting. We chatted about TV: the latest drama on Dallas and Geraldo Rivera's doomed opening of Al Capone's empty vaults. Dad and I washed dishes and we both laughed as he did his Pee-wee Herman impression. Afterwards, he kissed my forehead, and went to his den to finish work. I reveled in the simplicity of being daddy's little girl —no complications or secrets. It was a nice distraction from constant thoughts of Teddy.

My insides still stung, and every step I took reminded me of him. I felt stupid and naive to think Teddy would dump my sister for me. A whole week passed with no signs of him.

The next morning, the house was soundless except for the hum of the refrigerator. The thermometer read eighty degrees. I ventured into the garage, where our pile of family bicycles lived. I took out my red Schwinn with the long white banana seat and pink streamers, the only dustless bike, and pedaled under a lemon-yellow sun towards the park.

Summer, in full swing, scattered the stretch of green with people. Moms chased their shrieking toddlers around monkey bars and jungle gyms. A group of kids smacked a Hacky Sack around, and a few boys played Frisbee. I rested my bike against the bike rack and headed to the broken swing set. Harper and I usually hung out there for privacy.

Sitting on a swing, I swayed back and forth, my toes brushing the ground. The space behind my eyes burned. I hadn't slept well in days. Each night, lying awake, I heard Isabel slip upstairs in hushed steps, coming in late from work or hanging with Abbey.

I drew lines in the dirt with my flip-flops.

"Hey there."

I jumped.

Like a ninja, he suddenly appeared.

"Oh my God! Teddy! What are you doing here?"

I scrambled to my feet before he could answer. The swing bobbed awkwardly and knocked the back of my knees. He towered over me, and I threw my arms around him.

"Hey, you," he whispered, "I've missed you."

I pulled away slightly, remembering my puffy eyes and unwashed frizzy braid.

"You have?" I asked, as my stomach churned with warmth.

"Of course," he said, scanning the park and letting me go. "Wanna go sit? I don't think these old-ass swings could hold me."

We found a spot under a tree. He was wearing black jeans and a white T-shirt with the sleeves rolled up. His tanned muscles swelled and sweat trickled down along the sides of his temples. He was so handsome it hurt.

He placed a hand on my arm, and goosebumps rippled my legs.

"Are you okay?"

I snatched a clump of grass and tore it into pieces.

I had rehearsed what I would say when I saw him, but now, I was tongue tied. I stared at the ground and watched black ants scurrying in circles.

"I wanted to make sure you were alright." He lifted my chin until my eyes met his. "I missed you."

"I'm fine, I guess. Where were you?"

"I needed to stay away for a bit. Isabel and I . . . well, we've been fighting . . . and showing up would look suspicious since she's trying to avoid me."

So, they weren't broken up.

"You and Isabel are fighting?"

I held my breath.

"Well," he sighed. "Yeah, she's being a bitch."

I flinched and smashed the last blades of grass, staining my palm pale green. A thick sourness formed in my stomach. Sure, my sister could be a bitch, but I didn't like the word rolling easily off Teddy's tongue.

"Wow, that's mean. Did you two break up?"

I wanted him to say yes, that he broke up with her for me, but calling her names made me uneasy. His cheeks deepened to the shade of my mother's ruby velvet chair in her bedroom.

"Not really, not yet. I mean, we've been on and off. She's just . . . okay, I won't call her a bitch, sorry. But she's getting super naggy and always complaining. She's always working or going out and doesn't have time for me. She's trying to boss me around, like my mom. I already have one of those and don't need another."

This was news to me. Isabel draped herself all over him, hanging onto his every word whenever he visited.

"Really? What is she nagging you about?"

"Annoying shit, like, 'get a job,' or 'go to college,' 'do something with your life,' blah, blah, blah. I wish they would lay off me. I'm never going to be my dad. College doesn't make you smarter than anybody. You can make good money learning a trade. School is a big waste of time anyway."

"What's a trade?"

He looked at me, his lips curling into his crooked smile. I leaned in, wanting him to feel my support and interest—everything he wasn't getting from Isabel—but the memory of his hands all over my chest and stomach flashed and almost involuntarily, I crossed my arms.

"It's a job you need special skills for, no college needed. Like, a plumber or an electrician. Or . . . maybe a . . . fortune cookie writer!"

I giggled, and he laughed.

"Yeah, right! You're making that up. There's no such thing!"

"How else do those sayings get inside? Do you think little fortune cookie elves make them appear?"

"Well," I giggled, "if that's true, then that sounds like a fun trade!"

His long fingers drew circles on my knee, and I forced every muscle to hold me steady before I melted into the grass.

Thwack!

A soccer ball smacked the ground next to us. A little boy with wild brown hair ran towards us, stumbling and laughing.

"Sorry about that!" the boy's father, not far behind, called out. "This one's got quite a kick."

"No problem," Teddy said, grabbing the ball. He smiled at the boy and handed it over.

"What do you say?" asked the dad.

"Thank you!" the boy said.

He dashed off, and the man looked from me to Teddy and hesitated a moment before he resumed chasing his son.

Our age difference showed, and it was our first time in public together, leaving me nervous and ashamed. Teddy, if he had noticed, didn't say anything about it.

"Actually, there's a refinery in Indiana that's always looking for people. I don't know . . . It's a dirty job with long hours, but it pays pretty good. And a couple buddies of mine are talking about backpacking in Europe."

My stomach dropped, and I felt all the oxygen leave my lungs.

Indiana? Backpacking? He couldn't abandon me! We were just getting started.

"What's a refinery? And when would you go?"

He saw my panic and put both his hands on my knees and held my gaze.

"Hold on, hold on. I'm not going anywhere yet. It's just a thought. My parents are being assholes about me not working or going to school, so I have to come up with some sort of plan. Whether I go through with it . . . well, that's not high on my priority list now."

"But why Indiana? Can't you find a job here?"

"Hey," he lifted my chin again. "Stop worrying! I'm not going anywhere yet. That's part of the reason I wanted to find you today."

"How did you know where I was?"

"Well, there's only a few places you would be," he chuckled.

"Home, at the pool with Harper, or here with Harper. I started here and got lucky."

I pictured him driving around in his IROC-Z, listening to music and smoking.

"Oh."

He picked a pack of cigarettes from his back pocket and flicked open his Zippo. It clicked when he opened it and snapped it shut. The woman on the front of it smirked at me, pleased with her large breasts and the fact she got to sit in Teddy's back pocket.

"How do you feel, you know, down there?" he asked, changing the subject.

"It hurt, but I'm okay. Do you still want to do it again?"

His face opened into a wide smile.

"As long as you do."

"I do," I said.

I straightened my posture, subtly thrusting my chest forward. I needed to be convincing; he was on the brink of leaving Isabel, and I had to prove worthy.

"I'm glad you do, because I came up with a plan for us to see each other. Can you keep a secret?"

"I'm getting good at secrets," I grinned.

He smiled and dug into his pocket, pulling out a shiny silver key. It glimmered in the sunlight.

"*This.* This is how we can be together. I made you one."

"What does it open?"

"My buddy Chad's apartment. He works so we can go during the day. Just say you're going to Harper's house or the mall or whatever. It's summer, you're not in school. It's perfect."

Joan Collins as Alexis from *Dynasty* came to mind. We would sneak around like forbidden lovers and meet and make wild, passionate love. I would wrap myself up in sheets while Teddy would bring me breakfast in bed and tell me how beautiful I was.

It *was* perfect.

Yet, what Teddy and I did in my bed did not play out the way it did on *Dynasty*. Maybe if my boobs got bigger and I wore lingerie and heels, I'd feel better about it.

"Okay! Yes!"

He put his hand on mine.

"And by the way, if he's ever home for some reason and you meet him, you're eighteen. Okay? Nobody would understand, and we don't need him knowing your real age. Shall we get this party started?"

I sat up tall.

"Alright. But, how will I know when to go, and how do we find each other if something happens?" Teddy swatted at a fly buzzing around his ear.

"We just need a day and time that we always meet. Is there a day your folks are gone during the day the most?"

"My mom is gone until Sunday. I'll tell my dad I'm going to Harper's."

"Are you sure?"

Was I sure? My heart was pulsing. I fought back the thoughts of the repercussions of getting caught. But it was too exciting, *and* he chose me over Isabel.

"I'm sure."

I wanted his kiss again. I ached to learn to be seductive and for him to fall in love.

"Fuck yeah! How about tomorrow? We've been apart too long. I want to touch you all over again."

"It's going to hurt again, isn't it?"

I already knew the answer. He stroked my knee with his fingertips. Chills sprinkled down my legs.

"It might a little, yeah. As we keep doing it, you'll loosen up. I swear you will enjoy it soon."

I thought of the blood.

"I think it was too fast last time."

"I know, Hazel. I got too excited. We'll go slower."

I smiled.

"Alright, baby girl, here is the info." He handed me a folded-up paper with an address and an apartment number on it. "Tomorrow at noon?"

"Yes!"

"Okay, then." He looked around and kissed my cheek. He stood up, wiping grass from his jeans. "I'll see *you* tomorrow, Hazel."

I watched him walk away, looking so tall, manly. A man, who wanted me. I stared at the shiny silver key I held tight in my left hand.

A little girl in a pink dress skidded down the slide, her bare legs sticking to metal. She lurched forward at the bottom and dumped headfirst into the dirt. Instantly, the tears came, and howls echoed through the park until her mother rushed over to scoop her up.

9

SEDUCE

ANN ARBOR, MICHIGAN 1986

A t 11:56 a.m., I was four minutes early. I had no clue what to wear for my second attempt at sex. So, I spent an hour trying different outfits and landed on pleated white shorts and a buttoned pink tank.

Was he in there?

The building was the color of sand, towered six stories high, and had identical rows of windows. Birds chirped in the trees that bookended the building. I locked my bike at the apartment's bike rack. My pink handlebar streamers flickered in the light breeze. *So babyish*. I would remove them soon.

Building 3, #24.

The paper with the scribbled address began to soften from the heat of my hand. Between breakfast bites of Fruity Pebbles, I told my dad I was going to the mall in the afternoon with Harper and Kathy. He was busy making himself coffee and buttering an English muffin. Lying was getting easier.

I pressed the number three button. It belted out a shrill buzzing sound, and I stepped back.

"Hello?"

"Yes, um, I'm here to see Teddy. My name is Hazel."

Laughter.

"It's me, Hazel. I'll buzz you up."

A staircase was to the right of the entrance. The heat and my nerves continued to push sweat through my skin.

"Up here!"

Teddy's head flopped over a banister one floor up. He was wearing a black Iron Maiden T-shirt and low-slung jeans, and he was barefoot. His hair was loose around his shoulders, and his face was scruffy with hair.

"Hi!"

Teddy pulled me in for a hug. The warmth of his skin leached through his T-shirt.

"Come on, let's go in," he said.

I nodded and followed. It was so tiny. The kitchen and the bathroom were on either side of the short entrance hall, and a big black leather couch was pushed up against one wall. On the glass-topped coffee table were bottles of beer, a pack of cigarettes, an overflowing ashtray, and car magazines. The bed was on the floor in one corner, an unmade mess of sheets and blankets, smelling like sweat and cigarettes. This was not what I was expecting, and Teddy read my face.

"So? It's not the Ritz, I know. My buddy's not great at the cleaning stuff, but at least it's somewhere private for us, right?" He pointed towards the kitchen. "I brought beer and wine and smokes, and we can order food later. We can pretend it's our own place."

Does it come with a pretend maid too?

He seemed so excited, and I didn't want to disappoint him.

"Um . . . it's great."

He led me to the couch. An old air-conditioning unit protruded from the window, growling out cool air. My sweaty shirt clung to me and I felt gross.

"I got wine and beer so, you know . . . to help you, us, relax. It might make it easier. The more relaxed you are, the more you'll like it. Maybe it won't hurt."

I hated beer, all sour and bitter and bubbly. But maybe wine? My mother certainly loved wine. I hated how she acted after too much wine. But that didn't mean I would act the same way. And if it would get me through the next couple of hours, it was worth a shot.

"Alright. I don't really like beer, so maybe we could try the wine?"

If I was going to be his girlfriend, I had to drink. I couldn't give him reasons to stay with Isabel.

"Okay!" He went to get drinks in the kitchen. The refrigerator door made a sucking sound as it opened, and sounds of clinking glass echoed as Teddy dug through the pile of dishes in the sink.

What a small, dirty place.

"I have to clean a couple glasses, hang on."

I stared at the rumpled bed, feeling a glob of panic in my stomach. *What if I was terrible at sex? What if this place had roaches?*

"Yeah, sure."

Teddy came back carrying short water glasses filled with pale-pink wine. *He got the pink kind!* He plopped down, handed me a glass, and held his up.

"Cheers to our new secret hideaway!" he said with a sly smile. We clinked glasses, and I took a sip. It was both sweet and sour, better tasting than beer, so I drank more. Teddy swallowed a large gulp and then turned to me.

"Do you like the wine? It's called white Zinfandel. My mom has a big supply, so I grabbed a bottle."

I debated mentioning my concerns. My mind leapt all over the place. His mother drank wine too? Do all moms drink wine? But, if I was going to be a woman, I had to act like one too. I had read that women should "express their feelings" to really be heard by men.

"Teddy," I sighed, "I don't know what I'm doing. I mean, you've been with Isabel . . . and, I'm afraid to disappoint you."

Teddy put his glass down and scooted closer. He caressed my face with his thumb.

"Oh, Hazel, baby. Don't worry. It takes time and practice and now we'll have that. Listen, we have a connection, you and me. You don't judge me like everyone else. Do you know how rare that is? You listen to me and make me feel good about myself. You're not demanding or demeaning. You respect me. And I respect you.

You're fun and easy to talk to. It's hard to find those things in a girlfriend."

"Girlfriend?" I whispered.

I was afraid to breathe. His eyes glowed the color of burnt toast, and I felt gooey, like marshmallows melting in a fire.

"Well," he glanced at the floor, "yeah, I mean, I need to break up with Isabel, but she hasn't been around for us to talk. I think she's avoiding me."

The pink wine pleasantly coated my stomach, and my head floated above. Today, I wouldn't question him about my sister. She wasn't here, I was. So, I boldly made the first move.

I grabbed both sides of his face like they do in the movies and pulled him towards me. I pressed my lips to his. He was surprised; his body tensed up immediately, but quickly he eased right in. He didn't open his mouth wide and shove his tongue inside. He gently kissed my lips, his facial hair prickling my face, and tenderly tugged my bottom lip with his teeth. His were so much bigger than mine, but the kiss was less jarring than the first time. He slowly pulled away.

"Look at you getting all assertive coming in for the first kiss." He raised his eyebrows.

"Oh, God. Was that stupid?"

I blushed, embarrassed. The air conditioner whirred its constant heavy hum. The room felt silent and loud at the same time.

"Not at all. I think we should have more wine and take things slow. I want you to be totally relaxed. Music?"

Teddy stretched around the coffee table, his legs like a daddy longlegs spider, and in two steps he reached a boom box perched on a milk crate.

"I made a mixtape for us," he said.

"Live to Tell" by Madonna floated from the speakers.

He brought the bottle over and refilled our glasses. I smiled and took a hefty gulp. My muscles were softening into a bowl of pudding. I now understood why my mother enjoyed wine so much. I searched the catalog in my mind of soap opera scenes and *Cosmopolitan* magazine articles on how to be seductive. I considered pouting my lips and gazing longingly into his eyes like Erica Kane on *All My Children.*

"How ya feeling?" Suddenly, his fingers were massaging my neck, kneading my skin.

I was tingly all over, as the wine rushed through my body.

"I'm good . . . better . . . definitely better."

"Excellent," he whispered in my ear.

I felt bolder. I gently pushed him away, swigging the last of my wine. The pink liquid slid down my throat easily.

"Whoa, okay, let's maybe order some food," Teddy said, and pried the glass out of my hand. "A bottle of wine on an empty stomach is not a good idea."

"Oh, yeah, probably," I shrugged.

My eyelids were heavy. The possibility of throwing up this morning's Fruity Pebbles in a rainbow of colors seemed horrific. Teddy went to the small round table cluttered with mail, loose change, and a couple lighters. He picked up some takeout menus and fanned them out in front of me on the coffee table.

"Mexican, Italian, Indian, Greek, or Thai?"

I squinted hard at the menus as the words slid around. Was this what drunk was?

"Um, I don't know? My parents love Thai, but I don't know what they order. Some noodle thing?"

"How about Chinese? My favorite is Hunan spicy beef. Do you like spicy?"

"I can handle any-fing," I slurred, and I narrowed my eyes to look sexy. "Can I have more wine, please?"

"You can have whatever you want, Hazel," he chuckled and nuzzled the nape of my neck. My stomach fluttered. "Just give me a minute to order."

I noticed a stack of travel guidebooks on an overturned red milk crate that served as a nightstand. *Spain, France, Germany, Italy.* A small knot formed in my stomach recalling his backpacking plans with friends. Teddy was captivating. He read books, watched documentaries, ate spicy food, and dreamt of world travel. No boy my age compared.

~

My tongue throbbed from the spicy food, and when we laughed my eyes watered. My body happily floated above itself as the intensity of the sweet wine and spiced food flowed through it.

"If You Leave" by Orchestral Manoeuvres in the Dark purred from the speakers as we cracked open our fortune cookies and reminisced about the "trade" of stuffing them.

Teddy's: *"Hard work pays off in the future; laziness pays off now."*

Mine: *"Be on the lookout for coming events; they cast their shadows beforehand."*

I was drunk with wine and emotion. Teddy's hands wandered around my body in tickling movements, slower this time. I closed my eyes as his fingers traced my back in light strokes, lingering around the bottom of my shirt, stopping short of trailing into my shorts. His other hand was on my cheek, drawing my face towards him and kissing me, gently prying my mouth open with his tongue. It wasn't darting into me; it was more like a slow dance, caressing mine with his. I was dizzy with excitement and fear.

He stopped and stared into my eyes.

"Hazel, this is how it's supposed to be. I want you so bad . . ."

My head was swimming, but I couldn't stop now. He was happy, and this is what he wanted. And what I wanted was for him to "make love to me," like in my soap operas.

Teddy glanced at the bed. *That filthy bed.* Everything in this apartment looked like it felt sticky. My mother would be horrified. *Oh, God, don't think about Mom.*

"It looks kind of um . . ."

"Chad is an asshole. I thought he might have the decency to wash the sheets once in a while. If you want, we can take the sheets off and put the blanket down."

"Okay, yeah, that's a good idea."

He started ripping the blankets and sheets off.

"Do you want some help?"

"Nope, I got it . . . but can you grab us some beers? We killed that bottle of wine already, and I only brought the one, sorry."

"Sure."

I stumbled slightly and crawled off the couch. I didn't want beer, but at this point, it might go down easier. I was drunk and giddy. I felt free. Free of my mother's criticisms, her frosty touch, the cruelness she showed my father; it all slipped away. Isabel and her snide remarks and bossiness; it was nothing. I felt nothing for any of them. I didn't need any of them; I only needed him. I swung open the refrigerator door with drunken force, smacking the wall. I giggled.

"Oops!"

Teddy laughed.

"Be careful! I've got these gross sheets off for my princess."

Princess. I sucked in a sharp breath and thought about how I couldn't wait to tell Harper. I was his princess now. I grabbed two bottles and slammed the fridge shut with my foot, almost falling forward into the sink.

Stumbling into the next room, Teddy was in bed, wearing just his underwear. His stomach was tan and packed with muscles. "Mad About You" by Belinda Carlisle played from the speakers. *How fitting.* He had lit a cigarette, and the smoke filled the room. The smell was horrible, and another thing I'd have to get used to.

I panicked, remembering my young and awkward body.

That morning, I examined my growing breasts, my butt, and between my legs. What parts were appealing to Teddy? I attempted shaving my legs carefully like I saw my mother do, but the hair remained. A second messy try did the job as I flinched, squeezing one eye shut and steadying my other leg on the tub.

Teddy patted the side of the bed and smiled. He opened the beers with a bottle opener from the crate. As I tipped the neck of mine into my mouth, cold, frothy bubbles exploded within. I coughed. *Well, that was sexy; good start.*

"Hey, hey, slow down. It's not smooth like wine. Are you okay? I don't want you to get sick."

The room was out of focus, yet I felt invincible. I pouted my lips and hoped I didn't look ridiculous.

"I'm fine, won't get sick. Feel grrrreat, don't worry."

My words spilled together, slurring like my mother on her heavier wine-soaked nights. He took one more drag from his cigarette then put it out in an ashtray on the floor.

"Okay, just be careful. I'm going to keep you busy anyway . . ."

He pulled me towards him, sloshing my beer and spilling droplets on my shirt. I giggled.

"Oops, sorry. Here, give me that." He put the beers down and put his arms around me. He lifted my shirt halfway. I tried to protest, but he began to run his tongue across my stomach. Goosebumps traveled from my legs to my neck; a brand-new sensation. I didn't stop him.

"You like that?" he whispered, and met my eyes.

I nodded and closed mine. Teddy fell back onto the mattress and drew me with him. I was now on top and clueless what to do. His hands kept busy—squeezing my butt cheeks, pushing me into his hips, petting my face. I struggled to keep up. He was quick and precise. His breathing was rapid as he inhaled sharp gulps of air and exhaled soft moaning sounds, all while probing my mouth with his tongue. *Cosmo* magazine instructed to never "fake it," but I did not know how to "make it" either. I would have to follow his lead.

His penis strained against his underwear. I feared it might transform into The Incredible Hulk and bust out, giant and green and riddled with big veins. A hard penis was supposed to arouse women, but I felt nothing. In one swift movement, he pulled me underneath him, his body heavy, and his mouth everywhere. I had to steal air between kisses. It became difficult to relax. I stared at a poster of the Duran Duran *Rio* album cover on the wall. A woman with short dark hair, red lipstick, and long pointy earrings looked out vacantly in the distance. Colors of magenta, teal, and gold slashed through the frame. Despite her eyes staring ahead, I felt like she was watching us. She smiled with a bright-cherry mouth, and I focused on that while Teddy began to undress me.

His skin was glistening now, and he set about lifting my shirt over my head.

"Wait!"

"What?"

Teddy's arms pinned me on both sides as he gazed down at me, his hair falling forward. He was so much bigger than me. Even if I wanted to leave, how could I?

"Nothing," I whispered.

"That's my girl."

He slowly unsnapped each button of my tank top, and my hideous training bra lay across my breasts like a sad sack. Teddy lifted it quickly, exposing me, and I attempted to cover them, but he snatched my wrists and stared with hungry eyes. The bulge in his underwear swelled as it struggled against the fabric.

"They're beautiful, Hazel," he exclaimed.

I nodded and pinched my eyes shut as he unbuttoned, then slid my shorts down. He kissed my stomach as he removed my last layer, my underwear. He kissed my legs and parted them and ran his tongue down my inner thighs. *This was supposed to feel good.* I was utterly frozen in fear and fully exposed.

I was drowsy and unable to form rational thoughts.

"You are perfect, Hazel. Just perfect." He ran his hands up and down my body.

Perfect.

"Do you want more beer before . . . you know, I go inside you?"

I nodded, still keeping my eyes shut.

"You can open your eyes now," he said laughing, as he retrieved our beer. "In fact, drink the beer, it's probably a good idea."

I exhaled deeply. *This will all be worth it in the end,* I thought as he guzzled his beer. He set the empty bottle down and slid his hand under the mattress.

"Here," he said, holding up a bottle filled with clear goopy stuff. "This should make things easier too."

Oh, lube. Harper had educated me about that. It made everything slippery and easier going in. The label had strawberries on it.

"Okay, if it will help, sure."

Teddy squeezed the bottle above his hand, and goo oozed out. The scent was similar to my strawberry lip gloss. *Great. Now every time I put that on, I will think of sex lube.*

With the other hand, he tugged at his underwear, one side at a time until his penis sprang out. It was huge. No wonder it hurt so much. I wanted to look away, but I was also fascinated. It stuck out like his body was holding a gun. And below it, were his two hanging balls, nearly hidden in a tangle of hair. Teddy seemed pleased that I was gaping at his manhood. He smiled and jutted it closer. He rubbed the lube all over it, moaning a little.

He slipped his underwear off with his feet doing the work.

"Okay, Hazel. I'll be nice and gentle this time. Open your legs up."

By now, I thought I would have been enjoying this. I was mad at my soap operas, mad at how this was nothing like on TV. Maybe he was doing it wrong.

Maybe sex just wasn't great for the girl. Maybe this was only for men's pleasure. If he loved me and was nice to me, I could probably get used to it. He did slide into me easier this time. And he stayed propped on his elbows—so I could breathe. The hot tearing feeling burned, but slightly less intense.

"Oh, God, you're so tight . . . you feel so good, baby . . ." he kept repeating, as he rocked back and forth. How did something so big fit inside me? The blankets began to chafe my skin, but I didn't dare move or talk. I didn't know what to do with my hands, so I held onto his arms and counted my knuckles over and over again. I wanted this over with so he could tell me how great it was. I moved my focus to the smiling woman in the poster.

This is love! she said, without speaking.

Then, just like the last time, it ended with a grunt and long moan, and he was on top of me, sweating and gasping for air. His heartbeat raced through my chest. A slick wetness coated the inside of my legs. Teddy rolled off me, still breathing heavy, but gazing at me, a stupid smile on his flushed face. He was so hot. No matter what it took, I would have to keep him. He draped the blanket over me.

"Better?"

I nodded, happy to be covered up and done. I was disappointed. It still hurt, and I didn't have this "orgasm" that I had heard so much about. Thanks for nothing *Cosmopolitan.*

"It's going to take time, Hazel." He gave me a soft, melty look, and I relaxed into the bed. "And we have this apartment whenever we want. I know it still hurts, but it will get better, I promise."

He sure made plenty of promises. This had to be love, I was sure of it.

10

SMASH

ANN ARBOR, MICHIGAN 2005

Old Town Tavern was also overflowing with patrons. It was Friday night, and the snow wasn't slowing down the drinkers. The hostess took us to the last open table, a small corner booth. I was grateful that we were out of view of eyes that might know me. Ann Arbor was a small town.

Teddy ordered a beer. Me, gin on the rocks with lemon. My stomach twisted in nerves; I needed something strong as his snakelike charm drew me in.

Stay focused. Talk about Phil. Your kids. Happiness. Make him regretful. See what he's missing.

I glanced at my watch. Nine thirty. Eight thirty in Chicago. Mitchell would be asleep, Phil reading in bed. Hopefully my mother had put Maddy down hours ago. I had more faith in her grandmother abilities than her mothering skills.

"So," Teddy said, his muddy-brown eyes captivating, "you look great, Hazel. How do you like Chicago?"

"How did you know I live in Chicago?" I narrowed my eyes, feeling violated that he knew about my life.

"Ah, my dad. He talks to your dad occasionally."

"Oh, right. Your dad talks about me? He doesn't know—" My face flushed, and I stared at a series of grooves in the wooden table.

"No, no. He filled me in on what happened while I was gone. Your dad talked about your family in general. And then *they* moved, so I don't hear much anymore. The last I heard, you were working with Isabel in Chicago as a pastry chef?"

"Wow," I said, my hands shaking. "Yeah, I'm a pastry chef and I lived with her and Abbey, initially. They started a catering business, and I do all the desserts." I paused. "How do you like being here again?"

This conversation felt stupid and awkward, like an interview or first date. I should either be asleep at my parents' or helping Harper, not at a bar with my former *boyfriend*, or whatever he had been. Teddy shrugged and scraped his beer bottle label.

"It's alright. Boring. A lot of memories," he said, his eyes meeting mine.

A loud roar startled me. A group at the bar downed a round of shots, followed by shouting and cheering. I silently scanned the room. I longed to be either with the jovial group at the bar or at the table next to ours. A family of four ate dinner amidst the noise; a teenage boy scarfed down french fries, another boy slumped, bored with an empty plate. The husband and wife looked tired, chatting between bites. I missed the banality of the family unit while hating myself. Here I sat, across from Teddy, flustered and blushing, potentially the fool again.

"Yep, I bet," I breezed over the comment. "Um, yeah, Chicago is great. I'm married—his name is Phil—I have two amazing kids, Mitchell and Maddy, and I'm a pastry chef—"

"—*Two*? Wow, the last time I talked to your dad, you only had one. That's so crazy. Two kids and a husband. Are you happy?"

The question bounced in the air like moths throwing themselves into a streetlight.

"Of course, I'm happy."

Why had I paused? Was being with this man for one evening making me reconsider this question?

I felt the heat of his legs when our knees touched. What would life be without diapers and formula and cartoons and grocery shopping and thousands of loads of laundry? What would life have been with Teddy? Would we have traveled the world as he once promised? Where would we have settled in Europe? Would we have gotten married on a cliff overlooking the ocean somewhere? And would that have made me happy?

"You sure about that?" his eyes questioned me.

"Yes, Teddy, very sure! I won't discuss my family with you. You can tell me about you, though.

Since you and your needs are your favorite topic.

"Wow, harsh! Can't we talk like adults?"

"Oh, because I finally am one?" I sneered.

I drained my gin with shaking hands. I signaled the waitress for another round. I closed my eyes and focused on the sounds around me.

"Ouch," he said. "I know I hurt you, Hazel. I've apologized a million times. And, I explained why I had to leave. If I hadn't, you wouldn't have your family. I did you a favor, believe me."

What a hero he was. I thought back to something my therapist, Diane had said.

"He's a narcissist, Hazel, arrogant and manipulative. He charmed you as he damaged you, brainwashing you to believe he was your hero. You were too young to decipher this. These are adult actions and you were a child. We want to get you to a place now, as a grown woman, to recognize this type of behavior quickly and keep distance from people like him."

Bubbles of irritation formed in my gut. Before I could respond, he leaned in and resumed talking.

"Hazel, my life has been a mess forever," he said, as he kept peeling the beer label, forming piles of sticky goo on the table. "And I am serious about doing you a favor. I ran away when things got tough and shouldn't have. I should have stayed and got a job or went to school, the right thing to do, and also what you wanted. Instead, I ran off to see the world. Which, I don't regret either. I had to get the fuck out of Michigan, and it was amazing. People who stay here and never leave miss out on life. I'm glad you got out too. Sure, I wish you had been with me. But, Christ, you knew our issues. You were too young. The timing was shitty. I couldn't take you but couldn't stay either. I was fucked in the head. And then, seeing you years later at my party, well, yeah, we shouldn't have gotten together. I missed you, and when I saw you, it all came back . . . and I needed you."

"What do you want me to say?" I asked, as I leaned back. "Thanks, I guess? While you were out traveling, I was alone. You made promises, then disappeared. Do you know what that does to a kid? I *lied* for you; I *lied* for me, and lost everything."

Beads of sweat rolled down the back of my sweater. Anger melted off my body like butter in the sun.

"My childhood was a series of mistakes. I didn't enjoy the fun things kids do at that age," I continued, "I should have been playing with friends and having crushes on boys my own age. You saw my vulnerabilities and took advantage. For God's sake, Teddy, I was thirteen. What you did is basically considered child abuse."

The first time I said it out loud.

"Well, I mean—"

"Yeah, yes, it is. It makes me sick to think of a grown man touching my daughter."

"Hazel, I—"

"—On top of that," I interrupted, "you broke my heart. And just when I had found happiness with a boy my *own age*, you show up again. So, I felt I had to—"

"Break up with him?" He leaned back, smirking.

"You're an asshole." I wrapped my scarf around my neck, ready to leave. How stupid I was to be here right now.

"Wait, Hazel, hold on, please?" Teddy grabbed my hand and bolts of electricity erupted.

I slowly unwrapped myself and slumped into my seat. That split second of his touch made my entire body tingle. I flashed to his lips kissing my neck, his hands traveling over every inch of me. That connection he always mentioned was still there. The gin soothed my pounding head, and I was becoming too relaxed.

"Fine, but I have to leave soon."

"Hazel, listen. I'm sorry. I'm an asshole. I truly loved you. We had an incredible summer. But, things just . . . got out of control."

My emotions were weaving back and forth.

Keep your distance.

It wasn't all his fault. I should have said no, a thousand times over. I tried to imagine Diane sitting across from me, telling me to run. The door was right there, I could get up and leave and never look back.

But. I could feel he still loved me. I could feel it. My inner adolescent spun irrational thoughts.

Now, he sat here, drinking as if we were just old pals, seeking forgiveness to ease his guilty conscience. If he even had one.

"What part was out of control, Teddy? The part where you came to my house all the time and sang to me, and we talked for hours, and you read me poems by Oscar Wilde? Or maybe the part where you supplied me with liquor and drugs? Or, do you think taking my virginity might have been out of control?"

His face softened, and he put his hand on my forearm.

"Listen, it's really loud. I'd really like to talk more. I have a place we can go and talk easier if you want."

I was drunk. My head and body were liquefying into a puddle. Before I could stop, I shook the last drops of gin from its ice and nodded.

"Fine, let's go."

11

PRY

ANN ARBOR, MICHIGAN 1986

M y mother was a shell, only showing her outer layer. We longed for her full attention, but it wasn't ours to have. Girls were supposed to learn about sex and love from their mothers. *Weren't they?* Harper's mother had shown her diagrams of vaginas and explained how menstruation cycles worked, how babies were made, and how to avoid pregnancy. Her mother needed a cigarette after their talk.

"Mom?" I found her in bed reading pages of her novel. She was scrutinizing her words, moving her lips, silently.

"Hmmm?"

"Can I ask you something?"

"Mmmm Hmmm."

She frowned, reading, barely listening.

"Can I ask you a question?"

"I said yes, honey. What is it?"

I waited for her to look up at me. She kept reading, and then finally, as if just noticing me, glanced up.

"Well? What is it, Hazel? I have a lot of work to do."

I picked at my cuticles and searched for words.

"Well . . . um . . ."

She took her glasses off and threw her hands in exasperation. "Hazel!"

"What is love?"

"*That* is your question? Well, geez, darling. Why don't you ask me where babies come from too!"

I flinched.

She sighed.

"Oh, Hazel. That's a monumental question. Do you *need* to know today? I wasn't expecting questions like these for a few years. Is there a boy you like? I hope to God you are not thinking about sex yet. Tell me you are not pregnant. That would be the worst thing that could possibly happen. You are not pregnant, right?"

Her anxiety escalated, her face flushed, her pupils dilated, and she fidgeted.

"Are you pregnant, Hazel?"

"No, Mom, gross!" I rolled my eyes. "I'm not asking about sex! I just . . . wanted to know if . . . you know . . . how will I know if I am in love?"

"Oh, thank God!" She relaxed and melted back into her pillows. "Because that's the last thing this family needs. Okay, well, love. Love . . . hmmm . . . okay, what is love? Hand me my coffee, sweetheart. God knows I'm going to need it."

She motioned with bangled wrists for her favorite coffee mug, a colorful terra-cotta piece from New Mexico, near a plate with a half-nibbled croissant.

I carefully handed it over, flinching slightly at the smell of alcohol mixed in milky brown coffee.

"Well . . . the ancient Greeks called love, 'the madness of the Gods.' Because, frankly, love can make you go mad. At first, you are infatuated, and you can't sleep or eat; you want to spend every moment with that person. You actually *crave* them. You want to crawl inside their skin and live there. You can't think straight, and you make stupid decisions. Really stupid decisions."

She paused and sipped.

"I won't address the level of sex drive. That's for another time. But you simply cannot live without them. You become possessive, and you might disregard friends, family, work, everything. He will follow suit. And every little thing that person does is simply adorable! Oh, he leaves a little trail of socks from the bed to the closet, even though the hamper is right there. That's okay, because it's the cutest sock trail! And he can only drink expensive wine? How cultured he must be! I'm so lucky!"

"And then, some women—not me, mind you—but most, get this intense motivation for total emotional union. You two must be forever! You must be married quickly! What shall we name our children? We shall have a boy and a girl and a dog and a cat! It's totally alright that he's socially awkward and sometimes says stupid things because you can change him! Women always think they can change a man, and Hazel, if you learn nothing else, know that you cannot change a man. He is who he is. No sense in trying."

She shifted and took another sip.

"Down the road, that sock trail and that social awkwardness and the stupid comments, well, you just want to explode. It's no longer adorable. It's downright maddening! You start to resent each other. Because there are things about you that bother him too. And he will let you know all about it; trust me."

She took a frenzied sip.

"And then, more years go by, and you settle. You just give up and settle in. The grass isn't greener, even though your lawn is looking pretty brown. You end up doing your own thing and then, occasionally, you mesh together for a few good times. That, Hazel, is what love is."

My mother stared expectantly, as if I owed her gratitude for this depressing revelation. Instead of feeling grateful, I was disappointed and confused. *Did my father feel this way?*

"Hazel?"

I should have known better to expect her to be sweet, loving, and supportive—now or ever. She could have shared some gooey love story about her and my dad. Instead, she had turned one of the most important questions of my life into her bitter version of reality.

"Okay, well . . . thanks, Mom."

She blinked twice, adjusting her focus.

"Oh . . . yes! Of course! Do you have any more questions regarding love?"

"Nope. I'm going to go shower."

As I walked out, her loud words followed me.

"Are you sure, Hazel? You better not be having sex or thinking you're in love, young lady! You're just fooling yourself . . . love is for fools!"

I needed my dad. It was Saturday, his gardening day. I headed outside, shielding my eyes from the bright-lemon sun. I searched the backyard and headed out to the pond. He was churning up dirt with a small shovel.

Coconut was near him, rolling around, contentedly rubbing his face into the soil.

"Hi, Dad," I said and knelt down.

"Hi, honey. What's up?" he said, wiping his forehead.

"Um . . . I had a question for Mom and she . . . well, I wanted to ask you too."

"Okay. This sounds serious."

"Yeah, it's . . . well, when do you know when you're in love?"

He raised his eyebrows and laughed.

"Hazel, do you have a boy you like?"

I felt myself turn pink. I began to pull dandelions scattered around the garden's border.

"No, I was just wondering. Friends at school will sometimes say they love a boy, and I just, well, I don't know what that means exactly."

"Okay, then." He put his shovel down and wiped his hands on his shorts. He removed his sunglasses. "That's not an easy question nor is there an easy answer or one that fits everyone. But I can tell you that love is exciting. You don't choose love; it chooses you. It's unexpected. Once it hits you, you have to surrender. You can love people that you don't even like sometimes. It turns your insides out until your stomach is sick. It's wonderful and terrifying all at once. You want to always be with that person, and you might even ignore those closest to you. But, it's part of the process. It's a wonderful thing, love."

His blue eyes flickered, and drops of sweat streamed down his tanned and whiskered face. The cat came over and began to rub up against him.

"Hey there, boy. You're filthy! We're going to have to dust you off before you can go inside."

"So, do you stay in love forever?"

His jaw tightened now, and the twinkle faded. Coconut ambled away and found a spot under a large cabbage and plopped down beneath its shade.

"Hmmm. That's the funny thing about love. It starts out exactly like I said, but," he hesitated, "the thing is, over time, that jolt of excitement, the butterflies in your stomach, they sometimes fade. And what happens after that, is, well, companionship. There's nothing wrong with companionship, Hazel. No one wants to be alone. Being able to lie next to someone at night, reading a book and talking about your day, well, that's a comfortable way to live."

Suddenly, the window in my parents' bedroom slid open and my mother's head popped out.

"Richard? Richard! Could you please come upstairs? I need to talk to you, please."

My dad sighed and looked at me with flat, dull eyes.

"Sorry, Hazelnut, duty calls."

12

RIPEN

ANN ARBOR, MICHIGAN 1986

They called it the "afterglow." According to the latest *Cosmo*, it was the elated feeling of floating on air after making long, passionate love. All your senses would be heightened; the air would smell like a spray of gardenias as you walked along the sidewalk.

Teddy and I had not made long, passionate love. We had drunken, awkward sex on a dirty bed in a stranger's apartment. I wasn't driven home and kissed good-night. I rode home on my Schwinn with the rainbow streamers flapping in the wind, legs wobbling and sore and sticky between them.

But, none of *that* mattered. I had *the afterglow*.

"The fucking nerve of *him* to break up with *me!*" Isabel complained one night before work. "I've been blowing him off and avoiding him, and *he* says we should 'see other people.' Um, duh, I've already been doing that! Anyway, if he changes his mind and drops by, tell him from me to eat shit!"

My mother looked up from her legal pad, pen in hand and reading glasses perched on her nose, clucked her tongue and furrowed her brow.

"Isabel, really! I would appreciate you not using that language in the house. You are a lady and not a truck driver for God's sake."

Isabel and I both rolled our eyes. Our mother swore all the time, just apparently, not this evening.

"And, that Teddy is quite charming. What did you do to make him break things off, dear?" She sipped wine, feigning interest for a moment.

"Mom!" Isabel bellowed as she gathered her keys and purse. "You have no idea who he is. Dad may be friends with his dad, but I can assure you, Teddy will never amount to anything close to his father. Just because he brings you flowers does not mean he is a keeper."

And with that, she stormed out. My mother raised her eyebrows at me, shrugged, and went back to writing. I, however, danced on invisible clouds.

~

Back at Chad's apartment, the sex was getting easier. I was more comfortable with my body and building confidence. I began caressing the back of Teddy's head the way soap opera lovers did. My touch always excited him, and he would moan softly and bury his lips into my neck. I arched my back while he kissed my stomach and breasts. My body contoured and shifted to ease him inside me. The pain still pinched when he went deep. At times, I thought I might split apart, but I never stopped him.

He did sweet things for me. He went to the apartment before I arrived to wash and dry Chad's sheets. He emptied the ashtrays and attempted a little tidying. He once brought me stargazer lilies in a pink vase.

Then one day, Teddy suggested a boat outing. His family belonged to the Barton Boat Club, where members could rent sailboats for Barton Pond. The small-scale boats were ideal for children and beginners. According to Teddy, it had been the fun family activity of his childhood.

"We used to all go out together—me, my sister, Mom and Dad

—and my dad taught us how to sail," he said, as we shared an almond chicken dish at Chad's one night. "Dad loved the water. He grew up on the lake and sailed all the time as a kid. My mom would strap our life jackets on us and just try to keep us from falling overboard. And then, we'd have lunch by the boathouse. It was pretty cool."

He smiled as he reminisced. I cherished the rare times he spoke fondly about his family and felt special to be his audience.

"Anyway, we should go and sail around the pond. It'll be fun *and* romantic," he said, and kissed me lightly on the nose, "and I know my stuff so don't worry about tipping over or drowning."

"Really? I mean . . . we would be in public together. Are you sure?"

He looked down at his nails gnawed to the quick.

"Yeah, I've thought about it. We'll be careful. If anybody asks, you're my niece. No one will suspect anything."

I sighed. His *niece*. He confirmed to me earlier that he and Isabel were done. This was in no way romantic to me to be seen as his niece, especially since *I* was his girlfriend now.

He recognized my frustration and softly kissed my lips.

"Don't worry. We'll go during the week. There's hardly anybody there except junior teams learning to sail. They usually stick with their instructor, so they won't notice us. We can sneak in some kisses. It will be romantic, you'll see," he winked, and curled me into his lap, sliding down the straps of my tank top.

～

"**M**om, I'm leaving now."

I was on edge and fidgety because usually when I snuck out, my mom was gone. Today, she was gardening.

"Yeah?" she squinted up at me. "Where are you going again? My mind is a damn sieve today."

"Me and Harper are going to the pool. Her mom's going to take us."

This was much riskier, and I had to play the thirteen-year-old virgin who didn't drink or lie. I could barely recall the traces of my old self.

"Harper and I," she corrected.

"Harper and I."

She looked at me in my shorts, flip-flops, and a pink top with tiny flowers.

"Where's your suit?"

"It's in my backpack. I'll change there."

"And you have sunscreen?"

"Yes."

"Are you alright?"

"Yeah, why?"

"You just seem . . . different. More grown up," she said, digging up a slug in the soil and flinging it towards the pond. "Damn things. You're sprouting like these weeds."

"Mom . . ." this time I rolled my eyes.

"Okay. Go on. I can pick you and Harper up when you are done."

"No! I mean . . . that's okay. Her mom already planned to drop me back off."

She sighed. "You're sure you're okay?"

"Yes, Mom. Can I go now?"

"Yes. Have a good time and mind your manners."

"I will! Bye!"

"Give your mother a hug. Or are you too old for that now?"

I bent down for a small squeeze. A stale cigarette smell hung to her sundress.

I sprinted back. Teddy planned to meet me at the end of the block. I grabbed my backpack and rushed out the door.

Nestled inside Teddy's IROC-Z, I sank into the velvety black cloth seats, pulled my flip-flops off, and propped my polished pink toes on the dashboard. My hair was hiked in a high ponytail and white Wayfarer sunglasses covered my eyes. On my lips was hastily applied red Estée Lauder lipstick I swiped from my mom's purse.

This game of deception felt sexy. I was ablaze with certainty that this was the new me.

"You look amazing, baby girl," he whispered and kissed my neck.

"Thank you!"

Teddy was preppy today: plaid shorts, slip-on boating shoes, a short-sleeved powder-blue Ralph Lauren Polo shirt with the collar popped, and Ray-Ban sunglasses. I couldn't believe this man was mine.

"Wow, I dig your outfit!" I gushed.

He smiled and slid his glasses down the bridge of his nose, exposing his dark eyes.

"At the boat house, I better fit in so we don't stand out."

The engine growled along winding Huron River Drive. Banana-colored rays of sun burst through the rows of trees. "Sweet Dreams" by The Eurythmics wailed through the speakers and emptied out through our open windows.

Teddy smoked cigarettes, and I took occasional hits from them and didn't even cough. They were disgusting, but his eyes were hungry, and they traveled over my bare crossed legs and watched as I put the cigarette to my red lips. I knew the sacrifice was worth it.

The river surged below with tiny ripples of current, sapphire in color and glistening like sequins. Perfection.

As Teddy predicted, the nearly empty parking lot indicated a slow day. A few sailboats scattered the water: a group of students in lessons and a young couple in a boat by themselves, drifting along the shore.

"I'll be right back," he said, and pecked my cheek. I popped a piece of Bubble Yum gum in my mouth and blew a pink bubble.

Teddy and a man in khaki shorts and a yellow polo shirt went down the dock to inspect the boats. The man made some hand gestures and Teddy signed something on a clipboard, shook the man's hand, and headed back. He smiled through the windshield and waved.

"We're all set! Let's grab our stuff and go."

"Okay!"

He clicked open the tiny trunk and pulled out a duffle bag.

"What's in there?"

"It's a surprise," he grinned and glanced back at the man. "I told him I was taking my niece out, that my parents were away in France. So, we're cool."

I resented all this niece crap and struggled to mask it.

Keep your mouth shut.

"Got it."

We were alone on the dock with ten empty boats, lined up side by side.

"This little lake gets the perfect amount of wind for sailing. Once we get onto the water and situated, it will be a smooth ride."

"Sounds good."

The boats were small, inverted shells, barely big enough for us and the gear. Teddy threw the bag in. It smacked with a thud, pitching the boat back and forth. My nervousness conjured up images of me losing my balance and falling in and dying of embarrassment.

"It's alright, I'll help you in. It's not going to flip over," he said, quickly interpreting my thoughts.

I exhaled and nodded. He stepped in first. It rolled again and splashed little laps of water against the dock.

"Are you sure?"

He held out his hand.

"Yes, Hazel, I'm sure. Take my hand and step your foot right there," he pointed to a flat spot inside the boat.

"Take this, first," I said, and handed him my LeSportsac bag.

He tossed it on top of the duffle and reached out again to me.

Stop acting like such a baby, you're a woman now.

I gripped his hand and lurched forward. I landed with a soft thump, and he held onto my shoulders until the boat stopped rocking.

"You okay?"

"Yeah, I got it."

"Okay, have a seat, and I'll get us pushed off. Oh, and put this life jacket on, just until we get out of view. We're supposed to have them on at all times, but you know me and rules."

Oh, I did.

As I snapped my jacket closed, Teddy loosened the ropes, shoved off the dock, and hoisted the sail. He settled in and steered with a long pole that controlled the rudder. The wind kicked up once we got farther from the dock, and the sail made a whooshing sound before popping into place and then ballooned like a small parachute. And then, quiet. The water was flat; the only sound filling the hushed air was the soft rippling streaming alongside the boat.

Towering trees clustered around the lake, and two red-tailed hawks scouted for prey. Kayaks and fishing boats came into view, along with the ducks and geese that snugged close to shore. Logs submerged in shallow waters served as perching spots for big gray herons and white egrets. The sky was washed in a cornflower blue and cloudless. I exhaled a long-held breath and drank in this perfect moment with my next inhale. I put my hand into the cool water and let it spray gently up my arm.

"So, you like it here?" he asked, as I gaped at my surroundings.

"It's awesome, I love it."

"Good, I figured you might," he smiled.

Teddy picked up the duffel bag.

"You okay still?"

"I'm good, really."

He smiled and unzipped the bag and handed me a thermos.

"Soup?"

"No, it's wine," he said, laughing. "This time, Chardonnay."

A small stab of worry came as I thought about my mother draining bottles per week. At the rate we were drinking, would I end up like her?

"Never heard of it. Is it French?"

"Nah," he chuckled, "It's from California, like the white Zin. My mom and sister drink a lot of wine. They call it 'oaky' and 'buttery' but you be the judge."

Teddy produced some Styrofoam cups and took the thermos back.

"Here, you hold, I'll pour."

We raised our cups.

"To us!" he said.

"To us!" I said and tapped his.

The wine wasn't sweet and citrusy like the white Zinfandel. I didn't know what oaky tasted like, but the texture was creamy, and I liked it from the first sip. I felt sophisticated drinking oaky, buttery Chardonnay.

"What do you think?"

"I like it. It's like drinking popcorn," I said.

He grinned, and his lips melted into mine. I tasted wine with a hint of cigarette. Butterflies fluttered deep in my stomach.

"You know, Hazel, this has been a great summer."

I sipped, edging the Styrofoam in red lipstick smears.

"The secret we share," he continued, "will bond us forever. No one feels the way I do about you. Ever. I was your first, and that's an honor, Hazel."

"Really?" My head was feeling dizzy from the wine, but I felt bold and alive.

He leaned over and breathed into my ear, "Yes."

Goosebumps popped all over my body.

"Can I ask you a question?" I examined my cup.

"Of course."

"Have you ever . . . um, been with someone, you know, younger? Like me?"

Teddy shook his head hard and looked at his feet.

"No. Never. I mean that, Hazel. I'm not a guy that goes after little girls. And you're not a little girl, that's not what I mean, you know what I'm trying to say . . ." he was stammering now, "but, there's something about you that I can't resist. You're an old soul. You're smart and like me, ignore the rules. You're saying fuck you to the world by being with me. Our connection is real. Your face, your body, your mind . . . I love you, Hazel."

"I—"

Before I could speak, he pressed his lips against mine. My body went limp.

"I have something for you," said Teddy.

"Another surprise?"

"Hold my cup for a second," he nodded.

He lifted a small square box with a red Christmas bow which made me laugh.

"For me?"

He took the cups from me as I lifted the lid. Thousands of rays of light showered me in the form of a gleaming, shimmering diamond bracelet on a fluffy bed of cotton. The sun caught every individual facet, casting a glow within itself. It was stunning.

"Oh my God, Teddy! What the—"

He picked up the bracelet.

"Give me your wrist."

Dumbfounded, I stuck my arm out. He looped it around my wrist. It was so loose, and I was scared it would slide off with any movement.

"It may be big now," he laughed, "but you'll grow into it."

"Teddy, this is just too much. This must have cost a fortune! How did you afford this?"

He slid the bracelet off and placed it in my palm.

"Don't you worry about that. I wanted you to have something as beautiful as you and to remind you of us.

I stared at the sparkling band of light.

"I won't be able to wear it. Even if it fit," I said.

"I know," he frowned. "You're going to have to keep it safely hidden until you move out. But you can bring it when we're together."

"Well, can we get it sized?" My mother had a couple of watches resized when, after her cottage cheese diet, she bragged that she was too thin, and they were dangling off her.

"Sure, yeah, let's do that at some point."

Some point? When?

"Okay."

I kissed his cheek.

"Thank you. I love it. And I . . . I . . . love you too."

He brushed my face and looked into my eyes.

"I know you do."

He loved me.

I wanted to cement this moment. I gently pried myself from him and his lipstick-stained lips.

"Hold on, one second," I said. He raised his eyebrows as I pulled out a Le Clic camera from my purse.

"Can we just take a couple pictures?"

"Hazel, I don't know if that's a good idea," he said.

"Please? I'll keep them hidden. I won't show anyone."

He considered it and then relaxed.

"Okay, sure. Anything for you."

I grinned, and we took a series of photos. First, one of him with a wind-blown ponytail, holding onto the sail. Then me, draping myself in the tight space, proudly displaying my new treasure. He projected the camera, and we kissed, hoping it would capture our faces. I took pictures of the lake, the boat, and one of him blowing a kiss at me.

~

L ater that afternoon, after my mother quizzed me about the pool, I lied expertly. I told her I was tired and was going to shower and lie down. Once in my room, I searched for a hiding place. This bracelet—diamonds!—was such a shocking surprise I still didn't know what to think about it.

I examined it top to bottom. It was a tennis bracelet, very in style with older girls and the rich women who volunteered for Junior League and well, played tennis. It was an extravagant gift for a girl my age, but maybe he thought of me as a woman now. Teddy couldn't have told the salesman it was for a thirteen-year-old. This was no "niece" gift either. He must have lied and said it was for his girlfriend—an imaginary age-appropriate woman. And now I had to hide it.

The moccasins that Mavis had gifted us that weird weekend

seemed like a good spot. I had never worn them. I examined the bracelet once more and wrapped it inside a pair of socks before I stuffed it in.

Everything in me was glowing.

~

My mother had finally relented to take me bra shopping after I pestered her that I needed a new bra. I was mortified that I had to go with her, but I really needed one.

I yearned for a sexy red lacy bra like Joan Collins would wear, with matching underwear. But I knew Mom would flip out and demand to know why I would want such a thing. I sauntered around in the lingerie section while she skimmed racks of plain-white cotton and beige no-lace teenage bras.

As I took off my shirt in the dressing room, she sat outside, drilling me with questions.

"What have you been doing all summer, Hazel? You're never home."

I hooked the bra in front of me like the saleslady showed me and then spun it around, cups facing front. It was ugly, and I frowned as I pulled the straps over my shoulders.

"Hanging out with Harper, going to the pool, the mall, the usual stuff. You've been gone too, you know."

She had been traveling a lot. I relished her trips to conferences. It was one less obstacle to Teddy, and she was becoming more suspicious and harder to lie to.

I heard her rummaging through her purse.

"Yes, I know. It's been a busy summer for me too. We haven't been able to spend much time together, which makes today more special. How's it going in there? Are they fitting?"

"Well, they fit. They're kind of ugly though, don't you think?"

"Well, Hazel, you're thirteen. You don't need anything fancy yet. You're still growing. And besides that, who will see it?"

Ha. If only you knew.

I put my T-shirt back on and turned sideways. I definitely looked better.

"Yeah, but *I* have to see it. Can I just get one pretty one, please?"

She sighed.

"Fine. But no lace. You can get a nice color to add to the white ones."

I rolled my eyes and shook my head at my reflection.

"Alright. I want red."

"Red? Why red?"

"I like red. It's bright and cheerful," I said, hoping I sounded believable.

"Hmm. Alright, I'll get the salesgirl to bring one."

She rooted through her purse again.

"What are you doing out there?"

"Well, speaking of red, I'm missing a red lipstick. I can't figure out where in the world I put it."

I froze thinking of the stolen lipstick and how pretty it made me feel and how I had forgotten to put it back. Another lie rolled out easily.

"No idea, Mom. Can you get the lady? I want to try a red one."

∾

I awoke one Saturday morning to a mixture of dried and fresh blood in my underwear and on my sheets. Was it from the previous day with Teddy? I hadn't bled from sex for quite a while, and that was the only blood I had ever seen down there.

I panicked and stripped the sheets off and balled my underwear up inside them.

Memories of my first night with Teddy and my bloody bedspread bubbled to the surface. It was so different then; he didn't love me yet, and it had been terrible. I yanked on some sweatpants and hid the mess in my closet.

I refused to go to my mother. She would embarrass or disregard me. Obviously I couldn't talk to my dad about it. That left Isabel.

I knocked quietly on the bathroom door.

"What?" Isabel yelled.

"Can I come in?"

"I'm almost done; can't you wait?"

"I need to talk to you."

"Like, right now?"

"Yes, please. Can I come in?"

"Fine! But don't let the hot air out."

I squeezed through the door and entered the steamy room.

"Geez," I waved my hands around the thick air. "It's summer out, why do you need it so hot in here?"

"I just like hot showers. What do you need so badly?"

Behind the curtain was the faint outline of her shaving her legs.

"I need your help, Isabel . . . with so many things . . . and now I just woke up with blood in my bed. I think I got my period."

She thrust open the curtain and gaped with dripping wet hair and a razor.

"Are you serious?"

"Yes. In my underwear and on my sheets."

"Okay, hold on." She drew the curtain closed and rinsed her legs and hair.

"I just . . . well. . . I don't want to talk to Mom about it and I don't know what to do."

"Hand me the towel, please."

I jerked the towel from the rack and handed it to her.

She dried off, slid the curtain aside, and stepped out wrapped in the towel. She had become obsessed with Annie Lennox and had chopped her long brown hair into a cropped style. My mother hated it. Isabel had laughed and said, "Wait until I dye it bleach blonde!"

"I don't blame you. Mom would either make you feel stupid or throw you a weird party."

"Ha, ha," I grimaced.

"Hand me my robe, please," she said, pointing to the back of the door.

As her towel fell, I saw flashes of breasts and a mound of pubic hair and averted my eyes. Teddy had seen Isabel's womanly body many times. Her hips were proportioned with her shoulders, and she had a small waist in an hourglass shape. The body that I wanted and probably Teddy wished I had.

Isabel opened the sink cabinet and pulled out a box of maxi-pads.

"Here," she held one out.

I shook my head.

"Don't you have any tampons?"

She raised her eyebrows at me.

"Really? You want to try that?"

I figured after months of sex with Teddy, how bad could a tampon be? I was uneasy, but I refused to put another one of those pads on.

"Yeah, how do I do it?"

She reached back into the cabinet and pulled out a couple Tampax.

"Does it hurt?" I asked.

Would the pain of the tampon be like the pain and pressure when Teddy climbed inside?

"No, you don't even feel it. The cardboard is the shittiest part."

She unwrapped one of them and held it up.

"I'll reenact how to put it in without doing it because that would be weird. You can try after I show you."

"Okay," I sighed.

"Alright, so, you can sit down, stand up or bend over, whatever floats your boat. A lot of girls use the toilet."

She gave me a thorough demonstration with plenty of instruction.

"Are you ready to try?" she asked.

"I guess?" I shrugged.

"Okay, I'm going to leave so you don't get stage fright, nor do I need to witness this, but I will be waiting outside the door."

I saw fright as I gazed at my reflection. I was having sex with a grown man, but this piece of cardboard was terrifying. I was uneasy touching myself down there and braced myself for pain.

Ten minutes and five tampons later, I got one inside me. It pinched my insides and I let out a little yelp. But it was in.

Isabel was getting impatient.

"I need to blow-dry my hair, Hazel. Did you do it?" she said through the door.

"Shh," I whispered. "I don't want Mom to hear."

Too late.

"Girls? What's going on up there? Do you want bagels? Your dad's going to Zingerman's."

"Yes, please!" I yelled.

"Sure!" Isabel yelled.

"Alright. What are you girls doing?"

"Nothing!" we both yelled again.

Now she was interested.

Soon, my mother would be snooping.

"Hurry up!" Isabel whispered, and stomped away.

I buried the tampon applicator deep in the garbage, put on sweatpants, and opened the door.

My mother was standing there, in her long royal-blue robe, with a cup of coffee in hand and a shocking white face mask smeared on her face.

"Jesus, Mom!" I jumped. "What the hell?"

"Language, Hazel!" she scowled, lines of clay crackling around her eyes.

"Sorry! Then don't sneak up wearing that crap!" I pushed past her, wondering if she could tell I had a tampon in.

"I came up to say good morning and see what you were doing. What a grouch!" she said, following me.

I faced her.

"Good morning, Mom! If you must know, I kicked Isabel out so I could poop!"

A look of disgust crossed her bright-white face.

"Hazel! That is disgusting!"

I shrugged, "You asked."

∽

W hen I told Teddy about my period, he looked worried.

"Shit, it was bound to happen sometime. We're going to have to be really careful now. Condoms or maybe birth control for you?"

"Yeah, right," I laughed. "My mom would freak out!"

We were at Chad's, smoking and listening to Blondie. I smoked now and was getting used to the taste and the light-headedness. I had been working on blowing out smoke rings but hadn't mastered it yet.

It was hot and muggy outside. The window air conditioning unit hummed loudly, and we were drinking wine. I felt so cosmopolitan.

"I guess she probably would. Maybe I could take you to the clinic?"

I shook my head.

"I think I have to have a parent with me?" I could not risk having pills around for my mother to find.

"Can't you just wear a condom?"

He flicked cigarette ash into an empty beer bottle.

"I mean, yeah, but that's not 100 percent protection."

"Well, either is the pill. It's like 98 percent or something."

Teddy shifted around on the couch and started peeling the label off the bottle.

"I guess I could wear one and then pull out."

His mood was shifting and I sensed his irritation, but I wasn't going to let him make me feel bad. I was not only too young for sex, but a trip to Planned Parenthood would raise serious suspicion. He was going to have to step up and protect us.

"I guess so then." I blew out a rush of smoke.

"That just kind of sucks," he said, taking a gulp of wine.

"Yeah, well, being thirteen and having an eighteen-year-old boyfriend that I have to pretend is my uncle sucks too!"

I was angry now. Harper had warned me about this. Guys never wanted to wear condoms and wanted the girl to take care of the protection. Condoms didn't feel as good for the guys. Too bad. Sex never felt good for me at all.

"Hey! That's just when we're in public, and you know that we have to do that!"

I looked down. Teddy and I had discovered the tennis bracelet fit well on my ankle. As I turned my ankle from side to side, admiring its sparkle, I wondered if we were having our first fight.

"I'm just saying that hiding in secret is harder than wearing a condom. What's the big deal?"

He shrugged.

"It just doesn't feel as good. I like my skin next to your skin."

I yawned and looked around the apartment. I was feeling defiant; I wanted to go out in public and yell to everyone that we were together. I was sick of this messy apartment and all its secrets.

"Well, I can't get pregnant or go on the pill. So, I guess you're going to have to deal with it." I crossed my legs and bounced my foot up and down and blew smoke up to the ceiling.

Teddy raised his eyebrows.

"Wow, geez. So bossy and independent! You got your period, so now you're a badass?" he said with a smile.

I blushed, feeling stupid as well as surprised. The truth was, I did feel different, confident and a bit cocky.

"Yeah, I guess so."

He plucked my cigarette from me, smashed it out, and pushed me onto the couch.

"I like this new you . . ." he grinned, unbuttoning my cut-off shorts while kissing my neck.

"Whoa, whoa," I pressed my hands to his chest and craned my neck out of reach. "What did we just talk about? Do you have condoms?"

He hung his head down, his hair falling in my face.

"No," he murmured.

I propped myself up on my elbows and threw my head back. A ray of sun blazed through the windows, hitting my face. I squinted.

"I guess you have to go to the store then."

He groaned and rolled off me, a hard lump pressed against his jeans.

"Fine. Anything else, my princess?"

I glanced at the empty pack of Marlboro Menthols.

"Another pack of cigarettes?" I batted my eyelashes, and he laughed.

"Sure."

He kissed me on the forehead and grabbed his wallet and left.

I had spunk now, and Teddy liked it. I could snap my fingers and he'd do anything. I was drunk on power. Womanhood was shaping up to be just what I wanted.

13

CAUTION

ANN ARBOR, MICHIGAN 1986

Harper blew smoke rings into thick summer air, reminiscent of the chunky onion rings at Ponderosa.

She had been practicing for weeks, chain-smoking until her clothes reeked of a combination of stale smoke and her favorite perfume, Love's Baby Soft. We were under the football bleachers at school, and through narrow openings of the steps, we watched high school boys practicing preseason football—throwing, running, and grunting.

Harper stared wide-eyed, her lids covered in deep-blue eyeshadow. Her former blonde ringlets had been replaced by an asymmetrical bob. She tucked pieces of hair behind her ear, framing her lightly freckled, summer-kissed, beautiful face. I was envious of her perfect complexion, which never housed a single pimple, smooth like a freshly frozen lake.

"I will never understand sports," she said, inhaling deeply. "How is chasing a ball around a big field so fun? They run full speed and tackle each other and break their bones, all for a stupid ball. Women would never do something so, *asinine.*"

Lately, Harper had been using words like *asinine, pedestrian, and pedantic.*

"Melissa and Erin are pressuring me to try out for cheerleading. What do you think? Should I do it?" she asked.

"No way!"

Shouting out silly chants like, "Ready, set, go!" and "Go, fight, win!" seemed so fake to me. I couldn't imagine pulling it off with any sincerity—and couldn't imagine anything worse. Harper took a hit and exhaled a blast of smoke—no rings this time. Harper handed the cigarette to me, her eyebrows forming question marks. One end had fresh embers, the other, covered in her sticky pink lip gloss. I took a hit and attempted a smoke ring, unsuccessfully.

"I mean, why not? Being a cheerleader would raise my value as a hot chick. It's too bad we aren't in the same grade; you could join me."

I didn't care about being a hot chick, or a popular cheerleader trying to snag make-out sessions with high school boys. I did not have middle school girl dreams of dating a senior, becoming a varsity cheerleader, and then of course, being voted king and queen of the prom. I had Teddy. I had an actual man.

"That doesn't even sound like me, I said.

She shrugged, stubbed the cigarette on the bottom of her K-Swiss sneaker and flicked the butt towards piles of beer and whiskey bottles in overgrown weeds.

"It's a door to parties and the hot guys. And once I'm in, you can come with me.

"I don't care about parties filled with immature guys. Everybody gets drunk and acts like idiots."

Harper raised her eyebrows again.

"Geez, who pissed in your Cheerios?"

"Sorry, that's just not my thing." She was right. I was being mean. "You would be a great cheerleader though! I've had a lot going on this summer that I haven't told you—"

"—Oooh?" Harper smiled and scooched closer. "Sounds juicy! You have been M.I.A., but so have I with Steve. He's driving me crazy though. He acts like my boyfriend when we're alone, and then when his friends show up, he acts like a jerk. Boys are so annoying! And then, we went on that family vacation to North Carolina and—

sorry, back to you. What is going on? We *have* to catch up. Dish, please."

Not confiding in her about Teddy seemed like best-friend betrayal, but he swore me to secrecy, not even Harper. Even with our lifelong friendship, I feared her reaction.

Our bond began in our innocent youth. As kids, we pitted Barbie against Skipper in their quest for Ken's love, and we braided each other's hair on the merry-go-round. Once, I accidentally knocked over a bucket of deep-indigo dye on her garage floor while tie-dyeing shirts. We scrambled to wipe up the blue river with kitchen towels while Mandy, her floppy-eared basset hound, waddled through the mess. The tips of her draggy ears were blue for a week.

"I know, it's been a crazy summer and, um . . . well . . . I have to tell you something. And it's kind of a big deal."

"What?" Harper's smile faded. "What's wrong? You can tell me."

I took a deep breath, then blurted it out.

"I lost my virginity, and I've been having sex all summer, and I have a boyfriend."

"Wait, what!" Her eyes popped open. "With who? Holy shit, Hazel! Seriously? Why didn't you tell me and who is *this guy*?"

"You don't know him . . . well, you know *of* him."

"*Of* him? What do you mean? Who is it? Tell me the details!"

"Teddy," I whispered. I had not said his name out loud to anyone until now.

"Who is Teddy? Wait, wait. Teddy? Your sister's boyfriend?" Her voice rose several octaves, and I looked around nervously.

"Shh! Not so loud!"

"You cannot be serious! That dude is like . . . old! He's already out of high school!

"Not that old! He's only eighteen."

"Only eighteen? Are you kidding me? What happened? And what about Isabel? Does she know? Jesus Christ! You better start talking, Hazel! Holy shit!"

Harper grabbed her pack of cigarettes. She put one in her mouth and handed me my own.

"This must be serious. When did you start smoking by the way?"

She lit my cigarette, and I exhaled a long corkscrew of smoke and grimaced. She didn't smoke Menthols, and my tongue felt dirty.

"Okay," I started, "well, I've been smoking and drinking all summer. Sometimes smoking pot too. It started when Teddy started hanging out at our house a few months ago since he was dating Isabel, and well, his dad is friends with my dad, and so it was never weird that he was over all the time."

"Uh huh, keep going."

"Um, it all started back in May, I would sometimes hang out with them, and he would play his guitar and we would all watch movies—me, him, and Isabel—and sometimes, when Isabel wasn't home, he hung out with just me. And, we just sort of became . . . close."

"Whoa, this is crazy. What do you mean, close? Like, you had sex?"

Harper loved reading her mom's self-help psychology books, especially the ones about codependency. She considered herself an expert in dysfunctional relationships. Instead of feeling relief, I felt like I was on trial, convincing the jury of my innocence.

"Okay, hold on, you're asking a million questions. One—"

"—Sorry, but, Hazel, get to the point . . . the sex."

Just then, a group of kids plopped their backpacks on the bleacher steps and began talking about a party some senior was having on Saturday while his parents were away. A girl with permed hair sipped from a bottle hidden inside a paper bag, giggling and blushing as she passed it to one of the boys. They couldn't see us, but Harper fluffed her hair out anyway.

"See, Hazel. That could be us at parties and dating popular boys if we tried out for cheerleading. But . . ."

I rolled my eyes, "Do you want me to finish or not?"

"Sorry, yes, keep going."

In whispers, I told her everything—how it started innocently, talking about books and documentaries and how that formed a *connection* between us. I told her about our first night together, about how it hurt, and how I bled all over my comforter. I told her about the apartment, the boat ride, the diamond bracelet, and that we loved each other.

"He's so totally hot, Hazel! I cannot believe this! Although, he is way older. Does that weird you out? I think you're too young to have sex with him." She sighed and placed a hand on my knee. "I'd have to ask my dad, but it kind of sounds like statutory rape."

Harper's father was a lawyer and discussed cases at the dinner table. He never minced words or tried to sugarcoat his version of the world. Sometimes, it was great to have a friend with legal knowledge to help our future selves out of trouble, but it was not what I needed right now.

"He did not rape me! Rape is . . . Jesus, he's not a rapist. That's ridiculous! Rape is against someone's will. I *wanted* to . . . I mean, it hurts, but it will get better over time. He didn't force me or anything."

Flashes of him holding my arms down and covering my mouth came and went. Suddenly I felt confused. My throat burned as I swallowed down the tears that were starting to choke me. Would my best friend understand, and, if not, could I convince her?

"Okay, okay, calm down," she said, keeping one eye on the bleacher kids who were now smoking pot.

So far, they hadn't noticed us. I sensed her longing to be with them rather than dealing with her best friend's possible rape situation.

"Listen," she went on, "I get it. You have feelings for him, but what about your sister? Does she know?"

"They broke up, and no, she doesn't."

"Okay," she contemplated. "I mean, of course he said you have a connection. He's what my dad would call a con artist, a smooth talker. I don't want you to get hurt, and it is illegal, Hazel! He could go to jail! Can you imagine what your mom would do if she found out? Your poor dad? Isabel? This is what they call high-risk behavior, Hazel. On both your parts. And, dangerous."

I mashed my cigarette into the ground.

"Maybe I like the danger."

There, I said it. Maybe I really did.

"Look, Harper, I knew you wouldn't understand. No one will."

I started to get up, but she pulled me back down.

"Okay, stop. I am your best friend. And I'm older, so you're sort of like my little sister, who I'm trying to protect."

"You're a *year* older," I said, rolling my eyes, "and I have a sister. You're my best friend. Stop being so—"

"—Okay, sorry. What did it feel like? It still kind of hurts when Steve and I do it, but, geez, you're fucking a grown man with a big old dick!"

"Harper! God! Really?"

I thought of Teddy pressing his entire weight into me and the searing hot pain that spread through my belly.

"Sorry, just wondering! I figure Teddy has to be big, and you're so tiny."

"Yeah, it did hurt like hell. It hurts me down there and inside my stomach. It burns. I wait for it to be over."

"Yeah, for me too. I think it's only fun for the guy."

I shrugged, "According to *Cosmo*, it's supposed to be amazing for the girl, but I think it's a crock of shit."

"Fuck *Cosmo*. I take those quizzes all the time, and they always suck. Real life experience is far better than what they tell you it's supposed to be like."

What *does* his dick look like?" she giggled.

"Harper!"

"What? I never look at Steve's. He makes me touch his to get him hard, but I don't look. Dicks are gross."

"Harper! Stop saying that word!

"Dick?" She shrugged. "What else should I call it? *Penis* is what doctors call it. You should start using grown-up slang since you're fucking an older guy."

"I guess. That word sounds so vile."

I hated many words associated with sex and body parts. Plus, my dad's name was Richard and sometimes when my mom was angry with him, she would say, "Stop being such a dick, Dick."

She rifled through her bag and pulled out her Bonnie Bell lip gloss. She slid the applicator over her lips, adding to the goopy, shiny lacquer already layered on. It smelled like Jolly Ranchers and plastic.

"So, are you really going to continue this thing with Teddy? Whose apartment is it anyway?"

"Yeah, I mean, I want to. And he wants to. We said we loved each other, but I've never been in love, so I'm not really sure what I'm doing. The apartment is his friend Chad's. He's never home."

"Damn! You are so lucky! To have a place that's private and not be caught by parents—or the cops, in your case—but, shit, Hazel!"

She grabbed my elbow.

"That also means no one, up until today, knows where you are. What if he's an axe murderer? If he kills you, no one would find you. Except me now, of course."

I rolled my eyes.

"He's not an axe murderer. I trust him."

"And, you think you might love him? I don't even know if I love Steve. They say love is very different for guys and girls. A woman usually feels a connection right after sex, while it takes a lot longer for a man to feel it. Are you sure he's feeling the same as you?"

"They" always pertained to the authors of her mother's books, but not usually any one in particular.

"I honestly have no idea. I tried to ask my mom and dad—"

"—You asked your parents? They're dinosaurs, Hazel. Of course they had stupid things to say. They've been married forever, and everyone knows, once you're married, all you do is fight, and you never have sex. At least that's how it seems in my house. I mean, ew, I doubt if mine have sex . . . I still can't believe you popped your cherry!"

"God, must you be so—" I grimaced.

"—vile?" she laughed.

"Yes, that. Anyway . . . I need your help with this."

What do you want me to do?"

"I need you to cover for me."

"Cover for you, how?"

"I've been telling my parents all summer that you and I have been hanging out by the pool, with Kathy. And, if for some reason, my mom asks, yes, we are always together."

Her face puckered.

"Geez, you could've told me sooner. Good thing your mom never called! Your ass has been lucky so far! But, sure. My mom is always at one of her do-gooder charity things, that Junior League crap, so she's gone a lot, and my dad is always in court. And, my brother is never home. He's got some skank girlfriend now, and he stays with her a lot. So, you're covered. Just think of how popular you would be if word got out you were screwing a man!"

I shrugged and smiled. Her obsession with being popular baffled me, but I didn't care as long as she kept my secret.

"What do we have down here?" One of the guys on the bleachers above peeked underneath to see us. "A couple of hot babes! You ladies wanna smoke pot?"

He was cute with blonde hair falling into bright-blue eyes. Now the entire group looked between their legs down at us. Harper smiled back and nodded.

I grabbed her arm.

"Stay, I've gotta go. Just remember, you and I are always together if my mom asks. But she won't."

"Got it," she said, her eyes fixed on the upside-down boy.

A strong stench of pot lingered in the air.

"Please be careful, Harper. You don't know anything about these guys."

She smiled and twirled a thick piece of blonde curl.

"Look who's talking."

14

FLEE

ANN ARBOR, MICHIGAN 1986

A ugust was winding down but summer's crushing heat wasn't. Maps were spread across the table at Chad's, along with an atlas and travel books. Teddy wanted to travel the world starting with Europe. And he wanted me to come with him. We often talked about an adorable apartment in Italy with thousands of stone steps circling our ivy-covered front door. We would bike everywhere with baguettes and bouquets in our baskets, read poetry in coffee shops, and throw pennies in fountains while making wishes. Most importantly, unlimited freedom to just be us. Like my Sea Breeze, I drank up his blissful promises.

The sweet concoction of vodka, cranberry juice, and grapefruit juice pleased my inner child, while the alcohol migrating through my veins feigned adulthood. Teddy poured all the ingredients in a martini shaker, shook it up and down, then poured it into tall glasses, the edges of the drink swirling in a thin foamy layer. Teddy said his mother drank them by the pool. It was delicious, the taste of vodka hidden.

The sound of a key fumbling around the door startled us both. A tall, muscular man with bronzed skin and blonde hair staggered in wearing a tight Def Leppard T-shirt, barely containing bulging biceps. The fringe hanging from his cut-off jean shorts brushed his beefy quads. It was hard not to stare. Right behind him, a leggy blonde with high, rat-teased bangs and a tight perm swayed in wearing the shortest shorts I had ever seen. A neon-blue cropped T-shirt exposed her flat stomach. She hiccupped loudly, then giggled.

"Aw, shit!" I assumed this was Chad. "I didn't know you would be here Tedster! And who's this? Is this Hazel? *The* Hazel?"

His half-mast eyes rolled up and down over me. The girl was snapping her gum, hand on hip.

"Dude!" Teddy stood up and gave Chad a pat on the back. "Yeah, this is Hazel. Hazel, Chad. The proud owner of this . . . dump. And, dude, we are always here on Fridays. What are you doing here? Not working today?"

Chad squinted at me and then my drink. He held out his hand, towering over me, and I reluctantly stuck mine out. His massive hand was sweaty and pumped mine with vigor as a blue vein popped up in his forearm.

"Well, well, pleased to finally meet the lady in Teddy's life." He spread his arms open wide to showcase the room. "How are you liking the . . . accommodations?"

"Nice to meet you too . . . yeah, your place is great—"

"—Ah-em," the girl behind Chad fake coughed, and he swung around and playfully grabbed her waist.

"Sorry, babe! This is Emily! Emily, this is Teddy and his girlfriend, Hazel."

Girlfriend. Finally, someone said it out loud.

"Hi!" she said, sporting a fake smile. Clearly, she had envisioned having the apartment to themselves and now, here we were.

"Okay if I grab us some beers, hon?" she asked her gigantic boyfriend.

"Sure thing, biscuit!" Chad said, ogling her ass as she sauntered away.

Chad quickly produced a joint. He raised his eyebrows, and Teddy smiled and nodded. Looking to me for approval, I simply shrugged.

"I took the day off, my friend! Em and I went to the 'rents place and hung out poolside, raided the liquor cabinet, and ended up here. Hope we're not interrupting your . . . um, maps?" he said, pointing to the mess on the table.

"No, problem, dude," Teddy said, scooping up the maps and piling them by the couch. "It's your place."

Emily returned with a beer for her and Chad and seated herself next to me.

"What are you *drinking?*" she asked, admiring the pink foam.

"It's a Sea Breeze," I said, sipping proudly. I had a sophisticated drink while she swilled beer.

"Huh . . ." She absently dug through her tattered leopard-print purse and found the prize—a Zippo featuring a blonde pin-up girl in a polka dot bikini—turning her admiration from my drink to her lighter. She lit her Virginia Slim. "Isn't she a doll? Chad got it for my birthday last week because she looks just like me." She chomped gum between inhales.

"Yeah, she's pretty. Happy birthday."

"Thanks! So, um, how long you been dating Teddy?"

I took another sip. *You do not look like the pin-up girl.*

"All summer."

"That's cool. Teddy's got that cool car, huh?"

"Yeah, it's cool."

"So, um, I don't want to be rude or anything, but how old are you?"

I gulped the last of my drink and set the glass down. The moment of truth—of lying. People who knew Teddy. People who could call the police.

"Eighteen, why?"

I looked her straight in the eyes as I spoke. Teddy told me when a person looked to the left when answering, it usually meant they were lying. He told me to maintain eye contact. But, all the lipstick, blush, and mascara could not camouflage my baby face. She squinted at me through glossy red eyes.

"Oh, okay. You just look real young, that's all. I mean, lucky you! When you're fifty, you'll probably look twenty-five! Teddy just normally dates . . . oh, you know, girls that look older I guess."

A pit formed in my stomach. What girls? My sister? Who else? I never asked him about past girlfriends because I was afraid to know.

Chad interrupted with a sloppily rolled joint.

"Who's first, ladies?"

The afternoon floated in and out of my consciousness. My muscles relaxed into jelly, and my skin radiated warmth. My senses heightened with the lingering traces of sunscreen and chlorine lifting from Chad and Emily's skin. Even Teddy's signature smell of leather and tobacco became muskier. The sound of the boom box bass resonated from my toes to my fingertips.

I latched onto some conversations, and others drifted away. Asia, Africa, Europe, backpacking, hostels, Machu Picchu, cross-country trains, hiking, ruins, caves. *Dude, we have to plan a fall trip! Totally! I've wanted to do this my whole life. Me too, dude. Let's do it!*

"I've just never felt this way before about somebody, ya know?" Emily's voice was loud in my ear. "I don't even want to go to college, my stupid parents . . . are you going to college next year? Are you okay, Hazel? You are so high!"

I remembered sitting on the bed but wasn't sure how I ended up *in* bed on my back next to Emily. She was much taller than me with big boobs and long legs, all emphasizing the truth that I was a child. She looked so pretty and trustworthy with her caked-on makeup flaking off, revealing freckles and light-pink lips. I felt a sudden urge to confide in this total stranger about everything. I reached out and touched her lips. She curled them together and kissed my finger.

"Are you sure you're eighteen, Hazel?"

Chad was hovering over us, a beer in his hand, grinning. He was swaying, and his eyes were bloodshot.

"Shut the fuck up, Chad." Teddy promptly pulled Chad away. "She just looks young. She gets asked that all the time. It's annoying, dude. Leave her alone. Are you sure you're not taking 'roids to get those muscles?"

"So original, asshole," Chad retorted.

I was rolling in pudding and couldn't answer Chad if I wanted to.

"Come on, babe, let's go." Teddy quickly picked me up.

"Where? You can't take me home . . ."

"Shh, shh. I gotcha."

"Where does she live?" I heard Chad ask.

"Not far, don't worry, I got it. Thanks for the smoke. Later."

Teddy folded my body up and into his car. The dashboard was hazy, and when I put my fingers out to steady myself, I saw double. In the daylight sun, the car's interior was hot and suffocating. He rolled down the windows and cranked the air, and I moved my face towards the vents.

"You okay?" he asked, petting my hair.

"I think so. How did I get so fucked up?"

"Sea Breezes and pot. You're tiny, so that's a lethal combo."

I flopped my head back and turned to look at him.

"What were you and Chad talking about? It sounded like you were going somewhere."

Teddy stretched back and pulled a pack of cigarettes from his pocket and lit one up with his Playboy Zippo. I thought of Emily's lighter and giggled. He blew a stream of smoke outside.

"Aw, just shit talk. We've talked about backpacking in Europe since junior high. But he's working now, and I got nothing but time; we wouldn't be able to make it work. We always fuck around with the idea when we're high."

"But . . . you said you would wait, for me . . ." My parched mouth and clumsy tongue made forming words an effort. "We go together."

He fidgeted and looked out his window. I said nothing and waited for his answer. Instead, he started the car. I tried remaining calm, but my head pounded, desperate for water.

"I don't see you as a backpacking kind of girl. Do you?"

"I could totally go backpacking!" I said, trying to convince both him and me.

"You think so, huh?" he smiled at me as he took another hit of his cigarette and rubbed my leg. "A fifty-pound pack on your back? That's about what you weigh!"

I happened to weigh 105 pounds. Did he think I was ten?

"No, but by the time I graduate, I could!"

"Yeah, probably then you could. It's just shit that Chad and I have talked about forever. Just stupid guy stuff. Don't worry so much."

He flicked his cigarette out the window. I adjusted my twisted denim skirt and smoothed out my shirt. I thought of Emily's perfect body and her skimpy outfit. My boobs were getting bigger now, growing fast, but despite the running, my legs were still string beans.

"We need to get you coffee before we get you home."

"No, take me home."

We drove the few blocks in silence, him rubbing my leg and me staring out the window fighting back tears. Safely parked a couple houses from mine, he pulled my face towards him and kissed me gently. Brushing the stray hairs from my messy ponytail, he forced me to look at him.

"I'm right here, babe, quit worrying so much. I love you, right?" he said, and kissed me on my forehead.

"Yeah. Okay." I said and got out of the car.

"Hazel!" he called to me. But I took off running.

Expecting him to get out and chase me like in a movie, I slowed down. I was almost to my house, and he couldn't be seen going in. I stopped and turned. Teddy just sat in his car, smoking.

The tears came easily now, flowing hot down my cheeks. He was lying; I could feel it. Or maybe he was telling the truth, and I was just drunk and high and overly sensitive.

Suddenly, the insides of my stomach wanted out. I felt a surge of nausea and liquid rising to my mouth. Red and pink juices gushed out violently as I sobbed and vomited into the bushes. I heaved and heaved, and it kept coming.

Once it was done, I rushed into the house and up to my room. I pulled my oversized diamond bracelet from my purse and slid it onto my arm. I asked Teddy last week if we could get it sized, and he rejected the idea. It was just too risky to be seen together at a jeweler. I wanted and needed it to fit so badly, to strut around with it and show it off. Show everyone what my *boyfriend* had bought me. It wasn't fair. None of this was fair.

❧

The next morning, I woke up puffy and exhausted, but still asked Isabel if I could tag along while she shopped at the mall for work pants. She was in a good mood and said sure. She didn't ask why I looked like hell. I put on makeup and sunglasses, hoping I was concealing my hangover.

While she was in the dressing room, I went to the lingerie department and picked out a lacy red bra and matching panties. The saleswoman raised her eyebrows as I opened my wallet but said nothing as I plunked down cash. Once paid, I stuffed my secret prize deep into my backpack. I bought a couple pairs of earrings from Claire's boutique as a cover story.

Back at home, and Isabel at work, I showered and tried the new red bra on. The snap was in front—*Cosmo* said men loved easy access—and this one actually gave me some cleavage. I couldn't stop staring at the bulging flesh. And the panties cut high on my thighs, showing off my running muscles. Teddy would not be able to resist me.

I wore sexy, ass-peeping shorts to compliment my hidden lingerie. I painted my lips in my stolen red lipstick and applied generous coats of mascara. I felt like a prettier version of Emily.

I rode over to Chad's and arrived first. I put in a mixtape and lit some scented candles I had smuggled from home and a stick of Nag Champa incense.

"Hey, sorry I'm late, babe." Teddy walked in to find candles glowing. He wore tight black jeans and a white T-shirt, despite the heat. He looked so good; I forgave his lateness. "Wow, candles and music, impressive."

On tippy-toes, I kissed him, inhaling his cigarette and Ralph Lauren Polo scent.

"What took you so long?"

He pulled a Chardonnay bottle from a bag and went to fetch glasses.

"Oh, a stupid fight with my mom and bitch of a sister. They ganged up on me."

"What about?" I asked and waited.

Teddy came back with a corkscrew and glasses.

"The usual. They want me to either go to college or get a stupid job. My sister is so high and mighty—but, how are you? I don't like how you ran off last night."

The cork slid out, and he poured the wine.

"I'm fine. I'm—"

"Good, I'm glad," he stood and began pacing, "They set a fucking deadline. I can either apply to college or get a *real* job before September. Can you believe that shit? I took one damn summer off. My job at the shop will wait but, fuck, I am sick of dirty car repair."

I took a sip.

"—And my dad's pissed too. Says he will cut me off if I don't get a real job. Whatever the fuck that means. He thinks putting on a suit and tie every day qualifies as real work. It's such bullshit. And, college, please! Do I seem like a nerd that will study all night? Fuck, no. Not happening."

My heart raced, and a brick weighed down my gut.

Tell me you're going to leave and take me too.

He snapped open his lighter, and he paced. The candles flickered from the drafts he created. Cyndi Lauper sang "Time after Time."

"Oh, and my car! They're also threatening to take my fucking car! Babe. It's total bullshit."

He was worked up like never before. I drained my glass and poured another, playing it cool.

"Well, shit, Teddy, I don't know what to say. This sucks."

Inside, I was thrilled. If his parents forced him to stay for college or a job, he couldn't go to Europe. He would be here for me . . . and maybe get his own apartment.

"I have some cash saved up. I don't spend all they put in my account; I have it stashed in another bank. They don't know that, obviously, but I knew this fucking day was coming."

"Oh, that's good. Maybe you could just crash here until you find a job."

Teddy snickered, plunked down on the couch and lit another cigarette.

"Yeah, right. Like I would stay in this dump. Anyway, I forgot to tell you. Emily's moving in here with Chad."

It was as if he had smacked me in the face.

"He told me last week, and I forgot to tell you. Sorry."

"Jesus! I can't believe you didn't tell me, Teddy! Okay, so why can't you get your own apartment with the money you saved? Then we'd be together whenever we want!"

He was chain smoking and smothering the mood I'd created.

"It just seems like too much to deal with, an apartment, a job, bills. I'm not ready for all that shit."

Was he serious? I was far from a bill-paying adult, but he was the one acting like a child.

He came over to the table and sat down next to me.

"Listen, babe, I will figure something out, I promise. I won't be like my folks or my stupid sister. I don't want to be a corporate guy, but not a blue-collar zero either. I need time to think. We might not see each other for a while until I figure out what to do."

"Teddy!" I stood up and nearly knocked my chair over. "That's not fair! You promised you would be with me until I graduated. You *lied!*"

"No, no, just listen. I know it's not fair. Calm down, babe. You haven't even started high school yet. Listen—"

"—You fucking lied, Teddy! When is Emily moving in?"

He stared at the floor.

"A couple weeks."

"How could you do this to me?"

I was sobbing now, tears and snot running down my face. He must not love me if he was giving up.

"Hazel, I'm not doing any of this on purpose. This is just my shitty life, Hazel! Shit doesn't work out for me, ever."

"Shitty?" I exclaimed. "You poor thing! I've spent my entire summer hiding in this dump, lying to my parents and drinking and smoking. For what? You were never going to wait for me! I wasted my whole summer on you and your lies!"

I ran to the bed like a child, curled into the fetal position, and cried into dirty sheets. He came over and sat on the edge of the bed and stroked my back.

"This summer has been awesome with you. I never expected anything like this in a million years. How did I waste your summer? You don't really feel like that, do you?"

I couldn't look at him as I shed tears on the sheets.

"I just don't understand why you can't . . . I . . . why you can't just get a fucking job and be with me?"

"Well . . ." He stroked my hair, pulling pieces of it out of my wet face. "Baby, give me time to figure it out. My life is out of control right now. I know it's total bullshit. I'm sorry. I really am."

"I just can't believe you're going to leave me."

"Hazel, come on. Let's not ruin this day. We still have wine . . ."

I could not stand his voice anymore.

"Forget it."

I pushed away and got off the bed. My hand brushed my shirt, and I felt the lacy bra beneath, the bra he would never see. *Fuck this place and fuck him.*

"You tell me you're leaving, and then you want to fuck me?" I slipped on my sandals. "If you really loved me, you would get a stupid *real* job or go to school and just deal with it! You're so selfish! I hate you!"

"Hazel!"

I threw the shiny silver key to the floor before slamming the door.

"Babe! Come back here!"

~

I was surprised to hear his deep voice the next day on the phone. My dad was mowing the lawn, and my mother was taking a bath to Joni Mitchell music.

"Hazel, it's me, don't hang up."

My heart dropped. "You shouldn't be calling here!" I whispered.

"Can you come outside? I'm parked down the street. You ran out before we could talk more. Please?"

"I can't believe you called me here!" I repeated, and looked around nervously.

"I know! But, there's no other way to talk to you. I got worried when you ran out. Obviously I couldn't come to your house."

I paused and thought for a moment.

"Hazel? Please?"

"Fine," I sighed, "I'll be there in a few minutes."

I hung up the phone and raced upstairs to quickly brush and pull back my hair and apply the red lipstick, now worn to a nub. I assumed it would be the last time I wore it for Teddy.

I moved down the sidewalk slowly, unsure of what to say to Teddy. How I loved him? How he was a jerk? Beg him to just get a job and stay?

His stupid orange car was parked at the usual spot. Teddy was inside, his arm dangling out the window, a cigarette between his fingers. His sunglasses masked his dark eyes. He smiled and kissed me behind the ear as I slid into the seat. Teddy removed his sunglasses and handed me a small bouquet of wildflowers, presenting them along with a sheepish grin.

"Hi, babe, these are for you. To say I'm sorry."

I couldn't help but smile. They were clearly hand-picked from some field and tied with twine. A small effort, but they were pretty.

"Thanks."

"I am really sorry, Hazel. How are you doing?"

"I'm fine."

Teddy took a hit off his cigarette and sighed his exhalation.

I picked at the petals, letting them fall between my legs onto the seat, not caring about the mess.

"Listen, I know you're mad. I wish I could make it all better. But, like I said, all this is happening at once, and I have to make some quick decisions."

"Why can't you just get a job and an apartment?"

"And do what? I have no skills, no college degree."

"What about that trade thing you told me about?"

I kept plucking at tiny petals and felt sad about ruining them, but nothing mattered anymore. And they were already dead anyway, cut from their homes.

"You're going to destroy those flowers I picked for you." I heard the smile in his voice but refused to look.

"Don't change the subject."

"Hazel, the trade thing will probably eventually happen, but for now . . ." He motioned towards his back seat.

I hadn't noticed the large duffel bag and backpack sitting on the seat.

"What is that?"

"I'm leaving."

No, no, no, no!

"Teddy! No! Are you really doing this? Where are you going?" I wailed, tears spilling down my cheeks.

He tried to brush them away, but I backed away.

"This trip is to help me figure out what the hell to do with my life."

"I thought *I* was part of your life! Are you going with Chad? Where are you going and what happened to waiting for me?"

"Of course you're part of my life. This is just temporary, I promise. No, Chad can't quit his job, and plus he's moving in with Emily. I'm going alone."

"What?" I was sobbing now. "By yourself? Where?"

Teddy reached out again, and this time I let him touch my cheek. His soft, warm hand made my insides flip-flop.

"I'm going to Europe to bounce around a bit, see what's good. Then, I'll get a game plan and come back for you."

I shook my head in disbelief. His hand stayed on my face.

"You won't come back for me," I cried. "You just won't."

"I will, I promise. It's just for a little bit. Look, you're starting high school this year. It's a big deal. You should hang out with friends, with Harper, and have fun. Hiding out with me all the time won't be fun for you, ya know? And by the time you miss me, I'll be back."

"I can't believe this."

The flowers were almost picked clean, and I rubbed at the twine.

"I'm going to send postcards from everywhere. I'll figure out where we'll go together once you're done here. I'll take pictures and send them."

Speaking of pictures, I had yet to pick up the ones from our boat adventure. Maybe it was better if I didn't.

"It's not good-bye forever, Hazel. I'll keep you updated."

"How long will you be gone?"

Teddy began fiddling with the stereo knobs despite the lack of music.

"I'm not sure. Look, you'll understand this when you're older—"

"Stop it! I won't understand it. Stop treating me like a fucking kid. I know you're not coming back. I'm not that stupid."

He sighed, and I felt his rising irritation. He wanted this over.

"Hazel, look, I love you and you love me, and we'll be together again soon. I promise. But . . . I came to tell you, and now I have to go. I got into another huge fight with my folks. I tried to reason with them, and they basically kicked me out. I have to go catch a plane outta here. Like, right now."

This was unbelievable. He was getting on a plane today. No last day together. This was it. There was nothing I could do to stop him. This was my good-bye.

"Well, then . . . ." I wiped my eyes and set the flowers by my feet. "Have a safe flight, and I'll look for your first postcard."

"Hazel, kiss me please. We can't leave like this."

I was so angry, but I still had a sliver of hope inside me that he would keep his promises. And I needed to feel his lips on mine one more time. I leaned over and into him. Teddy held my face and kissed me gently. Salty tears mixed between our lips. Then, he pulled away.

"This isn't good-bye. This is just, see you later. I will be back for you, I promise. I love you, Hazel Walczak."

Without another word, I got out. He slid his sunglasses back on and blew me a kiss.

The car rolled away slowly at first, and I could see him watching me in the rearview mirror. I stood with arms crossed, no childish waving or chasing the car.

At the end of the block, he turned with a squeal, and the engine roared away. He was glad to be gone.

15

HOLLOW

ANN ARBOR, MICHIGAN 1986

Lockers opened and slammed as the 8:00 a.m. bell shrieked throughout the hallways. The piercing voices and sounds irritated both my mood, and eardrums.

I glumly hung my book bag in my locker. Unlike my classmates, the inside of my mine was barren. My plain long gray metal locker reflected my vision of the next four years. No *Teen Beat* poster boys, team sport paraphernalia, magnetic mirrors, or anything cutesy pink or bubbly adorned my mandatory space.

"Hey, there you are!" chirped a voice behind me.

Harper stood close, holding some textbooks, wearing head-to-toe acid-washed everything. The jeans and the jacket. Her pants were pegged and rolled up to her ankles, and her loafers sported pennies.

"Wow," I blinked, "that's . . . a lot of *denim* for one day."

"Well, duh!" She scrutinized my outfit, "*I* am very *in* right now. Besides, who died, Hazel? Jesus!"

I was wearing all black—black jeans, black Converse, a black T-shirt, and black cardigan.

"My soul," I said with a smirk.

"Hazel, seriously. Teddy was an asshole for leaving you, but you can't let him ruin high school, and you cannot wear black for four years. Christ, you're oozing depression."

"Thanks," I said, starting down the hall.

"Oh, come on!" she followed, her loafers clicking in step with me. "This is high school for God's sakes; the supposed best time of our lives according to my mother. Listen, I'm a sophomore, and I will guide you through your messy first year. We have epic parties to go to, boys to date, cheerleading, football games, skipping class—"

"—Harper," I faced her, "I don't give a shit about cheerleading and parties, and I certainly don't care about boys in high school. I was with a *man*."

She rolled her eyes.

"So, let me get this straight. You're gonna walk the halls like Morticia all the time?"

I regarded my outfit.

"Morticia? I hadn't even thought of her, but thanks, I take that as a compliment."

"Please, don't." She frowned at me and glanced at the big wall clock near homeroom. "Okay, fine, Morticia, I hope this is just a phase. You are way too pretty for this look. Anyway, I have to get to Algebra. Ugh. I hate it. I just know I'm going to fail it."

"You don't fail at anything, Harper. I'll see you later. I gotta go catch some sleep in social studies."

"Do you want to hang out after school? Meet my new cheer friends? We're going to—"

"—Umm . . . no thanks. I just want to be alone."

"Okay, fine," she said, trying to mask her hurt, "but forget about that asshole already, Hazel."

Harper strode off down the hall with a bounce in her step.

I stood alone outside my class at the end of the hall. I couldn't relate to my classmates' enthusiastic chatter about their exciting summers and upcoming fall football fun. Teddy was gone. I was alone, and this was high school. *Fuck.*

Shortly after Teddy left for backpacking in Europe, I went to the photo mat to get the pictures from our boat adventure. After pedaling three miles in the blistering sun, a guy working in the kiosk handed over the photos, emotionless and sweating.

As I folded over the envelope and saw the tops of our heads, I smiled. I slid the photos out farther, and there was Teddy and me, partly cut off from bad angling but laughing and kissing, the sun glinting off the water. The twinkling diamond bracelet dangled loosely from my waif-like arm.

My other hand was holding a Styrofoam cup, filled very obviously with wine, the dark- yellow, piss-colored Chardonnay. I sifted through the rest—the woods, the boat, the one with just me looking like a kid on Christmas day, and the one of him, all crooked grin and strands of hair falling in his beautiful face. Tears streamed down my cheeks.

I shoved the photos into my backpack and pedaled back home, wiping the snot from my nose. Despite cutting the streamers from the handlebars, little stubs of their existence bristled in the wind.

After weeks of checking the mail, I finally got my first postcard from Teddy, three days before my birthday. It was tucked inside an envelope, and luckily I had gotten the mail:

Greetings from Madrid! Feliz cumpleaños! That means happy birthday in Spanish! How's 14? How's high school? I hope you like it better than I did.

It's beautiful here and everywhere I look, I see you. I miss you. Madrid is awesome, Hazel. I am using what little I remember (which isn't much!) from Spanish classes (smiley face) and learning flamenco and watching bullfights. I'm looking for our best place to land together. I'm off to France soon, been mostly staying in hostels. They're kind of dirty, but getting dirty and figuring things out is why I left. I'll try to call when I can get to a phone. I'll send another letter when I can! Love you! Teddy

He wrote in tiny, neat handwriting to fit it all. The postcard was a photo of The Royal Palace. I raced up to my room and fell into bed, gripping the postcard.

It was hard to cling to the belief he loved and missed me. He left me. He went to Europe without a thought to my feelings. We fought and then off he went. No good-byes. He probably only sent the card out of guilt.

I shoved the postcard deep into my sock drawer and vowed not to look at it again.

~

A few days later, I celebrated my fourteenth birthday. My mother said since it was not a milestone birthday, we shouldn't make a big fuss. For once, we agreed. There was no comparison to my thirteenth year, when my happiness bloomed and then disappeared over the course of a few months.

I didn't feel like celebrating, but my grandparents, Dad's parents Lolly and Oscar, came over and gifted me an ugly sweater, some socks, and fifty bucks in a card. Isabel stopped by for dinner and cake. College suited her well. She spoke to my mother happily several times, prattling on about classes and the new friends she was making. Dorm life gave her freedom from the dysfunction within our walls. She bought me a copy of *It* by Stephen King, and when we were out of earshot, told me it was creepy as fuck.

I read it a few chapters the next day then road my bike to the cemetery to meet with Kathy, my summer alibi "pool and mall friend," and her friends. Kathy had long bright red hair and wore a black leather jacket stuck with endless amounts of safety pins. Then there was Tracy, with peroxide-dyed hair and black lipstick and see-through mesh shirts exposing black bras; Laura, who was passionate about crystals and Wicca, casting spells on boyfriends and cheerleaders; and Michelle, with her huge black mohawk that required tons of hairspray and hair paste and two hours to perfect. She wore Doc Martens, always, and I never saw her without black eyeliner circling her eyes. I felt at home with the Goths and their curated moodiness.

For weeks, I stuck to wearing black clothes and black lipstick. I often met up with Kathy and her friends at the cemetery after school where we'd drink Apple Blossom Boone's Farm or Spiked Melon Mad Dog 20/20. Not the Sea Breeze crowd.

Harper and I still hung out occasionally. Cheerleading practice, dating Steve, and moving up the popularity ladder kept her busy.

We didn't like each other's cliques, but kept a truce between us. She prattled on about football players, cheerleaders, and which seniors threw the "best" parties. I had little to contribute since my world consisted of witchcraft, crystals, and drinking shitty alcohol on the stones of dead people. In spite of her preaching to get over Teddy, my funk persisted like a scab.

～

The next envelope arrived in January without a return address, but the postage said "Italia" on the stamps. I peeled off my hat, the crackle of static prickling my ears. We had around a foot of snow, but today had been unseasonably warm, enough for a six-mile run.

The sky was crisp and blue, and thawing icicles fell from houses and landed with plinks and splashes. It felt refreshing.

Ciao Bella!

That means, hello beautiful in . . . Italian! Yep, that's where I am now. I didn't spend much time in France, since I went there a lot as a kid. How's high school? Making new friends? A new boyfriend? I'm sure those little assholes are chasing after you. (Smiley face) I couldn't blame them. You are a beautiful, amazing girl and anyone would be lucky to have you.

I have some news that really sucks. My parents have pretty much disowned me and told me again that if I come home, it's either college or a job. I'm still not ready for either.

I am in Florence now, learning some Italian and staying at a nice hostel. I have picked up some odd jobs. I really hope you will understand.

Nothing is the same without you, but I need to find out what I really want before I come back and face the real world. I'm sure that makes me a coward in your eyes but know that it's not you keeping me away. Again, I hope you understand. You will more when you're my age.

Anyway, I will write more when I can. I love you and hope that you can forgive me. Arrivederci amore mio! (That means good-bye, my love!)

Teddy

My head screamed but my mouth was silent.

Mother Fucker! Asshole! You prick! Who the fuck do you think you are, Teddy?

His neat penmanship, the way it slanted, spewing false promises, selfish requests, and permission to date other boys. No talk of our future.

I ran to the bathroom to dry heave.

I ripped the letter and envelope into a thousand pieces and flushed it down the toilet.

I stayed in bed for three days, with no appetite. The temperatures had become artic, and the endless blankets of January snow further deepened my mucky depression. My grades slipped, and my mother grew impatient. I slammed doors and ignored her. She persisted, imploring me to stop wearing black and moping. And to wash off the "obscene" makeup, get a part-time job, and start shaping up. My grades would improve in another environment, she said. I would learn something new, and school might become interesting again.

I had been growing weary of the Goth group. I didn't believe in witchcraft, and my burgundy hair had faded to a weird pink that clashed with my green eyes.

The group was also becoming risky. Tracy was caught shoplifting silver rings from JCPenney while Laura and Michelle often skipped school after boozy nights in underground bars that served minors.

My summer of lies, secrets, and sneaking around had taken a toll, and ultimately exhausted me. Taking risks with these girls was not worth it.

So, in early May, I took my mother's advice to find a job. I traded the dark makeup for a fresh clean face with just some mascara and lip gloss.

My first job—a veterinary assistant—abruptly ended after holding a black schnauzer to be put down. I sobbed along with the family, and then discovering the horror of the freezer housing dead animals put me over the edge.

The job Harper helped me get was not much better. She worked part time at a nursing home and warned me that it smelled like a combination of the Goodwill and shit but that the old people were nice, and she felt kinder for helping them. She filed papers, called out bingo numbers, painted nails, made beds, and applied lotion to the hands of the female residents. I was hired to serve food, complete with a hairnet and white kitchen jacket. Plopping instant mashed potatoes and canned peas onto plastic trays was gross and depressing. By the end of May, I quit that job too.

Still no word from Teddy since January. Five months of nothing.

My parents kept grilling me on what was wrong with me, so I concocted a story that I had been dating a boy named Aaron, and he moved to Ohio and only told me two days before he left. Sounded familiar enough.

Over Sunday dinner, my dad tried alleviating my hurt, stating this boy wasn't worth it, that I deserved better, and I should move on.

Per usual, my mother showed little compassion.

"Hazel, for God's sakes. How important could he be if you never introduced him to us? You're too smart and *young* to mope around for a middle school crush. High school will prepare you for the real assholes. I told you love was painful, and this isn't even real love yet. Get over it, and get another job."

She had no idea that I had already been with an asshole.

"Though clearly, you can't even accomplish that," she said. "My former colleague, Marjorie, owns a bakery in town. I've spoken with her, and she is happy to have you work for her. But you can't quit when the going gets tough like the others."

"Mom!"

"Don't, 'Mom' me! This is an excellent opportunity. It's a bright, sunny place, and you'll meet people, and Marjorie is extremely smart. She could stand to stop eating her inventory, if you ask me— you'll see—because you will need to watch your weight while working there too. So much sugar. But the best benefit is that you will learn a trade!"

Learn a trade. I wanted to throw up.

～

The bakery, Marjorie's Sweets, was annoyingly adorable—just as my mother described. It was bright, with yellows and pale pinks customizing the décor. Expansive floor to ceiling windows radiated with light, and a center display showcased every cake, cookie, and pastry imaginable. A big chalkboard with the "Pie of the Day" hung on the wall.

Marjorie was short and plump—as my mother had insinuated—with a brown bob haircut and an apron decorated in pies and cupcakes. She was funny and friendly, and I immediately felt at home. She had retired from the English department at U of M a few years ago to open up the bakery. The selection Marjorie sold was endless—cookies, brownies, cakes, pies, custards, tarts, Danish & French pastries, scones, croissants, and donuts. I stood in awe.

She showed me around—all the supplies, the fryer, two large double ovens, and a refrigerator with a door so heavy I could barely open it. I'd be working with Cleo and Maggie—Marjorie's pastry chefs—and a couple high school girls working part time at the register. I was overwhelmed, but to my surprise, excited. Isabel and I baked occasionally, but I never thought it could be a job for me.

Now, admiring the edible artwork designed by the chefs and the intoxicating smells of sugar and dough, I couldn't think of anything I wanted to do more.

My head spun trying to remember everything Marjorie babbled about as I gauged how to taste a bite of everything without getting fat. I would need to run more.

On Saturday and Sundays, I headed to the bakery. I rang up orders, cleaned, and learned the basics of baking. Saturdays were very busy, and among the scant bakeries in town, Marjorie's was the local favorite. I grew particularly fond of Maggie, who happily taught me everything. I learned the differences between raw vs. baker's sugar, how to blanch the skin off of fruits and nuts by boiling them, and how to perfect stiff peaks of meringue.

I was hooked. In this place, I was surrounded by sickening cheerfulness and laughter. I felt a new person emerging inside me. School ended, and barely having passed, I promised my parents I would do better next year. My only focus now was working full time for the summer.

I hung out with Harper when I wasn't working, attending parties, and lounging by the pool that I never made it to last summer.

Isabel and Abbey sublet an apartment for the summer, so she was around more now. One night over dinner, she stated that she and Abbey planned to open their own catering company after graduation.

My mother balked at Isabel, claiming it was ridiculous, a waste of money, considering they were paying for her bachelor's degree. Isabel just shrugged and ignored her.

College had morphed my sister into a different person. Her hair was platinum blonde and chopped super-short, like Madonna. She painted her nails black, and her outfits consisted of leather jackets and shirts embellished with studs. She was half-Goth, half-pop star, and overall, happy. She oozed sexuality and was cocky in a way that I admired. When she was home, she asked me about boys and work and how I tolerated living with our "whack-job" of a mother. She even took me to R-rated movies.

Things began to normalize for me, and for all my protesting, Harper had been right. Going to the right parties—parties with her —made me popular. I never wanted status, but I was soaking up the attention nonetheless. Girls thought my bakery job was cool, and the boys loved my boobs. I started having sex with a junior named Pete who knew what he was doing and made me feel good. There were times, though, that I cried in the dark, but he never knew.

"You really do have a thing for older guys," Harper teased.

"I guess I do, fuck." I said.

~

By mid-July, I was the one opening the bakery up, and frying the donuts all on my own. Harper would pop in, cheerleaders and football players in tow. They would stay and chat and boys would flirt with girls. I blushed at the cute juniors who flashed smiles at me. It felt odd, yet refreshing—interacting with kids my own age.

One Saturday morning, Maggie taught me to pipe perfect roses onto a sheet cake. The afternoon had been slow, with few customers. She went home, and I was left to close down the bakery.

The bell on the door jingled, startling me.

I looked up from my practice cake. The unmistakable pair of misfits stood in front of me.

Tanned, ripped muscles towering above short shorts and a Motley Crue T-shirt with the sleeves rolled; there stood Chad. He looked the same, except now his skin resembled a leather bag. Emily's hair was darker and longer, with grown-out blonde ends, and looked terrible. Chad's eyes widened when he spotted me.

"Holy shit . . . Hazel?"

Inhaling deeply, I forced a smile. Flashes of his apartment whipped across my brain, and I felt nauseous. The bed. The dirty sheets. The wine. The kissing. The fucking.

I wiped my hands on my apron.

"Hey, Chad. Hi, Emily."

She snapped her gum, a blank stare, and finally, recognition.

"Oh my God! Right! Hazel! Hi!"

"You work here?" Chad asked.

"Yep."

"Wow. Surrounded by sweets all day. Dangerous!"

"Well, I've been in worse danger before," I smirked.

"Ha! That's funny. Teddy's not too dangerous. Have you heard from him?"

"Nope. You?"

Chad and Emily exchanged glances. She shrugged and moved over to look at the selection of pastries.

"Nah," Chad said, "not lately. He was in Venice the last time he called. Boy, I wish I could've gone. He's doing what we always talked about!"

Emily rolled her eyes. My stomach roiled and flipped.

Teddy *called* Chad. I guess a phone call was too much to ask of my so-called ex- boyfriend.

"Venice?" I hoped I didn't sound like I was seething. "No, but maybe I will soon. How did he seem?"

"Happiest I've ever heard him!" Chad slapped his hand on the counter while gazing at the pastries inside the case. Emily elbowed him. "Right. You know what I mean. He's away from his folks, exploring the world, that's all. I know he misses you."

"He does?"

My heart raced, and I could feel sweat on my brow.

He doesn't, you idiot. He's just saying that. Even Emily knows that.

"Well, sure!"

The door jangled, and a group of teenagers headed towards us.

"Um, what can I get you guys?" I said, professional again.

"I want one of those cupcakes!" Emily squealed, pointing through the glass at my newly frosted batch.

"I'll just take a chocolate chip cookie," Chad said and fished for his wallet.

I handed off the cupcake and the cookie and took Chad's cash.

"Did he say when he's coming home?" I asked as I plucked his change down.

"No, he doesn't know yet. He needs a plan to come home, his parents are still pissed. And, well, you know, he's not really a planner."

"Oh, yeah, I do know that about him," was all I could think to say.

Chad took a bite and grinned.

"These are awesome! Look, I'm sure he'll call you. He's not around phones a lot. You know? Mostly out in the wilderness and shit. Living the dream. I'm so jealous."

The teens were growing anxious and the door opened and a young couple with a toddler came in.

"Yeah, well . . . I hope you guys have a great summer."

"Thanks, you too, Hazel!" Emily said in between licks of frosting.

"Yeah, hang in there, kid," Chad said.

"Thanks, Chad."

Kid?

16

RANSACK

ANN ARBOR, MICHIGAN 1988

I came home one day during the first week of tenth grade to my mother, rear end up in the air, rooting through my closet. Piles of clothes, shoes, and old toys were strewn everywhere.

"Mom!" I yelled, tossing my backpack on the bed. "What are you doing?"

"Oh good, you're home." She stood and wiped her brow. "I'm throwing out stuff you don't need, and you certainly don't need your toys anymore. It's all going to Salvation Army."

I looked at the piles and then at my mother. She had pulled her hair back in a red bandanna and was wearing an old T-shirt of my dad's and jeans. Her feet were bare, with polished red toes.

"I still wear this!" I said, pulling a pink angora sweater from a pile. It indeed was tattered, but I wasn't ready to let it go.

"Hazel, it's a ratty mess!"

"And, these!" I grabbed a pair of jeans that were at least three years old and definitely didn't fit. None of that mattered, I felt violated.

She squatted down and picked something up from the closet floor.

"And, how about these?"

I froze. My moccasins—the bracelet's hiding place.

"Are you attached to these too? Because I have never seen you wear them once." Her eyes flickered in the familiar way, daring me to lie to her.

She knew.

"Oh! I *totally* forgot about those," I stammered. "I should wear them, you know, since Mavis gave them to me. But, how about those jelly shoes? Jellies are so out of style and babyish and too small. We can get rid of those!"

"Nonsense, Hazel. I'm going to give you one last chance to tell me why I shouldn't get rid of these boots."

Her eyes had turned gray, and her tone was edged with annoyance. I was busted. She dropped one of the shoes and stuck her hand into the other, pulling out the bracelet. It twinkled in the light.

"Where in the hell did you get this? These are real diamonds! This costs thousands of dollars! Where, young lady? Did you steal this, Hazel? And don't you lie to me. I know when you're lying to me."

You have no idea, Mom. I lie to you all the time.

"No, I didn't steal it, geez!"

I shook my head and rolled my eyes.

"Do not roll your eyes at me, Hazel! Answer the question!"

"It was a gift."

"A *gift*? Who do you know that would gift *you* a diamond tennis bracelet?"

"My . . . ex-boyfriend, Aaron."

"That boy who moved to Ohio?"

"Yes, Mom, *that boy* gave it to me last summer."

"I don't believe you."

"You don't think a boy could like me enough to give me real diamonds?"

My hands were sweating. I sat on my bed with my eyes fixed on the roller skates that I hadn't worn in years.

"These are *real*, Hazel. Where did he get the money? Do his parents know he gave this to you? Did *he* steal it?"

"For God's sake, Mother! Nobody stole anything. You're being dramatic."

She rolled the bracelet around her fingers and a small distorted Cheshire Cat smile crept up.

"I think his mother should know about this. What is his phone number?"

She put her hands on her hips, the bracelet dangling from her fingers.

"Mom! Stop! He moved to Ohio, remember? We broke up. I have no idea what his phone number is, and I wouldn't give it to you if I did!"

"He didn't want this back? Seems suspicious. I'm going to have to tell your father about this."

She played with the clasp.

"No, you don't! Just give it to me!"

She ignored me, looping it around her wrist.

"What are you doing?" I thrust my hand at her. "That's mine! You can't wear it!"

"Oh, Hazel, calm down. I just want to try it on. It really is beautiful. Your father never got me one of these."

Anger washed over me. Her cruelty knew no bounds. I wanted to punch her.

"Mother!" I yelled. "Take it off now!"

Her eyes narrowed into slits like the snake that she was and she rested her wrist on her chest.

"Don't you yell at me, young lady! You still live in this house and under my rules!"

"It's mine! It was a gift for me! Stop being such a bitch!"

"Excuse me?" her mouth pinched as she inched towards me.

"I . . . I . . ."

"Don't you ever call me that again. Do you hear me?" Her breath was in my face, and the odor of wine seeped out.

"Yes, I'm sorry."

She headed for my bedroom door, then paused.

"I will discuss this with your father, and we will decide together if you get to keep the diamonds. You are far too young for such an expensive gift."

"Mom, no, please! It's all I have left to remember him by. Please give it back!"

"Hazel, what did I tell you about love? It's messy and often heartbreaking. And look, that's what he did, and it nearly ruined your whole first year of high school. Why on earth would you like a reminder of such a nasty young man?"

The sting of tears brimmed hotly.

"Because I loved him."

"Well, there's your first mistake. And he won't be your last. I'm doing you a favor, Hazel, helping you move on."

Flashing a fake smile, she shut the door behind her, leaving me with the mess of clothes and toys. I crawled on top of it and cried into the pile of my youth; the youth my mother was determined to take.

~

My sixteenth birthday was coming up, and I had no interest in celebrating. I remained bitter towards my mother as she had not given the bracelet back in over a year. I begged, cried, stomped, and swore. She wouldn't budge. Instead, she pranced around in her bedroom, wearing her sexy nightgowns, drinking wine, no doubt wearing my diamond bracelet, imagining my father had given it to her. My father kept telling me to "ride it out."

Harper couldn't believe I didn't want a party. Sweet sixteen, the door to impending womanhood—I must have one! It was all she talked about. I reminded her that I had become a woman two summers ago.

"We could have a party at the roller rink this weekend!"

It was a slow day at the bakery, and Harper ignored my resistance.

"The roller rink? Are you high? Plus, I think the old crotch threw out my skates."

She rolled her eyes.

"No, duh, we would get drunk and stoned first! And they rent skates there, remember? I know the gang would be in. It's like our last time to be kids, you know?"

"That ship has sailed. I don't care about it at this point."

"Your mom still has the bracelet?"

"Yep. I hate her."

"Man, I can't believe she's still being such a bitch about it. It's so wrong, Hazel. It's too bad we weren't older. We could have my dad take her to court and get it back. But you'd have to tell him that Teddy gave it to you, so that wouldn't work."

"Yeah, too bad. I would love to sit in court and tell a jury my mom is a drunk asshole and a thief. Then they could throw her in jail. I would love—"

"Oooh, how about bowling and drinking?" she cut me off. Her pile of blonde curls was pulled into a side ponytail with a leopard-print scrunchie. "Or get drunk and go to the arcade?"

"Shit, you're an alcoholic," I laughed. "I honestly don't feel like doing a damn thing."

"First of all, I am not an alcoholic. Alcoholics go to bars and drink hard liquor and never go home to their wives." She applied lip gloss while looking in her hand mirror. "And second of all, you have to get over this bracelet thing. Teddy hasn't contacted you in forever, and frankly, he's an asshole and a loser for that. Maybe it *is* best you don't get the damn thing back!"

I bit into the cupcake I was frosting. She wasn't completely wrong. Sulking around was getting boring. I hadn't even run in days. My shorts were getting tighter. Still, it was more about my mother, the thief, more than anything.

"No party," I said. "But maybe we all could do something Saturday night."

"Fine. But I am going to make sure you have fun."

My father was equally disappointed with my no-party decision. He offered to make his specialty, homemade pasta and Bolognese sauce on Sunday night, my actual birthday, so we could celebrate as a family. He asked if he could invite Isabel and Oscar and Lolly.

I shrugged.

~

Six girls—me, Harper, Kathy, and three of Harper's cheerleading friends, plus Rita—Kathy's sister who was driving—piled into the Chrysler Caravan and drove to the movie theatre. On the way, we passed around a joint and drank Chardonnay—my drink of choice—in paper cups and cranked Van Halen through the speakers.

Harper decided on the Saturday matinee showing of Die Hard. We swooned over over Bruce Willis in his black tank top scaling the side of a building. We gorged on tubs of buttered popcorn and whispered, "He's so hot!" and covered our eyes during the intense fighting scenes..

We had burgers and fries at Casey's Tavern in Kerrytown—a perfect birthday dinner. It was loud and raucous, filled with happy slobbery drunks at the bar, tables occupied by families, and couples on date nights.

I envied the bar customers—the freedom to drink whenever they wanted and escape their problems. In a few years, Teddy and I could've been a couple having cocktails, intertwined at the bar. He would whisper something naughty in my ear, I would throw my head back, laughing. Then he'd pull my bar stool closer and pull me in for a kiss.

"You okay?"

It was Harper not Teddy, whispering in my ear. "Aren't you having fun?"

"Huh? Yeah, sorry, I'm high, but it's fading, and I'm thinking too much. We need to leave. I need more drinks and shit."

"Got it!"

In minutes, we all piled into the van, back to Kathy and Rita's.

Blue Lagoon was on TV. We drank more wine, smoked another joint, and lounged around, talking and watching bits of the movie. We made prank phone calls to guys we liked, and hated. We howled in laughter as the four cheerleaders drunkenly performed sloppy routines.

Rita and her friend introduced us to drinking games, and Harper brought cupcakes compliments of Marjorie.

By ten thirty, I was shit-faced, and a deep sadness overtook me. I wanted to be home—and alone. Rita offered to drive me.

"You okay, Hazel?"

"Mmm Hmm."

"Are you too fucked up to see your parents?"

"Nah, I'm fine," I said, shaking my head. "They'll probably be asleep."

I wasn't fine though. An intense feeling of abandonment was creeping in and a strong desire to cry for hours was pulling at me.

"You sure? We can stop and get some coffee."

"No, I'm alright, really," I said, staring out the window.

We rode in silence. Rita smoked a cigarette and blew the smoke into the night.

"He must've been some guy."

"Huh?" I asked.

"I know the signs of heartbreak, girl. It will get better, eventually. Trust me, a new guy will make you forget all about this one. He's not worth the trouble, believe me."

"That's what everyone says," I mumbled.

She pulled into my driveway, a glow illuminating the living room window.

"Shit," I said.

"Should we go back to our place?"

"I can handle it. To be honest, I don't give a fuck. Thanks for everything tonight."

"Alright, if you say so. Have a good night, and, happy birthday, Hazel."

Slowly, I twisted my key into its slot and tried not to stumble. I willed myself to become sober. No one was downstairs; they must have left the light on for me. I poured myself water, guzzled it, and refilled before heading upstairs.

Sneaking up the stairs, I approached my bedroom when my

parents' door opened and out peeked my sleepy-haired mother. She squinted with a wan smile.

"Oh, you're home, she whispered. "Good. We left the light on for you."

"Um, yeah, I saw, thanks."

"Of course. You can tell me about your night tomorrow. Don't want to wake Daddy. Sleep tight and happy birthday, Hazel."

"Thanks," I rushed in and shut the door behind me.

How can she act normal when we were still in a bracelet war?

～

S unday morning, I was a slug, hungover and head pounding. I slept like a rock yet felt sleep starved, and my mouth tasted like a wet ashtray.

Coconut scratched my door. I flipped the covers back and let him in. He sauntered in like he owned the place and jumped up to display his belly.

"It's my birthday, but you want all the attention, huh?"

I smothered his face with kisses, wishing all my relationships could be this easy. I flopped back, closing my eyes.

"Good morning, birthday girl!"

My dad popped in suddenly, with coffee in one hand and a gift bag in the other. I was going to have to talk to him about busting into a teenager's room with no warning. "You're sixteen and all grown up now! How do you feel?"

I feel like absolute shit, Dad. Thanks for asking.

"Dad," I rolled my eyes, "you ask me the same exact question every year. You gonna ask me that when I'm thirty?"

"Maybe." He chuckled, set the coffee cup down, and sat on the edge of my bed. "Whenever my little girl gets a year older, I want to know how she feels different."

"Hmm," I took a sip of coffee; it was hot and swirling with cream, and I desperately needed it to get through the day. "Well, I guess I feel . . . old. Is that how I should feel?"

"I know what might make you feel better."

He nodded toward the gift bag.

"Open the top one first," he said, as I retrieved two little boxes.

It wasn't wrapped, and when I lifted the lid, there it was, my bracelet.

"Dad!" I threw my arms around him, "How . . . what . . . how did you get this for me?"

"Compromise," he smiled. "Sometimes I can get through to your mother. You've been punished enough. It is a very elaborate gift, and we don't completely approve of this, but the boy is gone. No matter how he acquired it, it's still yours."

"This is the best birthday ever! Thank you, Daddy, so much!" I slipped it onto my wrist. It was still slightly big, but fit enough to finally look somewhat normal, and now I wouldn't lose it.

"You're welcome, honey. Now open the other box."

The diamonds slid down to the meat of my hands and then stopped as I pulled the other box from the bag. This one was wrapped in pink paper with a rose-colored bow on top.

"Did you wrap this?"

"Yes, your old dad can handle wrapping a present, Hazelnut," he smiled. I carefully tore the paper off and opened it. Another bracelet. This one was silver, with charms dangling from it.

A heart, a cat, and a dragonfly dangled from the chain. I loved it immediately.

"Oh, Dad! I love it!"

"Are you sure?"

"Yes!"

"I . . . well, I know this Aaron boy gave you *diamonds*, but I wanted to give you something more personal. I hope that someday you will cherish it as much as you do the other one."

"Oh, I love it!" I hugged him tightly. "I really do."

"I'm so glad, honey. Okay, listen, we are going to have dinner tonight. Grandma and Grandpa and Isabel are coming. That's still okay, right?"

I nodded as I stared at the two bracelets dangling from my wrists. I wanted to soak in the moments before I faced the reality of the whole family being together tonight.

"Alright, then. Grandma and Grandpa will be here around six. They are picking up a cake from Marjorie's. German chocolate. That's still your favorite, right?"

"Yes. Thanks, Dad. Really."

"Of course, sweetheart," he kissed me on my forehead and headed for the door. "I hope you have a great day today."

So did I.

～

At five o'clock, the doorbell rang. Lolly and Oscar arrived with my cake and presents. I spoke to my grandmother Elizabeth—my mom's mom—who lived in Florida. She called to wish me happy birthday and verify I had received her card and forty dollars.

We didn't see her often—just once a year when she trekked north for a week. My mom told us that her mother was "difficult" and that distance between them was a good idea. We had only been to Florida a few times to visit. My mother complained about all the bugs and the "disgusting" humidity.

"Why don't you show your grandparents your beautiful bracelet?" my mother announced, the minute I got off the phone.

"Um . . ."

She grabbed my wrist and held it up under the dining room light. The diamonds sparkled in all their splendor.

"Oh, my, that is quite beautiful, Hazel," said Lolly. I jerked my wrist under the table.

"Yes," my mother said, "this is what boys buy for girls nowadays. Can you imagine? I mean, that is a *very* expensive bracelet. I don't know where he got—"

"—That's right," my dad interrupted, glaring at her, "a keepsake forever."

I gave my father a grateful smile and lifted my other arm up.

"And, look, Dad got me this bracelet. I love it!"

Everyone oohed and aahed while my mother seethed and buried her mouth in her wine glass as we enjoyed my dad's delicious dinner. After cake, came presents. Isabel got me an Andy Warhol print of Marilyn Monroe, instantly becoming the coolest thing I owned, along with a bottle of Boucheron perfume. Oscar and Lolly gave me a fifty-dollar check.

"I know we didn't get a chance to go school shopping because I had so much prep work before classes started," my mother said, bringing over a stack of neatly wrapped boxes. "So I do hope this makes up for it."

Predictably, there were a couple of sweaters from Esprit, a pair of cute black-and-white espadrilles, some button-up shirts from the Gap, and a skirt from Benetton. I had to give her credit for her good taste and knowing my style.

"Thanks, Mom, everything is really . . . cool."

"Ohh, did you hear that, everyone? Cool! I got her *cool* stuff. I'm so pleased that I'm so *hip*! Is that what the kids say these days?"

She twirled her wine glass and looked around the room for approval.

"Not really, but good job on the clothes, Mom," said Isabel.

Grandpa went to the living room to watch the football game. The Detroit Lions were getting pounded by the Green Bay Packers.

"Well, kid, I need to head back," Isabel pecked my cheek and picked up our cake plates. I've got a quiz tomorrow, and I haven't even cracked the book yet."

I followed her into the kitchen.

"You can't stay longer?"

I pleaded with my eyes. "Sorry, no. Walk me to the door?"

I shuffled alongside her to the front door.

"What is up with that bracelet? Do *I* know this boy that got you that?"

You certainly do.

"No, never brought him around. Mom would have humiliated me."

"That's for sure. Well, the guy's got good taste. Sorry it didn't work out. Okay, I gotta go study. And, happy birthday."

She gave me a hug and slipped out the front door.

17

CREATE

ANN ARBOR, MICHIGAN 1990

"Congratulations, Hazel. You've earned this!"

Marjorie handed me a new name tag that read "Store Manager" beneath my name.

"Thank you," I said quietly. "This means a lot."

"And," she grinned, and pointed to a framed plaque by the kitchen door, "now it's official!"

A picture of me in the bakery uniform—white polo shirt and khaki pants—smiling and holding a pan of cookies. My name and new title were typed below the "Marjorie's Sweets" logo.

After two years, she had promoted me to wedding cakes. Since I had been decorating cakes with such elaborate designs, she said I was a natural talent and wanted to invest in me. Saying I loved the bakery was an understatement. The mixing and measuring gave me much needed focus and structure in my life. The designing nurtured my creative side, and when the last petal on a flower or a pearl on the base of the cake was complete, satisfaction and pure joy washed over me.

Tracing my fingers across my name tag, a wave of awareness struck me. *This was it.*

I was meant to be a pastry chef. My insecurities and loneliness disappeared whenever I created desserts. Each bite represented something different to people: a celebration like a birthday, a wedding, a new baby, a graduation, and sometimes, an ending—saying good-bye to a favorite teacher, a death, a sickness, or even a breakup. Either way, my handiwork became a part of people's lives and memories. It was going to be a good summer.

I didn't care that I'd gained a few pounds. My mother, on the other hand, did care and commented that my face was chubby and that she refused to buy me clothes in a bigger size.

"It's not that difficult, Hazel," she would say. "Discipline is a practice, and you are in the perfect setting with that sugar and junk in front of you daily—just imagine each cookie or cupcake showing up on your thighs—trust me, it's for your own good. And, imagine how hideous you will look as a fat girl. It's not pleasant."

She wasn't completely wrong, and I hadn't gone running since our bracelet stand-off, so I made a plan to run every morning before work so I could slim down before twelfth grade. And indeed, within weeks, I regained my leaner, more muscular shape.

"I knew you could do it, darling," my mother said one day after she brought home a new outfit for me. "I'm proud of you. And this little job of yours is turning out quite well, I must say. Aren't you glad your mother pulled some strings? Now, let's keep those grades up."

Surprisingly, I not merely tolerated school but enjoyed it again. I had been a stellar student before Teddy, so I eased into the predictable world of education and the gratification of "As" circled in red, showcasing my homework.

That April, I started casually dating a boy from school. Harper's boyfriend Steve introduced me to Nick. A *boy*, not an older man. Nick was my age, charming, witty, and oddly responsible for his age. He had a slight, lanky build and parent-approved short brown hair with blue eyes and adorable deep dimples.

My parents were ecstatic that I had moved on from "Aaron" and found Nick. He was my savior, and theirs as well. My mother resumed her self-absorption. My dad whistled more. And my sister, one year left of college, stopped by for dinners occasionally, and asked about my life—and boys.

I had all but forgotten that she had no clue her former boyfriend was also my ex.

Sometimes, I wanted to confide in her in hopes of bonding over our shared failure with Teddy, and to ask the dangerous questions. *Was I special? Did he ever even miss her? Did he tell her he loved her?* Questions with answers that had the potential to destroy us.

But I couldn't risk her telling my parents or the police. I knew Harper was right; in the eyes of the law, my love affair with Teddy was statutory rape. And despite Teddy breaking my heart, I didn't want him imprisoned for giving me the best summer of my life. Harper was the only one who could ever know.

Nick and I became serious, and thoughts of Teddy faded. His family lived in a huge mansion in Barton Hills, the same neighborhood as Teddy's family. Regardless of spending a whole summer with Teddy, I had never seen his home. Whenever I was at Nick's, I had this heightened sense of anticipation. What if, while winding through the hills to Nick's house, I spotted Teddy in the yard of another mansion, smoking a cigarette.

But in those moments, when reality reminded me that he was gone, I would touch my bracelet—the one my father got me for my sixteenth birthday—and squeeze the dragonfly charm to shake off the thoughts, because I had a nice, sweet, hot boy who adored me.

With my manager job, I worked full time, but we closed at 1:00 p.m. That left time for parties on the weekends. Nick and Steve had friends whose parents had vacation homes with boats and jet skis on Whitmore Lake. Every Sunday, a group of us would head up to the lake to water ski, float on blow-up rafts, and dive off the bows into deep dark water.

Music blasted from boat radios, and girls bopped from boat to boat in bikinis or perched on boys' shoulders for games of chicken. Shrieks of laughter pierced the air as opponents crashed into the water. The boys threw footballs and tossed Frisbees, leaping to grab them and splashing down with their prize in hand.

My lake-soaked hair air-dried as night fell, and Nick and I

cuddled by the fire. Clad in one of his sweatshirts, sun-kissed skin, and hair drying in waves, I felt sexy in the glow of the orange embers. It was the perfect ending to a glorious day on the water.

I loved leaning into Nick's lap, wrapped in a blanket and wedged between his legs. Pulling my hair to the side, he would kiss my neck tenderly and tell me he loved me. These nights were magical.

It was fun and exciting, and my parents trusted Nick, allowing me to stay out until midnight.

And he *was* trustworthy, always careful not to drink too much, sober before he drove me home. We would cruise down US 23 in his brand-new black Mustang GT and sing to Cat Stevens and James Taylor.

Nick was a hit at the bakery. Some days he would stop in as we were closing and bring flowers. A tactic that Teddy used, but Nick was genuine.

"Marjorie," he gushed, "your pastries are out of this world. Flowers are the least I can do!"

She would blush and smile coyly. Cleo and Maggie exchanged smiles and continued kneading dough.

Nick and I double-dated with Harper and Steve. Nick was a romantic, and I drank it all in, hoping it would never end. This was normal life, to do all these things, in public, with my friends, not having to hide our relationship.

I was falling hard. Harper, too, was in love with Steve. I liked him, and he met two of her requirements: he treated her like a princess, and he was a football player. Nick, thank God, had no interest in football. Like me, he was a reader, and tennis was his only sport.

His parents had enrolled him in lessons when he was little, hoping he would compete professionally.

"They would love for me to be the next Jimmy Connors, but I want to enjoy school and not be practicing constantly, you know?"

"Are they mad about it?"

"Nah. I mean, they wished I was more into it, but they also want me to be happy. So right now, that's you, friends, and school.

Right now? I could feel myself panicking.

"And who knows," he said, kissing my forehead, "maybe we'll be one of those high school sweetheart stories that live happily ever after."

Happily ever after. Words I never thought I would hear. I gazed up at Nick, his smile, his dimples, the softness around his eyes, and relaxed. I could trust him, and now maybe I could trust myself as well. Nick wouldn't hurt me. He just wouldn't.

"I love you, Nick."

"I love you too, Hazel," he grinned and kissed my nose.

~

College.

It was senior year, and I dreaded the upcoming conversation with my parents. The last two years had flown by, a cyclone of studying, working, parties, and blissful adventures with Nick. I kept my grades high, which pleased my parents. Probably congratulating themselves because despite the chaos in our family, their daughters made it through high school, and one was in college.

I saw no need for college. I knew what I wanted. I was going to be a pastry chef—either in a high-end restaurant or my own store, specializing in wedding cakes. I absolutely loved designing them. From perfectly round pearls piped around the edges of a three-tiered cake to the elaborate ribbons cascading from crest to pedestal, finished with delicate flowers, each petal a precise, smooth layer of sugared delight, showcasing any flower the bride loved.

My parents would never understand a career of baking cakes. Even my father, my biggest fan, would be disappointed. They both believed strongly in higher education and the tangible benefits and social status it afforded.

"College creates life-long connections, girls," my father said. He included Teddy's father as one of those life-long friends. How horrified my father would be to discover his close friend from college bore a son who stole his daughter's virginity.

Nick and I frequently discussed how my parents would take the news, and he tried to reassure me that they would understand. Or, eventually, accept it. I would be graduating high school and an adult. They couldn't control me forever.

Nick supported my choices with no judgments either way. He, however, did want a college degree. Both of his parents were lawyers, his mother in real estate law and his dad in environmental law. Nick planned on following suit, his interest in intellectual property law. This meant less time together as he would be studying constantly. While my life at the bakery probably wouldn't change much, I worried about the time apart. Nick assured me about our future, and I began to believe life would be amazing.

"What on earth are you talking about, Hazel?" demanded my mother, scooping an olive from her martini and biting down.

It was one of our Sunday family meals, she with her vat of gin and ridiculous outfit—a Japanese silk kimono, exposing a low-cut black lace negligee beneath. She made no attempts to hide her ample cleavage—which resembled a plumber's butt-crack—and her long legs tapered into fuzzy pink high-heeled peep-toe slippers showcasing perfectly pedicured feet. She held her head high, smiling, and sipping her drink like the goddamn Queen of the Nile.

Sipping on red wine, my dad ignored her as he was busy preparing clams casino as our appetizer. Isabel was in the living room, painting her nails a dark-blue color.

"Hazel," my mother persisted, "don't be absurd. You are going to college. No daughter of mine will just have a high school diploma."

I never should have brought it up. We may have survived a family dinner night with low-level drama if I hadn't mentioned my plan.

"Yes, Hazel, what *are* you talking about?" my father asked, slipping the clams into the oven. "The plan was always for you girls to go to college. Your mother and I don't understand."

I peered into the living room, and Isabel rolled her eyes. We had spoken earlier that week, and I told her I was going to break it to them at dinner, and she promised she would support me but couldn't guarantee saving me if the ship started sinking fast. The ship was sinking.

"I know, but . . ." I started.

"Isabel is almost done, and she's loved it, right, Izzy?" my dad said, waving a spatula towards her, dripping butter on the floor.

"Dad, I already know what I want. And Michigan doesn't have a culinary program, so I wouldn't want to waste your money earning some useless degree that won't benefit me in the long run. I can't even think of one profession I would go to college for."

"Hazzzzel," my mother slurred, draining half of her martini and munching on her second olive. "There is no such thing as a useless degree. Well, unless you count *Communications*," she rolled her eyes, "but, either way, you are not going to waste your life making cakessss. I know I got you that job, and I'm glad you have enjoyed it, but don't be ridiculous. You can't make *real* money doing that and well, you'll just always be the help. Don't you want better for yourself?"

Her words stung.

The help?

She was drunk and angling for a fight. I reminded myself of the short memory she conveniently had the next day after any bad behavior.

"Joanne!" my father scolded her. "That's enough. Stop demeaning her."

My mother pouted, shrugged, and sipped. I knew her silence would be fleeting. Isabel sprung from the couch, holding her wet nails up in the air and came into the kitchen.

"Hey, you guys, listen, I'm with Hazel. She doesn't need to go to Michigan. It would be a waste of money. Shouldn't she do what she is passionate about? *Dad?* You always told us that as kids, right? Shouldn't she follow her *dreams*?"

Dad backed out of the fridge, retrieving brussels sprouts and began chopping off their ends.

"This sounds risky, Hazel. Everyone should have a degree to fall back on. What if you open a business and God forbid, it fails? I'm not saying it will fail. But everyone needs a backup plan—"

"—Richard, you're dropping that shit all over the floor," barked my mother. She was perched on one of the adjacent counters, legs crossed, half-empty glass in hand, her spine perfectly arched. He immediately began picking up leaves off the floor.

"Dad," I said, ignoring my mother, "plenty of people don't have degrees and have done just fine, great in fact. I'm not worried about failing."

"Of course you're not!" my mother said loudly, and slid off the counter and towards her bar cart in the living room. "You're young and stupid. No one your age ever thinks about consequences. You've had it easy! We've given you everything." The three of us turned from her as she mixed another cocktail.

"I'm not saying you're going to fail," my dad repeated, his attention now on the steaks marinating on the countertop. "I just want you to have a backup plan. College is always the best backup plan."

If I heard the words "backup plan" again, I would scream.

Isabel shot me a look that told me we had to go in strong, no time to chicken out.

"Dad," she said, sitting down and blowing on her nails, "Look. Here's the deal. Once I graduate in June, Abbey and I are planning to start our own catering business in Chicago. We've been doing it for years now and know how it's all done. Hazel could join us at some point as our pastry chef."

I beamed at her plan. The only problem was Nick being left behind. Isabel said if I wanted to wait for him, we could both come to Chicago when he finished college. There were surely more opportunities there than in Ann Arbor. It would be a minimum of four years before he began law school. I hadn't even presented this idea to Nick yet.

"Wow, really?" My father set down the steak he was holding and turned to face us. "So, this is what you two have been talking about?"

I couldn't tell if he was mad. Wearing his "Kiss the Cook" apron, it was sometimes hard to take him seriously.

"Yeah, I—"

"Oh, hell no!" my mother shrieked. "That is a foolish and ridiculous idea! No girls of mine are going into the catering business! You are educated—well, one of you is—smart girls, and this whole half-witted plan is insane!"

She was spitting now and enunciating every word as if we couldn't understand English.

"Mom!" Isabel yelled. "Chill out! It's not up to you! She's going to be eighteen soon, and, shit, I'm already gone, so you can't do anything about my choices. Thank God."

Isabel picked up her wine glass and gulped down half. I wished I had one. I also wanted a cigarette.

"Isabel, that's enough!" my father yelled.

Yelling at his daughter, but not his drunk wife. The dynamics in this house were so fucked up.

My mother glared at me through drooping red eyes, daring me to speak. The oven timer dinged, and my dad pulled the clams out. They smelled divine, crispy and bubbling over with browned butter simmering around the edges. Sliding the clams onto a platter, he brought them over making eye contact with no one. He was quiet for what seemed a hundred years.

"Clams casino!" he announced. "Dig in!"

Isabel and my mother and I exchanged looks of uncertainty. My mother shrugged and took a gulp of her second drink, dribbling drops of gin down her chin and neck and into her robust breasts.

"Looks good, Richard!" she said, breaking the silence.

She plucked one from the platter and onto her plate. Dad came over, and we all sat down. He took a clam, scooped it from its shell, chewed it once and then swallowed. We all waited. My mother grabbed at another clam, chewing it too voraciously as if it were her last meal.

Isabel and I ate a few in the stark silence. Ella Fitzgerald crooned from the jazz station on the radio, her voice miles away.

"Okay," he finally spoke after eating four clams and washing them down with wine. "You're right. I can't tell you what to do. If this is what you really want to do, then I will support you. But, at any time you want to go to school, the funds are available."

"Thank you, Dad!" I exclaimed, and jumped from my chair to hug him.

My mother glared at me as she slowly chewed on a clam. I glared back, victoriously.

~

My mother scowled around me for the remainder of the school year. As seniors, most of my friends were planning for college, filling out applications, and taking tours—according to Joanne. But it was business as usual. I studied, worked, and spent time with my boyfriend.

We planned out prom. I had picked out a pink dress—to my surprise and Harper's—with lots of lace and shoulder pads and pleated satin at the bottom. I completed the look with white pumps and a white purse and highly teased hair. Nick would wear a pink bow tie and cummerbund with his suit. Harper and Steve decided to crash our prom and go with us. We all ponied up for a limo and a hotel.

I never told Nick about Teddy and lied that I had lost my virginity to "Aaron, the boy from Ohio." I felt horrible, but he could never know. He would never understand. His parents were lawyers, and who knows how he would have reacted to my extremely underage sex scenario.

Instead, we had long discussions about moving to Chicago after he graduated and passed the bar, and I would take classes to continue my pastry skills. He thought Chicago would be a great change; he had been there often with his parents and loved the city. Loyola had a great law school. We could get an apartment together in Ann Arbor until then.

I was on track for the perfect happy ending, the one Harper always dreamt about and I had doubted could ever happen to me: go to senior prom with my hot boyfriend, graduate with my high school sweetheart, move in together, and pursue our career dreams.

Prom night was "mind-blowing," as Harper described it. We got ready at my house, applying heavy coats of makeup and spraying our teased-high hair with copious amounts of hairspray. My parents took embarrassing amounts of pictures in front of our limo. The boys gave us corsages, and to my relief, my mother was on her best behavior—not drinking.

My dad beamed with pride and insisted on several dad and daughter shots. In the limo, we drank and smoked pot (the driver got pissed and threatened us, but Steve tossed him a couple twenty-dollar bills and he backed off) and then we snuck flasks into the gymnasium and danced for hours until the limo took us to the after party at the hotel.

There were nearly a dozen of us crammed into one room playing drinking games. We smoked pot out of a ridiculously big bong. A boom box blared our favorite bands until around one o'clock when a knock on the door came, and the manager told us to cool it.

Nick and I went outside, and he kissed me against the side of the building.

"Guess what?" he asked, coming up for air.

"What?" I nuzzled into his neck, inhaling his Liz Claiborne for Men.

"I got us our own room."

"What?" I looked up at him. "Really? No way! How?"

"Yes, way," he grinned.

"What are we waiting for then?"

We spent the next few hours exploring each other's bodies. We smoked a joint and every sensation was heightened. I felt amazing and loved and completely safe wrapped in the nook of his body.

"Promise me you'll always love me," he whispered, snuggling under the polyester covers. He gazed at me with his pretty blue eyes, bleary from partying.

"Of course I will." He held me so close, I had to breathe slowly. "Nick, I love you, always. I promise."

18

FORSAKE

ANN ARBOR, MICHIGAN 1990

"Hey there, my sexy graduate."

I jumped and spun around. It was Nick, in his gown, beaming at me. He looked handsome as ever, even wearing what was essentially a dress.

"Hi!" I leaned into his arms and kissed him. "You scared me!"

"Sorry about that. I just wanted to see you before they lined us up. Good luck out there."

"You too," I hugged him, and Harper, who had snuck backstage, stepped in.

"Okay, love birds, this shit show is about to start," she nodded towards the side of the stage.

Our principal came to stand in front of the group and told us to start taking our seats. It was time to graduate.

Speeches were made, most of them boring, and me and my classmates walked across the stage to accept the rolled-up paper that declared we were officially done with high school. My family stood up and cheered as I shook the principal's hand and posed for the school camera.

When it was over, we threw our caps into the air and cheered and laughed and congratulated each other.

Nick and I parted ways to go have celebrations with our families. My family went to Knight's Steakhouse in downtown Ann Arbor, while his had a catered party at their house.

We sat around the table in the boisterous restaurant filled with families and graduates. We ordered drinks while I opened my presents. I opened my dad's first—it was a tiny diploma charm for my bracelet, and it came with a card.

My dearest Hazel,

Words cannot express how proud I am of you and your accomplishments. You have grown into a lovely young woman, though I never doubted that you would.

You have shown your independence in beautiful ways and that responsibility is not a burden for you. You are strong, yet humble, tough, yet delicate.

Hazel, you are my dragonfly nymph, all grown up. You have climbed up that reed out of the water and are entering the new world. I wish for you only love and happiness, success and mistakes. Yes, mistakes. They teach us lessons, and we all need to learn every day.

You are my Hazelnut, my brave girl who has to be older than she should be sometimes, and I am full of pride today as you are not only my wonderful daughter, but a bona fide high- school graduate. Congratulations on all your accomplishments.

I love you, Dad

"Thanks, Dad," I said, choking up a bit, "I love you too."

I hugged him and he helped me hook the charm onto my bracelet.

My grandparents gave me a nice card with two hundred dollars in it and a gift certificate to the Gap, no doubt my mother's idea, and Isabel gave me a cool photography book by Annie Leibowitz with a card that congratulated me on "getting the hell out of high school." She and Abbey would be heading to Chicago, and Abbey's parents were giving them the money to start their business.

"Hazel, dear," my mother said, "I think you will find both of these beneficial to you."

She handed me two books she'd wrapped in a bow—*The Art of Loving* by Erich Fromm and *Siddhartha* by Hermann Hesse.

"Relationships between you and men and you and yourself are very complex. These might shed some light on both areas."

She was genuine and unpretentious as she said it—she was on her best behavior and had been lately. She had started practicing yoga and meditation. Some days I would come home and find her in her bedroom upside down on her head, chanting, surrounded by flickering candles. Naturally, though, a bottle of wine was nearby on her dresser. I knew nothing about Buddhism, but I was pretty sure it had nothing to do with wine.

"Thanks, Mom. I'll let you know what I think."

She smiled, raised her glass of red wine to me, and took a sip. She set it down and slid it over to me.

"Go ahead, you've earned it. Just a couple sips though. And don't let your grandparents see."

"Really? Okay, thanks," I said, and took a couple swallows.

"Sure. Cheers, Hazel. To you and your new future!"

~

I t was the end of August and the rolling swelter of another hot summer was here. Nick would start classes at Michigan in a couple weeks, and I was signed up for an advanced cake decorating class at the community college. We had barreled through a lightning-fast season of boating, swimming in his pool, barbecuing, working, and daydreaming. Nick's parents adored me and the same went for my parents about Nick. His folks went to Paris for the summer and gave him permission to let me stay over as often as I liked. Astonishingly, my parents seemed to have no problem with this either.

In our private moments, the way Nick touched me was insane. He took his time, his fingers were light and delicate, grazing over every inch of me. It took a while, but I started moving past the insecurities of my body. I was so in love with him. Often, we were having sex in his pool house or at someone's cottage up at the lake in the daytime, so I had to learn to be okay with nakedness not hidden in the dark. His penis, my boobs, flesh everywhere, exposed. Our skin, wet beneath bathing suits, sprang up in goosebumps as soon as we removed them. The smell of chlorine or lake water lingered on us as we lay down together and explored each other's bodies. I no longer had to fake pleasure; Nick had guided me into it.

After years of not being able to relate to *Cosmo* and these so-called orgasms, I was finally there. Something Teddy was never able to accomplish. Nick had just turned eighteen and it made me sick to think of him hanging around a playground, giving an eighth-grade girl a key to an apartment to spend the summer plying her with drinks and having sex with her. He would never do such a thing.

My bracelet sat in my jewelry box untouched. It was just another something shiny, no longer holding a grip on me.

It was a Friday night, and one of Nick's friends was throwing a party at their parents' house. This weekend was our last real time to party and hang out with friends and be together until his first semester ended. After that, we would start to look for a place together.

I ran every day, sometimes five miles, and my body was a sheet of muscle. My legs were my best feature, strong and sexy. Plaid was very in style, and that night I wore a short plaid skirt to show off my toned legs , paired with a white T-shirt and patent leather Mary Jane shoes. I brought along a cardigan sweater in case it cooled down. I wore my hair straight and parted to one side. I felt amazing. I looked it too. Nick told me so when he picked me up. The party was at a house not too far from his. He picked me up and we sped through the winding roads in his Mustang, music blaring, windows down, and my hair blowing wildly around my face.

We pulled into a long driveway and parked in the line of cars already there. The house was palatial of course, like all the other mansions in the neighborhood, this one a Tudor style with steeply pitched gable roofs and elaborate stone and brick that outlined the windows and the detailed mahogany front door. I could see silhouettes of people through the drapes, with drinks in their hands and heads thrown back in laughter.

Inside, dark wood, timber ceiling beams towered above the vast great room, lit by table lamps and the dim of orange glow crackling in the fireplace. Couples filled the room, knitted around each other on anything soft they could land on; some making out, some whispering in each other's ears, some laughing. Dozens, maybe even a hundred people were scattered in every room, drinking out of plastic cups, lying on velvet couches, and sitting in high-backed chairs. A billiards room with wall-to-wall built-in bookshelves was off to the right and a group of boys were playing pool. The shelves seemed as if there were a million books lining them. It was a beautiful home and I wondered with some envy what it would have been like to grow up in a place like this. "Elegia" by New Order echoed through speakers in one of the two living rooms, and the dark instrumental inflection drifted throughout the other rooms of the main floor. I recognized many of the kids from school, but also loitering about were older kids, past their high school years—adults. Must be friends with the older sister, I thought.

About an hour into the party, and quite a few drinks in, I decided I wanted a cigarette. We had thrown back Jell-O shots, played a couple games of beer pong and had shared a joint with a group of friends. I was pretty fucked up. I poured myself another beer from the keg in the kitchen and sauntered back over to Nick, who was in the billiards room, laughing and talking to a couple of guys he knew, and kissed his neck.

"I'm going to go smoke out by that goddamn ridiculous pool in the backyard," I announced.

I breathed into his ear. "Wanna come?"

He turned and raised my chin delicately up to his lips, kissed me lightly, and shook his head.

"I'm having the most interesting conversation about Sue the T. Rex they just discovered with these boys. Who knew anybody still cared about dinosaurs? I'll come find you in a few."

"Dinosaurs." I rolled my eyes and then smiled seductively. "Alright, but don't wait too long. Who knows, I might jump into that pool naked. You wouldn't want to miss that."

One of the guys laughed and slapped him on the back.

"Whoa, dude, you wouldn't want to miss that!"

"No, shit, Nick!" He was poked by a pool stick by another. "Sure, you want to talk about dinosaurs?"

"I'll be out in a few."

"Okay, but don't take forever," I bit my lower lip and ambled off, swinging my small hips, aware they were all watching me.

The "backyard" was ridiculous, a massive pool surrounded by a wraparound stone wall with fountains that spilled into the pool. A Jacuzzi in the corner was filled with people. Girls were wearing just their bras and underwear; others were naked with their tits bobbing around.

The water in the pool was smooth and still, and I was surprised no one had jumped in it by now. I sat down at the deep end and plunked my toes up to my calves into the water. It was luxurious as silk and warm as bath water. All my nerve endings were tingling. I lit a cigarette and blew out a large ring of smoke up to the ink-black sky smattered with millions of stars. I leaned back to rest on my elbows, taking in my happy drunkenness, the beautiful night sky, and the toasty water caressing my legs. I closed my eyes and smiled.

"Hazel?"

The voice was miles away, years away.

"Hazel."

I felt like I'd gone back in time. *Was I that stoned?* I opened my eyes and looked up.

There he was. *Theodore Michael Spencer.* Teddy, in the flesh, staring down at me, with a bottle of beer in his hand and a cigarette in the other. I jerked my legs out of the water and pushed myself up to stand. *Was I hallucinating? Was I that fucked up?* I wasn't. There he was, at this house, by this pool. And there I stood, taller now just slightly above his chin.

"Oh my God," I said.

The cigarette in my hand was down to the filter. I took one last hit, turned away from him, and walked over to a table with an ashtray.

"Hazel, how are you? What are you doing here? Holy shit, I can't believe it's you!"

I should have bolted out of there. Cold blood ran through my veins as my stomach flip-flopped like a fish gasping its last breath.

This is not happening. I'm high. I'm delusional. You're not thirteen anymore.

Nick was still inside with his friends, and I willed him to walk outside and look for me. *Find me. Take me away from Teddy.*

For so many reasons, Nick knew nothing about Teddy. I kept my relationship with "Aaron from Ohio" vague. I lost my virginity. We dated briefly. He went to high school in Ypsilanti. He moved. I hated that I had to lie to Nick.

"Do you think we could go talk? In private?" Teddy asked, now standing beside me at the table.

Still no Nick.

Was he really still standing there talking about fucking Sue the T. Rex?

Actually, no. In fact, through the windows, I could see Nick and his friends in one of the living rooms, standing around a grand piano. They were singing and laughing as some girl was smashing her fingers along the keyboard and swaying her head. I couldn't hear what they were singing.

"I don't think that's a good idea," I said, keeping my gaze on the window that held Nick in view.

I could feel the heat of his body travel to mine, the way it did on my couch so many years ago. I felt beads of sweat spring up all over my body. My mouth was dry. I took a swig of my beer. I finally lifted my eyes to look at him. He was different somehow. He had always been muscular, but the years of travel and backpacking and hiking or whatever else he had been doing had turned his biceps into mountains. His appearance was that of a weathered man. Not just because he was chronologically older or that there were tiny lines around his eyes from too much sun; there was something captured in his face that had changed. *Experience, maybe? Love? Had he fallen in love overseas?* His hair was shorter now, and streaks of blonde ran through it. His eyes, those dark and penetrating eyes, remained the same. The light-yellow iris sparkled around the deep brown of his pupils.

"Why not?" he said. "I can't believe you're here! I didn't want to have this party, but my friend Matt practically begged me. I had no idea you would show up. How did you even know about this? Whatever, doesn't matter. I'm glad you did."

"Wait, what?" My stomach was empty and tightening around itself and blood raced through my limbs. "This is *your* house? You've got to be kidding me!"

How did Nick know about this party? Did he know Teddy?

They did live on the same street.

God, did their parents know each other?

"Well, my parents' house, technically. But, yeah . . ." He grinned at the party going on inside. "This, Hazel, is the place that drove me insane for years."

"Where . . . where are your parents?" I asked, gulping in air.

I was in Teddy's house. This whole night. I had been admiring his mother's taste, touching objects that he had touched, making out in a dining room where they probably had had family dinners . . . and his bedroom. I never made it upstairs that night. I'd missed my opportunity to see Teddy's bed, perhaps lie down on it, and inhale his smell . . . I was slipping. Drowning, near a giant pool filled with water, on dry land.

"I don't know, I think somewhere in Asia. My sister keeps tabs on them, but I stopped doing that a while ago."

"Is your sister here tonight too?" I asked, wondering if I had rubbed shoulders with her tonight while filling my cup up with beer.

"Nah, she lives in Texas with her new husband. She's got herself a big old rich dude."

"And," I was stammering now, "what . . . ta . . . a . . . about you? Are . . . are you living here?"

"Hazel, come on, let's go talk." He took my beer from me, and before I could stop him, he was leading me away with his palm in mine. I looked back at the house again, giving Nick one last chance to stop me, but he didn't come. Teddy had pulled me from the patio and out onto the perfectly manicured grass, down to the street, and there we stood in front of his car—the IROC-Z, still orange, still ugly.

"You still have this car?"

"Yeah," he smiled his crooked grin, "it was in storage while I was gone, so she's still running!"

He put his hand on my shoulder. The hairs on my neck sprang up. Just the feel of his skin next to mine weakened not only my knees but any resolve I had left in me to run back to the house. I made a lame attempt to turn around, but Teddy swiveled me back and opened the passenger door for me. The realization that I might actually want this smacked me in the face, and suddenly I felt sober. And guilty.

Why would I put myself through this? *Because he owes you an explanation. And because, you still love him.*

The familiar sensation of nervousness and insecurities crept in, and then flashes of the last day I ever saw him again—those stupid flowers and his flimsy, shitty good-bye in this very car washed over me. A lump formed in my throat; I pushed it down with a swallow of beer. I was thirteen-year-old Hazel again, and Teddy slid into his seat and smiled. His lips were perfect. I had waited so long to kiss them again.

"Damn, girl, you look amazing," he said, tracing my body from head to toe with mischievous eyes. "I've missed you."

"Teddy, what the fuck is going on? Where have you been? Are you back now? You just *left!* Fuck, I have a million fucking questions. I cannot believe this."

I pulled a cigarette out from the pack in my purse and dug around for my lighter. Magically, Teddy's Zippo with the Playboy Bunny flipped open, the flame flickering in front of my face. I sighed and leaned in, glaring at the woman who had traveled around the world with him. It was supposed to be me.

"Hazel, I know. I'm sorry, I really am. I was a shit boyfriend and even shittier man to drop off like that. But, you gotta get it by now, the timing of our relationship, well, you know, it sucked." He put a hand on my bare knee and the logical voice in me told me to swat it away, but instead, I melted into it. "I had no choice, and I couldn't take you with me. You were too young, and you needed to finish high school without me fucking up more of your life. I didn't want to ruin all that for you."

I sucked at the cigarette until smoke filled my lungs. I could barely breathe.

"Thanks, Teddy. Like I didn't know all of that. I may have been a kid, but I wasn't a stupid one. Not only was I too young, but what we were doing was *illegal*. You could have gone to jail. But, fuck, don't act like you did me any favors by leaving and *allowing* me to finish out high school. I knew I couldn't come with you, but the fact is, you never even considered it, even after all your promises. You're just a liar. A manipulative liar who broke my little teenage heart."

"I'm—"

He sighed. My muscles tightened as he ran a finger over my thigh, dangerously close to the edge of my skirt. He stopped short of the hem and then lifted his hand to touch my cheek. Tears were pooling at the corners of my eyes. I hated him, or so I had convinced myself. And I had waited for his touch again for so long. I felt a tingling between my legs.

"I know, baby, and I'm sorry for that. I never meant to hurt you."

"Where were you? I thought you were just backpacking for a summer or something. You just disappeared."

I took a sip of my beer, which was almost gone and getting warm.

Teddy took his hand off my leg and sat back in his seat, running his hands over his face.

"Everywhere, Hazel, I was everywhere. All over Europe. Spain, France, this little town in Germany. A week in Ireland. I went to Asia for a while; it was amazing, a once in a lifetime experience. Oh, and then Amsterdam—"

"Well, fuck, Teddy, I'm so fucking happy for you that you got to gallivant all over the world while I sat here and—" I stopped. I refused to tell him how miserable I had been. Clearly, he had been happy, happy without me, having his own selfish once in a lifetime experience.

"And, what? How was high school? You're graduated now, you can do whatever you want! I would have ruined it. We'd have been sneaking around for years. Did you really want that?"

I thought about it, the way I had thought about it over the years. I would have missed out on working at the bakery and my career. I would have missed out on all the parties on Whitmore Lake. I would have snuck around and lied and lied for all of high school. And, most of all, I would have missed out on Nick.

Nick. Oh, shit.

He must be missing me by now, wondering where I was. If he would ever leave that damn piano and come . . .

"I . . . you could have at least sent me a card telling me to move on, to forget about you. But, don't worry, I have moved on."

The lights from the house illuminated up into the dark gray sky. I should have stayed inside with Nick. But, God, what if Teddy had come up to me at the house, while I was with Nick? What would I have even said?

"Hazel, I know. I just thought it might be better for you if I just ripped off the Band-Aid and stopped all communication. I knew you'd hate me, but like you said, I guess you moved on."

"Listen, Teddy, I gotta go. I shouldn't be here. Yes, I have a life now and you and me—we ended a long time ago, and I have . . . friends inside that are probably looking for me."

I didn't want to tell him about Nick. Nick was all mine, and I wouldn't let Teddy ruin my relationship with him.

"Don't go, Hazel."

He cupped the back of my head and pulled my face to his. I knew I should resist, that this was wrong, but his lips were pressed against mine now, and his hands were on the small of my back, drawing me closer.

His tongue slid inside my mouth, and I let out a little moan. I thought about the way he had made me a woman, the way he looked at me from the first day I met him, how we hid from the world, cocooned inside Chad's apartment. I had ached for this for so long, and he was here now, touching my skin, my lips liquefied against his, his hands all over my new adult body.

~

I have no idea how long it lasted. The pot and the beer and his hands and his mouth created endless time in my mind. But now it was over, and I was pasty with sweat and in full panic mode. I had been transported back to 1986 in the same car with the same smells, sticky tar from too many cigarette butts smashed in the ashtray and the musky film on his skin. There was an unfamiliar scent of a new shampoo that hung in the air, and I knew if I ever smelled it again, I would think of him.

My skirt was bunched up around my waist, and my bra was unhooked, the straps having fallen off my shoulders. There was a heat in my belly that hovered around my groin and crept down my legs where globs of semen seeped from my thighs. I felt dirty, ashamed, and yet here I was, still drawn to this unbearable man, his body awkwardly straddled over me, one leg smashed against the back seat and the other kneeling on the floor.

"God, baby, you have changed. You're so . . . sexual now. What exactly have you been up to?" he said, grinning.

Teddy's penis hung limply outside of his jeans, and I refused to look at it. I couldn't look at him. I was disgusted with myself.

I just cheated on Nick. My wonderful, faithful boyfriend. I've ruined my life in a matter of minutes.

I struggled to prop myself up on my elbows and pushed his chest from me. I desperately wanted to cover myself up. I felt violated, even though I had stupidly, and without a sound, given my permission—again.

He looked surprised, as if he expected some post-coital snuggling and me professing my unwavering love for him. His once long dark hair that used to hang in his eyes was now shorter and tucked behind his ears. *Still, so hot.* I wriggled my bra back on and tussled to pull my skirt back in place.

"I don't know what you want me to say. It's really none of your business."

"Shit, so sorry! I thought maybe you'd be happy with a compliment. You've grown up so much. I thought you might have missed me. And God, you've changed, you're so hot and this body—"

You've grown up so much? I wanted to vomit. That was something your grandparents said to you, not an ex-lover.

"—Hmm. Well, should I say thank you, Teddy, for noticing that I'm not the child you used to fuck? Thanks for noticing that I have tits and an ass, now—and *experience*. Does that sound right to you? Is that what you'd like to hear?"

He huffed out a sound of exasperation.

"Hazel, what the fuck is wrong with you? I'm back! I told you I'd be back. I thought you'd be happy and want to—"

"Want to what, Teddy? Fall back into your arms and be your girlfriend? Fuck you in your precious car?"

"Well, no, I mean, I didn't know you'd be here. But now that I am, and we still have that same connection, maybe we could—"

I laughed and pulled out my compact mirror to reapply pink lipstick over puffy red lips.

He hadn't expected to see me.

"No, Teddy. You can't just show up after four years and think I'm going to run back to you. What kind of idiot do you think I am?"

I snapped my lipstick shut and looked at him.

"Actually, *I am* a fucking idiot. Teddy, this was a mistake. A really big one. No one can know about this. Just like every other time. The story of our lives. I have to go."

"Aw, come on, Hazel. We just had this conversation. I told you why I left. I had to. It just took longer than I thought it would. I couldn't call you, and I got scared your folks would find the letters in the mail. And then, like I said, it was just better for you that I cut it off, since I knew I wasn't coming back for a while. But, now, you're old enough and we wouldn't have to hide anymore!"

I looked at his face. His stupid brown eyes and his stupid

crooked smile now responsible for the second biggest mistake I'd ever made. My mind zoomed to the first time he came to my bedroom and invaded my life. I thought of the day he gave me the key to Chad's apartment, the summer days rolling around in bed with him, drinking Chardonnay. And the boat and the bracelet. And the complete abandonment I felt when he left me. I loved him so fully as a child. But I was a woman now, and my life was different and good. My future was paved in gold in front of me, with Nick.

Nick.

"Fuck! I have to go!" I scrambled to find my shoes. I needed air. I needed this to never have happened. Nick must be looking for me. What would I tell him? More lies. Yes, lie.

"Jesus, what is your deal? What the fuck, Hazel? I thought you would be happy to be with me again."

I needed another cigarette. I grabbed his Zippo from the ashtray.

"I'm going to take this as a memento of your homecoming if you don't mind. Also, I have a boyfriend."

"Sure, I guess. Hey, where are you——"

I threw open the door and rushed up the hill, raking my fingers through my hair, hoping I didn't look like what I had just done. I could hear Teddy's voice in the distance calling my name, but I kept running. I rummaged around my brain for a lie to explain my disappearance. My cheeks were flushed, and I could feel the slime of sex between my legs. I would need to go to the bathroom immediately to wash it off. Luckily, I had a bottle of Exclamation perfume in my purse, and I squirted myself liberally with it.

As I got closer to the house, my stomach churned, imagining Nick's reaction if he found out. How utterly disappointed he would be in me, how hurt. He would break up with me immediately; his morals and values outweighed mine by oceans. He would never understand. Add in the fact that Teddy was really "Aaron" and now a twenty-two-year-old man. None of it would make sense and I would have to explain my whole childhood filled with lies and secrets and he would never forgive me. No, he could not find out.

I could see Nick, standing by the pool, talking to a group of people. He was craning his neck around, probably looking for me. I took a deep breath and then put both of my hands on my stomach, hung my head down, and put on the best miserable face I could.

"Hazel!" Nick was running towards me. "What happened? I've been looking for you. I was worried!"

I smiled as he put his arm around my shoulder and helped me walk to a patio table. The same one that held my snubbed cigarette.

"It's so stupid, Nick." I feebly sat down. "I had to pee really bad and I didn't feel like coming back inside, so I walked down the hill to pee in the bushes and . . . I guess I'm a little trashed because I fell down the hill! And, if that wasn't stupid enough, I got sick and starting puking. Nearly peed my pants. The whole thing was a mess!"

I laughed lightly, hoping my story full of lies would fly.

"Oh, babe . . ." He rubbed my back, "I'm so sorry that happened! You sure you're okay? I was calling for you, you didn't hear me? You *are* drunk."

"No," I shook my head, avoiding his eyes. "I think all those shots were a bad idea. I just need a shower and to go to bed I think."

He smoothed my hair with his free hand.

"I'm so sorry, babe."

I wished he would stop being so sorry.

"*I'm* sorry I worried you. I feel like a fucking wastoid loser."

"Oh, stop. Shit happens. I'm just glad you're okay. I got caught up in the piano singing in there. I should've come out sooner, I'm sorry, Hazel."

He laughed as he steered me towards the house.

Yes, if only you had come out sooner. We could have avoided all of this.

"It's okay. Oh, do we have to say good-byes? I just threw up and fell down a hill. I'm not in the mood for answering questions and being laughed at."

"Of course not. I have to grab your sweater though. Meet me in the car?"

He held out his keys.

"Thanks."

"I'll be there soon, I promise," he kissed my forehead and headed into the house.

I felt like I wanted to *actually* throw up now. I just betrayed Nick in all the worst ways possible and then lied to his face after he had been nothing short of a perfect boyfriend, and now he was even going back for my cardigan. I saw that Teddy's car was still parked on the street. He was inside it, smoking a cigarette, and when he saw me, he just nodded.

He must have another lighter. I touched his Zippo buried deep inside my purse. Somewhere in the depths of my insanity, I had wanted Teddy to stop me and tell me to leave Nick. Tell me we would go away together, maybe somewhere in Europe that he loved. I would learn another language. We would swim in the sea and one day marry atop a cliff overlooking the ocean.

But, he didn't. He had stared at his hands and said that he was happy for me, that I had found someone to love, that I deserved it.

Tears had sprung to my eyes when he said that; clearly not the words I wanted to hear. That's when he told me what his "plans" were.

He was moving to Indiana. He had already interviewed there and was offered a job. He would learn a trade, just like he had planned all along. Indiana was a horrible place, he assured me, but he was just doing it to save up some money and maybe go back to Europe.

He hadn't come back for me. I don't know why I even thought for one second that he had. Running into Teddy at the party was a dirty trick being played on me by some terrible God. He had moved on. Having sex with me was just some nostalgic reenactment of the past. Teddy wanted me to miss him. He wanted to be wanted. We were alike in that way.

Nick sprang down the driveway and hopped in next to me. I refused to look out the window. I knew Teddy was watching us.

"Feeling any better, babe?"

"Um, sort of, but I really need to go to sleep I think."

"Okay," he put his arm behind the passenger seat and turned his body to look out the back window to reverse the car, "we'll be back to my house in just a few."

He and Teddy were yards away, Nick facing my ex-lover as he backed the car up, with Teddy's face in the shadows.

Once he straightened out the car, I snuck a peek out the side mirror, Teddy's face fitting perfectly inside of it. He lifted his fingers from the steering wheel in a small wave and nodded.

I continued to stare at him as we drove away, his face growing smaller and smaller until he was no longer in view.

19

SPARK

CHICAGO, ILLINOIS 1990

I t had been a hell of a couple of days. The event we were prepping for was our biggest account so far. It was a Christmas party for two hundred guests. The clients were Robert and Suzanne Smolnik, owners of Smolnik's Meat Solutions, a meat-packing company and slaughterhouse.

They were Polish and requested traditionally Eastern European desserts. Being Polish myself, I enjoyed the flavors and textures and had plenty of experience creating them at Marjorie's.

Spread across the long stainless-steel counter was an array of my creations. Rows of Kolaczki, cookies made with cream cheese dough and filled with varieties of fruits and nuts; Chrusciki, also known as angel wings, deep-fried, sweet crispy pastries shaped into thin twisted ribbons and sprinkled with powdered sugar; and finally, Polish rum balls, a mix of pecans, rum, vanilla, and sugar rolled into balls, baked, and covered with powdered sugar.

I smiled at my labor of love, proud of how far I had come. Five months ago, I had fled Michigan, struggling to escape the guilt and shame of my betrayal to Nick. I had tried, really tried to push it down and continue with him back home, but it was impossible. I worried that Nick and I would be out and Teddy would appear. My intense paranoia was punctuated by daily stomach aches. I also wanted out from under Joanne's roof, her scrutiny and questions becoming less manageable. The lies of omission surrounding my infidelity and betrayal gnawed at me daily, and a few weeks after the party, I broke it off with Nick.

I told him about Isabel and Abby starting their business in Chicago, how they wanted me to be their pastry chef, how I wasn't sure I could wait another four years to go join them. This was an excuse of course, my sister could easily hire a pastry chef, but I needed a reason to leave.

It was heart wrenching to watch his face distort in hurt and confusion. The promises I made to love him forever, disappearing within a matrix of selfishness and disbelief. Being the amazing man he was, he said he wanted me to be happy, to follow my dreams, that he understood. I must have seemed one-dimensional, a child eyeing a toy and not seeing anything else around me. He deserved better.

Abbey's parents, the perpetual travelers and disinterested parents in their children's lives, had easily handed over a large check to her to start her business. After she and Isabel graduated college, they moved to Chicago and rented out a space in a warehouse right on the river across from the abandoned Montgomery Ward building. They named the business AbbeBel's Catering, a mash-up of their names. It had a commercial kitchen with vaulted ceilings and large stainless-steel countertops and appliances. It was a dream space to build my fortress of sugary desserts.

Isabel and Abbey had welcomed me without a hitch into the three-bedroom apartment they shared in "Boystown," a large gay community within the Lakeview neighborhood. The apartment was on the thirtieth floor of a high-rise, encased in floor to ceiling glass windows. It had a large modern kitchen, stunning décor that Isabel and Abbey both picked out, and a gorgeous view of Lake Michigan and the twinkling lights of downtown Chicago. I was taking classes at the Kendall School of Culinary Arts part time to earn my associate in baking and pastry.

My final step in reinventing myself was therapy. Harper convinced me to go after I exposed my betrayal of Nick to her. I had been inconsolable. My deception to him was the tipping point in the cyclone of chaos Teddy had sucked me into. I needed help to step out of the storm. With the guidance of my therapist, Diane, I began to understand my past, and the necessity of forgiveness. I kept her advice tucked into the pockets of my brain whenever I lacked trust in myself and needed reassurance.

It was the fresh start I had needed.

Now, here I was, running my own department, and I even had my own staff for the event.

Abbey and Isabel hired a few high school kids to help with mixing ingredients, putting things in and out of the oven, and cleaning up. I saw them through my eyes, the way I had learned so many gifts from Marjorie. The student was now the teacher.

Two of the girls were applying the buttercream on the logs as I had instructed them, and another was plating the cookies for the dessert table later.

There were sixteen Yule logs which, by definition, are French, not Polish. But the client wanted them anyway. Their proper name is Bûche de Noël, and making them was fairly simple: spread buttercream over a thin layer of sheet cake, carefully roll it into the shape of a log; next, cut off a piece of the log and place it on the side of the rolled log, like a chopped off branch; spread more buttercream over the log, run a knife through it to simulate bark; and decorate with edible red poinsettias and holly.

I had prepared the Yule logs, hundreds of cookies, and four-dozen rum balls myself. It was my first large event, and I was proud that I had accomplished it single handedly and that it all looked and tasted delicious.

"Okay," Isabel said, rushing through the kitchen doors. "Frank is almost done arranging the flowers, and the party guests should be coming any minute. I've got to get back to the main kitchen and check on the rest of the food. All good? Will everything be ready in time?"

Her brow furrowed in worry.

"Yes," I sighed, "I already told you. The logs are filled and rolled. I'm about to start the design soon. Please stop nagging me."

"Sorry." She softened her shoulders and came to stand by me and dipped a finger into a bowl of buttercream. "I'm just nervous. This is a big account for us."

"Keep your fingers out of there, please!" I pushed her hand from my bowl. "I know you're nervous, but as Abbey would say, 'Every account is a big account.' They are all keeping us afloat."

"Yeah, yeah," she rolled her eyes, "okay, I'm going to do final checks on everything."

I nodded and turned back to my work.

The party was at the Hilton hotel on South Michigan Avenue in an enormous and exquisite ballroom. Dazzling chandeliers as large as cars and adorned with thousands and thousands of teardrop-shaped crystals trailed down the expansive ceiling. Large panels of velvet curtains, trimmed in braided gold silk, hung from arched floor-to-ceiling windows. Elegant Christmas décor gave the ballroom a cozy feel. Trees dripping in white lights and lavish ornaments towered in the corners. Candles glowed on each of the white-clothed tables, surrounded by vases of amaryllises. High-backed gilded chairs upholstered in gold brocade nuzzled into each of the round tables. All of it so breathtaking.

The majesty reminded me of Teddy's home. Many times since moving in with Isabel, as we drank wine and stared at the lake, I ached to tell her about Teddy. How guilty I felt and still felt about it. How I lied to her and my parents for an entire summer. How the lies followed me to Chicago. How I cheated on Nick with Teddy, destroying my one healthy relationship.

But I didn't dare. I was in a good place, doing what I loved most —baking—and spending quality time with Isabel. Our relationship had grown. We were more than sisters; we were good friends now. We worked together and lived together and laughed and were adults together. I wasn't ready to destroy our developing bond with the truth.

Traditional Christmas music piped through the speakers, and I found myself absently humming along. I longed to be a guest at the party instead of being there—as what my mother called, "the help." I envisioned what Joanne would wear—a long, sleek gown covered in sequins, hair in a French twist, drinking a martini and laughing at men telling terrible jokes.

The Smolniks had spared no expense; packing up flesh seemingly paid well. I watched as servers put the finishing touches on the tables—inspecting glasses for water spots and polishing the silverware—and saw Frank, our new operations manager, clad in a black Armani suit, running around with a clipboard, stopping briefly to turn a candle or wipe an invisible crumb.

Isabel and Abbey had hired Frank a month ago to deal with booking the events, meeting the clients, and all paperwork involved. Isabel had met him one night at a gay bar in the neighborhood. He was a bartender at night and now worked for us during the day. He was flamboyant and funny, ensuring a fun vibe in the business.

"Hey, Hazel, hon?" he hollered.

He grinned with perfect white teeth as I came toward him in my white chef's coat and black pants covered in flour. My long hair was pulled up in a high ponytail with a small red bow at the base of it. I sported some new sparkly eyeshadow to fit the holiday theme and my classic red lipstick.

"Well, my, my, don't you look just ravishing this evening!" He purred and squeezed me. "Well, thank you!" I said, with a curtsy. If a gay man thinks you look amazing, then you definitely look amazing.

"Of course, darling." He scanned the room. "So, what do you think? The tables? The decorations? Is it too much? Is it too *me*?"

I chuckled and put a hand on his arm.

"It *is* absolutely you, but thank God. It's gorgeous, Frank, really."

"Thank you, honey," he let out an exasperated sigh. "Let's hope these gratuitous flesh eaters agree with you."

We laughed, and suddenly a couple strode through the ballroom doors.

"Showtime." I said, silently throwing my head in their direction.

"I see! Okay, off you go!"

Frank air-kissed me and began his way to them. I assessed the couple as I retreated to the kitchen. An older woman, possibly Mrs.

Smolnik, wore a long brown fur with a matching fur hat, and high heels peeking from beneath. She removed the hat revealing a blond bob, fashionably cut.

The coat check girl took the woman's array of dead animal apparel and handed her a ticket. The woman smiled warmly and they chatted amiably. A portly man accompanying her handed over his gray overcoat and wool scarf, but just gave her a nod in exchange for a ticket. I assumed that this was Mr. Smolnik. He stamped the snow off his dress shoes.

Isabel and Abbey were at the front host podium now, smiling and shaking hands with the man and distributing air kisses on the woman's cheeks. The evening was commencing, and as I turned back around for the kitchen, a man came in behind them. He was young, probably around my age, with sandy-brown hair. He wore a pale-pink button-up shirt with a gray sweater over it, dark-gray pants, and shined shoes. He turned over a camel-colored trench coat and plaid Burberry scarf to the coat check girl.

I couldn't help but stare, feeling invisible for some reason when he met my gaze. I froze and smiled with my lips pursed, embarrassed he caught me staring. He grinned, flashing beautiful teeth to match his gorgeous face. I felt a hand graze my waist.

"Oh, would you look at that?" Frank was walking back towards me. "Is someone in love already?"

"Frank!"

Heat rose to my face as I shoved the kitchen doors open and hurried inside. He was close behind.

"What? I can see it all over your pretty little face!" he whispered. "But be careful, honey. These rich fucks can be dicks. No matter how wonderful your desserts are, he could still break your heart."

Before I could respond, he blew another air kiss and exited.

I frowned and went back to the kitchen. My assistants had cleaned up most of the mess and added decorative hollies to the Yule logs. My part was pretty much done. But I needed to stay until dessert was brought out, so I had a block of free time. I snuck a peek out the round window in the kitchen door and saw the guests pouring in.

More fur coats, diamond jewelry sparkling on women's hands and ears and wrists rivaling the chandeliers above them. Men in expensive-looking suits shook hands and patted each other's backs.

All these people were in the business of slaying animals? Evidently providing bacon and steak was very lucrative.

A server pushed through one of the doors and whisked by with a tray in hand, nearly colliding with me.

"Excuse me," she said, without a glance.

"Sorry," I mumbled, and shifted out of the way.

I peeked again into the dining room, searching for the hot guy. I couldn't find him. I was a goldfish in a tiny bowl, looking out, possibly to a world I didn't belong.

～

Three hours in, after the main courses had been served—beef tenderloin, prime rib, cider-glazed carrots, pork loin, brown-sugar brussels sprouts, and butternut squash—my desserts would be going out.

I sat on a turned-over milk crate, bored, chewing on a straw, and reading old magazines in the back office. *Cosmopolitan* was still trying to teach me how to be a "tigress in the bedroom" and how to achieve multiple orgasms.

I listened to the boom of raucous laughter escalating, drowning out the Christmas music, as the flow of alcohol inebriated the guests. It was loud, and I was annoyed—mostly because I couldn't be a part of it.

"Okay, Hazel, you're up." Isabel came in looking tired. "The entrée dishes have been cleared, and the coffee is being poured."

Finally. I replaced my dirty jacket with a clean white jacket embroidered with my name and retrieved my high school girls from the back alley. They were smoking cigarettes and gossiping. I advised them to scrub the stink of smoke off their hands.

One by one, they picked up platters of cookies and Yule logs and paraded out to the dining room. I followed behind with a special Yule log, larger than the others, with "Merry Christmas from Smolnik's Meat Solutions" written across it in white icing.

As I exited the stuffy kitchen and entered the fresh, cheery air of Christmas in the ballroom, I felt a calm wash over me. I smiled and followed my procession of girls to the long table covered in white and green tablecloths, adorned with pinecones, candles, and statues of sad angels playing harps. A massive wreath peppered with sparkly ornaments hung above the table.

I scanned the room, searching and squinting until I finally saw him. He was seated at his parents' table, drinking something amber on ice. Glass in hand, he tilted his head back to drain the liquid, and on the way back down, he caught my stare. He put his empty glass down and smiled at me.

I blushed and quickly turned to focus on the work at hand. *What the hell is the matter with me?* I had never had problems flirting or talking to men.

"Hazel?" one of the girls touched my shoulder. "We're all set, you can put that down now."

I nodded and strode over to the table, placing the grand log in the center. Flickering candles glowed around it, creating an air of elegance to the whimsical log. Stepping back, I admired my work. Isabel, in her tight black dress and kitten heels, snuck up next to me and briefly laid her head on my shoulder. Her hair was still short in a pixie cut but dyed deep auburn now.

"Everything looks great!" She squeezed my arm.

"Thanks," I said, "I hope they like everything. The first people who arrived—are they the clients?"

"Yep, Daddy Warbucks and his sweet little wife."

"Um, how about the young guy with them?"

A wicked smile spread across my sister's face.

"Why? You interested?"

"Who is it? Their son?"

"Yes, his name is Phil, and he happens to be single."

"How do you know that?" I turned slightly and felt his eyes on me.

She rolled her eyes. "His mother. She loves to gush about him.

And especially how he needs to meet a nice girl and settle down. She even tried to pawn me off on him!"

"Seriously? And?"

"Not my type," she said."A little too uptight for me. But, you . . . on the other hand? Could you deal with an accountant?"

"An accountant? Really? Shit, that seems super boring!" I said, but then remembered Nick had been studying to be a lawyer. Reliable. Something stable.

"I know, right? Anyway, everything looks great, and I'm sure these fat cats will descend on desserts soon. They're going to love everything! I'll let you know," she said, as she gently pushed me towards the kitchen.

"Thanks."

I was always being pushed into the back room it seemed.

I glanced back and saw that he was still watching me. He raised his hand, smiled, and gave me a little nod. I smiled back.

That made two smiles, a wave, and a nod. I returned to the clatter of the chaos behind the swinging doors.

As I helped the girls cleaning up, a voice called out.

"Hazel? Hazel? You back there? You have a visitor."

Abbey's voice rang through the hallway

A visitor?

I wiped my hands on my apron.

"Who?"

Practically anyone I knew in Chicago was here with me. And then, "hot guy" suddenly appeared in the flesh, smiling, eyes the color of a robin's egg. Abbey waved and winked from behind him.

"Hazel, this is Phil, the Smolnik's son. His mother sent him to tell you how great the Bûche de Noël was, and she loved the cookies too. I, um, have to run back out. Phil? I'm assuming you can find your way out of a kitchen?"

"I think I can manage that, yes. Thank you for bringing me back."

Abbey click-clacked away in her heels, pleased with herself.

"So, you're the amazing pastry chef everyone's been talking about?"

Excitement and anxiety hovered in my stomach. I hoped I looked okay.

"Really? Everyone?"

"Well, yes, the whole group is impressed, but my mother, she thinks she's died and gone to Polish heaven."

He relaxed his stance and leaned against the wall, hands in pockets. Heat flushed my cheeks. His confidence was effortless, lacking cockiness or pretense. I was the one struggling to find my old self, the charmer, the enchantress. But I was awkward, with sweaty hands.

"She didn't want to come thank me herself?" I managed a coy smile. "So, she sent *you*?"

"Well, my mother is still hobnobbing with friends and employees, so I offered to come meet you myself. I'm sure she will find you once the guests leave. But she wanted me to find you and ask you to stay, so she can shower you with praise. You know, I'm just here doing her a favor," he declared, and rolled his eyes in mock annoyance.

"How nice of you," I said, feeling more at ease. "She obviously raised a nice boy."

I stared at his cashmere gray sweater. Perhaps a reflection of the man who stood before me; it was both elegant and sensible. I fought the urge to touch it, to touch him and pull him in for a nuzzle of comfort.

Was love at first sight possible?

It had felt like that with Teddy, but I was thirteen. I knew now that all teenage girls were convinced that any boy who paid attention to them was instantaneous love.

"Hazel, I'm going to go out on a limb here and assume you don't normally make beautiful desserts for old men who cut up meat for a living."

He said my desserts were beautiful.

"No, not usually," I laughed, and nervously twirled a piece of hair. "The catering company is owned by my sister Isabel and her friend Abbey. I moved here a while ago and started working for them, but no, I've never made desserts for butchers before." I paused and smiled, "Normally I'm out living a fantastic, amazing life, but tonight, duty calls."

"Wow!" he laughed. "I don't doubt that! And what are you doing after this tour of duty tonight? Do you have something fantastic and amazing planned, per usual?"

I hesitated as a server muscled her way toward us. Phil and I both pressed into the wall as she squeezed by us, irritation across her face.

"Actually, no," I said, turning to face him, "I had to rearrange my amazing social calendar for this night. So, yes, I am free."

"Great!" he smiled mischievously. "First, I must schmooze more with those meat slayers, but maybe once you're done, you'd be up for some debauchery?"

"I'm always up for some debauchery." I fiddled with the bracelet from my father. "I have to wrap up leftovers and finish cleaning up. Once you get your barbarians out of here, I'm free." "I have a mission then, because I'd like to take you out for a nightcap. I'm staying in the hotel tonight, and the bar downstairs, Kitty O'Shea's, is a fun little spot. How about we meet for a drink when you're done?"

"Sure. That sounds fantastic and amazing. Just what I'm used to."

"Alright then, Hazel," he said, lightly touching my shoulder, "I'll rally up the troops and get them out. I'll see you downstairs soon." His foreign hand felt oddly familiar. And safe.

~

It was near midnight when the guests began filing out. They were loud and sauced from all the booze. The coat check girl was frantically gathering furs and overcoats while the servers hustled to finish clearing tables. The automatic dishwasher was churning soap around dishes. Isabel and Abbey thanked the guests, shook hands, and gave hugs.

I delegated my high schoolers to wrap up cookies and Yule logs and put them in the walk-in refrigerator. I hurriedly wiped down all the counters, swept the floor, and headed to the back office to shake my hair free and change into street clothes—an oversized cashmere turtleneck, tight blue jeans, and chunky-heeled lace-up boots.

As I grabbed my jacket from the coat check closet, Isabel called out to me.

"Hazel! Hey, good job tonight! Everyone loved your desserts, especially Mrs. Smolnik."

"Thanks," I smiled, realizing the woman never did make it back to speak to me. "It was fun. Glad they all liked it."

"And Mrs. Smolnik wasn't the only one who liked your desserts." She smiled slyly. "What happened with sexy Phil? Details, please!"

"No details to give yet, but I'm going downstairs to meet him for a drink," I said, blushing once again.

"No way, that's awesome! He's so cute!"

"I know, I'll see you later, at home, okay?"

"Or, maybe you won't." She smiled again.

"Or maybe I won't," I said and kissed her cheek and headed out.

～

The roar of intoxication overpowered the lobby as I approached Kitty O'Shea's. I pushed through the rowdy crowd congregated in circles and searched the bar. I found Phil with some of the partygoers. As he sipped his drink, he caught my eye. His mouth stretched into a playful grin, and he kept my gaze as I shoved my way towards him.

Once I arrived, he immediately took my jacket and draped it over a nearby barstool. The others were pretty lit up now, and the forced politeness from the event was replaced by haughty laughter, slaps on the back, and swearing. He gently placed his hand on the small of my back.

"Well, hello there, Hazel. I'm glad you made it."

My body naturally melted into the warmth of his hand.

"What, and miss an exciting adventure with a complete

stranger?" I said with a demure smile. "I'm glad you waited around."

"What would you like to drink, now that you can indulge in some debauchery with me?"

"I think I'll start with an Irish car bomb."

"Are you serious?" Phil laughed, and his whole face lit up. My tension began to melt away. His laughter was warm and soothing, like a hot bath, and filled up the emptiness inside me.

"Totally and completely. Full on debauchery."

"Well, okay then. Destruction, coming right up."

He leaned over the bar to order our drinks, and I fussed with a ponytail that I couldn't see and observed my scruffy nails with ragged cuticles and flecks of red polish chipping off. Between baking a million cookies and putting on and taking off gloves, a manicure would have been useless. Phil turned to me with two beers and the shot.

"Could you hold the beer for a sec?" I asked.

"Yes. This, I need to see."

I dropped the shot of Jameson and Baileys into the glass of Guinness. Once the shot glass clinked the bottom, I gulped the concoction down. The sweet and bitter taste coated my entire mouth and the sting of alcohol assaulted my stomach.

"Ahhhh." I smiled and handed him the empty glass.

"Good stuff."

He laughed and placed it on the bar.

"Very impressive."

"Well, I don't fuck around with my drinks."

"I see that. I like that you know what you like and aren't afraid to go for it."

"Wow, we just met, and you know me so well!"

"If you let me, I'd like to learn more."

He didn't appear drunk, and seemed sincere.

"If you're lucky, maybe you will."

Phil drained his glass, placed it on the bar, and turned to me. He took my hand in his and looked towards the door.

"I have an idea. Will you come somewhere with me?" He

squeezed my hand when concern colored my face. "Don't worry, it's not to my room."

I relaxed and nodded. He grabbed my jacket and my hand and left a twenty on the bar.

"But I just got here, and I'm only one drink in—okay technically two I guess, but still—" I started to protest.

"Don't worry, there are more drinks where we're going."

My head was swirling with intrigue. In the main lobby, majestic curved staircases spiraled up to other banquet rooms. With a hand at the small of my back, he guided me up the stairs, which opened up into a quaint bar with lounge chairs, plush couches, and a gorgeous Steinway grand piano that gleamed beneath the chandeliers. Small groups of patrons sipped on cocktails in elegant glassware, speaking in hushed voices and laughing quietly.

I suddenly felt exposed in my casual street clothes amongst a social standing I did not belong to. Certainly no one would notice my chipped nail polish or flour-laced hair, but I clenched my hands into fists to hide them anyway.

"What do you think? I do prefer it up here. It's quiet, and well, less obnoxious, don't you think?"

"It's stunning," I said, as we walked towards the bar. He ordered a Manhattan and for me, a gin martini. I felt a sudden itch inside; I was channeling Joanne.

"It's one of my favorite places," he said, his eyes smoldering, "and much easier to get to know you without all the shouting."

"I've never been, but I'm so glad you showed it to me."

The gin was warming everything inside me, and I was transfixed by my surroundings.

"Cheers, Hazel," Phil raised his glass close to mine. "It's an honor to be with you tonight when you *could* be out doing something fabulous."

I smiled and rolled my eyes.

"Oh, stop it already. *This* is fabulous," I smiled at him over the rim of my glass. And, it was fabulous. I wasn't the help; I was special. Everyone in this room had a story, real or imaginary, and I was living a fantasy, sipping on a martini in a beautiful hotel with a gorgeous man.

"Come with me," he cupped my hand, and led me to a lounge chair next to the piano. The mahogany in all its glossy splendor was exquisite. I sank into the plush velvet chair, unsure of what was happening.

Phil positioned himself on the piano bench.

I looked around, wondering if we were allowed to be doing this, but no one paid any attention.

"I hope I don't embarrass you, but I have this undeniable desire to sing and play for you," he chuckled. "I cannot continue to walk past this work of art and not play it. I haven't had a real reason, or well, *inspiration*, to play until tonight."

I sipped my drink and tried not to explode.

Who was this man, and where did he come from? *I* was the reason that qualified a performance from him? An actual serenade?

Breathe.

"By all means," I said, as nonchalantly as possible and smiled, "I would love to see what you can do."

"Fantastic," he grinned, tracing his fingers over the ivory keys.

"First, I'm going to make an observation. If you were a run-of-the-mill sappy girl, I would sing you some Eric Clapton. Or perhaps Billy Joel. But, you, Hazel, are special. I think you are the kind of girl who is inclined to enjoy a more meaningful piece."

"I would say you are correct. So, yes, please, piano man, don't play "Piano Man" for me."

We both laughed and he feigned relief.

"Oh, *thank* God. Let's get down to it, then."

His fingers danced lightly over the keys, sending magical melodies into the air. Several people stopped talking and turned to watch.

Only a couple notes in, I recognized it. Goosebumps prickled my skin as he began to sing "A Groovy Kind of Love" by Phil Collins.

Eyes closed, a tenderness and warmth flowed from his lips as he belted out the lyrics. I forced myself to breathe. This was sexy, deliberate, pure bliss.

I imagined so many delicious things—kissing his lips, his body— I wanted him and knew I would have him.

Phil continued to sing, closing his eyes at certain stanzas, and, at others, staring at me with his intense blue eyes.

Vibrations of emotions washed over me and finally, I could not contain myself any longer. As I pushed myself up and walked towards him, he did not take his eyes off me. I was buzzed now, and I felt my sexual prowess rising. I slid onto the bench and placed my hand on his leg.

Phil eased into ending the song as his eyes melted into mine. His oval face tapered down into a small, perfect point at his chin. His lips curled into a seductive grin, and I longed to kiss him. He grazed his thumb on my face and lifted my chin up to meet his lips.

He kissed me slowly, deliberately, and heat rose from every cell in my body. My body seemed to float away, absorbing his soft lips and bourbon-rinsed tongue.

Applause erupted around us, jolting us both. We had forgotten about the crowd, now all watching and listening and clapping. Smiling faces peered at us, lifting drinks to cheer us on.

"Well," he said softly, "I guess we shouldn't disappoint them?"

"No, we shouldn't." I shook my head and leaned in for another kiss.

20

UNION

CHICAGO, ILLINOIS / ANN ARBOR, MICHIGAN 1995

M y courtship with Phil had been swift. He took me to the movies, dinner, ice skating, and trips to The Art Institute, where he became my teacher. He educated me on eras and styles of painters and sculptures, and I cherished the works of Monet, Degas, and Renoir. I was drawn to the thick layers of paint, lending texture and presence to each anchored painting. I carried an incomparable calm with me as we wove through hallways of exquisite sculptures by Donatello, Da Vinci, and Michelangelo.

We relaxed in oversized booths, sipping on martinis and soaking in the thunder of jazz and swing at The Green Mill in Uptown. I thought of my father every time a Miles Davis song was covered. We went to Kingston Mines, one of the oldest blues bars in Chicago to watch Phil's favorite blues legend, Linsey Alexander.

Phil's world was luxurious, dripping with cultural sophistication. My parents were academics, intelligent and refined, but this was different. I flip-flopped between soaking up Phil's kindness and stability, and at the same time, feeling like I didn't deserve it.

I was giddy and happy. To resist him was unkind to the part of me that believed I was a good person. He remained unaware of the part of my past that included Teddy. As I created this new and improved version of myself, he would never need to know. And just maybe, I could have a life that I had always craved.

When we finally had sex, it was beyond my imagination. It wasn't raw and scary and manipulative like with Teddy. Nor was he a loving high school boy with inexperienced hands like Nick. Phil was a gentle, sexy man who brought me previously unattainable levels of sensual pleasure. He was a slim five foot eleven with a surprising layer of muscle that rippled down his stomach.

He first told me he loved me as we sat on the banks of the Huron River after a picnic and a bottle of wine. I rushed in, with watery eyes and whispered, "I love you too."

Our love affair moved quickly after that.

The proposal came in the form of baking. Phil asked me to teach him how to make the Polish cookies his mother loved so much.

I was in the middle of rolling out dough when he snuck up behind me, slipping his hands into my apron pockets.

He nuzzled close and whispered, "Can we take a little break?"

His breath moved down my neck and I tried to focus.

"Are you serious?" I smiled. "You're going to make a terrible baker. We can't just leave the dough sitting out—"

He took the rolling pin from my hands and set it down on the counter and spun me around.

"No, I am not trying to get you to the bedroom, yet," he smiled. "I want to talk for a minute."

"Okaaay . . ." I said, as he led me from the kitchen and to the couch.

"Hazel."

He took his hands in mine and stared into my eyes.

"There are so many things I love about you."

Oh God. Here comes the but . . .

"The way you bite your bottom lip when you're anxious, the way you twirl your hair when you're flirting, the way you organize your spices, the way you color coordinate your closet, how you stack plates when we're done eating as if you are working a catering job . . ."

Jesus. I didn't realize I did all this weird shit.

"But . . ."

Oh God, here it comes. I grappled with the blanket to brace myself.

"But also, the thing I really love about you is your kindness. You're as sweet as your desserts . . . sorry, corny comparison," he laughed nervously. "You're passionate about your career, and you are really, really *good* at it. I love that you strive daily to be a good person. And I love how you make me feel, like I'm one of the rare edible flowers on your cakes, and almost, well, magical. I've never met someone like you."

My mouth dried up like a wrung-out sponge.

"Don't even get me started on how sexy you are. Those lips of yours . . ."

He leaned in for a soft, lingering kiss. Every cell in my body liquefied and rose to the surface.

"So, Hazel, please reach into the right pocket of your apron."

"What? Why?"

"Just, please, do it."

My body trembled as I dug into the pocket, where a tiny object was wedged. The pit of my stomach rose and fell. A familiar, yet foreign object that I only observed in other's lives, never my own. I knew what it was, but it felt surreal. I stopped envisioning this moment after Teddy left, and never again once I abandoned Nick.

The ring sparkled in the low candlelit room. Phil gently and silently pried the ring from me, and lifted my left hand. He slid the ring onto my finger—a gold band with a large, single round-cut diamond. My mouth was agape, still speechless.

"Hazel, I can't imagine a world without you. I need your smile, your face, and those beautiful green eyes to wake up to every morning. Hazel, will you marry me?"

Sloppy, wet tears fell from my eyes. This was it. Finally. All the heartache, the mistakes, the lies, the pain; it all fell away, like rocks tumbling from a mountain. The weight lifted. Security. Love. Trust. Everything I had desired endlessly, but could never grasp and keep, was here in front of me. And he wanted *me.*

"Hazel," Diane's face came into my mind. "When true love comes, you will

know it, and feel it. And when it comes, know that it's okay to accept it. You are worthy. It's okay to embrace it when it's healthy. You've worked so hard, don't let the past define you."

"But, how will I know it's right?"

"By trusting yourself."

The tightness that had gripped my body for years unwound and melted, one muscle at a time. I was safe and loved, and it was pure and real. This was right. Diane was right.

I threw my arms around him, holding tight onto my new, wonderful future.

"Oh my God. Yes, of course I will!"

I threw my arms around him, holding tight to my future husband.

∼

Sparkling in the sunlight from the windows of my childhood bedroom was a stunning diamond necklace that hung from the nape of my neck. It was a gift from my grandmother, Elizabeth. It had arrived in a beautiful box with a note.

Dear Hazel,

Despite what your mother's wishes are, I will not miss my granddaughter's wedding. This necklace was my mother's and I would like you to have it, and if it goes well with your dress, I would be honored if you wear it on your special day. See you soon.

Best, Elizabeth

My mother flew into a rage when she found out. I had no idea she had banned my grandmother from my wedding. My father was furious when he found out and forced my mother's hand. Elizabeth would attend.

I gazed in awe at my reflection in the long oval mirror. Hugging the length of my body was my wedding gown. It was champagne-colored satin, swathed in a beaded off-the-shoulder, lace-on-tulle overlay, tapered down into the slightest mermaid flair and fastened tight by ivory buttons sinching the back.

My long dark hair fell in loose curls around my collar bones, and a thin, sheer veil, attached to a dainty beaded band, adorned my head.

Phil and I chose my parents' backyard for the wedding, with the gardens and the pond and towering trees as our backdrop. The leaves were September-crisp with burnt oranges, mustard yellows, and cranberry reds. The ceremony would take place at sunset, and tents draped with tulle and flowers would hold the reception.

I peered at a black velvet bag on my dresser. I scooped it up and sat on the bed, reflecting on my wedding tradition items. The something old was the necklace from Elizabeth. The something borrowed was a vintage compact mirror that Isabel bought in The Village in New York City. The something new was an Yves Saint Laurent lipstick in the shade of red my mother and I favored, and the something blue was a tacky lace garter from Harper that I had no intention of wearing.

From the little bag, I lifted the loop of diamonds and draped it around my wrist. It finally fit perfectly. It was always meant for a woman, and I would probably never know who the rightful owner was, a prior girlfriend or stolen from Teddy's mother or sister.

I suddenly felt foolish as I flashed back to the day on the boat when he gave it to me, and it slipped off my wrist and continued to for all my adolescent years, and then I resorted to wearing it as an ankle bracelet.

I wondered how many times my mother had worn it after she confiscated it. As I watched this small piece of history dangle and shimmer, an idea came to me.

"Hazel, sweetheart?" my dad said, startling me from outside my door. "You doing okay in there? It's almost time."

I unhooked the latch and placed the bracelet back inside the box.

"Yes, Dad, come in!"

He was wearing a tailored black suit purchased just for my wedding. His cerulean eyes complimented his ash-gray hair; the wrinkles in his face branched out farther and deeper, and yet, he wore it with distinguished grace.

"Oh, honey, you are beautiful!" he beamed with pride. "Look at you. I'm a real proud papa today."

He came over, put his hands on my shoulders, and kissed my cheek.

"Thanks, Dad. What's going on down there?"

I looked out the window to see guests hustling about, chatting, some taking their seats.

On the groom's side, Phil's mother, Suzanne wore a goldenrod-hued A-line dress splashed with large white flowers and oversized round sunglasses. She was, essentially, the mother I had wished for, sweet, generous, funny, and best of all, stable.

"Oh, you know, your mother is running around barking orders at everyone and rearranging perfectly arranged flowers."

I rolled my eyes and laughed.

We hired catering staff, but Isabel and Abbey were supervising. I felt a pang of anxiety for them.

"Can't she just relax and leave them alone? Why does she have to—"

"—Be so controlling? Come on now, Hazel, would you expect anything else?"

"No, you're right, she can't help herself. It's embarrassing." I faced him again and smiled. "How does my cake look?"

Marjorie designed and baked the cake. It was gorgeous: a white butter cream three-tiered work of edible art with sugared dragonflies circling around each tier. The border of each layer had light-blue pearl beading piped on top, and delicate yellow and green marzipan flowers represented the sun and pond reeds. Silvery petal dust was sprinkled over the entire cake, adding sparkle and sheen.

For my theme, the colors I had chosen were dark blue and green, reminiscent of dragonfly wings. Notebooks with dragonfly stationery and a gold pen decorated each place setting for party favors. "I haven't been allowed in the kitchen, but I hear it's beautiful."

"And Grandma Elizabeth? Have she and Mom killed each other yet?"

"No," he chuckled, "your grandmother has been talking to Lolly and Oscar, drilling them on what she's been missing all these years."

I felt sorry for Elizabeth, the way my mother had kept her from us with only vague explanations.

"Well, I'm sure she'll get an earful," I said. "And how is Phil? Is he nervous?"

"A little," he smiled, "but all grooms are, honey. He has a lot to live up to, to make my daughter happy."

"He does make me happy."

"He's a good man." He kissed my forehead. "This is it, Hazel. You are all grown and you found your partner in life. You're no longer that baby nymph crawling from the water."

"I love you, Dad, thank you."

"I love you too, Hazelnut."

⁓

The day was a blur, like everyone predicted. Isabel was my maid of honor, and Harper, swollen with her second child, was my bridesmaid. She and Steve married shortly after high school and had their first daughter, Samantha, a year and a half later.

I drained several glasses of champagne after the ceremony, followed by hugging and chatting, dancing and eating, all intertwined into what felt like the end of a romantic comedy.

My father toasted us with a tender speech, while Harper and Isabel told embarrassing and funny stories. Phil and I danced closely, and Isabel and Abbey and I danced and laughed to some old new-wave music favorites. We gorged on leftovers in the kitchen and helped ourselves to more cake. I chatted with Marjorie about the shop and thanked her profusely for my beautiful wedding cake.

Late that evening, I had a brief conversation with my grandmother, Elizabeth. I wanted to learn everything I didn't know about her—my mother, their relationship, and the grandfather I never knew. But she insisted that this was not the time or the place.

She clutched her diamond necklace and with hesitation,

remarked, "Your mother had been a stubborn child with an egregious lack of empathy, even at a young age. She's always been this way."

I was taken aback by the comment; it wasn't so much a surprise as it was jarring. This bluntness brought a clarity to many of my mother's actions and words to both me and my sister. I almost felt sorry for her.

I caught a glimpse of her slow dancing with my Uncle Paul— her brother-in-law—her arms looped around his neck and her eyes narrowed into drunken slits. He held his hand steady on her back, but he glanced nervously at his wife when my mother tried to pull him closer.

"Unfortunately, she hasn't changed much," I said, turning back to Elizabeth.

"Oh, yes, dear, I know. And it is unfortunate. She's very smart, and cunning. Too much of that keeps one safe. She's terrified of being hurt, so she severs everyone first. It's a disturbing protection mechanism that she learned as a child. Heaven knows why. She was not abused or starved. If anything, her father and I quite spoiled her."

Weaved in between the waves of words she had just poured out was a concealed history my mother had managed to keep hidden. I had to restrain the curiosity clawing its way out of me.

My mother was done dancing and was sitting cross-legged at a table, her dress hiked up to expose her striking legs, a cigarette dangling from her long fingers, and a glass of wine smeared with red lipstick at the rim in hand.

I joined Phil on the dance floor and beamed as he whispered how beautiful I was, that he was the luckiest man alive and that he couldn't wait to get me alone.

I curled into him, knowing I had finally made a good decision in my life.

～

After eleven, most of the guests were gone other than stragglers drinking in the yard.

I found my mother upstairs in her room, propped up on shammed pillows on the bed, with a glass of red wine. Her dress was crumpled, shoes kicked off, and a box of photos dumped out in front of her. She was staring at a photo.

"Hi, Mom," I swooshed to her in my gown and sat at the foot of the bed. "What are you doing?"

"Hmm?" She gazed at me with eyes stained red and wet from old tears.

"What's wrong?"

I peered over to see what she was looking at. It was a photo of her and my father, on their wedding day. She, in a simple white dress with no shoes and flowers in her hair, and my dad, in a simple flowy white shirt and linen pants, no shoes.

"Oh, nothing, honey. Just reminiscing a little. Look at how young I looked! Not a wrinkle or hair out of place!"

I smiled. It was so typical of her to comment on how she looked first, rather than on the moment. It was selfish and pitiful, but I couldn't find it in myself to be mad about it. This was who she was, to the core. She was in a constant flux of depression and elation. None of us could control it, and apparently neither could she. And if she could, she didn't want to. It was hard to accept it, to the full extent of unconditional understanding, but it no longer made sense to fight with her.

At twenty-three years old, I was happy now, and I didn't have the energy or desire to resent her for every one of her flaws anymore.

"You look beautiful, Mom. And, Dad, well, he's still as handsome as the day you were married. You look happy. Were you happy on your wedding day?"

She scrunched her forehead together and gave me a baffled look.

"Well, of course I was, Hazel! We were so in love and so young and so full of hopes but . . ." She took another sip of wine and continued to stare at the photo.

"And, what a life the two of you have had!" I was not going to allow her to go down the dark rabbit hole on my wedding day. "You certainly raised two amazing kids, if I do say so myself!"

She smiled and took another sip.

"Yes, of course, we did," she said, placing the photo on her lap. "And what a wonderful day for you! You are married now, Hazel! Tell me, has this been the happiest day of *your* life?"

"Of course it has," I said. "And I have something to give you."

"You do?" She put her glass down and sat up. "But, it's your wedding day. What could you possibly need to give me?"

I had entered her room with a little velvet bag in the palm of my hand, but she hadn't noticed. I opened my hand now and extended it to her.

"Go ahead, open it," I said.

Like a child on Christmas morning, she quickly loosened the string on the bag and poured its contents into her own palm.

My diamond bracelet caught slivers of kaleidoscopic light, despite the dim room, and sparkled as bright as it had ever been.

Her eyes widened as she looked from the bracelet to me. I unhooked the clasp, and it fell effortlessly into my palm. I admired it one last time and held out my hand to her.

"This used to mean something to me for so long. It was first love for me; I was young and naive I know, but it meant everything at the time. But it doesn't anymore. I know how much you liked it, so I want you to have it."

"Really? Hazel, you *must* be kidding!" She rolled the diamonds around between her fingers and her thumbs caressing each one. "But . . . Well, maybe . . . maybe I never should have taken this from you. However, you must now see how you really were far too young for such an expensive, extravagant gift. You understand that now, right?"

That was my mother's version of an apology, almost a decade later.

"Sure, Mom, I get it. It was definitely over the top."

"You are of course old enough *now* to wear it, so why on earth would you give it up?"

Exhaustion from the day was lulling my senses, and I just wanted to go to sleep with my new husband.

"I have enough memories of that time in my life. I'm starting a new one with Phil, and I don't want or need a bracelet to continually remind me of the past. And, who better to give it to? I'm pretty sure you still like it, right?"

"Well, yes, of course. I mean, diamonds are just so beautiful." She looped the bracelet over her wrist and motioned for me to clasp it. "And, well, you were so young to have it, and you're right to forget the past. There's never any sense dwelling on what might have been. You've found yourself a good man, be sure to keep him happy. Oh, my, look at how great this looks on me!"

I stifled a laugh. She was actually going to pretend she had never tried it on a thousand times when she took it from me.

"It fits you perfectly."

"Yes, yes, it does," she continued to smile and stare at it until I finally touched her arm.

"Okay, well, you enjoy it, Mom. Everyone is almost gone. Phil and I are going to head to our hotel soon."

"Oh, yes, of course!" She broke her gaze momentarily to notice me, her child, the bride. Smiling, she placed her hand on top of mine.

"Thank you, Hazel. I will take excellent care of it. You go on, I'm going to clean these up, and I'll be down to say good-night in just a few minutes." She reached across the bed and began to scoop up the photos, brief snapshots of her once happy past, and pack them away into their box. Glimpsing at the bracelet for the last time, I silently said good-bye to Teddy and my own past, hoping for good this time.

21

DOUBT

CHICAGO, ILLINOIS 1997

"Phil!" I squealed, my voice echoing into the cavernous three-story brownstone on Halsted Street in an affluent Chicago neighborhood, Lincoln Park. "Three-thousand square feet? It's so big!"

A perma-grin had been stuck to my face from the moment we breezed up the steps and into the spacious dwelling. It was gorgeous. The floors looked as if a mass of forest had been sliced up and spread throughout the house. They were peppered with intricate inlay designs. Ceilings soared above, my voice echoing with every exclamation I made. The kitchen, dining, and living rooms converged seamlessly to construct a feeling of unity.

My mind rearranged furniture we didn't own yet like chess pieces. I placed couches and overstuffed chairs and lamps to face the fireplace, my favorite feature in the living room. I fantasized about snuggling up with Phil on the couch, wrapped in a plush blanket, light and heat roaring around us while I lay in his arms.

"Hazel?"

Phil and the real estate agent, Mandi, a perky blonde with huge breasts, were staring at me.

"Oh, sorry," I smiled. "What was the question?"

Phil chuckled and touched my arm. "I said, we will fill this place up with furniture, no problem, I'm sure. Are you ready to see the rest?"

"Yes! It's just so beautiful . . . I got lost for a minute."

"It's quite alright!" Mandi chirped, writing on her clipboard. "I can't blame you. It's a fantastic place, in a fabulous location. Now, let me show you the upstairs!"

We trailed behind Mandi through the rest of the brownstone: three bedrooms, two-and-a half bathrooms, and an attached two-car garage.

"This third room is just perfect for a nursery!" Mandi gushed. "And just look at the light that pours through these windows! Any child would love this room!"

Phil and I exchanged glances.

"Well," Phil said, "it will be my office for right now. Kids are a ways off."

"Oh! Of course! I completely understand. My husband and I feel the same way. No need to be like our parents who all had kids at eighteen, right?"

"Right, yes," Phil said, changing the subject, "let's take a look at that garage."

～

We moved into the brownstone on a drizzly, chilly March day. I watched as Phil, his friends Jack and Rich, his father, and some of his employees unloaded the U-Haul and carried boxes up and down the stairs, each of them saturated from rain and sweat.

Most of the belongings were Phil's. We had been living together at his bachelor pad, and I didn't have much at Isabel's, just clothes, books, and records. I cringed at his overstuffed couch with big, rolled arms, and ugly hand-me-down lamps from his mother. He promised a shopping trip for new pieces when we were settled.

"Well, at least he has furniture." Isabel said, her eyes scanning the room. She was here to help me unpack and begin organizing.

"I know, right?" I sipped on a Heineken. Phil and I put our honeymoon off to save money, and now, getting out of his cramped apartment into this fresh space was another positive step in our marriage.

The sidewalks below had a constant flow of life. Women hurriedly pushed strollers and popped in and out of the boutiques that lined Halsted Street. Men strode by briskly, with briefcases in hand, and runners jogged by with sprinkles of rain dotting their T-shirts. I smiled, excited to lace up my own running shoes soon.

And the dogs. Great numbers of people walked their dogs, congregated with other dogs and their owners, and scooped up poop with plastic bags, leaving sidewalk smears behind.

"So, do you think it's a requirement here to have babies, shop at those fucking expensive stores, and get a dog?" I frowned at my sister and chewed at a cuticle.

"Fuck no. But you are now living in the snottiest neighborhood in Chicago. Those people down there are loaded. You are now too, I suppose. But, please, do not get a dog. You are a cat person. You have to walk dogs and pick up their shit all the time. Remember how hard it was for you to even clean Coconut's litter box?"

Poor Coconut. He was so old now, and he spent most of his time sleeping in the garden. I dreaded the day he would die.

"I was a kid, Isabel! What do you expect?" I laughed.

"That's true," she said, smiling, and grabbed another beer from the fridge.

"Well," she held up her beer bottle, "cheers to your new fancy lifestyle! I hope Phil and this place are everything you dreamed of and more!"

"Thanks, sis." We clinked bottles and smiled. She was growing her hair out a little, into a short blonde bob cut, punctuated with streaks of purple. Her nose was pierced, and she was dating a girl named Roxanne, whom I hadn't met.

"And, thanks for all your help, Izzy, really. You let me stay at your place, helped me move, and I would never have met Phil if we weren't working together and now, look at me! I managed to get a good guy, I love my job, and I think a great life is ahead of me."

I gathered her in my arms, and squeezed tight.

"You're welcome, Hazel. I'm glad you found your guy. You do have a great life ahead of you! Congratulations, sis."

～

M y stomach churned one afternoon when I came home to find Phil at the dining room table covered in maps, highlighters, and notepads. The déjà vu sucked the air from me, and I touched the kitchen countertop to keep my knees from buckling.

"Wanna plan the honeymoon, honey?" he said grinning.

I exhaled relief. The maps and highlighters and notes all involved me this time.

"Paris?" I said, nodding.

"I had a hunch that's what my bride would say," he said, and handed me the pamphlet.

Paris. Fantasies of eating baguettes and sipping espressos at little outdoor cafés and riding through the streets on bicycles had been building since Teddy had mentioned Europe years ago.

I could see that the maps were all of places in France. Now was my chance to go with Phil to erase those fantasies of Teddy and me, and replace them with real moments—with my husband.

I cried the night we arrived. Paris was so romantic, breathtaking. We had dinner on a charming houseboat restaurant, La Nouvelle Seine, on the Seine River, which had a view of Notre Dame cathedral. As the tears of unexpected bliss spilled, Phil kissed them tenderly and told me how much he loved me. All of my senses and every nerve ending in my body buzzed with pleasure.

Paris marked the beginning of our adventures. Since we both had autonomy with our jobs, we could explore the world. For the next year, we traveled. I soaked in every culture and language and nuance of each place we went: the flavors and architecture of Italy; the pubs, fashion, and royalty of London; the stunning countryside beneath the Alps of Switzerland, along with melt-in-your-mouth chocolate and cheese; and then there was Spain.

I was extremely anxious about going there, thanks to Teddy and his postcard. But, once we soaked in the sun on the gorgeous beaches, stuffed ourselves with jamón ibérico, plates of tapas, and tempranillo wine, I forgot all about him.

The vivid colors, the bluest seas, the majestic mountains. The decadent food and wine, the crisp air, the trains, the planes; I was living an opulent lifestyle, and I was invigorated every time we treaded new soil. I was so grateful for my amazing husband. He was thoughtful, generous, funny, sexy, and adventurous. I couldn't believe he was mine.

Did I really deserve him?

I would never make the same mistake again. Would I? The shame of giving in to Teddy for a second time and betraying Nick permeated every follicle of my skin. I tried to convince myself I was just a kid, but the truth was, what if Teddy showed up at my front door? No. I was a good wife, attentive and caring; the opposite of my mother. Her ongoing behavior towards my father had been unacceptable, and he deserved better. There would be no repeating of her behavior; I would break the cycle.

～

Nearly four years into our marriage, we began the baby discussion. I knew he wouldn't want to wait forever. I was terrified. The maternal instinct to have children was an apparition, appearing during happy times, and then disappearing during times of sadness. It was an incredibly hard decision. My childhood landscape—filled with a neglectful mother, a passive father, and the scars from Teddy—gave me little confidence that I could handle children.

"I'm just so scared, Phil," I told him, during one of our talks.

"I know, babe. It's a very scary thing for everyone."

"No, it's different for me. You know, my mother, she—"

"—Oh, I know. She's, well, Joanne. And—in your words—she wasn't the best mom growing up."

"Exactly. She's just so self-absorbed and was never there when I needed her, especially for the important stuff. I couldn't go to her for anything, really. I don't want to be like her. I can't, I just can't," tears trickled down my cheeks.

"Oh, honey," he pulled me close. "Trust me on this, you could *never* be like Joanne. You are nothing like her, I promise you."

"Well, thank you. But, even so, that doesn't mean I'll be a good mom. It's not like I've been around kids much. I've never even changed a diaper!"

"Oh, Hazel," he laughed and squeezed me tighter, "neither have I! Books and classes can teach us the fundamentals. You have so much love to give. You're probably more patient than me, and regardless of how you were parented, you're stable."

Stable. If only he knew my past transgressions.

"Listen," he continued, "I don't want to pressure you. But I wouldn't even think of having kids with you if I thought you were going to be a 'bad' mom, as you put it."

"You said kids, plural. Just exactly how many is that?" I thought about childbirth and clutched my stomach.

"Two at the most," he chuckled. "Growing up as an only child, I was lonely. I would love for our first child to have a sibling."

"Well, you know, just because you have a sibling, doesn't mean they like each other. Look at me and—"

"—Hazel," he put his hand in mine, "why don't you think about it? No pressure. Whatever you decide, I will support you."

"Really?" I paused. "I'm not used to having support when I need it most."

"Well, you have it in me. You're a great, loving person and a great wife. You'll have no doubts coming from me. I love you."

He kissed my hand and I kissed his cheek tenderly.

"Thank you, I love you too."

～

"So, what should I do?" I asked Harper.

"Tell me exactly what he said and what you're thinking."

She took a bite of her chicken flatbread and washed it down with ice tea.

Harper was in town, a trip planned weeks ago, but yet perfect timing. We sat on the sidewalk patio of an Italian restaurant a few blocks from my house. It was a beautiful Chicago summer Saturday, hot, humid, and teeming with people.

"Well, he's leaving it up to me, but I don't want to disappoint him if I say no."

"Yeah, I mean, he would be disappointed. But, that's not the point. There's no sense in having a baby if you think you'd be miserable. He wouldn't want that."

Lately, every parent and child caught my eye. Strollers passed by, and Harper smiled and cooed at each chubby little face. A family of four were window shopping across the street, and the father had his son perched on his shoulders, bouncing him up and down. Phil would be a great dad; I knew that for sure.

I thought about my family. Joanne, always pre-occupied with herself, skirting her responsibilities and building a wall between us. Isabel, innocently ignorant of what I was doing with her boyfriend, our own walls stacked high from a silent betrayal. And, my father, in his blind love for us, clueless to the chaos around him, busying himself with work and his garden. A sad portrait of a broken family devoid of communication, trust, and respect. I could not and would not have that kind of family. I vowed to do better.

"Don't you think I'm too young to be a mom?" I shoved a forkful of Caesar salad into my mouth.

"Absolutely not. You don't want to be an old mom. It's fucking hard work, Hazel, I'm not going to sugarcoat it. You want to have the energy to play with them. I have a six- and three-year-old! I could never do it if I was like forty or something."

"Yeah, I guess you have a point. What about sleeping? I love my sleep."

"Ha!" she laughed. "Forget about sleep for a while. Everybody loves sleep. You have to sacrifice things to be a mom. You can nap, make Phil take over sometimes."

"Sacrifice," I scoffed. "Something my mom didn't do," I said sipping my water.

"Well, yeah, that would make you different than Joanne. Shit, *any* sacrifice would make you a better mom. You are not her."

"No kidding."

A child inside the restaurant wailed at the top of its lungs. The mother quickly picked him up from the highchair and rocked him, his head to her shoulder.

"What about travel? I can't imagine that's easy with kids."

"God, no," she rolled her eyes, "you can forgo that for the first year, maybe two. But, shit, Hazel, you guys have been all over Europe already. Another temporary sacrifice. Travel will always be there. They're better as they get older, of course."

"Okay, then," I sighed and picked at my salad, "tell me *why* I should do it. So far—"

"Hazel, it's the greatest love you will ever know. The minute they are born, they are yours, and you have a fierceness to protect them from that day forward. Their smiles, their smell, the way they look at you like you are the only person in the world . . ." she trailed off, a smile on her face.

Inside, the little boy was back in his highchair, smashing a crayon onto the tray.

"What's giving birth like?"

"Fucking passing a goddamn watermelon through your vagina. It fucking hurts!"

"God," I moaned. "Also, I don't think I can eat watermelon again."

She laughed and took another bite. "Well, I'm not gonna lie to you about that!"

"You really think I would be a good mom?"

She put her fork down and put her hand on top of mine.

"I do."

"Okay, then," I held up my water glass, "let's cheers to Mommy Hazel then."

"Yes!" she squealed. She clinked my glass and we hugged.

"You're going to be great! Mommy Hazel!"

~

P hil was ecstatic. He twirled me around and showered me with kisses and hugs. He sent flowers to Harper, a thank-you gift for her timely encouragement.

"Okay, I'm flushing the little guys tonight," I told Phil as he put his jacket on.

"Wait, tonight? I have to go through some papers with Dad at work. I wanted to be here to say good-bye to them!"

"Don't be silly," I laughed. "I will tell them good-bye on your behalf. A quick flushing, and they won't know what hit them."

"Alright," he zipped up his coat, "but, reassure them we will need them again in the future."

"Don't worry, I will. I'm not having seven kids!

"I love you," he leaned in and kissed me. "This is just the beginning. Great things to come!"

I went into our bathroom with a bottle of Chardonnay. I poured myself a glass and took out my packet of birth control pills. This would be the end of my freedom. I took a sip. I would answer to a small human being that needed me more than anyone has needed me. Another sip.

Maybe it would be good to nurture a vulnerable being. Maybe the neediness of a child would help my past fade away. *There was no reason why I couldn't be a better mother than my own, right?* My father would be so proud, he would see how I didn't let my mother affect how I raised my children. Another gulp. They would be loved and cared for. I wouldn't hide in my bedroom, sulking. There would be no wild mood swings. I would never embarrass my children the way she did to us.

Could I really do this?

Phil will be an amazing father.

Yes. Yes, I can do this!

I drained my glass and opened the toilet lid. One by one, I

pushed the tiny little baby-blockers through their silver foil and watched them plop into the water.

I flushed the toilet, and in an instant, they were gone.

~

Phil and I were in the kitchen with a bottle of Château Mouton Rothschild Bordeaux. We each held a glass of this ridiculously priced wine and stared at the stick.

I reminded myself to breathe.

We glanced at each other nervously, taking sips of wine and staring at the lines of pink to appear on the stick.

"It's okay, Hazel, if it doesn't happen. You know that, right?"

He was looking at the stick.

He was being sweet, but I knew he really wanted a positive test.

"Yeah," I nodded, "I do."

"If it's meant to be, it's meant to be."

I put my glass down and rubbed his back, not sure who I was trying to reassure.

His eyes grew big, and he bent in closer to stare down at the stick. "Oh my God! Hazel, look! I think there's two!"

There they were. Two little pink lines. I felt the blood drain from my face.

"Are you sure?"

There was no mistaking it. I was going to be a mother.

"Yes, yes!" He picked me up and twirled me around the kitchen. "I mean, we'll have to get blood tests done at the doctor's to make sure, but this is good enough for me!" His entire body was a rubber band of excitement.

He picked up our glasses, handing me mine.

"Okay, this is the last wine you'll be able to drink for a while, so just a couple sips for you tonight. Let's have a toast!"

Shit. I had completely forgotten I wouldn't be able to drink for a year.

"Right!" I said, and stared sorrowfully into my glass.

"Here's to our new family, Hazel! We're going to be parents! I will be by your side through all of it. The classes, the doctors' appointments, the delivery room, every tear, every laugh, every moment. We are going to be amazing parents. I love you so much! Here's to us, baby."

"To us!"

We clinked glasses, took a sip, him never taking his eyes off me, and then he pulled me close and kissed me gently. "This really is the best news. I am so excited to start a family with you, Hazel."

"Me too. I'm scared, but it will be great. I love you."

He hugged me, burrowing his face into my neck. I stared at the stick, now resting next to the stove and slowly exhaled. I was twenty-seven years old, and pregnant.

22

NURTURE

CHICAGO, ILLINOIS 2002

The toilet smelled like yesterday's puke. I heaved again, strands of my hair falling in my face, and waited. Nothing. Just ropes of snot stretching towards the bowl.

"Shit."

I dragged myself up, my rotund belly scraping the toilet, and flushed.

Day eighty-five of morning sickness.

I swiped a Kleenex and blew my nose, catching a glimpse in the mirror—dark circles ringed my eyes, my skin sallow. My hair—which my stylist cut into a short, shaggy bob for ease—was dirty and matted. I hadn't showered in two days.

"Mommy! Mommy! I *need* you!"

I sighed. It never ended.

"Coming, honey," I yelled, and stood sideways. I was huge, like my first pregnancy. Baby number two was growing fast, and I was strangely shocked to feel a new transformation happening inside, stretching my skin and pushing at me, trying to escape.

"Now, Mommy!"

His hands beat on the door. I opened it to my little man, red in the face, filled with frustration.

"Yes, Mitchell?"

The pint-sized version of Phil and my father, with sandy-brown hair and blue eyes, was grabbing at my shirt with tiny, sticky hands and hopping on his feet, the signal that he wanted to be picked up.

"No, honey. I told you, you're too heavy for mommy right now. We have to be careful not to hurt the baby, remember?"

"But, *I'm* the baby!"

I squatted awkwardly down to his level.

"I know, but you are also a big boy! You'll be in preschool soon, remember? Only big boys go to preschool!"

"I don't want to go to *preschool.*"

I stood up and gently led him out of the bathroom.

"Sure you do! You're going to love preschool, I promise. Now, why don't you go color while I make you some noodles?"

"Noodles!" he grinned and took off to the living room, where the *Mighty Morphin Power Rangers* blared from the TV.

Unlike my mother who didn't allow us to watch much television, I welcomed the built-in babysitter. It allowed me to do things like laundry and clean and sometimes, if I was lucky, take a shower.

Motherhood had hit me like a tsunami. I didn't know what to expect, but certainly, it was harder than I imagined. The relentless lack of sleep, changing what seemed like ten thousand diapers a day, cleaning spit-up from my robe, the hours of crying (both me and Mitchell,) and sheer exhaustion. I missed my freedom.

Harper had been right, though. The second the nurse placed Mitchell in my arms, I became overwhelmed with emotion. This tiny little person, who had been rolling around in me for nine months, kicking me, making me throw up, causing crazy hormonal swings, was perfect.

His face was scrunched up angrily at being seized from my warm womb, but then, a calm washed over him, and he made quiet little grunting sounds.

I instantly felt fiercely protective of him. I didn't want the nurse to take him away. Phil stroked his face and kissed my cheek with tears in his eyes.

Did my mother not feel this flood of love for me and Isabel at our births? What was in her DNA that pulled her from us instead of propelling her forward into deep, unconditional love? Did she feel it at first but became overwhelmed and was able to turn it off?

A feeling of relief came. I was not like her. These were not fleeting feelings that I would ever lose contact with. This boy was my flesh and blood, encompassing all the goodness that was me and Phil. As I gazed into Mitchell's eyes, he curled tiny fingers around mine, cementing our bond, and I knew I would break the cycle.

Everything he did was amazing and brand new and adorable. I didn't even mind the lack of sleep, initially. Even in the middle of the night, scooping up his little body, beet red from crying, I just smiled and cooed and tried feeding or calming this perfect little specimen with tiny little fingers and toes and a light smattering of hair. At times, I couldn't stop kissing his face.

Phil was a remarkable father, as I expected. When he wasn't at work, he was hands on with Mitchell. He often relieved me from baby duty, and I carried a glass of wine into a hot bath, reveling in the soapy bubbles and heat and the pure privacy.

Childbirth was excruciating. Phil was by my side, holding my hand as I gripped it with enough force to break bones, kissing my forehead and bringing me ice chips. The image of a watermelon squeezing out of me, made me simultaneously laugh and cry.

My mother and father arrived in Chicago the day before, anxious to meet my son. Isabel was a natural, begging to hold him, smothering him with kisses. She excitedly agreed to be Mitchell's godmother.

My father glowed with joy as Mitchell's fist curled around his thumb. He held onto the baby with ease and rocked him, cooing and singing nursery rhymes.

"I'm so proud of you, Hazelnut," he said, never taking his eyes off Mitchell. "Just look at this little guy!"

Joanne—fighting aging with overdone makeup and a stylish new haircut—was surprisingly docile with Mitchell. She didn't make her usual large gestures or project her booming voice. She was simply hypnotized by her new grandson, smiling when he made little grunting noises and bobbed his head back and forth. This was a side of her that I had not seen before.

Of course, she insisted she would not be called Grandma or Grandmother or Nana or anything else that indicated an elderly woman.

"Mitchell may call me JoJo, I've decided," she stated, as she rubbed an age spot on her left hand.

Isabel and I exchanged glances and smirked; Mavis Flowers would be pleased.

Lolly and Oscar flew in to see their great-grandson, and Elizabeth sent me a beautiful silver Tiffany baby spoon and fork set with a note:

Dearest Hazel & Philip,

Congratulations on the birth of your first child! I hope to meet him someday. In the meantime, here is a set of first silverware to nourish little Mitchell's soul.

Best,

Elizabeth.

"I can't believe you have a kid!" Isabel kept saying, shaking her head.

She was thirty-four now and in a relationship with a woman named Adele who was in advertising. They met a year ago when Isabel catered Adele's company Christmas party. We thought it was both bizarre and awesome that we had met our other halves at Christmas parties catered by Isabel and Abbey.

My sister relished being an aunt. She would stop by often, showering Mitchell with gifts—stuffed giraffes and elephants, tiny boots that resembled Doc Martens and OshKosh overalls. His closet was stuffed with clothes, and the pile of toys he was gifted could have filled an entire Toys R Us aisle.

But, then, the bliss of fawning over a newborn faded. At a year old, Mitchell began to walk, and eventually run around the house, then fall, and then the crying began. Howling that lasted far beyond reasonable. At times, he was inconsolable. No amount of hugging or kissing his invisible boo-boos could pacify him.

"No!" was his favorite word. He put tiny objects in his mouth. I had to call 911 twice, after I managed to fish out the LEGO pieces, and was scolded by operators to not let him have tiny toys. They made me feel like a bad mother.

"No! Don't want it!" when I offered him yogurt, pureed vegetables or sliced fruit. He only wanted rice and bread and Goldfish crackers. He threw tantrums and screamed until I finally gave into his carb addiction.

Phil read books on parenting during his lunch hour, trying to problem solve what was, just normal.

"It's so frustrating. Some books say don't give in, others want us to comfort him and talk to him," he would say, scanning the words of our most recent book.

"I know," I sighed, "why isn't there just one big master manual?"

We tried both ways. Depending on the day and Mitchell's moods, they both worked, or neither worked.

"Just chill out," Isabel would say, as she held him, bouncing him on her lap. "This is what babies do. Just wait until he's two, the teenage phase of toddlers."

"Gee, thanks. How do you know so much about babies?"

"Uh, who do you think took care of you half the time as a kid?"

"Oh, right," I said..

Mitchell did calm down eventually. He shadowed me in the kitchen when I attempted new desserts. He pounded his fists in flour, banged on steel bowls, and crammed cookie dough in his mouth. We both laughed and laughed as he chased me around, slapping his little flour-filled hands on the back of my jeans, leaving lasting impressions. He thought that was hilarious, and I agreed.

"I see my son is taking after his old man, a butt guy!" Phil would grin when he saw Mitchell's handiwork on my backside.

"Indeed," I smiled.

At two years old, he could be trying, but in general, we were surprisingly evading what many parents called a nightmare. Mitchell and I went to the park daily. He made "Vroom, vroom" sounds in his stroller as we whizzed by trees and people.

We played in the sandbox, slid down slides, played hide-and-seek behind trees, and rolled in the grass. Mitchell loved hugs. He wanted to hug dogs, cats, even furniture. He was sweet and kind. It was surreal, having this experience with my child.

My mother had bored quickly with playtime when we were kids. Isabel and I learned to entertain ourselves and stick together. This bond I had with Mitchell was unexpected, and the love I felt for him was an emotion I had never experienced before.

I had bad days too. Depression washed over me on days that Mitchell wouldn't behave and I was so exhausted, I just wanted solitude. I empathized with my mother in those moments, wishing to retreat from my child.

Whenever I lamented to my mother about Mitchell, she said it was because boys are so different and more demanding than girls, that they have endless energy and want to smash things constantly.

"Which is why," she said one day over the phone, "I was so relieved when I had two girls. I don't know how you do it, Hazel, but you've got your hands full."

As usual, she was so helpful.

But then, I would see Mitchell, sprawled out, gently petting our cat, Sylvia Plath, and whispering to her. My sweet little boy. Life without him would be colorless.

Now, we were having a girl. Phil was ecstatic. I felt ready this time. I couldn't wait to dress her up, put bows in her hair, and be her best friend.

I strained the noodles and plopped a pad of butter on top.

"Noodles?" Mitchell asked, peeking over the couch.

"Yes, my big boy! Noodles!"

I rubbed my belly. My daughter would be here in six months. I thought about that day at the park with Teddy. The little girl who fell at the bottom of the slide, only to be scooped up by her mother. Her protector. That was me.

23

CRUMBLE

ANN ARBOR, MICHIGAN 2005

T he roads were clear at least. Mounds of heavy snow piled high on either side of I-94, and the bare branches of trees swayed wildly from the bitter wind.

"Snooooow, Mama!" babbled Madeline behind me.

I glanced in my rearview mirror. A shock of her blonde hair stuck straight up and was donned with a red-and-white polka-dot bow. I couldn't see her face in her rear-facing car seat, but I knew she was smiling.

"I know, honey! Lots of snow!"

I felt secure snuggled in our Ford Explorer, gunning along the stretch of highway and headed to Michigan with my two-year-old in tow.

Harper needed me. Her marriage to Steve was a complete mess. She had sobbed over the phone, begging me to come home and help her figure out her next move. He had cheated on her with a bartender from a local bar he frequented. Harper said she might have forgiven him had it been a one-night stand, but apparently, it had been a full-on affair, and Steve claimed he was in love with the woman.

My heart ached for her. Never had she been cheated on or

humiliated so deeply. They had been so in love in high school and through the first decade of their marriage, but after he began losing interest in his computer software job three years ago, he spiraled into an early midlife crisis. He was only thirty-four, but he had been working for the same company since high school and was bored.

Between depression and drinking, he slowly turned into a lousy husband. He was spending more and more nights at the bar with his friends and then coming home drunk and apathetic towards her. He wasn't a mean drunk; he just lost interest in Harper and doing things as a family. She overheard him on the phone with a friend lamenting that he probably got married too young.

"I swear to God, he's just staying with me because of the kids," she told me the week before, "and sure, he comes home at night, but I don't know where the fuck he's been."

"Shit, I'm so sorry. I never saw this coming from Steve," I said.

"Yeah, well, we haven't had sex in months, and now I know why!"

"How did you find out?"

"I was looking through the desk for something, and I found a credit card statement sitting right on top. I saw all these charges to the Red Roof Inn. All during the day! And a couple after two in the morning."

"Oh, Jesus."

"Yeah, the dumb fuck left the evidence just sitting there! Almost like he *wanted* to get caught."

"What an asshole. He didn't even use cash!"

"Exactly. I buy fucking groceries with that credit card! It's embarrassing. I feel like a fool. He didn't bother to even hide it."

She blew her nose and then told her kids to turn the TV down.

I was shocked. Her husband of fourteen years, her prince charming and the father of her children, was done with her.

My heart broke for her and I felt equally horrible for their two daughters, Samantha, she was twelve now going on twenty-five according to Harper, and Hannah was nine. Preteen ages were an awful age to have your parents' marriage falling apart.

"So, what did you do?"

"I flew into a rage at him, and he didn't deny it at least. He's in love with a fucking bartender. I guess the way to his heart is through his liver," she laughed bitterly.

"Shit," I didn't know what else to say.

"Then I acted like an idiot and started begging him, saying we could go to therapy; we can't throw our life together away for a fling. I tried to guilt him about the kids, but he's changed. He's not the Steve I married. He doesn't want counseling. Or me. Or the kids."

She said he packed up a few things and moved out. He didn't move in with the bartender (again, probably for the kids, she suspected) but was renting a studio apartment in Ypsilanti. I told her I would make the drive in a few days, that I would be there for her.

Madeline was babbling again, this time humming and making up songs and holding onto one of my old Barbie dolls.

"We're going to see Auntie Harper. Are you excited?"

"Yes, Mama! Auntie Harpa!" she squealed.

Harper was Madeline's godmother, and the two adored each other.

Madeline was babbling and happy, but I had a queasy feeling in my stomach. I wasn't sure how I would console my friend, considering I had cheated on Nick with Teddy. Granted, it hadn't been an affair, but my delusional love for Teddy made me a hypocrite. I turned my emotions off to Nick after that to drive him away. I could barely look at him, and eventually it worked. Steve was being stupid, the way I had been, cheating on an amazing person to pursue a twisted sort of comfort.

I looked at the clock on the dashboard, two more hours to go, and so far, Madeline had been an angel the whole time. But she had always been an easy baby. She was all joy and love from the minute she was born. She loved baths, kicking at the water, and screeching in baby laughter. As I ran the washcloth over her tiny little arms, we would lock eyes, and I knew she trusted me and felt safe.

She was my new sidekick, chasing after me while I did laundry, climbing up my legs as I sat on the couch, and she always wanted to go with me in the car, wherever I was off to.

Phil and I had completed our family. Madeline had him

wrapped around her finger, and Mitchell was four now and into cars and trucks. Phil taped out roads on the floor, built a city of blocks to drive for Mitchell to drive cars through, and even constructed ramps out of cardboard boxes.

I had come so far. I did what I had set out to do. I built a family on love and trust and had embraced motherhood. This felt natural, where I belonged. I wasn't my mother. I couldn't imagine pushing my children's lives aside to pursue whatever I thought I deserved. And Phil wasn't my father. We were in sync with so many things and made all decisions together. Mutual respect was what made a marriage work.

I left Mitchell at home with Phil to go to Michigan. He would have been bored in the car, and Harper and I had too much adult talking to do. Maddy was easy with just some animal crackers and crayons. Plus, my parents couldn't wait to see her and would watch her while I spent time with Harper.

A light snow smacked against the windshield. I hated driving in snow or rain, which was part of the reason we got the SUV; I needed to feel safe.

"Just a couple more hours, Maddy!"

Silence. I peered in the mirror again and could see her head lolled to one side, the naked Barbie upside down on her leg. My perfect, sleeping baby.

~

"I can't believe this is my life right now, Hazel!" Harper cried and blew her nose. A pile of snotty Kleenex was sprawled across her dining room table. A half-empty bottle of wine and a pack of cigarettes sat next to her. She was already drunk, and it was early afternoon.

Both of her girls were at Harper's mother's house until Sunday, and Madeline was still sleeping in her car seat.

"I can't either. I'm so pissed at him right now! I would strangle him if he were here!" I took a sip of my bottled water.

"Trust me, if I were strong enough, I would have already. I can't even look at his face. His fucking face. I just keep imagining him coming all over her and making those stupid sounds he makes."

Water spat from my mouth, and I coughed and gasped for air.

"Jesus Christ, Harper! I don't need to hear about his fucking orgasms! You almost made me choke!"

She managed a quiet chuckle and picked at her cuticles.

My poor, beautiful Harper. Her usual perfectly coiffed bouncy, curly, gleaming hair was pulled back in a matted bun. Unshowered and in sweatpants and a soiled Led Zeppelin T-shirt, her porcelain skin was ashen now. Her blue eyes were disguised by angry-red veins from a constant pool of tears.

"Sorry," she mumbled, "but I can't get the image out of my head. And it didn't happen just once. Or twice. They've been fucking for months! Could be longer, I don't even know. He's such a liar now, this could've been going on for years. I just don't know what I'm going to do. He moved out, Hazel! Like, gone. He left me alone with our kids. And do you think he has come by to talk to them about this mess at all? Fuck no! I've had to cover his ass until I think of something."

"What did you say?"

Madeline stirred in her seat, and I put my finger to my mouth to quiet Harper's ranting down.

"Sorry," she whispered, tilting her head and smiling at Maddy. "It's been so long since my girls were babies. She's so precious, Hazel. You're just so lucky to have a perfect husband and two great kids. I told the girls he's depressed and that men go through midlife crises, and it's very childish, but it happens to some men. My girls are smart. I told them he was staying at a hotel to work his shit out, and I didn't know when he was coming home. I didn't know what else to say. I couldn't tell them he was fucking a bartender. For fuck's sake, I'm lying to my kids about my lying husband."

"Yeah, well," I sighed, and glanced at Maddy again, "nothing's ever perfect, Harper. You know that."

"I know, I know, I just thought that my life would turn out like a fucking fairy tale. I was a decent kid, got pretty good grades, only did a handful of drugs and didn't drink myself to death. I married my high school sweetheart. I should be a winner! That's the fucking problem. I gave it all to him! My *life*, Hazel. Fucker didn't deserve me."

Lopsided, sparse lights lilted off a small dying Christmas tree in the corner. It was February now. Some of the lights blinked, others did not.

"No, he doesn't!" I said, placing my hand on hers, "But, you've had over a decade of great years with him and two beautiful girls! Can you imagine your life without them?"

"Of course not," she said, and began pacing around the kitchen. "I just wish—oh, fuck, I don't know what the fuck I wish. I wish my husband wasn't an asshole."

"Are you thinking about divorce?" I asked, afraid of the answer. Her girls were both at that age of extreme vulnerability—especially Samantha—where any small event could change the course of their lives. The way Teddy had pulled me in and spoiled my childhood, making me feel grown up and sexy with some version of love that no child needed to experience at that age.

Harper looked around the house, her eyes settling on a framed photo of her and Steve and the girls at Cedar Point years ago.

"I mean, probably. What choice do I have? He doesn't want this life anymore. He wants to keep banging that slut. He actually told me he feels alive again! *Alive?* I'm so sorry that while he was out working every day with *grown-ups* and going out to lunch at restaurants, I stayed home to care for his kids and do his laundry and make him dinner, that he somehow *died* inside." She stomped over to the patio door and cracked it open.

An abrupt blast of cold air blew through the kitchen. She lit a cigarette and leaned against the door jamb.

She shook another one from the pack and held it out to me. I hadn't smoked in years. But maybe just this once, a solidarity cigarette to show support for my best friend.

"I'm so sorry, Harper," I said, and then, with my mouth formed in an "O," I blew out a perfectly round smoke ring. I still had the skill that took us weeks to perfect. The cigarette was delicious, and I closed my eyes for a second. "What can I do for you while I'm here?

Do you want me to take the girls out for a while so you can rest or take a bath or burn his clothes?"

"Ha! I already threw his clothes out the window the day I found out. Not a stitch of any of his shit in the closet anymore. That bitch can do his laundry now," she paused. "Nice smoke ring! No, I just need you here as a friend. My mom can take the kids whenever I need her to. I need a girls' night out, I think. Maybe we could go get some dinner and get shitty drunk and talk about old times? I could use some laughs right now."

"Sure, that sounds like a great idea. I'll take Maddy to my parents and pick you up around six?"

"Yes, please!" she smiled weakly and gave me a hug. "Thank you for coming, Hazel. I don't know what I would do without you."

⁓

"**W**hat a bastard!" my mother exclaimed, while yanking dresses and blouses from her closet and throwing them onto her bed. "That poor girl. She's always been so sweet, that one. It just figures that this would happen. When you get married out of school and don't take time to date around, men start to get the itch. They get older and wonder 'what did I do? I missed out on screwing so many girls!' and then they get bored and then they cheat."

I furrowed my brow at her and sipped on my cup of tea.

"Well, that's a great viewpoint, Mother, and I'm sure you don't know any of this from personal experience, so where is all this bitterness coming from? And, could you watch the language?"

Maddy was running around the room with two naked Barbies in her hands flying them like airplanes.

My mother glanced at her grandchild across the room and rolled her eyes.

"Language? I said *screwing*, Hazel. That precious little girl has no idea what that even means. And, well, *bastard* is a word she should get to know, in all honesty. You worry so much." She plucked a dark-blue dress up from the bed and held it up to her in front of her full-length mirror. "And anyway, that's just how high school sweethearts end up usually. Too much time together and not enough rolling around with other lovers. What do you think of this one?"

Lovers. The way it rolled off her tongue made my skin crawl. I didn't need to imagine my mother being a lover to anyone, even my dad. I let the bastard comment go. I would not get into it with her today.

"It's nice. What is all this mess going on? Where are you going?"

"Oh! Your father and I are going out to dinner on Monday night to a new restaurant in town, and I'm trying to figure out what to wear."

She continued to skim through the clothing on the bed and started humming. I sat down on her bed and wrapped my tea-bag string around twice and placed it on the saucer on the dresser.

I watched her glide from her closet to the mirror, holding up more dresses. She was sixty-six years old now and aging rather nicely. Tiny creases around her eyes and shallow grooves along her forehead displayed the fortunes of her regimented skincare routine. Her hair was still a flame of red, but a small stripe of gray peeked from her roots and around her hairline. She was slimmer too. I wondered which crazy diet she was on now.

Maddy dashed across the room to me with both dolls above her head, yelping and making "zooming" noises, and slammed into my knees, giggling.

"You're so cute, you little weirdo," I said, as I bent down to kiss the top of her head. I stood back up and turned to my mother.

"It's only Friday, and you're shopping your closet for Monday night? You and Dad are going out to dinner? And with friends? That's something new!"

She frowned at me through the mirror as she held up a red blouse that clashed with her auburn hair. "Actually, Hazel, it's not. Things have changed a lot around here. Your father and I are spending a lot more time together. It's quite nice."

A sly grin slipped across her face, and I couldn't help but smile.

"Really? Wow, that's good to hear. I'm so happy for you guys!"

"Well, we've been living the 'empty nesters' life for a long time now. We try our best to get along more. You girls took up a lot of time and energy of course, as children do, and marriages often fall apart from that. We've been trying to get back to the way we were when we were first dating. Silly, I know. And, I think having beautiful grandbabies has softened us both."

I could hardly believe my mother's words.

Had she really changed? Softened?

I bit my tongue about the "time and energy" it took to raise us. I would not spoil the moment. She was actually giddy over having dinner with my father.

"Well, that's great, Mom. I'm really happy for you, honestly," I glanced down at Maddy who was now pulling at my shirt. I knew that signal; she was getting bored. "You can still watch her tonight though, right? While I go to dinner with Harper?"

My mother came over and scooped up Maddy and placed her on her hip. It was always strange to see my mother being motherly.

"Of course, dear. Go, go help Harper out. You know, you got so lucky with Phil. Things could be so much worse. Thankfully, it's not you going through this. I'm glad she has you to comfort her. Unfortunately, comfort only comes from knowing pain in the first place."

~

I found my father in the garage, breathing heavily, red faced, as he pulled the snowblower inside. Space heaters hummed around the corners of the room.

"Hi, Dad!" I gave him a hug; his jacket was stiff and felt like cardboard. He had waved to me when I first pulled in the driveway, but this was my first conversation with him since I arrived.

"Hey there, kiddo," he said, while starting to unravel his scarf and remove his gloves. "How are you doing? Did you find your mother?"

"Yes, I sure did. She is upstairs trying on dresses because apparently the two of you are going on a *date* Monday?" I said, with wide eyes.

"Oh, yeah, we've been doing that lately." He looked away, like an embarrassed teenager, and pushed the snowblower to a corner in the garage.

"Well, I think it's very sweet and about time! Things have always just been so . . ."

"Difficult?" he said, smiling.

"Yes, difficult."

"Well, your mother has been doing yoga again and meditating and apparently 'finding herself' and realizes that she hasn't been the best wife—her words, not mine—and she says she wants to make it up to me. So far, it's been a good few months."

"Wow. So, no crazy mood swings?"

"Don't tell her I told you this—she would kill me—but she's also been going to a therapist, and she's taking some medication. Hazel, she's like a different person."

"What?" I was astonished.

My mother became self-aware? A therapist? She always said therapy was for the weak. And medication?

"Now, don't get me wrong, she still has her moments, and nobody's perfect—nobody. But it's been a really big improvement. Although," he bent down and brushed snow from his boots, "I think sometimes whatever they gave her makes her kind of loopy too. But you know what? Loopy is better than moody, right?"

He laughed, and I rubbed my arms to keep warm.

"I guess so. But you don't know what she's taking?"

"She told me in the beginning, but I can't remember the name offhand. Hey, hand me that broom, would you?"

I wasn't sure if my mother taking prescription drugs was such a great idea, but it didn't seem to faze my father, so for the moment I let it go. I was here to help Harper. I couldn't take time from Harper this weekend to see if she had a pill-popping problem.

"Um," I handed him the broom, "well, I need to get over to Harper's. We're going to dinner, and Maddy's up with Mom. Don't overdo it on the snow blowing, okay, Dad?"

"Don't worry about me, honey, I'm fine. I'm all done, for now. Might snow again later. It's not that hard to push that thing, and it's a lot easier than shoveling. Be careful driving out there, okay? And, give Harper my best. I hope she and her husband can find a way to fix this. It's a shame."

"Me too, Dad," I smiled, and shut the door behind me.

~

Harper and I sat in a booth tucked away in a corner of Cottage Inn, a famous pizza place downtown Ann Arbor that originated in 1948. It had the feel of an Italian courtyard. Exposed brick remained on some of the walls, and leading up the stairway was a painted mural of intertwined grapes and leaves. It was a cozy place, and the pizza was awesome.

Harper had cleaned herself up; the sweatpants were gone, replaced by jeans and a low-cut black top. Her blond curls were clean again and cascaded around her shoulders. Her makeup was done, and dangly gold earrings hung from her ears. She sipped on red wine and I had a gin and tonic while we waited for our salad and pizza.

"What's with the slutty top?" I asked, grinning.

She looked down at her boobs.

"What, these old things? Hmph. I figure if my husband can go out and get laid, so can I!"

"Good God," I said, rolling my eyes "You are not getting laid tonight! You are hanging out with me, and also, that is not going to solve anything."

She jutted her bottom lip out into a pout.

"How about the fact that I haven't had sex in months? How is *that* fair?"

"Harper, this is serious. Having sex with a stranger is not going to make you feel better."

"Whatever," she rolled her eyes, and rolled her napkin around her fingers. "I just don't know what I'm supposed to do! If I get a divorce, I will have to start dating again, and I have no clue how to do that!"

"Well," I motioned to her shirt, "I guess that's one way to catch a guy. But, come on, we really need to talk this through."

As the salad and pizza came, we went round and round in a frustrating conversation that led to one conclusion; she was angry. She didn't want to talk about how she would approach the future, what to tell the kids, if she should file for divorce, and she still hadn't told her parents. All she wanted to do was slam Steve and the "bitch" bartender and tell me the variety of ways she would get even with them.

Her goal in high school had been to get married right after, have children, and live happily ever after. There was never a plan B. No one who gets married thinks they'll ever need one. Her coping skills for this situation were zero. I tried to pull out some real emotions from her, some sort of reality check, but she was tuning me out. Steve had moved out a month ago, and she was still in revenge and anger mode.

The melty, gooey comforting pizza was also lost on Harper. She was eating and drinking rapidly, in between complaints and moaning, while I silently savored every bite.

I felt pangs of guilt for my successful marriage while Harper was borderline hysterical, blowing her nose and gulping down beer and swearing loudly in the restaurant. I suggested we go to a bar. At least she could be angry and yell obscenities there without turning heads. We decided on Red Hawk on State Street. It was a bar-slash-restaurant and had a long wooden bar that was always lively and filled with people.

It was a quick walk there, both of us smoking a cigarette on the way. It was freezing outside, and my fingers went numb as I puffed on it. There were spots on the sidewalks that were slick with black ice, and we looped our arms together to keep from falling.

We grabbed a couple seats at the bar, and as usual, it was noisy and a perfect spot for Harper to vent and my last chance to try to get through to her.

"Shit," she said, rummaging through her purse.

"What?"

"I thought I had more smokes. We just smoked the last two," she frowned and kept digging.

"We *just* had one, Harper, Jesus. I thought you quit smoking anyway?"

"Hazel, don't be ridiculous. My drinking game is on now. You know I'm going to need to smoke like every five minutes. I can't believe this. I totally thought I had another pack."

"Okay, okay," I pressed my hands on hers to make her stop. "I will go down the street to the party store and get more, alright? Just order me a gin and tonic and I'll be back in a flash."

She sighed and dropped her shoulders and smiled.

"That would be great. Thanks, babe, you're the best!"

I leaned over the bar and shouted to the bartender, "Hey, keep an eye on this one, will you? I'll be right back."

"Sure thing, Miss," he smiled, glancing from me to Harper's boobs.

"I don't *need* a babysitter!" Harper shouted at me.

"Just stay put!" I smiled and kissed her cheek and walked out of the bar and into the dark night.

24

RETURN

ANN ARBOR, MICHIGAN / CHICAGO, ILLINOIS 2005

S quashed into a soft mattress, I was entangled in a mass of sheets and blankets with a familiar odor. Faint light sifted through dirt-stained windows and cast shadows in the darkness. A radiator hissed in the corner of the room. It was a recognizable sound, but I couldn't place it.

I heard a click and a splash, and the swoosh of a toilet flushing startled me. Suddenly, glaring white light splashed across the room.

I know this place, but what is it?

I squeezed my eyes shut and put a hand up to shield them. A silhouette stood in the doorway, the orange smolder of a cigarette glowing. His face was blurred around the edges, and he stood silently.

He was naked, and it was then that I realized I was too. I yanked the covers up, horrified. He took a drag of his cigarette and threw it in the toilet. It hissed as it hit the water. He turned the light off and joined me in bed.

Pushing me back gently, his hot breath traced the outline of my neck. I moaned softly and relaxed as he peeled back the blankets and covered my body with his. He entered me. I closed my eyes and scratched my nails along his back.

"I love you," he whispered in my ear.

"I love you too."

~

Time stood still in the tiny apartment. An oversized black leather couch pressed against one wall, and a glass-top coffee table trimmed in chrome sat in front of the couch. The mattress was still on the floor. The same Patrick Nagel prints in smudgy glass frames decorated the walls, the women still flat and colorful. Even the print of the Duran Duran album cover remained, ends frayed and curling. A black halogen lamp cast a wide circular shadow on the ceiling.

How did I get here?

My head throbbed.

Why can't I remember anything? How much had I had to drink last night? Last night.

My clothes and purse were strewn on the couch. The coffee table was cluttered with bottles of beer, a bag of weed, and a vile of white powder lay near an overflowing ashtray.

"Hey, hey, look who's awake! Morning, baby girl."

Teddy was naked, holding two cups of coffee.

"Oh my God. What happened? How did I get here? And why are we in Chad's apartment?"

I sipped too fast and burned my tongue. I needed to wake up, and fast. As I set the coffee down, my diamond wedding ring set sparkled.

He sat down next to me. His penis hung limply between his legs and I turned away, blushing. Wet snow pattered against the windows, and squiggly lines trailed through the dirty panes.

"Well," he took a gulp and smiled, "we left Old Town, I drove us in your car—you were pretty drunk—and we came here. The roads were a shit show. And, then, as for this place, turns out Chad and Emily sucked at living together. She moved out, he took some manager job at a vitamin chain company, and he travels. He's got some girl in Colorado, so he's not home much. Kinda like before."

"What? Why didn't we just go to your place?"

"Too far. My place is in Ypsi, and like I said, the roads were shit."

Nothing had changed. It was sealed up like a museum of bad taste. It seemed impossible that a person would not change one thing in twenty years.

My head was throbbing again, a slow ache starting at the back of my neck and moving to the top of my skull.

How much did I drink last night?

"Did we do all those drugs?" I nodded towards the table.

"You really don't remember? You were pretty out of it," he scratched his head, "but, yeah, things got crazy last night. Crazy good."

"Oh, God, no. Fuck."

He tried to kiss my cheek, but I pulled away.

I was exhausted, physically and mentally. This place, filled with memories unraveled me. *I did not remember snorting cocaine and smoking a joint. Everything was a blur. Had he drugged me?*

Hazy images swirled in my head of his hands and tongue all over me, inside me, and music in the background. He had told me he loved me.

And, I said it back.

I glanced at the alarm clock on the floor. Nine o'clock.

"Shit!"

My parents must have been freaking out. I told them I would probably stay over at Harper's, but I never confirmed with them last night, did I?

"Teddy, I have to go." I shoved my half-empty mug into his free hand, "I have to go get my daughter and head back to Chicago. This was . . . a mistake. A terrible, terrible mistake. You know that, right? And, fuck, Harper! I came here to help her, and she left to go fuck some stranger. She could be dead for all I know."

My eyes welled with tears while I gathered my clothes together to leave.

"Aw, come on, I wanted to take you to breakfast. Don't go yet," he said, taking the mugs into the kitchen.

"Breakfast? Are you serious? Teddy! I am married! I have kids! I'm not thirteen anymore!"

"That's for sure, babe. You are *all* woman now. I mean, last night—"

"Shut up! Shut the fuck up, Teddy! You can't wreck my life yet again! I won't let you."

He chuckled at my outrage and pulled me close. He gently cupped my face and kissed me.

My knees melted.

"No, Teddy, stop it, really." I pushed him away and went to the bathroom.

With shaking hands, I pulled on my jeans, shirt and sweater, and socks. I had no clue where my underwear was, but I had no time to look.

"You sure?" he asked through the closed door.

"Yes, Teddy, I am very sure."

"This was not a mistake, you know. We still have that connection. It's even hotter now."

I avoided the mirror as I combed my fingers through my hair. The vows I made to Phil were shattered. Images of Mitchell chasing a screeching Maddy around the living room flashed in my head. I wanted to hold them, kiss them, forget this had happened.

That connection.

"Hazel, despite how you interpreted it there was no healthy connection," Diane's voice echoed inside me. *"He manipulated you into believing he had genuine feelings. And, Hazel, I know you believed they felt real, but you were too young to reciprocate."*

"But I should have known better," I had said. *"I will make sure my daughter knows better."*

"Of course you will. Times were different then. I doubt your mother would have helped, even if you had come to her. But you will be there for Maddie. You are a different mother than Joanne. Don't blame young Hazel, she had no one there for her. Together, you and I will work on forgiving that young, innocent part of you and put the blame where it truly belongs. Squarely on adult Teddy's shoulders."

Opening the door, I squeezed past him and grabbed my coat

and purse. I faced him and sighed.

"We can't have that connection anymore or ever again. This was wrong. Take care of yourself, Teddy."

I stood on my tiptoes and kissed his cheek lightly. I inhaled him and shut my eyes, momentarily.

"Okay, fine, Miss Suburbia with hubby and kids. Go on. But I have a feeling we're going to see each other again, real soon."

He pulled a cigarette from behind his ear and flipped open his Zippo. It was the same one, from 1986, with the pin-up girl.

How could that be?

I shook my head.

"Good-bye Teddy."

~

My cell phone showed three missed calls and two texts. Three calls from my mother plus one text and the other text from Harper:

Holy shit! What a fucking night! His name is Greg and he is so hot. We had sex at his place. He's divorced, just like I'm about to be 2! Don't worry, I'm home and fine. Sorry I bailed. Where did U end up?

I rolled my eyes and called my mom while the car warmed up. The windows were thick with fresh snow. I apologized for not calling. She had assumed I stayed at Harper's, and Maddy was fine, just missing her mommy. I missed her too, incredibly.

The windows defrosted, revealing the brick and windows of Chad's building. Frozen in time, yet so fresh in my memory. I could picture myself parking my bike that very first day.

~

As soon as I arrived at my parents' house, Maddy ran to me, wrapping her arms around my legs. My precious, innocent little girl already bathed and dressed, with a bow in her hair. I fought back tears as her tiny pure body pressed against mine.

I had failed her. Her big blue eyes blinked up at me in adoration, and my guilt surged as I squeezed her.

"Well, there you are!" My mother drifted from the kitchen wearing a paisley-printed caftan and a cup of tea in her hand.

"Hi, sorry, I should have called last night," I smiled weakly as Madeline's little hands clutched at clumps of my hair. "Harper is a total mess—"

"It's alright, Hazel, really," she said, waving her free hand dismissively before settling it on Maddy's back, stroking her and practically purring. "We had a wonderful time last night, didn't we?"

"Mama!" Maddy whined, squirming to get down.

I slid her down, and she took off to the living room.

"The croissants are in the kitchen, and there's still coffee," her eyes looked glazed, and I remembered that she was taking medication now, "and that poor, poor Harper. What kind of monster has an affair with a *bartender*, for God's sake, and leaves his family for her? He ought to be sterilized, that one."

New meds, same Joanne.

"Yeah, well, Steve turned out to be a real asshole. She's not great, but I did my best to distract her and just be there for her. Um, I think I'll just take a croissant and some coffee for the road. I'm already behind and should get back home to the boys."

I could barely face her. I wanted to slink into a corner and hide. I *was* Steve. I basically fucked the bartender.

But I will not leave my family for him.

"Oh, are you sure you have to go already, Hazel? I barely spoke to you this weekend. And, I know your father would like to spend a few minutes with you."

She headed back to the kitchen, and I followed, sighing deeply.

"Unfortunately, yes, it's a five-hour drive with the bathroom stops, and it's already late. Sorry, Mom, next time. Where's Dad?"

I took a bite of a croissant. No longer warm, light, flaky pieces fell to the floor.

"The usual, the garage. In the summer, it's the garden, and the winter, it's out there. Hazel, really, could you get a plate please? I can't be cleaning up after your daughter *and* you. It's just too much."

"Sorry," I grabbed a plate and poured myself some coffee and headed to the garage. "Could you just watch Maddy a bit more while I talk to Dad?"

"Of course, dear, and I'll get these crumbs for you too."

I rolled my eyes and went into the garage.

"Dad?"

"Yeah? Out here!"

He was where I found him when I first arrived, stuffed into winter gear, tinkering with the snowblower.

"Hey, kiddo!" he smiled, and put down his wrench. "Damn thing. It stopped working."

"Hi," I leaned in as he kissed my cheek. I averted my eyes and pulled away.

I must have stunk of booze, cigarettes, and sex. The imprint of Teddy's hands all over my body prickled my skin. I needed to shower and wash it all down the drain.

"Everything okay? With Harper?"

"Not really. I tried to help her, but she's really pissed right now and determined to get revenge. She's not thinking clearly. She isn't ready for my advice, or anyone's to be honest."

"That's too bad," he said, shaking his head. "Cheating is something impossible to get over, no matter how hard you try. If she can't forgive and forget, then it is best for her to move on."

"Um, right, yeah, cheating is pretty unforgiveable," I said, almost choking. "She has a lot to decide and she's far from ready. Besides, Steve seems to be in love with this girl, so the decision may be made for her. She's going to have to face it as hard as it is. I feel terrible for those poor kids."

"That's a tough situation alright. I hope she gets through it. Anyway, we had fun with Maddy. She's just like you were—spunky and funny and full of giggles. She sure loves those damn naked Barbie dolls though!"

We laughed. I loved how much my father enjoyed being a grandpa.

I finished the last bite of the croissant and washed it down with the coffee.

"I know! She's a weirdo! Well, Dad, we have to get going. I'm going to take a quick shower and then head out."

"Okay, sweetheart. Be careful driving home. It's slick and dangerous out there."

It's okay, Dad, I already went to the danger.

≈

The drive home was tortuous. The roads were fine, fully plowed and salted and Maddy slept most of the way. But, my stomach ached, and my insides were hollow and numb. *Why couldn't I remember what had happened last night?*

My head still ached. I hoped the shower would snap some recognition back to me, but nothing came. I sobbed quietly while the hot water poured down onto me.

My last recollection was going to get cigarettes for me and Harper and going to Old Town with Teddy. After that, I woke up naked, in Chad's apartment, having had sex with Teddy during the night and then woke up next to him in the morning.

I could not have been that drunk. Did he drug me? Did he rape me?

A chilling thought ran through me, something I had suppressed for years, Harper's voice under the bleachers that day:

"I hate to burst your bubble, but I don't think this is love. I'd have to ask my dad, but it kind of sounds like statutory rape. You're way underage for him to be having sex with you . . . He's what my dad would call a con artist, a smooth talker . . ."

Over the years, I ignored her words. But they were etched in my memory, and dredged up every time I thought about Teddy.

It wasn't just statutory rape; it was child molestation. Teddy had barely flinched when I said 'abuse.' Had he done this before?

I glanced in my rearview mirror to see the back of Maddy's tufted blonde hair. She would be thirteen someday. The thought of a full-grown man touching her, manipulating her and stripping her of her innocence made my skin crawl. I would definitely kill that man.

And just hours ago, I had slept with that man.

~

"So," Phil kissed me as I put my suitcase down, "how did it go? Did you save a marriage?"

Bile swelled into my throat.

"Unfortunately, no, she's beyond listening to anyone right now, even me. She wants revenge."

Maddy giggled as her big brother made funny faces, and drove trucks over her sausage-like legs. Mitchell babbled to her about how he and Dad played ball all weekend. She just laughed, as if she understood.

"That sucks, babe. I'm sorry to hear that. Cheating is tough to get over, and really, can you blame her? I'll order Chinese, and you can tell me all about it. Wine? You deserve it after this weekend."

He kissed me again. His lips were warm, safe. My husband. I smiled, so grateful for him, but now I could barely face him.

I deserved nothing. But I did need wine. Phil fished in a drawer to get the takeout menu, and I sat on the couch with my glass.

I was already numb, but now I wanted to evaporate. Closing my eyes, I took a few sips. The liquid slid down, coating the tears I had swallowed all the way home.

I wasn't ready to be a liar again. It had been so long; I had been so good. Acid churned in my stomach as I absorbed the emerging fear of being caught. I was out of practice with deceit; how could I pull it off?

My house was filled with love. Mitchell was building a LEGO castle, Madeline was *finally* dressing Barbie, and Phil smiled at me as he ordered moo shu pork. This was what I had worked so hard for. Security, trust, admiration, and unconditional love. I closed my eyes and shook my head.

What have I done? I've ruined everything.

25

UNVEIL

CHICAGO, ILLINOIS 2005

"I still can't get over the view up here," I said, sipping from a glass of red wine and staring out the window of Isabel's thirtieth-floor apartment. Sometimes I really missed living here. I bent over to grab my cigarettes and lighter from the walnut coffee table.

The crinkling of the plastic snapped my sister's head up from the carrots she was chopping.

"Don't even think about it. No smoking in here, you know that." She took her knife and scraped the carrots into the pot of soup she was making. Her girlfriend, Adele, was joining her for dinner, and she invited me to stay.

"Fine, sorry, I know. I'll go downstairs to have one."

Having to take the elevator all the way down and stand out in that cold air to smoke sounded as fun as sleeping in an igloo.

I rolled my eyes and threw the pack onto the table. The lighter fell and skidded across the glass top. It was Teddy's lighter, the Playboy girl was scratched up a bit, but she was still smiling. I sighed and peered out the window.

Since returning from Michigan, I started sneaking cigarettes again. I was stressed out and convinced that Phil would find out about my transgressions, and my life would be over. So far, things had been normal at home. Maddy and I had been home for two days, Phil was back at work, and Mitchell in school. I was scheduled at a catering event with Isabel this coming weekend.

The four of us had gone to dinner last night. Phil rubbed my back, my leg, and kissed my neck. I was terrified he would want sex, but he was exhausted, and I pretended to be too. I wasn't ready to make love to my husband after what I had done.

Tonight, I told Phil I wanted to hang out with my sister. He took Mitchell to baseball practice and brought Maddy in her stroller. Everything was business as usual, but it all seemed distant and foreign, and temporary. Isabel's apartment and the cat, DJ Jazzy Jeff, brought me familiarity and comfort.

Cars small as ants zoomed by below on Lakeshore Drive as light, fluffy snow fell from the sky. Angry white ice caps smacked the shoreline, heaving floods of icy water to pool along the rocks.

Isabel resumed stirring the pot of soup.

"Why are you smoking again? Was your visit with Harper that bad?"

Yes, yes it was.

"Um, well, I guess, yeah. She started smoking after this shit with Steve went down, and with all the drinking and talking we did, I started up again. But—I'm going to quit. It's disgusting, I know."

Everything about me lately seemed disgusting.

Isabel raised her eyebrows, "Well, I sure hope so. It's gross. What is she going to do about her marriage? I mean, cheating is really shitty, so I imagine she'll get a divorce?"

I know, I know, it's really, really shitty.

Isabel put a spoon to her mouth and tasted the soup. With a small satisfied grin, she put the lid back on and reduced the heat. I flopped down on the couch while the cat rubbed up against my legs, purring loudly. I scratched his ears.

"I don't know. She's fucked up about it and needs time to cool off. She's not listening to me, that's for sure. And it's not like I come from a normal childhood where my parents were a good example. Who am I to tell her what to do?"

"Huh. Well, yeah, true, but you do have a great marriage, so you have experience on how to make it work, right? You're a success story."

A hard lump formed in my throat. I drained the wine from my glass and poured us some more.

"Yeah, I guess, but, it's her life, I can only offer advice. And right now, she's just too angry."

"I know, but God, can you imagine? That life is all Harper ever wanted, and then she gets it, and he fucks some chick and abandons his family? Seriously, what a mother fucker!"

She put the lid on the pot and started emptying the dishwasher.

"Yep, he sure is. Um, I'm going to go have a smoke now."

"Gross. Okay, fine, but make sure you air-dry the smell off you before you come up. Adele is allergic to cigarette smoke. And don't freeze to death while puffing on your death sticks."

I rolled my eyes.

"No such thing, but, got it. I'll be back in a bit."

I stuck my tongue out at her, and she shook her head as I grabbed my jacket and purse. I was getting a headache. I needed fresh air and a cigarette; what an oxymoron.

~

I slumped against the mirrored wall in the elevator and stared at myself. My long, limp hair was in need of a haircut. My complexion was sallow with dark circles rimming my tired eyes, the green dull and flat. I was just so tired. And why, two days later, did my head still hurt? I rarely got headaches. Maybe the cocaine mixed with the pot and the booze? Clearly, I was too old to bounce back anymore.

The elevator doors opened, and I headed to the front of the building.

"Good evening," the doorman greeted me.

"Hi," I mumbled, and propelled myself through the revolving doors.

The frigid air smacked me with flakes of soft snow and bitter wind. My hair whipped around my face, and the cold crushed through my jeans, penetrating every muscle.

Jesus, this sucks. Just for a cigarette.

With fingerless gloves, I rummaged through my purse for my cigarettes.

Fuck. I left them upstairs.

"God dammit!" I whispered.

Sorting through the mess, I was stunned to find several items at the bottom: a small vial of cocaine, a half-smoked joint, and a piece of paper with an address scribbled on it.

There was no name printed on it. Just one sentence:

Meet me here for a Sea Breeze.

Overwhelming dread punched my gut. I hadn't gone through my purse since coming home.

Teddy put drugs in my bag? Why would he do that? And what was this address?

I realized these drugs were in my bag the whole time I drove home from Michigan with Maddy. I pictured myself in a jail cell and my mother having to come retrieve Maddy.

What the fuck was he thinking? Why would he do this to me?

A Sea Breeze.

My mind swirled back to Chad's apartment when I had been a young impressionable child, drinking Sea Breezes with my eighteen-year-old lover. I saw his devious smile, heard his soft laughter, and felt his arms wrapped around me, promising me everything.

I studied the paper again. It was a local address.

He was here, in Chicago?

I can't. I won't. I shouldn't.

"Fuck!" I yelled out.

I circled back into the building to the doorman's desk.

"Hi again," I said, "could you call me a cab, please?"

He nodded and pushed a button, turning on the cab light in front of the building.

While waiting for the cab, I went back outside, the wind biting on my skin. I took out the joint and lit it, inhaling deeply. I needed to relax and *think.*

❧

H eading south down Lakeshore Drive, I stared out the dusty window through a whir of snowflakes at the waves surging the shore. We drove through the section of the River North neighborhood nicknamed "The Viagra Triangle," because gold-digging young girls often found rich old men to buy them drinks there.

The snow splattered the windshield as the driver weaved between cars, talking into his Bluetooth earpiece. The joint had worked—I was high. I looked at the paper again.

Why was Teddy here? We were together two nights ago, and he's in Chicago now? Had he mentioned coming here?

My memory remained locked up and missing altogether.

I pulled the coke from my purse.

Had Teddy convinced me to do it last night? Why would he do this to me?

He didn't care about the consequences for me. Or maybe this was his plan, to ruin my marriage, so we could be together.

The cab headed south, passing the Shedd Aquarium and the Field Museum. I smiled thinking about how the penguins excited Maddy and the way the flowing rhythm of the sharks captivated Mitchell as he pressed his face to the tank.

"What neighborhood is this?" I asked the driver.

"It's the South Side. Rough area. Been there before?"

I grimaced, "No, I don't think so."

"Yep. Not a great place for a girl like you. Are you sure you want to go?"

I thought about going back to Isabel's. I should have stayed and had soup and wine and hung out with her and Adele. Also, I should have told Isabel I left. She was probably frantic by now.

I should call the kids, talk to Phil. Come to my senses and go back.

But this address.

It lured me to the South Side, to Teddy, and I abandoned all capability to make good decisions.

Did he finally want a future with me?

The concept of leaving Phil and my kids seemed inconceivable. I could not imagine going through a custody battle, being torn from my kids, to just see them 50 percent of the time? Maybe not even that, since I had been unfaithful.

And Teddy. Could he be trusted with my children? *No, definitely not.*

Maddy would be thirteen someday, what if he started having desires for her . . . no, no, I was just high and paranoid. He would never do that.

Would he?

"Yeah, I do. Thanks," I leaned into the seat again.

"Alright, then. We'll be there in about twenty."

~

I must have dozed off. The cab driver gently tapped on the window divider and pointed to a dilapidated building. Blinking, I gaped at it. It didn't look familiar. I picked up the paper that had fallen between my feet. The address matched. I sighed, dug out some cash and handed it to him.

"Thanks, lady. Be careful out there. Here's my card if you need a ride back. Just give me fifteen minutes, and I can come get ya."

I put the card in my purse, thanked him, and got out. The snow had slowed, flakes fell in light whispers now. He drove away, leaving me alone in the street. It was quiet. Streetlamps dotted the icy sidewalks, and cars were cloaked in snow.

The sable sky twinkled with millions of stars, struggling through the snow to illuminate the city below. I was entranced by the silent sound of snow falling and the plume of my frosty breathing.

The building stood on brown bricks and was six-stories tall. Two broken windows on the top floor were flanked with cardboard and plastic tape. Blinds and curtains covered the remaining windows, dim light peeking from their edges.

It seemed impossible that Teddy was inside.

Every muscle in my body tightened as the bone-crushing bitter air seeped through my jeans. I trudged up the thick walkway, my boots crunching in the snow. A sense of unknown familiarity washed through me.

Had I been here before?

Whatever it was, it was forcing me forward.

Stairs leading up to the door were shrouded in thick snow, as if no one had come or gone for days. A man sat on the top step, bundled and hunched over, staring at his feet. His presence startled me.

I squinted at the man, searching for recognition. He wore a heavy winter jacket, slacks that were too worn and too thin for the weather, boots, and a wool hat pulled down to his eyebrows. Tufts of sandy-brown hair peeked from beneath the hat.

"Hello? Sir?" I called up to him.

Bleary blue eyes peered down at me. His weathered skin was leathery and brown.

"Yep?" he grunted.

"Um . . . this may sound weird, but do I look familiar? Have you seen me here before?"

I must have sounded like a lunatic. My mind raced to remember the sights and smells and the *lack* of sounds around me—nothing. He focused on my face for a moment, and then roared with laughter.

"You were here last night, Miss! Don't ya remember? And ya asked me the same thing! Ya on drugs or sometin'?"

His voice was gravelly, with a heavy Irish accent. He shook his head and laughed again.

What in the hell was he talking about?

I was with Phil and my kids last night. He must have me confused with someone else. *He could be a loon; just walk past him.* I searched the corners of my mind, and tiny fragments of memory jolted me. A face. A shadow. The street. Slipping away in darkness. Laughter. Bare legs. A blanket. Beer bottles. Cocaine, snorting. Laughing. Teddy. Oh, God. Teddy's face.

But, wait, that was Saturday night. Maybe both me *and* this man were loons.

I grabbed the cement baluster at the base of the stairs and steadied myself.

Shit, shit, shit.

"You gonna just stand there, missy, starin' at the snow and starin' at me or ya goin' inside? I don't much like people starin' at me."

I looked at the building and winced.

What should I do?

The cab was long gone, and I was freezing. Maybe I should call the cab driver back. Just wait in the doorway until he got me the hell out of here. I could go back to Isabel and Adele and the warm apartment, eat some soup and drink some wine. Then fall asleep watching reruns of *Cold Case*. The night I should have had.

Just ring the buzzer, get into the hall, and don't go upstairs.

"Um, yeah, sorry. I'm going in. Thanks."

My feet sank into the deep snow, and I struggled to climb up the steps. Where were my footsteps from last night if I had been here?

I read stories to my kids last night and tucked them in. Phil and I had wine by the fire, and he fell asleep on the couch. And then, I— oh, right, I called Harper and *then* went to bed.

Didn't I?

I reached the top and looked over at the man, now standing and descending the steps but watching me from the corner of his eye.

"Be careful in there, Missy. He will destroy you. He will whisper things in your ear that are untrue. You will believe those words. You will carry them around for the rest of your days if you're not careful."

I whipped my head around.

"Wait, what? What are you talking about? How do you know?"

But he was halfway down the street, treading through the snow, and he never looked back. I stood there, speechless.

I am losing my fucking mind.

The wind whistled through the trees suddenly, and my teeth began to chatter. I scrounged through my purse again and pulled out the paper. Next to the address, *#24* was scribbled. I found it on the panel of buzzers.

If I hit that button, I was entering the darkness again.

How could I be so confused?

I had a husband I adored and children who meant everything to me. My world was with *them*. Nightly cuddling, reading bedtime stories, and drinking hot cocoa. Not this. This was insane.

But the secrecy, the illusion, the blind appetite I had for my childhood paramour left me restless and searching. I closed my eyes and pressed the buzzer. Dread traveled up my spine as I waited for his voice.

"Yeah? Who is it?"

My knees buckled, and I fought to stay standing. The voice from forever ago, the voice from two days ago. And, last night? The man I ran from, the man I run to. He was the scar from my past and the source of my weaknesses. Every fiber that connected to every muscle begged me to flee down the stairs and back to my family.

Don't do it. Don't do it.

I pressed the button again to speak. Any good intentions I had drifted away, and I was a child again, offering my predator his prey.

"It's me."

∼

S tanding in front of apartment twenty-four, the hall smelled of cigarette smoke and stale carpet.

There was still time to flee. But my wet feet stuck in place. I tried rationalizing my irrational thoughts.

It's too cold to go back outside. I'll just stay a few minutes to warm up. I need to find out what happened last night. A beer or two won't hurt.

The chain lock slid across its grooves on the other side of the door, and then it opened. There stood Teddy, holding a beer and smiling. He looked different from the other night, older somehow. Deep lines arced his dark-black eyes, and parentheses outlined the corners of his mouth.

"Hey, baby girl, I see you got my note."

He pulled me to him before I could breathe a word and kissed my lips softly. My back melted into his hands. I was pudding.

"Hi, yeah I did," I whispered. He stared into my eyes as he unraveled my scarf, slowly, intentionally. Then he peeled off my jacket. Despite the cold, a trail of sweat ran down my back.

"Well, come on in," he said.

The layout of the place was identical to Chad's. It was a studio with the galley kitchen to the right, the bathroom to the left, and the living space all in one area. But, everything else about it was different.

The kitchen gleamed with shiny stainless-steel appliances. There were granite countertops, bare and spotless. No dishes piled up in the sink, and no garbage can overflowed with beer bottles.

End tables with lamps cast a soft glow and bookended a sleek dark-gray couch with decorative throws. A gorgeous Oriental rug lay beneath a walnut coffee table, which housed neatly stacked coasters.

The bed had an actual frame, complete with a head and footboard. A small bedside table contained a stack of books and an elegant clock. Where milk crates had been stacked with records in Chad's apartment, this place had an entertainment center, doors closed, contents hidden inside. Light wooden blinds folded down the windows. Lit scented candles peppered the apartment. A high-top dining table against the wall held a bouquet of fresh wildflowers. I was stunned.

What was Teddy doing in a place like this?

"I . . . I . . . what is this place?" I stammered, easing myself onto the couch.

"What do you mean?" he cocked his head.

"I mean, what is this place? We were just at Chad's apartment the other night in Michigan, and now we're here in this . . . exact replica of his place, only beautiful! I'm so confused."

"Hazel, are you okay? You were here last night after your kids went to bed. You said you couldn't handle your life anymore."

"What are you talking about? I did not! Whose place is this?"

"It's mine, remember?"

The familiar clinking of ice, a cap untwisting, and the

unmistakable *glug, glug, glug* pouring from a bottle echoed from the kitchen.

"Yours?"

How could that be? And what did he mean I was here last night, complaining about my life? God, did I drive over here after drinking an entire bottle of wine?

"Yes, I told you last night,"—another cap removed, the trickling of another liquid, finished off with the stir of a spoon,— "When my parents died, they actually left me some money. Surprised the shit out of me."

"Your parents died? When?"

Teddy reemerged, gripping two glasses of colorful booze.

Sea Breezes.

He handed me one, and I suddenly felt paralyzed by confusion, guilt, and shame. I stared down into the glass filled with swirls of grapefruit and cranberry juice.

"Hazel, are you sure you're okay? We had this conversation last night. Are you just really hungover?" he joked. His eyes had a soft, milky glow that melted my insides.

I sipped the sweet concoction of my childhood and tried to think.

Maybe I shouldn't drink.

Was he drugging me? How did I get here last night and back home again?

He led me over to the couch and sat down next to me, his leg touching mine, a gesture that lured me in as a child.

"I don't know what's going on," I said, "None of this makes sense. I left you behind in Michigan two days ago! What are you doing in Chicago? And why didn't you tell me about this place?"

"Well, you *were* pretty sauced by the time you got here. You said, and I quote, 'I need to not be a wife and mom tonight' and I was happy to oblige."

I swallowed hard.

"That doesn't sound right. What else?"

"Okay, well," he smiled over his glass at me, "then we drank more, I played guitar, some of your favorites. I told you about working in Indiana and getting a place here. Nobody wants to live in shithole Indiana. Hazel, I've been living in Chicago for a while like I told you last night. You seriously don't remember any of this?"

My stomach knit into tight knots, and a wave of gluey panic coated my insides.

What was he talking about? This was absurd.

This cruel story was a lie and didn't mesh with the one he told me a few nights ago.

"That is not what you told me in Michigan. Your parents are in Florida, not dead. You moved back to Ann Arbor, and you live there. You—" I waved my arms around the pristine apartment —"don't live here. This is not your place."

I licked my lips and tasted the sweetness of the drink. I tried to breathe. Beads of sweat flowed down my back.

"Hey, hey, Hazel," he scooted closer and put his hand on my knee. I flinched but made no attempt to move it. The heat of his hand was fire on my cold jeans. "Calm down, it's okay if you don't remember. It was a long night, and you wanted to do some blow, so after that—"

"What?" My legs came alive, and I jumped up. "Are you out of your fucking mind, Teddy? There is *no* way I asked for that! Wait a minute."

I rushed over to the high-top table for my purse, fished through it, and pulled out the stub of the joint and the vial of cocaine.

"This!" I yelled at the contents in my palm. "You put this shit in my fucking bag! And then I drove all the way home from Michigan with my *daughter* in the car! You asshole! Did you think it was *funny* or *sexy* or that this is some kind of sick game?"

"Whoa, whoa, settle down! I don't know what the fuck you are talking about. I haven't been in Michigan in years, and definitely not this weekend. And, you're the one who asked me for the blow last night. You wanted 'to escape.' I didn't hide that shit in your bag. Jesus Christ, Hazel, you took it with you! What the hell is going on with you?"

My head was spinning; the room was spinning. Teddy's face was blurry.

"No way! I would never put my kids in danger like that. And—

what do you mean you've been living here, in Chicago? Have you been following me? All this time?"

Teddy examined his hands; they were cracked and dry with ragged cuticles. He was quiet, as if waiting for me to get it all out before he responded.

"Well? What the fuck, Teddy! Answer me!"

He drained his drink, sucking on an ice cube and chewing it quickly, and then finally spoke, an intensity in his eyes.

"Hazel, I think you might need to get some air, maybe stop drinking. The fact that you can't remember anything from last night, and you think we were in Michigan together two nights ago is freaking me out."

"Freaking *you* out? Fuck you, Teddy!" I stormed into the kitchen, poured a hefty dose of vodka and downed it.

The liquid snaked through me quickly. The high from the joint was wearing off, and my mouth felt sticky like jam.

Beep. Beep.

"What's that noise? Jesus, Hazel, calm down!" he said, as his body filled the doorway.

"Fuck! It's my phone. Probably my sister. Wait, unless, maybe now you're going to tell me I live here with you? What other surprises should I know about, Teddy?"

My headache was floating away, but my surroundings were becoming murky.

I pushed past him and picked up my phone. Three texts from Isabel.

Where R U? Adele and I went downstairs looking for U. The doorman said U left in a cab. Are U okay? Let me know!

Hazel! Where R U?

I shook my head. I was a goddamn adult.

I quickly typed out a response:

Sorry, I'm fine. With a friend. Going home soon. Call U tomorrow.

My legs were wilting stems, and my eyelids cumbersome. I wanted to sleep.

"That's my girl," he nodded, and the lead weight of his arm was soon around my waist, leading me to the bed.

"No . . . no, Teddy, don't . . . I can't."

"Did you move here for me?" I whispered, the words extracting slowly, like a needle pulling blood. "Have . . . you been . . . watching me?"

Beep. Beep.

"Isabel," I mumbled.

"Don't worry about her. Just close your eyes. You need your rest now, Hazel."

"But—"

"Shh, shh, just rest."

His lips lightly grazed mine, and he bent down to whisper in my ear.

"Listen, we don't need to talk about the past or present. Let's just enjoy our time together. Hazel, I can make you feel better, I always do." His tongue traced my ear, and his hot breath tickled down to my belly button.

His fingers fumbled with the button on my jeans. I couldn't breathe, couldn't open my eyes; every sense in me was heightened.

No. no. no. Don't. Not again.

But I couldn't stop him; I didn't want to stop him. I had neither answers nor resolve left.

26

POSSESS

CHICAGO, ILLINOIS 2005

"**A**re you fucking drugging me, Teddy?" I spat angrily into the phone.

"What are you talking about? What kind of monster do you think I am?"

"Ha!" I shrieked. "Do you really want me to answer that?"

My pulse raced with fear and excitement. His deep voice was a rope, pulling me to him.

I must have a mental disease of some sort.

Perhaps, it was exhaustion as I hadn't slept in days, and my headache was constant. I had fried an egg and ate the toast that Phil made me, but my stomach felt empty.

"Hazel, that's really fucked up, don't you think?"

I sighed and focused on Maddy who was delicately scaling the jungle gym.

"Sorry, but what else could it be? First, I'm in Michigan with you, then I'm home and at some fucking fancy apartment with you again? If you're not drugging me, then I'm going crazy."

"I mean, why would I need to drug you? I thought we were enjoying being back together."

Goosebumps smattered across my arms as images emerged of

his tongue tracing my back, kissing my neck, and his breath tickling my ear. "Mama, look!"

My eyes refocused to see Maddy at the top of the dome, pleased with herself.

"Good job, honey! Be careful!" I yelled. "Sit down now, please!"

She smiled and sat down. Then, repositioned herself to climb down. She loved to do this. Get to the top, stand up, go back down, and repeat.

"Yeah, I mean, no. I shouldn't be talking to you, Teddy. Let alone, doing—"

"—Doing what we've always wanted? As adults? Listen, come over tonight. We won't drink as much. You can bring your own wine if you think I'm drugging you. See what you remember tomorrow."

"No way! You know I can't . . ." I trailed off.

I wanted to. The way he touched me now was different. And if I brought my own wine, I could know for sure.

"I don't know. It's wrong."

"Wrong to who? Yeah, your husband, I guess. But this is about us. Let's just have one more night, and you can decide after."

"Teddy, I just—"

"—Listen, you know where I am now. I'll be here tonight. I hope you will be too."

∾

Arias from *Tosca* flowed through speakers in the living room, and the mouthwatering aroma of lasagna saturated my senses. The lamps were dimmed, and candles flickered on nearly every surface.

A large baguette, chunks of hard and soft cheeses, olives, fresh fruit, and two bottles of red wine were arranged on the table. Teddy emerged from the bathroom in nothing but a towel, his skin glistening, and his woodsy body wash permeating the air. I sighed. At thirty-seven years old, he was gorgeous.

"Hi there," he grinned, and pulled me into his wet body.

My knees weakened as he kissed me.

"Teddy," I gently pushed him away, "don't."

"Okay, fine," he put his hands in the air and stepped back, "dinner first."

I set my bottle of wine on the counter and inhaled deeply.

"You cooked for me? Wait, you cook now?"

He stretched a T-shirt over his head and stepped into the kitchen. He cracked open the oven door, and a waft of cheese and sauce poured out.

"There's a lot of things you don't know about me now. But, yeah, I cook. I took some classes in Europe." He closed the oven and smiled.

"Wine? Ah, you did bring your own. Good choice, given the suspicions."

"Teddy—"

"—It's alright. I'll try not to take it too personally. Let's get your bottle open then, shall we?"

I nodded, slipped my jacket off, and went into the main room. I selected a pick of cheese and nibbled.

"Here you are," Teddy appeared, with wine for each of us. "We have two things to celebrate tonight."

"Celebrate?"

"First, you made the right choice by coming over tonight," he raised his glass, "and second, I got my dream job today. Cheers!"

He clinked our glasses and I sipped. "A job? What kind of job?"

"I'm a boat dealer!"

"What? What is that?"

He still hadn't put pants on, and his towel slipped, exposing the skin below his belly button and above his hips. I looked away, but he saw and grinned.

"Well, just what it sounds like, selling boats to rich people, or regular people too, I guess. I've been wanting to be back on the water for forever, and I can't tell you how excited I am."

"Wow," I said, and popped an olive in my mouth. "Well, congratulations."

"I thought you'd be more excited," he frowned. "I'm going to buy a boat soon. Think of how amazing that would be for us!" He ran his fingers down my arm.

"Whoa, what? Teddy, just stop. I am *married*. I have *children*. What is this 'us' you're talking about?

"Aw, all kids love boats, don't they?" he grinned, and bit into a slice of apple.

Panic churned in my stomach.

"*Don't* talk about my kids, ever."

"Damn!" he said, backing away. "Jesus, somebody's a little touchy. I was just inviting them is all."

I gulped some wine and felt the pressure of tears building. This was too close to home now. My protection over my kids and Phil was setting in.

"No, that will never happen. Because this is ending tonight. I don't know what I was thinking." I drained my glass and stood up.

"Hold on, okay, sorry, sorry, please don't leave." He put his hands on my shoulders. "I won't mention them again."

"Please, don't," I croaked. "They mean everything to me."

"I'm sorry, I really am." He approached me, and kissed my neck, his breath leaving hot trails. I closed my eyes and leaned into him.

"Now," he stopped, "my lasagna is almost done, I'll go put some pants on and check it."

I let out a slow release of air.

"Right. Um, can I get a glass of water?"

"Of course. Cupboard next to the fridge," he said, and opened his closet.

I grabbed a glass and spotted a mug, shockingly out of place.

"Oh my God!" I whispered. My mug. A mug Phil bought me years ago. It was ceramic, in a combination of lavender, sea green, and pale yellow, and decorated with dragonflies.

Ten months into our marriage, Phil had passed a gift shop and the mug caught his eye. That night, he presented me with a gift.

"A gift? What's the occasion?" I had asked.

"Do I need a reason to buy my beautiful wife a gift? I just saw it and thought of you."

He took out a little bag from his satchel and handed it to me. As I unwrapped it, the pale colors emerged, and a dragonfly peeked out.

"Oh, Phil, I *love* it!" I looked at him and back at the cup, my eyes tearing. You know how much I love dragonflies and you—it's so—I love it! Thank you, babe."

"You're welcome I thought you might like it."

I got up and sat on his lap and kissed him. He smiled, inhaling me. "You're wearing that perfume I love." His eyes danced and his hands wandered. "How long before dinner's ready?"

I smiled.

"Oh, we have time."

He grinned and led me upstairs.

I was so happy that night, and every night since.

This was *that* mug. Why was it here?

"Okay, let's take a look." Teddy squeezed past me and opened the oven door. "This looks great!"

My heart pushed against my chest. I closed my eyes for a moment.

This isn't real. That is not your mug.

I closed the cupboard door.

"Great, but I have a question before we eat."

"Okay, shoot," he said, cutting into layers of pasta, meat, and cheese.

"Where . . . um, where did you get that dragonfly mug?"

"What mug?" he asked, piling a giant piece of brown and crispy lasagna onto a plate. I placed one hand on the counter to steady myself and swiveled my head around to look. It was still there. The dragonflies in flight, soaring through a magically colored sky. I was both relieved and unsettled.

"That one," I stammered and pointed to it.

He squinted, perplexed.

The dragonfly mug? Babe? Seriously, don't you remember? I saw it in that store window and thought you'd like it."

"No, no, that's not right. You weren't the one who bought that mug!"

"Hazel, what are you talking about?"

He reached for me, but I recoiled. In a sudden loud crescendo, the opera music boomed, startling me. I needed to focus; the mug was not real.

"I need to sit down," I said, and headed to the other room.

"Okay, come on," he said, and helped me to the couch. I began to cry.

"What is going on, Teddy? My husband bought me that mug, not you! Why are you lying to me? Have you been in my house?"

"Hazel, come on. That's ridiculous. I don't even know where you live! And, again, stop accusing me of shit! What the hell is wrong with you?"

I could see he was getting upset, but so was I. Still tired from the day, my eyes were heavy.

Maybe if I close my eyes, this will all go away.

"How did you get the mug, Teddy?"

"Forget about the mug, Hazel. Are you taking some meds that you shouldn't be drinking with?"

Something definitely was not right. That's when I noticed out of the corner of my eye, the maps.

What the hell are those?" I recognized them, the same folds of paper that destroyed me long ago.

"Oh, well, I did want to talk to you about something, but now, I don't think—"

"—Talk to me about what?"

He reached over and fanned them all out, seven continents stared back at me: Europe, Asia, North America, South America, Africa, Australia, and even Antarctica.

"Is this some sort of cruel joke? What the fuck, Teddy?"

"Wait, what? Why are you upset?" he said. "They're just maps!"

A flush of heat rose to my face, and I questioned why I was here. I set my wine down angrily, on top of Africa, crimson drops spilling on Zambia.

"Okay, tell me then, Teddy, why are there maps on your table?"

"Calm down, Hazel, geez," he said, moving closer to me. "No, actually, I am trying to make it up to you."

"What do you mean?"

"Well, I'm going to be making real money with the new job. I want to give you what I couldn't before, exploring the world together, finally. Not to mention, weekends on the boat I'm gonna buy. I want to give it all to you."

His words were thick in the air, and I wasn't sure I heard correctly. "What are you saying—"

Beep. Beep.

"Dammit," I said quietly, "my cell."

My head spun as I went to get my purse. The cheeses were lukewarm now, the olives glistened in the humidity of the room, and the candles were halfway burned down.

I rummaged through my bag and found my phone at the bottom, its red light blinking.

It was a voicemail from Phil:

"Hi babe. I know you and Isabel are going over a menu tonight. Could you possibly grab a gallon of milk on the way home. We'll need some in the morning. Okay, well, that's all, love you babe! Be careful driving, it's shitty out there."

The battle between fantasies with Teddy and the reality of my family was unbearable. I was groggy, and my chest felt tight.

"Everything okay?" Teddy appeared and we went back to the couch.

"Yeah," I nodded, and sipped my wine. How much had I drunk already? My glass was full again.

"Traveling together is what you always wanted," he said, gesturing at the maps.

"Teddy," I hugged a throw pillow and reflected. "Why did I want that?"

"What do you mean?"

"I mean, what is it about you that I even like? I barely know you. I never met your family. I don't know what you did all that time in Europe. I know nothing."

"Oh," he crouched at my feet, with that trademark crooked

grin. "Well, back then, I think you liked me because I made you feel special."

"Right, that still doesn't tell me why I would risk everything for you." I paused, "You're going to be selling boats, right? Why don't you sell me on you?"

He winced. "Ouch. Okay, fine."

Teddy ambled up next to me, squeezing his body into mine, trapping me.

"I guess back then, I was your escape from home. We had fun, didn't we? I taught you things, stuff you were probably too young to learn," he said, scratching at a spot on his jeans, "but, now, I'm starting a great new job. I can make you feel safe, Hazel. But I will also give you the adventure you've been missing."

"Hmm. I am already safe and have stability in my life. And, I have adventures. You know nothing about my life. I don't trust you. When it got tough before, you ran."

He frowned and stared at the maps.

"I was young and stupid back then. I've changed, and have more to offer."

I took a deep breath and sipped my wine, my gaze on the map of Barcelona. I recalled when Phil and I traveled to Spain. One day, we bicycled throughout the beautiful countryside, stopping at vineyards, stopping in for wine tastings and picnic lunches. Back at the hotel, we dumped the bikes and rented a room in a quaint eighteenth-century hotel in the heart of the Gothic Quarter.

We made love all day, and when our bodies were spent, we napped. Then, we roamed the streets and gorged ourselves on Spanish cuisine: paella, bombas—tennis ball-sized croquettes served with a white garlic aioli and a spicy red sauce, esqueixada—a salad made with raw salted cod, and for dessert, motó—a soft, sweet, and spreadable goat cheese topped with honey and walnuts.

Thoughts of that day brought a swelling to my eyes. I missed Phil, and his utter unapologetic love. It was honest and unflappable. He was the safe one.

"You can't give me anything better than I have right now. I would never destroy my kids' lives like that."

Beep. Beep.

This time it was the timer for the oven. Teddy hadn't turned it off after he took out the lasagna. He went to deal with it.

I sat alone on the couch, staring at the maps, thinking of Phil. *He* was the one who took me on the tour of a lifetime.

"Well, the lasagna is pretty cold now."

I shrugged and sipped more wine.

"Hazel," he said, sitting on the edge of the coffee table. "I know you have the kids, and you don't want me to talk about them, so fine. But, are you really, truly happy? Can you really push aside what we have for that life?"

My head ached. It had to be the wine.

Scanning the room around me, I had to agree, Teddy had changed over the years. He seemed responsible for the first time, and had a promising job. His world travels sparked desire to cook, dance the flamenco, and speak broken Spanish.

I was overwhelmed and rattled. The wine in my glass was new, a Zinfandel now. It was thick and chewy and coated my mouth. We were halfway through the second bottle.

"Teddy—"

"Hazel," he nuzzled into my neck and whispered, "don't decide tonight. I just wanted to start talking about it."

I stared through the flames of the candles. My vision blurred along the edges of every object.

I'm having a breakdown. That's what this is.

"And, if I decide I won't give up my life for you?"

"Well, that's the thing." He pulled away. "I'm changing everything in my life. I want to be out on the water; I want to travel again. I love being immersed in new cultures, learning languages. This country is just boring to me. Sure, I'll have a great job, but I want to keep exploring, and I want you with me."

At some point, the opera had ended, and now the eighties were back. "The Ghost in You" by The Psychedelic Furs echoed in the background.

I felt my lips moving, but no sound came out. Just a moaning sound. The lights were bright, and my head pulsed in pain. My head rolled to one side, and a blurry image of a mattress with a mess of blankets on the floor came into view, along with a beer bottle and a dirty ashtray next to the box spring. My eyes traveled up the wall and there she was again, the woman in the painting. She's looking at me, smiling at all angles, smiling at the bed. Chad's bed.

"Hazel? Are you okay?"

I shuddered. The room began to spin, and tiny bits of chewed bread and cheese were making their way up. I shoved Teddy with doughy muscles and zigzagged through carpeted quicksand to the bathroom.

"I have to throw up!" I yelled. From the corner of my eye, I saw the bottle of wine I brought, still on the counter, unopened.

27

MUDDLE

CHICAGO, ILLINOIS 2005

A throbbing pain gripped my forehead. My mouth was stale with gin and sulfur-soaked morning breath. On the end table sat a crumpled pack of Virginia Slim Menthols and a glass of melted ice with a lime wedge floating upside down. Bits of pulp left a film of sticky splinters around the edges. As I picked up the glass, a ring of boozy condensation left its mark.

I groaned, set the glass back down, peeled myself from the leather couch, and rubbed my eyes.

What happened last night?

The muffled noises of my children's morning routine startled me. Mitchell began opening drawers, and soon after, the showerhead began splattering the drain. Maddy's feet stomped as she whined for breakfast. She pounded her little hands on the bathroom door.

"Stop it, Maddy! I'm in the shower!"

"I want Cheerios!"

"Go ask Dad!"

I couldn't let anyone see me like this. I stuffed the cigarette pack into my purse, hid the glass of gin behind the lamp, and ran my fingers through my hair.

I heard the sound of Phil's Italian footwear clicking on the hardwood heading toward the den.

Shit.

"Hazel, honey?" The door opened, and Phil was holding a tray with hot tea and toast. "How are you feeling? Throat still hurt?"

"Um," I fidgeted, and tightened the blanket around me, "yeah, little bit."

"I'm sorry babe, here." He set the tray down and smiled. "You really didn't have to sleep here; I doubt you're contagious."

"Well, the kids—"

"I get it, you don't want to get them sick. Do you want me to stay home today with Maddy? I can call the doctor to—"

"—No! No, I mean, I'll be fine. Like you said, I'm probably not contagious. You go to work, I'm fine, really."

"Well, alright then." He stood there, perfectly dressed in a salmon-colored Brooks Brothers dress shirt and khaki pants. "I'll get Maddy her cereal and take Mitchell to school. And then, I'll pick something up for dinner tonight. You just rest up."

He leaned over and kissed the top of my head.

"Thank you," I smiled weakly, and he left for work. I breathed out a sigh of relief.

What is happening? A sore throat?

I scanned the room. Phil's desk was bare and polished, apart from his computer and a coffee mug labeled "World's Best Dad" filled with pens, each one imprinted with the family business logo, "Smolnik's Meat Solutions."

Throwing the blanket off me, I turned on his computer. While it booted up, I stared at the documentation of our lives. A collage of our wedding day photos—Phil and I dancing, cutting the cake, and laughing into the camera. Candid shots of Maddy and Mitchell caught mid-squeal with Goofy at Disneyland. A yellowing photograph from my childhood of me and Isabel, picnicking with our parents at Bandemer Park along the Huron River.

Our accomplishments—his diploma from Northwestern and my certifications as a pastry chef in master baking and master decorating—graced the wall behind the desk. My favorite authors—

Bukowski, Sedaris, Hemingway, Anaïs Nin, Henry Miller—
intermixed with his mystery novels and accounting textbooks.

I touched each one, my recollections abruptly muddled by
flashes of a dark room, echoing laughter, someone crying, and a
man standing in shadows. I clamped my eyes shut and shook my
head.

The computer chimed, and I climbed into the chair. I navigated
to Google and began to investigate.

*"Drugs that erase memory," "drug-induced amnesia," "forgetting entire
events."*

My search for answers was interrupted.

"Mommy!" Maddy barged in, and I quickly pulled the blanket
up again.

"Hi baby! How's my girl?"

"Why are you in here?" She pulled at the blanket, and I placed
her on my lap. Leaning in, I inhaled the scent of sleepy child, milk,
and fabric softener. She was still in her pajamas. I kissed the top of
her head and squeezed her.

"I'm just on the computer, honey. Why aren't you dressed yet?
Did you eat?"

"Yes, Cheerios!" She nodded her blonde head vigorously. "Don't
wanna get dressed!"

"Okay, that's alright. Should we go to the park?"

"Yes!"

"Well, then, you have to get dressed, now, don't you?"

"I guess," she giggled.

"Okay, Mommy will get dressed too."

She hopped off me and ran out. I looked at the computer screen
and sighed. I would have to resume the search after Mom duties.

Beep. Beep.

It was my cell phone, its text alert muffled from the bottom of
my purse. I dug it out and flipped it open:

**Hey babe. We need to talk about last night. U R making
a mistake.**

28

ESCALATE

ANN ARBOR, MICHIGAN 2005

Dusk was settling in and casting a long shadow across the bar. Cigarette smoke lingered above patrons sipping beer and slamming shots of whiskey. Newspapers were scattered, picked apart by old men griping about gas prices and arguing about President Bush and "fucking terrorists."

The owner, Dwayne, cleaned glasses, emptied ashtrays, and pretended to empathize with every customer's bitch and groan. They were a sorry bunch, but they always showed up and spent money. In his twenty years of ownership he had been robbed four times, shot at twice, and stabbed once.

Iris, an aging prostitute, was at one end of the bar picking at a scab. She coughed loudly between gulps of scotch and looked up nervously at the door often. She fixated on an old portable CD player, grappling with the earphones and cackled and snickered when she placed them in her ears. She removed them and repeated the process. She had a rhythm: scab, scotch, cough, music.

Perched at the opposite end was my mother, her auburn hair pinned up in a chignon. She dressed in cream-colored trousers and a pale-pink silk blouse. Large, dark sunglasses covered her eyes. She took dainty sips from a martini glass, swirling the toothpick of olives.

Dwayne introduced himself as he prepared her drink.

"Nice to meet you, Dwayne. I'm Joanne," she said, and smiled wryly as he set the glass in front of her.

He had tried to make conversation with her, but she was very vague in her responses, and years of experience told him to leave her alone. She had not removed her sunglasses, and he was puzzled why this caliber of lady sat in his bar. He wasn't about to ask.

"Damn! Fucking whores! Stupid. Damn," Iris cried out, yelling at her CD player.

Dwayne glared at her. She smirked, took a gulp of scotch, and picked at her scab. She managed to tear a piece, releasing pinpricks of blood. Joanne grimaced and slowly sipped her martini.

Light poured as the door opened. The bar vampires flinched, squinted, then looked away. A man came in, adjusted his eyes, and a crooked smile spread across his face. He sauntered over to Joanne and hopped onto the stool next to her. She did not acknowledge him but elegantly placed an olive into her mouth.

"Hey," Dwayne nodded, and went for the beer cooler.

"What's shakin' big D? You entertaining my lady friend here?"

Joanne flinched. Dwayne set a Budweiser down and glanced at her.

"You know this loser?" Dwayne asked with a smile.

"I wouldn't say we are friends," she frowned. "Hello, Teddy."

"Oh, don't let her fool you, big D," Teddy said, grinning. "This is my good buddy, Joanne. Joanne, this is big D. The D stands for Dwayne."

"We've met, but thank you," she said dryly.

Joanne tipped her glass back, emptying the last drop. She looked up at Dwayne through her shades.

"Could I get another, please?"

"You got it," said Dwayne, and he threw his bar towel over his shoulder.

Iris was getting agitated. She moved on to a scab on her face and was rocking back and forth.

"Bullshit, this is bullshit! Whores!" the old hooker growled.

"Shut the fuck up, Iris!" shouted one of the men. "Go outside and wait for your dealer! You're goddamn annoying.

"Fuck you, asshole!" she yelled.

"Both of you shut up!" Dwayne sighed, and shook his head.

Joanne's mouth twisted in frustration, and she scowled at Teddy.

"Your taste in drinking establishments is—"

"—Look, I've got to get back to work soon," Teddy interrupted, swigging his beer. "Not all of us can take a liquid lunch and go shopping. What do you want?"

She sighed and gave Dwayne a small smile as he supplied a fresh drink.

"Let's talk about Hazel and what you've been doing to her."

"What are you talking about?"

"Don't play stupid with me. Or perhaps, you *are* just stupid." She threw up a perfectly manicured hand when he tried to speak. "My daughter is married with two beautiful children, my *grandchildren*. You have lured her back and I want it to stop."

Shock crossed Teddy's face, and Joanne winked.

"What? You think I don't know you've been molesting my daughter since she was a child?"

Teddy rose from his bar stool, his mouth wide open.

"What do you mean?" he said, once he glugged down half of his beer. "You're . . . *crazy*. Isabel was my girlfriend, for, for . . . like, a minute. I think that vodka's going to your head. I mean, I haven't . . . . I haven't seen Hazel in years. Or, er . . . Isabel."

His nervousness amused her, and she spun casually on her stool to face him and removed her sunglasses.

"Sit *down*, Teddy."

Without a word, he nodded and sat back down.

"Don't bother lying to me. I know everything. You are the lowest form of human. You molested my child, and now you are trying to destroy her marriage. You are so very fortunate I never went to the police."

"I have no idea what you are talking about. I barely know her. Dwayne, a shot of Jameson please! Now!"

My mother shook her head in disgust, her mouth pinched in anger.

"You thought you were getting away with it all those years, didn't you? Touching my child in that nasty little apartment. Teaching her to lie and sneak around. You corrupted her and took away her innocence."

Dwayne set the shot down and Teddy slammed it, "Another, dude, please."

His hands were shaking now.

"But, how did you—"

"—Find out?" she sneered. "Don't you worry about that. I want you to slither yourself back to Indiana, and I absolutely forbid you ever seeing anyone in my family again."

Teddy leaned against the bar, lit a cigarette, and smirked.

"You *forbid* me? That's rich."

Dwayne slid another shot to Teddy from down the bar, his eyebrows arched up in curiosity.

"Yes, yes I do." Joanne yanked her purse from the stool back and pulled out a checkbook. "How much will it take for you to disappear?"

"Are you serious?" he laughed.

"Well, it's either this or the police. Your choice."

"If you knew it back then, why didn't you call the cops? She wanted to be with me. She couldn't stand being at home. You didn't even notice she wasn't there," Teddy hissed.

A few men at the bar stopped talking to gape at them.

"Now, listen here, you piece of trash," she whispered, her finger wagging in his face. "You may think you know what my child wanted and what went on in our house, but you have no idea. Nor do I need to explain anything to you. This ends today. If you come near her again, I will take you down, and you will be sorry you ever fucked with me. Do you understand?"

Suddenly, the door opened, and a large Black man wearing a leather jacket and jeans walked in. He had mirrored sunglasses on his shaved head. A large diamond stud pierced his right ear. He made a beeline for Iris, who stiffened and then smiled, exposing several missing teeth.

"Hey baby! I been waitin' for you."

Dwayne frowned and pointed to the door.

"Go outside, both of ya."

The man grunted and nodded at Dwayne. Iris scrambled off of her stool and followed him outside.

"Listen, Joanne. I have no idea what you are talking about. I haven't seen either of your daughters for years. And if you think—"

Loud shrieking from outside startled them, and Dwayne grabbed his gun from behind the bar and started for the door.

"Shit, not again . . ." he mumbled as he ran past them.

"I'm sorry baby . . . I'm sorry . . . I didn't lie, I swear." Iris's words leaked in through the open door.

Joanne's pulse quickened as she downed her drink and grabbed her purse. The last thing she wanted was to be caught in the cross hairs of a fight between a hooker, her dealer, and a bar owner with a gun in hand. She slipped the checkbook back into her purse as Teddy stepped towards the door.

From behind the door, a scream, and the boom of a gunshot assaulted their ear drums.

~

S tanding in the shadowy street outside a bar, I could hear my mother screaming. The only illumination was a blinking neon beer sign in the window and a couple of streetlamps. I followed the screams to find her lying in the street. Her expensive handbag and sunglasses were strewn alongside her jerking body as blood poured from a punched-out hole in her chest that she clutched at with panicked hands. The blood was crimson and thick, like melted crayons, oozing into her silk blouse. She tried feverishly to scoop it back inside the hole, as if she could pour it back into her heart.

An old woman, garishly dressed, stood above my mother, whooping and holding a large boom box almost twice the size of her above her tiny body. "Whatever Lola Wants" blared from the speakers. Yellow puss oozed from scabs on her arms. My mother managed to crane her neck to glare up at the woman as her wound gushed blood.

"Shut up!" she gasped between labored breaths.

A large Black man with a diamond earring busted out of the bar shouting something, but I couldn't understand him over my mother's wailing. She turned to me, and I was startled at my reflection in her sunglasses.

Dressed in a paper gown, snakes wriggled from my nose and ears. My hair was matted and wet. A heavy, cold gun dangled from my hand, black smoke wafting from its barrel. I opened my mouth to scream, but no sound escaped. I flung the gun to the ground and swiped at the snakes, unable to catch them. They squealed like pigs and melted at my touch. They were chameleon-like, some changing colors and shapes, others translucent and filled with liquid.

My mouth was dry and metallic, and my left ear began to ring. I couldn't feel my legs. My mother clutched her chest with one hand and reached out to me with the other.

Perched on a curb across the street, my father, clad in a polo shirt and khakis, was reading a newspaper with "Vice President Dick Cheney visits Iraq" splashed across the front page. He glanced up at me, smiled, and resumed reading. I wanted to run to him, but as I tried to wrench up one of my legs, they were lead and useless.

The sky was pure ink and millions of stars sprayed across it, lighting up mountains that appeared on the horizon. The air was crisp, and snow crunched under my weight. The rawness of the cold did not bother me. This place was foreign to me. I stared at the mountains. They spoke to me.

Choose.

Was I dreaming? Standing in the middle of a street, bare feet in the snow, half naked, with my mother bleeding to death and my father oblivious? Who was the man that looked like Ice-T from *Law & Order*? Where was Isabel? Isabel would help me. Maybe she knew what the hell this place was and what was happening.

Why wasn't my father helping? He just sat there, turning the pages of the paper and shifting occasionally on the curb. Suddenly, two dragonflies the size of hummingbirds circled his head. They fluttered gracefully, dancing along the paper's edges.

Miles Davis flowed through Iris's boom box now, and I searched for eye contact with my father, any sign of recognition, but he didn't notice.

"Hazel! Hazel, please, you have to help me!" my mother yelled, crawling towards me. "Why are you just *standing* there?"

Pain stretched across her face. She looked pathetic in her designer blouse and trousers, her flame-red hair disheveled and free from its updo.

"I don't know why, Mom. I just can't. My legs won't work."

My entire body was limp.

She managed to drag herself up to sit. The blood was turning indigo, and her face softened. Ringing began in my other ear now, and I pressed my palms to both.

"Please, sit next to your mother. We need to talk about this."

She was tiny and meek and lacking her usual poise. I checked on my father—he was halfway through the paper now, and the dragonflies rested on each of his shoulders.

"Fine. But just because I shot you and you are dying doesn't mean I'm any less mad at you. *Did* I shoot you?"

Joanne let out a loud laugh and wiped her bloody hands on her cream-colored pants that were now a myriad of shades of red.

"Defiant! Just like your mother! I wouldn't expect anything less. Honestly, I'm not sure who shot me."

My knees collapsed inward. I folded down into a cross-legged position and landed heavily onto the cement next to her.

"I am *nothing* like you, Mother!" I narrowed my eyes.

My mother began to rub the blood on her pants around like finger paint. She laughed again.

"Certainly not! I haven't been cheating on my husband. And with that *vile* man, of all people. Haven't you learned your lesson yet?"

The snakes were snickering in my ears. Mocking me. Agreeing with my mother. The man with the diamond earring leaned against the bar door and checked his watch. The heat of shame rose to my cheeks. I fiddled with one of the snake's smooth and shiny tails.

"I don't know what you're talking about," I stammered.

"You know, this is partly my fault. My obsession with beauty rubbed off on you and you found, at a very young age, that your beauty can get you anything. I know how good that feels. It's a self-fulfilling prophecy, really. You believed all the things that you did would make you a woman, and voilà, just like that, you were!"

"Wha—"

She held up a bloody palm and inhaled a choking breath.

"Did you think I didn't know about you and that disgusting Teddy? Running around, hiding and lying that summer, and letting him *do* things to you? You don't think a mother knows? I'm far from stupid, Hazel."

I stood in stunned silence. She knew? How could that be?

The blood had slowed down to a trickle now, her inhales smoother.

"Don't look so shocked. You went into that hovel of a building and didn't come out all day!"

A slight wind picked up and rustled my paper gown. My hands were shaking, and I was dizzy.

"How? How did you know? You followed me?"

"I did. And then when I saw you come out with that man, I wanted to kill him."

"Why didn't you say something?"

"I thought you would stop, that you would know it was wrong. I wanted you to come home and tell me, so I could call the police. But, every time you came home, you were happy. I could see that you thought you were in love."

Acid churned in my stomach. My head pounded against my ribs. I was losing control. Anger rose in my throat. I wanted to kill *her*, but I had already shot her, so that seemed a moot point.

"You, what? You knew the *whole* time and didn't say a word? How could you let that go on? What kind of mother lets their child have sex with a grown man?"

I was sobbing now, and she nodded her head and kept her eyes closed.

"I know, Hazel, I know. I was young once. I loved a boy so much, but my parents interfered and forbade me to see him, and I was devastated."

I stared at her.

"They didn't think he was good enough," my mother continued, "didn't have a family with money. I didn't care, I loved that boy. I hated my parents for that. I just, well, I didn't want to stand in your way and for you to hate me. I figured he would probably grow tired of the hiding; men are not good at these things and that—"

"—What? That he would break up with me? So, instead you let me fall in love with him and wait until he left me devastated?"

"I know it was wrong of me. I should have stopped it."

My eyes widened as I faced her. Tracks of mascara ran down her cheeks, and some pooled beneath her eyes. She had morphed into a rabid raccoon. Only a trace of her lipstick remained, and her eyes were swollen and red. A gold snake wriggled around my neck, slid down my gown and onto the street.

"I spoke to that despicable man, to tell him to stay away from you, or he would be sorry."

"What? When?"

"Well," she jerked her chin towards the bar across the street, "we were having a talk when, well, you shot me."

"I—I don't remember doing that. You talked to Teddy?"

"Well," my mother smoothed her shirt with bloody hands, "I think you did. I don't really know. I guess I deserved it."

My words snared and failed to form, so she continued.

"Look, Hazel, you've made mistakes, and so have I. And the worst of mine was letting you go to that monster every day and be violated." Tears fell down my mother's face. Her face was dissolving into a puddle on the ground. "You have to face what he did to you and stop all this. Go to your husband. Go to your kids. Stop this nonsense. Make your choice."

In the distance, the snow on the mountains started melting. I cried as it slid down in large chunks.

"Hey!" a puny voice called out from behind. I spun around and, through dark shadows, saw a young girl dangling something off her fingers.

"Who is . . .?" I whipped my head back towards my mother, but she was gone. Not a trace of her, or even a drop of blood.

"Hey!" the little girl yelled again.

"Hello?" I said, squinting my eyes.

She stepped under a streetlamp, and I gasped.

There stood thirteen-year-old Hazel with long brown hair swept up in a high ponytail and a short jean skirt, an off-the-shoulder T-shirt, and jelly shoes. Red lipstick traced her lips and black eyeliner rimmed her eyes. She extended her arm out. A bracelet—my bracelet—shimmered, hundreds of tiny diamonds glimmering in the light.

"Is this yours?" the girl giggled, and stepped closer.

I inched away, fear racing through my veins.

"Who . . . are . . . you?" I stammered.

"I'm you, *duh!*" she giggled again.

I knotted my eyebrows together and frowned. "That can't be," I said.

"Whatever," the girl said and rolled her eyes. "Do you want your bracelet back or what?"

"Where did you get that?"

"Seriously? From Teddy. You know that. That day, on the boat."

She—me? was next to me now.

"I am losing my goddamn mind!" I yelled up at the sky, overflowing with its own diamonds. "*What* is happening?"

"Stop yelling," she said, and took my hand.

She pried my fingers open and placed the bracelet in my palm.

"Why? Why are you giving me this? I got rid of this! My mother —wherever she is—has it," I said, looking around for her again.

"Well, I'm giving it to you so you can decide."

"Decide what?" I glanced down at the bracelet and then back at her green eyes. "How are you even real?"

She crossed one ankle over the other and leaned back onto her elbows.

"I'm real, because I'm you."

"Why are you here?" I asked, shaking my head.

"I'm here to tell you that it's okay."

"That what's okay?"

"Everything. What happened with Teddy. It wasn't your fault."

"Well, I never—"

"Teddy took complete advantage of you. It's *his* fault, Hazel. You need to know and remember that."

The wind cut into me, and I tightened my grasp on my gown, beginning to shiver. The bracelet edges carved into my palm, but I didn't let go.

"But, what about high school? When I cheated on Nick with Teddy?"

"He left, and then he came back, and you just wanted to feel happy again."

I began to sob, snotty, wet sounds escaping my throat. She rubbed my back while I spilled tears into the street.

"You have to forgive yourself, Hazel," said a man's voice. "Before you make your choice. You have to do that first. Forgive yourself."

The girl was gone, and Phil and his strong hands were rubbing my back.

"Phil!"

I struggled to stand. I was desperate to feel his arms around me, to take me away from this crazy universe I had dropped into, but my legs were frozen once again. Thick sand formed around my ankles like chains, and as I tried to get up, I stumbled.

I heard more giggling, but this time it wasn't from the little girl. Madeline and Mitchell were far away, under the streetlamp, holding hands. They were older though, Mitchell was a teenager, and Maddy looked to be about nine.

Was I in a fucking time machine? I used the slight strength I had left and pushed myself up. Sand fell from my hair. I spit granules from my mouth, and as they spilled to the ground, they formed glass shards and shattered.

My ankles were stuck solidly in the sand, and the best I could do was to turn awkwardly and sit sideways. A snake with scales the color of exquisite blue and green jewels slithered from behind my neck and slipped down my arm, and glided over the sand. Suddenly, a hole appeared, and the snake dove inside it and disappeared.

Beep. Beep.

Why was my fucking cell phone going off, and where the hell was it?

"Phil, what is going on? Maddy! Mitchell! Come here!" I called them, but they were busy building a sandcastle.

Phil dropped his hands from my shoulders and bent down to face me.

"It's time, Hazel."

"Time for what? I'm so confused."

"The kids miss you so much, you know," he said.

"But I haven't gone anywhere. They're so grown up, how long have we been here? Where is here? How do we get out?"

"Time is slipping away, Hazel. It's all up to you. We all love you and hope that you'll come back to us soon."

Phil had aged. His face was sunken and pale. He had a beard, and his hair was long and unkempt. He wore a powder-blue oxford with a gray striped tie. The shirt was untucked and dirty. A belt cinched in its last hole strained to hold up baggy khakis. Wrinkles spread across his forehead, and the sparkle in his blue eyes was gone.

Scanning my surroundings, my mother was now sitting on a lawn chair with her sunglasses on, reading a *Glamour* magazine and smoking a cigarette. A small table with a glass of wine was perched next to her. Multi-colored swirls of blood were smeared on her cream shirt, but blood was no longer pouring out.

My father was playing checkers at a card table under a streetlight with Iris. They were having a conversation, and she was flirting. She picked at her scabs as he made his move.

He chuckled deeply at whatever she was saying and gazed into her vacant eyes. A dragonfly the size of a small dog sat on my father's head reading a book called *Mr. Mosquito Put on His Tuxedo*, and it snickered as its little legs turned the pages.

"Hazel, are you listening? Phil asked.

I tried again to get up, but my ankles would not budge in the thick sand.

"Yes, I . . . I don't—what are you talking about? I don't want to be here. I don't even know where *here* is. I think I shot my mother. I did. I think. I don't know why. But now . . . what is going on?"

Phil stroked my face. I melted into his hand, and warm comfort washed over my tired body. It felt as if every cell in me was dying off, and the shell of me was hunched over a pile of sand. A gold snake squeezed out of one ear, and a lightning rod of pain shot through my head.

"Fuck! Ow!" I said, holding it with my hands. "Why are there fucking snakes crawling out of my body?

"I'm not sure, Hazel. This is your world. We are just inside it with you. We would all like to go home now too."

He crossed his legs and faced me. He slowly scooped sand away from my ankles.

"You should have been happy with what you had, *dear*. My son deserves better."

I covered my mouth in horror.

"*Mother*. Stop it. Stay out of this. Go home." Phil scowled at her.

"Humph. Fine. You'll be sorry young lady. And so will you, son." And then she and her pig were gone.

I took Phil by the shoulders and forced him to look at me.

"Did I take some kind of crazy drug, Phil? This is fucking nuts! Am I in the looney bin? Because I feel fucking crazy right now!"

I sobbed into his dirty shirt.

"Phil, how can I make this stop? I want to come home. Please? Tell me what to do."

A shattering sound startled us both. I spun my head to see my mother passed out on the chair, her wine glass in shards on the pavement beside the lounge chair in the middle of street.

A streetlight flickered on. It cast a ray of light, illuminating an orange IROC-Z. The door opened, a lit cigarette flew to the ground, and a boot swung from the car, smashing it into the pavement.

29

RISE

ANN ARBOR, MICHIGAN 2005

M y eyes fluttered open. My hand rested on a clean white slab of porcelain. It was smooth and cold under my fingertips, which resembled tiny, wrinkly prunes. I slowly lifted my chin, a dull ache throbbing from the back of my head.

I was naked, lying in a large claw-footed bathtub. Bubbles floated on the surface of the tepid water, the air fragrant with fresh lavender. Prisms of light bounced from a chandelier above, dripping with dazzling crystals. Pale-yellow curtains breathed in and out as a breeze from an open window carried the scent of fresh-cut grass.

On my left, a large pedestal sink held quaint squares of delicately wrapped soaps and an array of lotions in glass bottles. Warm air hissed from a radiator. It was a massive room, with space for a heather-gray loveseat and a vanity topped with crisp-white towels folded neatly into squares. A robe was draped over an elegant Victorian-style chair. Wildflowers inside a small vase on the windowsill caught my eye.

Where am I?

I stood up, sloshing water onto the fluffy shag rug under my feet. I felt faint and steadied myself on the side of the tub. I allowed the blood to flow back into my legs before I pressed back up. I faced myself in the beveled mirror above the sink.

My hair was wet and hung in smooth strokes. It was silky when I touched it. A pair of emerald-green jewels stared back at me.

My mother's eyes.

My skin was dewy and smooth as if I were young again.

A knock on the door startled me. I gasped and plunged back in, splashing water everywhere.

"Hazel? It's me, I'm coming in."

Isabel! Where had she been? A sigh of relief washed over me.

"Oh my God. Thank God. Where have you been?"

Isabel laughed.

"I'm right where I've always been, Hazelnut." She smiled, removing the robe from the door and handing it to me.

Trailing behind her was her cat. He sauntered in, weaving in and out of Izzy's legs, purring loudly.

"DJ Jazzy Jeff!" I exclaimed, reaching my sopping arms toward him. "Come here, kitty!"

Isabel laughed.

"I'm pretty sure he won't go near that water."

He jumped on the window ledge and eyed me suspiciously.

"See? Smart cat."

I stepped out of the tub and slipped into the robe my sister held for me. I sat on the loveseat, and Isabel handed me a plush towel.

"Would you like some tea?"

"Sure, I guess—whose house is this? Where are we?"

"I'm not really sure myself," Isabel said, as she pulled out the stopper in the tub. "This is your world. I'm just living in it."

"Why does everybody keep saying that?" I began mopping up the water on the floor with a hand towel. "And what do you mean 'you don't know?' I don't understand what is happening to me."

As I looked up, a white unicorn suddenly appeared. It was small, a rainbow horn protruding from its forehead, and it drank nonchalantly from the tub as the water swirled down the drain.

Isabel cocked her head and began to stroke its mane.

"What is that?— Nevermind." I shook my head and looked around. "Have you seen Teddy? Or Mom? Oh my God! I shot her!"

"*Teddy*? Wow. I haven't heard that name since we were kids. What made you think of him? And what do you mean you *shot* Mom?"

"I shot her. And Dad, he didn't get up to help. He just sat there. And, Phil, where is he? And where are my . . . *kids*?"

"What are you are talking about, Hazel? How could you have shot Mom? Do you even *own* a gun? And what does Teddy have to do with this?"

A photo of Phil and our kids in a beautiful silver frame materialized on the vanity.

"Come on, you need some sleep, Hazel. You're not making sense."

She helped me lie down. Closing my eyes, sleep came quickly.

30

LUCID

ANN ARBOR, MICHIGAN / CHICAGO, ILLINOIS 2005

B eep. Beep.

Cold air, a swoosh, footsteps.

"When will she wake up? It's been seven days for God's sake. I'm worried, Richard."

Voices muffled like I was underwater.

"I know, sweetheart. I am too. We have to wait. Her brain is repairing itself from the fall. She will wake up right, Hazelnut?"

Cold air, a swoosh, footsteps.

"Any changes? You guys have been here forever."

"No, honey, not yet. You and Adele should go home and get something to eat. We'll call if anything happens."

"No, Mom. I want to be here when she wakes up. Come on, Hazel, this is ridiculous."

A hand, heavy on my leg.

"Well, listen, if you won't go home, let's get dinner in the cafeteria?"

"Dad, that shit is nasty."

"Do you have a better idea?"

"No, I guess not. Adele is vegetarian now, and hospitals don't cater to that."

"Isabel, your sister is in a coma. Your girlfriend can eat shitty hospital food this once."

"Sorry, you're right. I'm just . . . I need her to wake up."

"We all do. Come on, let's go get nasty-shit hospital food."

Whispers of laughter.

Beep. Beep.

Cold air, swoosh, footsteps leaving.

Beep. Beep.

Cold air, swoosh, footsteps close to me.

"Hazel, it's me, Harper. God, please wake up. This is all my fault. I should never have let you go get cigarettes alone. It was so icy . . . and shit, I've been so absorbed with my problems I wasn't thinking right. Plus, well, I was piss-ass drunk. Oh, God, and I went home with a guy. Oh, what a mess. I can't stop crying, this is all my fault. I am just so—"

"—Uhhhhh," I groaned, my throat hoarse and raw.

"Oh my God! Hazel, you're awake! Shit! I should get a doctor!"

"No . . ." I croaked.

I struggled to open my eyes. My eyelids were heavy, thick like mud. I saw white walls, bright lights, but the edges were fuzzy. I was wrapped in snakes—no, wires—protruding everywhere. I was in bed. I tried to lift my arm, but Harper spoke again.

"Don't move, Hazel. Oh my God!" she shrieked. "I have to get a doctor. I promise I'll be right back . . ."

"Wait . . ."

Footsteps, swoosh, cold air, silence.

Beep. Beep.

I turned my head slowly to the source of that awful beeping—monitors with numbers and graphs hooked to the wires. I ran my hands across my arms and body. I wiggled my legs. I felt no pain, just exhausting grogginess and confusion.

Another swoosh of air, hurried footsteps.

"You're awake! Hazel, I'm Dr. Jankowski, I'm happy to see you're back with us. Do you know where you are?"

A bright-red light blinded my left eye, then my right. Voices elevated from all directions. I closed my eyes.

"Hazel! Oh my God! It's a miracle!" My mother rushed towards me. Her Opium perfume permeated the room. "You're awake." I felt my father's warm hand squeeze my shoulder, "Oh, Hazelnut . . ."

"Hazel, holy shit! You're awake! You scared the piss out of us!" Isabel's voice boomed.

I fluttered my eyes open. The familiar faces of my family circled my bed.

"Phil?" I searched the room.

"I'm here," said Phil, rushing through the door.

"Jesus, you scared the shit out of me. You're finally awake . . . you're okay. And the kids are at my parents—"

"—Okay, now Hazel . . ." the doctor interrupted. "Do you know where you are?" the doctor repeated.

"Not really . . . a hospital?"

Laughter. Relieved laughter.

"Yes, that's right, Hazel. Do you know how you got here?"

"Um, I fell . . . um, on ice?"

"I told her what happened," Harper said.

"Yes, you are in the intensive care unit. You slipped on ice and hit your head, hard," said Dr. Jankowski. "It caused a brain hemorrhage, or a bleed in the brain, and we medically induced a coma to keep the swelling in your brain down. Now, I'll need you to do a few tests for me. Follow my finger with just your eyes please, and, nurse—"

"I'll get her vitals," said an unrecognizable voice.

"Thank you, Alice," the doctor said, and as I trailed his finger, she wrapped a cuff around my arm. A clamp snapped down on my finger.

"One-ten over eighty, pulse is seventy-two," she announced once the cuff deflated.

"Great!" the doctor said. "Those are terrific vital signs, Hazel. Now, you're going to start getting your bearings as you recover from the coma. You all need to keep conversations brief with her. Don't overwhelm her. No stress, understand?"

"Yes, Doctor," many voices.

My vision sharpened. I could see outlines of everyone in the room. Smiling faces across the board. Excited noises.

"I'm so tired," I muttered.

"Of course you are," said Phil. "We'll let you rest."

He addressed the doctor, "This might be a dumb question, but, she won't . . . go back into the coma during sleep, will she?"

"No, she should be in the clear. She does need significant rest in the next few days. In fact, can you please head out and return later? Go out, get dinner. Get some fresh air. We'll keep an eye on Hazel."

Phil kissed my forehead.

෴

The beeping never stopped and invaded my sleep. I didn't dream, probably because I could never fall asleep that deeply. I moved to the step-down ICU unit with other brain-injured patients after waking from my coma. I thought sleep was important for brain healing, but it was impossible. The staff at the hospital talked so loudly, conversing about football or what they did the night before. The nurses and doctors came in and out constantly to adjust and check the wires and tubes attached to me and to write notes on clipboards. They flicked the lights on when they drew blood or gave me my medication or took my vitals. And often, someone lifted my ass onto a cold metal bedpan, encouraging me to pee or poop.

Isabel and Adele, Harper, my parents, and Phil came in and out all day too. I grew irritable from lack of sleep. I cried easily. Phil didn't want me to see the kids. I learned that they were back in Chicago—with his parents. Isabel and Adele were staying at my parents' house in Ann Arbor.

I never knew what day it was until the nurse wrote it on the whiteboard where my information was displayed. "Hazel: low-salt diet, Dr. Jankowski, Nurse: varies" and sometimes, a smiley face. On a Wednesday, I felt well enough to sit up and eat some suspicious-looking turkey doused in runny gravy, instant mashed potatoes, boiled carrots, Jell-O, and a carton of milk. Phil rubbed my back as I forced the bland food down.

"The doctor says you might be discharged in a few days, a week at most."

Another week. My coma had lasted seven days, and then two weeks more of being monitored. I wasn't on any good drugs, and no longer at major risk, but I was still stuck here.

I hated this place and not remembering how I got here. Only bits and pieces of memory were coming back. I remembered leaving the bar and Harper behind, and then . . . *nothing.* Something nagged at me though. Was there more?

"God, another week?" I wailed. "I can't take it anymore! I'm bored, the food sucks, and they won't bring me wine." I forced a smile. "Why do I have to stay longer?"

He laughed.

"Don't worry, babe, wine is just a few weeks away. It's the vasospasms. Remember what the doctor said—they can show up anywhere from four to ten days. It's precautionary and very necessary.

"But I've been here longer than ten days!" I pushed the potatoes around.

"I know, and I'm sorry you're miserable. I hate seeing you like this," he said, rubbing my back, "but they need to be sure."

I started to cry.

"I miss the kids so much. I've never gone this long without them. Do they even remember me?"

"Shh, don't cry, Hazel. I know this is frustrating. Of course they do. And they miss you terribly. And, *I* miss you lying next to me. And waking up to you in the morning. It's lonely without you."

He put his head in his hands and rubbed his face.

I wanted my life back.

∿

T hat afternoon, Phil went to my parents' house to catch up on computer work. Harper stopped by with goodies from the drugstore— a stack of magazines, hand lotion, a Kit Kat bar, mints, and moisturizer.

"You can still prevent wrinkles while you're in this dump."

I laughed as I flipped through the *People* that she had tossed on my lap.

"Thanks," I sighed. "Harper, I can't believe I left you at the bar that night. I should have dragged you with me."

"Why, so I could've fallen too?" she laughed. "Just kidding. No, I was being an asshole that night." She waved her hand in the air. "I had no idea that you even fell until your parents called me. Who knows how long you were lying on the cold sidewalk, unconscious. I feel awful."

"It's not your fault; stop it. Everything was a sheet of ice that night. I should've been more careful."

"Yeah, but you went out for smokes, for me, Hazel."

"We both wanted to smoke."

I froze. I remembered something. The convenience store, the face reflected in the glass.

Teddy.

"Oh my God," I murmured. "Oh . . . Harper . . ."

"What? What is it?"

Chad's apartment? Or was it Teddy's apartment in Chicago? Was that right? Was that possible?

"Harper, I've been having an affair . . . I think."

"Really?" She stopped and looked right at me. "Hazel. You think? What does that mean and with—"

"—Teddy."

"Uh, what?" She pinched her lips sideways, and a deep crease appeared above her eyebrows.

"Shit."

She quickly sat on the edge of my bed.

"Holy shit. Teddy? He's back?"

I let my head fall into my hands.

"He came back, I think," I shook my head, "and he has a place in Chicago. And . . . I've been sleeping with him and cheating on Phil—

"—Hazel, I don't understand. Teddy hasn't been around for years. What are you talking about? And what do you mean, you *think?* When did you see him? Was it before you came to see me? Or have you been seeing him all this time in Chicago?"

"No, no . . . I . . . I'm not sure, it's all so fuzzy."

I realized how confused I was. I couldn't remember when this started or how. I just knew I'd been sleeping with Teddy.

"Well, I must have been . . . His parents died and gave him money and he got this really nice apartment on the South Side, except the building's a real piece of shit . . . but he cooks now. . . and the place was so nice . . . and he was so different . . ."

"Hazel, you would have mentioned this when you came to town. I mean, I would hope you would have."

I shook my head.

"Shit . . . Hazel. What about Phil? Oh my God, does Phil know?"

I strained to remember how it started, where I fell. But all I saw were images of snakes and sand and my mother bleeding and a white unicorn in my bathroom.

"Hazel?"

"I was supposed to make a choice."

"Oh . . . Phil gave you an ultimatum?" Harper now settled into the pleather recliner opposite my bed, tucking her feet underneath her, preparing for a long story. "I didn't know you two were unhappy. Fuck, Hazel, this is what Steve did to me. How could you not tell me when we were together? This is really shitty. Really shitty."

Had there been an ultimatum?

Shame washed over me. Having Harper disappointed in me left me diminished.

"Phil's been a wreck and drove here immediately," she continued, twisting a piece of her curly hair. "He hasn't left your side. Why would you do this? And with that fucking loser?"

"I know, none of it makes sense. I mean, it started here, and then we were in Chicago, and then I woke up here. It's so confusing," I stammered. "He was going back to Europe, and he wanted me to come—the way we planned years ago. He wanted me to choose; go with him or stay with Phil and my kids. He was wonderful and—awful, as usual. He claimed he was the only person that could make me happy."

I choked back tears and sipped some water.

"Do you think he's right?" I asked. "I know what I did was awful and fucked up, but what if he was right?"

Harper sighed and unwrapped an Almond Joy. She took a bite, uncrossed her legs, and held my gaze intensely.

"Let me clarify. You've been fucking around on Phil for God knows how long, and you didn't tell me, which, what the fuck? With Teddy—the guy who has been fucking with you since you were a kid —and, he just shows up, *out of the blue* and decides that he's the answer to all your dreams. And he wants you to leave your husband and kids to travel the world with him? Is that right?"

I lowered my gaze to my thin hospital gown. A pattern of blue stars dotted the faded-cream smock.

"I guess so? It's still foggy, probably from my head, but also pretty vivid. I don't know why I wouldn't have told you. Or better yet, why I would have done this to Phil. He doesn't deserve this."

"Fuck, no, he doesn't," she said, shoving the second half of her candy bar into her mouth and chewing loudly. "What a piece of work, that asshole. You said he lives in Chicago now? How did he find you?"

I sat back in my bed. Her blue eyes were wild with anticipation.

"Yeah, he has a really nice place there, but first we were here, in Ann Arbor, at Chad's place? I can't exactly remember. This can't be real."

"Chad? That same apartment? Didn't he—Hazel, you're talking about shit from twenty years ago. This must be your brain injury. There's just no way Teddy would suddenly appear, and of all places, in Chad's place." She threw her wadded up wrapper on my nightstand.

I vaguely remembered driving to Michigan. Had Phil thrown me out? Had he found out about Teddy? My mind flashed to Harper's house and drinking and smoking cigarettes. I remembered going to the convenience store. But I couldn't remember Teddy before that. How could I have had an affair with him after the convenience store if that just happened?

"Hazel," she said, touching my arm. "None of this makes sense. Maybe we should ask the doctor about having delusions or something?"

I nodded. A vision of Teddy's apartment came to me. The drinks. The Sea Breezes. How I had been so tired.

"Drugs," I said, looking up at her. "I think maybe he was drugging me. That's why I was so sleepy . . . and why I can't remember now. God, what was he giving me?"

Panic filled my stomach as I searched for my cell phone. I found it on the nightstand and grabbed it. I flipped it open.

"I need to call the police. I need to tell the doctor. They need to drug test me. Yes, yes, that all makes sense now. He—"

"Hazel, stop." She stood up and grabbed my phone. "Let's talk to the doctor first."

"Okay," I blinked, and sank back into the pillow.

She squeezed my arm. "It's going to be okay. I'll be right back."

I was alone with the constant beeping of the machines and the uncomfortable pinch of my IV whenever I moved my arm.

Closing my eyes, I struggled for memories. I took deep breaths, in sync with the monitors. A slice of it came back to me.

The lasagna dinner with Teddy, my dragonfly mug, his ultimatum.

There had been a text on my phone.

Hey babe. We need to talk about last night. You're making a mistake.

My heart pounded against my chest, and the machines began to chirp loudly.

"Hi, Hazel, everything alright?"

One of the resident doctors rushed in with a nurse and Harper close behind. He pressed his stethoscope against my chest. The nurse pumped up the blood pressure cuff circling my arm.

"Yeah, I'm fine—" I glanced at Harper, at the foot of my bed, gnawing on a cuticle "—I just, well, did you drug test me when I was admitted?"

"Drug test?" He replaced the stethoscope around his neck, and the cuff was deflated. The nurse wrote the number down on a Post-it note for the doctor. He nodded and put it in my file.

"Yeah, I, uh, I think someone might have been drugging me before this happened," I said, and propped up on my pillow.

"Why do you think that?" he asked, as he began thumbing through my chart.

Harper nodded encouragingly.

"Well, I'm confused. I think some things may have happened, but I'm not sure if they did. And, I remember being tired all the time."

"Your chart does show a drug screen and pregnancy test when you were admitted, and both were negative." He set the folder on my bed and approached me, pulling a light from his pocket.

"Let's do your daily checks. Follow the light with just your eyes, please." A bright light hit my pupils, and I obeyed. "You had a brain hemorrhage and were in a coma. It's normal to be confused. And, understandably tired. Now, some patients do claim to dream while in a coma or even have strange dreams after a brain bleed, without a coma. Maybe that's what you're experiencing?"

"Dreams? I furrowed my brow and looked at Harper. "No, I don't think so. I was definitely with—"

"Hold on, Hazel," Harper interrupted. "This makes more sense."

"No, I'm telling you. I was with Teddy and not dreaming."

The doctor exchanged a look with Harper.

"Hazel, there is no indication you had drugs in your system upon arrival. There are explanations why you felt drugged. First, when placed in a medically induced coma, drugs are administered that reduce cerebral blood flow and the metabolic rate of brain tissue to relieve pressure on your brain.

Sometimes, these drugs cause hallucinations. Second, this dreaming—called lucid dreaming—is common. Do you remember, when you felt tired, having the sensation that you were dreaming? That things around you were unusual, or even, unrealistic?"

"Yes!" exclaimed Harper. "You think you had an affair and didn't even tell me? *That* is unusual for sure."

I stared at my chipped nail polish.

"Hazel?" he said, cocking his head.

"Um, yeah, I can think of some outrageous stuff. Unicorns, dragonflies playing cards, and shooting my mother. That's why I think Teddy was drugging me."

"You shot your mother?" Harper squealed and laughed. "She's not dead, we certainly know that."

I frowned at her and turned back to the doctor.

"So, what else happens during lucid dreaming? How is it different than regular dreaming?"

He pulled a chair to my bedside and sat down.

"Well, everyone experiences it differently, but in lucid dreaming, the images are usually influenced from memories ingrained in your brain. Many times, the same scenario will play out on repeat. And typically, you can control the dreams yourself."

"Really? How?"

"Well, say you're an apple in a dream, and you realize you're a person, you can mentally change back into a person."

"No shit!" said Harper, her blue eyes wide and shining.

"Um, yes," the doctor smiled, then continued, "and there are other factors. Sometimes being in a cold room can make these dreams—

"Snow! The snow never ended! And, oh my God, the beeping! I thought it was my—"

"—Cell phone?" he chuckled. "Yes, that's a common one. The beeping of the machines can invade your thoughts and manifest into objects like phones. One patient dreamed the beeping was a microwave constantly making popcorn. Some people liken it to an out of body experience, or, a movie of their life, playing out in ways that they really want their life to be. Many issues can cause this—PTSD, unresolved issues, trauma; all can be factors."

I felt the color drain from my face. Bile lurched against my throat. The air in the room was sharp and hard.

"Oh."

Was it all a dream?

Teddy's fingers tracing my stomach. His lips grazing my ear. The maps, the wine, the chance to escape with him the way I wanted all those years ago.

"Um, okay, thank you. I just can't believe—" I shook my head and gazed numbly at the ceiling.

"It's a lot to digest, Hazel. You've been through a lot. Rest up. Things will become clearer in time."

I nodded. He smiled at Harper, and left.

Harper came to my bedside and put a hand on my shoulder.

"That's great news, Hazel. You didn't cheat on Phil! It was all some crazy-ass dream—"

"Yeah, that's great," I mumbled, biting my lip. "Could you give me a minute? I'm feeling overwhelmed and tired."

"Yeah! Of course!" she replied, fussing with my blanket. "Get some rest. And, listen, this is good news. You are a good wife, and Teddy never came back. He's gone. He's been gone, and he's not coming back. But, *I*, however, will be back tomorrow!"

She kissed my forehead and left my room.

Unresolved issues.

A swelling ballooned in my throat. Tears fell. I gulped for air. I gulped again. The sobs became hiccups. The hiccups became moans. My body rocked back and forth. I was cold and sweaty.

So much loss from an absent person. He left me as a child, and again in high school. I recalled the boat ride, wind in our hair, Chardonnay in our cups. The way he touched me, and how his eyes seared into mine. My reality had truly been a dream. An unattainable, childish dream that I based my entire life around.

Now, the dream was gone again.

I sighed and breathed slowly in and out. I thought about Phil and my children. I had grown, despite Teddy nearly destroying me.

His power seemed so ridiculous now. I was no longer a child. I had my own children.

None of it was my fault. He had lured me in for some disturbing reason and captivated me with his charm and affection. If I ever saw him again, I would tell my parents and the police. Teddy needed to be in jail. He could be hurting other little girls right now.

My stomach tightened, and grief and disgust rolled through me. I sniffled and let out a quiet puff of exasperation.

"Fucking goddamn pedophile!" I said out loud.

I relaxed my shoulders and sunk into my pillow. I wiped my tears and blew my nose. It was over. It was finally over.

⁓

"I'm here!" my mother exclaimed, floating into my room, arms full of shopping bags. She set them down and joined me at my bedside. "I picked up some things since a few days here has turned to weeks. Just a few sweaters and jeans, and a little makeup."

I sighed. For my mother, buying us things made her feel like a good provider and kept up appearances simultaneously.

"Thank you. I called because I wanted to talk to you privately."

"Sounds so serious, Hazel, what is it?"

"Well, while I was in the coma, I experienced crazy things. I had an affair, contemplated running away with him, I shot you, I had snakes coming out my ears and eyes, and then woke up in a bathtub with a unicorn by my side."

"Wow," she laughed. "That's quite a dream. You shot me?"

I smirked. Funny how she glazed over everything else and went right to her being shot.

"I guess so. It wasn't fully verified. The blood dried up and you were fine, don't worry."

"Oh, well, thank goodness," she sighed, as if there had been real danger. "An affair? Do you know with whom?"

"No, it was all quite blurry," I lied, "but seemed very real. I spoke with my doctor and he said I was lucid dreaming, which many patients experience. It was quite scary to wake up and think it had all happened."

"I can imagine," she said.

"Well, in coming out of that, I wanted to talk to you about . . . our relationship."

"Oh?" Joanne asked, with expanded, panicked eyes. "And why you shot me in your dream?"

"I guess, yeah. Clearly I've been mad at you for a while."

Silence hung in the air, a dead weight between us.

"Listen, Mom, I can see you've been trying lately, especially with Dad, and I'm happy about that. You've been a great grandma to my kids, and I'm grateful because growing up, you built pretty high walls that none of us could get around. We all needed you, and you weren't available."

She started to speak, but I squeezed her hand.

"And, kids? I never wanted them. I was terrified. Isabel and I basically learned a lot of things on our own, or from Dad. I was so afraid of being absent in my kids' lives that I saw no reason to have them."

"Oh, Hazel, you're right," she said, her eyes glossed in tears. "I'm so sorry. I've been a horrible mother. Back then I was so consumed with myself, my work, the book I never finished. I tortured your father by withholding love, and I did the same to you girls."

I hadn't expected such a quick apology, or even one at all.

"I grew up with a cold and distant mother," she continued, "and my father traveled as a salesman and was often gone. She expected me to be perfect, and she was awful to me when I wasn't. I suppose I began building walls early on, trying to protect myself. My grandmother was the same way. The maternal gene was never passed down. Until you. You are an amazing mother, Hazel. You have broken the cycle. I know it's no excuse. Sadly, I don't know if I ever had a chance. Going into motherhood, I thought I could do it all. But I focused on the wrong things. Sometimes I am shocked at how well you and Isabel turned out. In spite of me."

Tears streamed down her cheeks. This was the most authentic I had ever seen my mother. Raw and sad, and genuinely sorry. It wasn't too late to have a real relationship with her, to prove that my childhood, and what Teddy did, had not destroyed me. I didn't have room in my heart anymore for anger and resentment. It was exhausting.

"Mom," I put my hand on hers and squeezed it. "You made a lot of mistakes, yes. In a lot of ways, it has shaped my values and how I am as a mother. I've carried around pain and sadness forever, and I never thought it would leave me. But then I met Phil and learned what real, healthy love is. He supports me, and we talk things through. I didn't see that growing up. It's given me the feeling of safety and comfort I never had."

"Oh, Hazel," my mother sobbed, tears and mascara smearing her face.

"Mom, just listen," I said, gently. "Being a mother is hard, really hard. There are days that I completely understand your actions. I've wanted to run in my room and lock the door for days. I've wanted to drink and smoke and go back to being single. But I have resources. I have a therapist; I've been on anti-depressants. There are ways to cope. You didn't have that. I need you to know, that the past, and all the hurt, it's a part of me. But, it's not all of me. And, I learned from it, I grew from it, and know who I am. And, most of all, I don't want to carry anger anymore. I want to rebuild a new relationship and work on forgiveness. Would you be willing to try with me?"

I was surprised at my own words. I had recited them to myself, but as I said them, the forgiveness poured out of me.

My mother embraced me. Her arms had grown thin, but carried great strength. She cried into my shoulder, her body trembling. Overwhelmed with this foreign affection, I leaned into her, and accepted it.

"Of course, I will, Hazel, of course. I am so sorry for all of it. Yes, let's begin again," she said, her voice muffled against my gown. "I love you. I love you so much."

~

The next morning, the sun broke through dirty streaks in the window. It was a new day. I was yawning as Phil entered my room.

"Hey, you! Wow, you look great today, babe!" he said, and kissed me on the lips. "You ready to head home? The nurse said tomorrow is release day! The kids are going crazy with anticipation."

"*Very* ready to go home," I smiled. He was so handsome, and so *good*. "This place is depressing, and the food is terrible, and I miss you, and I miss Mitchell and Maddy!"

"I know," he chuckled. "Soon. Back at home and our bed! And the kids miss you so much. They have so much to tell you. Madeline has been talking up a storm, and my mom says her counting is impressive. And Mitchell has new toy trucks to show you. He's really digging the excavator. Get it? Digging the——"

"——Yes, babe, I get it," I said, laughing. "First of all, he would tell you, 'Daddy, an excavator is *not* a truck' and I can't wait to hear all about it, but first——"

"——And I've been staying in a hotel for so long, to stay close, but now I'm so ready for both of us to go *home*, and we'll——"

"——Phil, babe, hold on for just a minute." I touched his arm. "I am ready to get out of here, believe me. And I have missed the kids so much. You are such a good man, and I am so grateful for you. But, if you could possibly go get a bottle of wine and sneak it in, that would be great. I have a story to tell you."

~

Three weeks later, I had eased back into home life. It was hard not to kiss and hug the kids constantly while I marveled at their changes. I never wanted to leave them again.

"Time for bed!" I called, after ending a call with my mother. We spoke on the phone every couple of days now, awkwardly trying to form our new relationship. I understood they would be surface conversations for a bit, but hopefully over time, we could connect on a new level. She was trying, and so was I.

I smiled as I wrapped my robe around me, grabbed my glass of wine, and went into the den.

"No, Mama!" Madeline yelled back. I sighed.

"Brush your teeth, both of you! Mitchell, help your sister!"

I touched a wedding photo of Phil and me. Back at the hospital after I told Phil everything, he had been shocked and hurt. He couldn't believe the secret I had kept from him. At first, he was angry and wanted to notify the police. I reminded him that too many years had passed, and legally, it wouldn't matter. I didn't want to revisit it again, especially to the police, my father or Isabel. All that mattered was my heart was with him and our children, and our beautiful life. He held me as I cried and let go of Teddy and the past.

༄

I sat down in front of the computer. I hadn't checked my email in a few days, and a catering job was approaching. Isabel had emailed the menu for my review. Resuming work was just the distraction I needed.

I yawned, rolled the mouse, and scanned the menu to see what desserts they requested. I sifted through the other emails. Nothing important.

I pulled up my MySpace page. I admired my profile picture with Phil and the kids. Cheerful smiles on all of us, eating donuts at a pumpkin patch. All my information was displayed on the right side of the page—college, hometown, status, and interests. It was all so odd. I was astounded by this new world of technology, where anyone could see into your life, if you invited them to. I had connected with some of the Goth girls from high school and Marjorie from the bakery.

To the left, I saw I had a "Friend Request."

Clicking open the screen, a photo of an attractive, clean-cut, middle-aged man on the bow of a sailboat popped up. He held a glass of wine as he flashed a crooked smile. Lightning shot up from the pit of my stomach. *Teddy.*

I stared at the photo. Was he still in Michigan? Indiana? Did he own that boat? He was looking for me. My hand trembled. My heart raced.

Theodore Michael Spencer.

The cursor blinked, awaiting my answer: Confirm or Ignore.

ABOUT THE AUTHOR

Richelle grew up on a chicken farm in Northern Michigan. The hens were grumpy, pecking at her fingers as she gathered eggs from their warm nests, but the environment lent itself to hours of crafting stories in her imagination. In her adult years, she transitioned from rural life to embracing the hustle and bustle of the vibrant cities of Chicago, New York City, and San Francisco. It was during these adventures she cultivated characters and a world setting to fill the pages of a novel.

Richelle graduated from the University of Michigan with a degree in science and has worked in the dental industry for seventeen years. When she's not working or writing, she enjoys reading, photography, kayaking, biking, traveling, and cooking.

She hopes that her novel will spark conversations about identity, relationships, and the power of acceptance. Richelle is a debut novelist living in California's Bay Area with her husband and their cat, Eleanor.

Printed in the USA
CPSIA information can be obtained
at www.ICGtesting.com
LVHW092332040923
757129LV00002B/5